A WOLF

AFTER MY OWN HEART

MARYJANICE DAVIDSON

sourcebooks
casablanca

Published by Sourcebooks Casablanca, an imprint of Sourcebooks
P.O. Box 4410, Naperville, Illinois 60567-4410
(630) 961-3900
sourcebooks.com

Printed and bound in Canada.
MBP 10 9 8 7 6 5 4 3 2 1

For Elinor –

Chapter 1

SHE WAS JUST GETTING THE HANG OF THE AMBULANCE WHEN she hit the wolf.

The thing was bulky and difficult to control (the ambulance, not the wolf), and whenever she got it back from its semiannual mechanically induced coma, it took her a few minutes to get the hang of driving it again.

She stood on the brakes

(*oh shit oh shit oh shit*)

and braced for the double-thump of the tires running over the animal, which didn't come.

Lila Kai collapsed back into her seat, her heart pounding so hard she could taste metal. She pulled over to the side of the street. A *street*, not a country road on the way from nowhere to somewhere. This was Lilydale, not Hastings. And even Hastings didn't have wolves in their streets. Just deer. So what the hell?

She put the ambulance in Park, kept the engine running, and hopped down. She checked the headlights—nothing. The side of the road—nothing. She even took a tentative couple of steps into the brown brush lining the ditch

(*don't think about the zillions of horror movies that start like this*)

—nothing. No wolf, limping or otherwise. Or…coyote, maybe?

Which made sense, now that she thought about it. Because whatever it was, it hadn't been just huge, it had been fast, too. It had come out of nowhere and to nowhere it returned, all in the space of half a second. Maybe she just clipped it.

Is that a metaphor for something? Life? Death? Taxes? Transitions? Romance?

Mmmm…probably not the latter. There was just no way to twist clipping a random wolf into an allegory about her nonexistent dating life. The fact that she'd given even half a second of thought to that was proof that she needed to lay off the Cosmos (the drink *and* the magazine).

She went back to her decommissioned ambulance, rebuckled her seat belt, put it in Drive, checked her rearview, ignored the urge to ponder more metaphors-that-weren't, then pulled out, and headed back toward her rental house. The adrenaline rush had been unwelcome as always, but—

"God *damn* it!"

Two kids had darted out from nowhere

(*what the hell is up with this street?*)

and were flagging her down, waving their little arms around so fast they looked like little bony windmills in a gale.

This time, at least, she didn't have to stand on the brakes, and once she had stopped, she rolled down her window. "What's going on, li'l weirdos?"

Both children were gesturing frantically. "C'mere, you have to help, she's hurt!"

And more than a few horror movies start like this, *too.*

Again with park, unbuckling, opening door, climbing out. The boy and girl who had jumped in front of her looked like they were about eight, dressed in the de rigeur kid gear of jeans and sweatshirts and battered sneakers. They had the corn-fed reddish-blond looks of many Minnesotans. "Who's hurt?"

"I dunno, she just is, we found her, come *on*. Bring your ambulance gear!"

"It's not an ambulance."

"'Course it's an ambulance!"

"No, I mean it's decommissioned, so it's not really an amb—"

Tiring of her explanation, the girl seized Lila's hand and started hauling her up the street. Lila looked behind her, half expecting to see the wolf creeping up on them and felt a little let down to see the way was clear. Which was insane. Strange enough to see such a creature under *any* circumstances, never mind smack in the middle of town. But she wanted to see it again; how was that for nuts?

I probably need a nap.

The girl hauled on her hand again and hooked left

"Jeez, kid. Do you work out?"

and then led her down a short alley, to where a small huddled form was curled into a blanket.

"See?" the girl asked, clamping down hard on Lila's fingers in her excitement.

"Yeah, see?" the boy, presumably her brother, added. "She's right there!"

"Isn't this a school night?" But she bent over the small figure, blinked as her brain tried to process the image, gently touched it on the shoulder, then pinched her own leg

(Nope. Not dreaming.)

and looked up at the kids. "All right, first, that's not a kid, it's a bear cub for some reason. Second, I'm not a vet. Most important, I'm not an EMT, either."

Instead of answering, the girl whacked the boy on the arm and hissed something that sounded like, "Unstable!"

"My high school guidance counselor would agree." Lila bent back over the curled up mass of black, fluffy, whimpering fur that cowered away from her and glared with dark eyes. "I'm not sure what it is you think I can do." She looked back up only to see the children's expressions had transformed; they were actually edging away from her. "Why are you doing that? You guys lured *me* here. If anyone should be uneasy, it's me. Shouldn't you have picked my pocket by now?" She looked around the utterly deserted alley. For the first time, she realized she couldn't hear anything: no bugs, no birds, nothing. And not much light from the lone streetlight. Downright creepy.

She checked the mouth of the alley for the wolf and was again disappointed to see nothing.

"You're right, sorry," the boy said.

"Yeah, sorrywebotheredyougoodbyenow."

Lila sighed. She was in it the minute she'd stepped down from the vehicle that wasn't an ambulance. "God *damn* it. Okay, so, just because I can't help doesn't mean someone else can't." She stood, only to see the children take several steps back. "Maybe call animal control?" She had to, she realized. You couldn't just leave a random bear cub in a random alley after random kids flagged down a random adult.

But in the time it took her to fish out her phone and begin looking up Lilydale Animal Control—or would that be Saint Paul?—the children had (cue the dramatic music) vanished. Like the wolf, her patience, and her faith in the good people at Apartment Guide.

"Nice quiet neighborhood," she muttered to the Realtor who wasn't there. "Lots of families. It's in the middle of a national park. Bargain."

She'd been a Lilydale resident for fewer than eighteen hours and had no idea who to call. And after a day of unpacking, she was standing in an alley at 8:00 p.m. After hitting a wolf. The one thing she did know: she—they—couldn't stay there indefinitely.

"You'd tell me if you were a metaphor, right, teeny tiny bear cub?"

She scooped it up, surprised by how light it was, given that it was the size of a small golden retriever

(*it must be mostly fur, the way birds are mostly feathers*)

then checked for the wolf one more time, and headed back to her nonbulance.

He had her, he had the cub's scent, he had to
    (*make her safe*)
do his job, he had to
    (*keep her safe*)
and that was fine, he could and he would but then
YOW!
    the big noisysmellything bit him and sent him tumbling and here came the Stable so he crouched down down down
    (*don't see me*)
in the dark hollow by the ditch and here she came
    (*don't smell me*)
and she was looking and he was he was downwind of her which was good which was perfect and
    (*oh*)
    the Stable smelled like berries and blankets, sweet and safe, and it was *wonderful,* and he didn't realize he'd followed her out of the ditch until he caught the scent of two more cubs and if they saw if they all saw
    (*if She saw*)
they would be scared and scatter and that would not would not do so he slipped back into the dark and watched and watched and watched and drank in as much of her scent and watched some more.
    And followed.

Chapter 2

"YES. FOR THE THIRD TIME, I FOUND A WOUNDED BEAR CUB about a quarter of a mile from my house. Well, someone else's house."

"What?"

"I'm just renting. And it's a bargain, or so they keep insisting."

"A bear cub." This in a tone that suggested the dispatcher was questioning Lila's sanity. Which was smart, frankly.

"Fourth time," Lila pointed out helpfully. "Yes. And don't forget about the wolf."

"The wolf."

"I can't shake the feeling that you've got a criminally short attention span."

"Can you still see the animal?"

"Which?"

"Do you have eyes on the cub?" the dispatcher asked.

Lila looked down at the animated ball of fuzz taking up her lap (and then some!) while licking honey off her fingers. For a wild creature (was it? maybe it escaped from a zoo? or was someone's pet?), it was gratifyingly vermin-free, as far as she could tell. It had interesting coloring, too... Most of its fur was a deep black, with a whirl of reddish-orange fur that curled down from its shoulders, forming a rough V-shape down the chest. Its face was broad, with a short snout, tiny ears, and it had cream-colored claws. It—wait.

Lila discreetly checked, then noted *she* was a little muddy, and *her* right foreleg was clearly causing her pain, but that seemed to be the worst of it. She didn't even smell bad, more like...old cotton? Dusty curtains?

"Ma'am? Do you have eyes on the cub?"

"Yeah, I can—ow!—see her. So anyway, my address is..."

"I'm afraid we don't deal in cubs. You need to call the IPA."

"Sorry, what?"

"The IPA. Do you need the number?"

"I need to know what an IPA is. The phone number is secondary."

"I'll connect you."

"God *damn* it! At least tell me what the acronym stands for. Important People Arriving? International Parasailing Accountants? Ow!" To the cub: "If you keep eating my hand, you won't be hungry for lunch. Get it? Of course not, you're a bear cub. Great movie, take my word for it." Meanwhile, the deeply unhelpful person at animal control had made good on her threat to transfer; she could hear phone ringing. "Whatever IPA is, I hope they make house c—*now* what?"

Lila viewed the front door, on which someone had just knocked, with deep suspicion. She was new in town, and she hadn't ordered pizza. The kids, maybe? Did they follow her back? The mama bear? No, an aggravated bear wouldn't have knocked. Was it an election year? She'd honestly rather deal with a frantic mama bear than someone shilling for city council.

The cub, meanwhile, was mewling and butting her with its hard little black head, displeased at the lack of honey on Lila's fingers. "Sorry, I'm cutting you off. You'll thank me in the morning." And, louder: "I'm coming!" She cast about for somewhere to put the cub, who had abruptly stopped being adorable and was now wriggling and scratching and bawling like a calf going through udder withdrawal. Lila could barely hold onto the ball of flailing, furry limbs. "Ow, shit! Okay, just...okay, I'm putting you down now— ow, *Jesus*, there, so you...uh..."

The cub rolled over and over, shaking its head and bawling and then

and then

and then

she wasn't a cub anymore. If Lila had turned her head, she would have missed it. Where the cub had been now crouched a little girl with the cub's coloring—long, wild black hair halfway down her back, and dark eyes with an upward tilt, with fair skin and golden undertones—who looked about ten. She was naked, so Lila could see how scratched up the

(girl?????)

artist formerly known as Cub was, and then something she could actually understand happened for the first time in the last twenty minutes: the child burst into tears.

"Never mind!" Lila shouted at whoever was still knocking. "If you're IPA, it was a false alarm. If you've got pizza, I don't want any." This was a rather large lie. A deep-dish pie loaded with sausage and mushrooms would go down just fine with a beer or five. "If you're stumping for a politician, leave the brochure in my mailbox. If you're the two random kids from earlier, go home, it's a school night. If you're a bear, there's no cub in here."

There. That ought to cover everything.

To the little girl sobbing in the corner: "Hi, I'm Lila. Don't worry, the noise and the situation definitely aren't getting on my nerves or anything." She took a deep breath and let it out slowly. *Calm. Calm-calm-calm. Project so much calm. Be fucking calm, dammit!* "What happened? Should I call someone? Do you know your parents' numbers? Are you friends with a great big wolf? Am I hallucinating? It's okay if I am. You can tell me. I won't be mad."

The little girl sniffled and wouldn't look at her.

"You're shivering." Because of course she was. The rental house was agreeably old, with lots of dark wooden floors and very little carpet, and the heater struggled, especially since it was only about fifty-five degrees outside. "Let's get a blanket on you, and a sweatshirt, maybe? Are you hungry? I could get you something more substantial than honey." That was another lie, she realized.

The fridge held a twelve-pack of LaCroix coconut water, a box of Little Debbie Swiss Rolls (they were better chilled), a half-gallon of skim, and the ingredients for Flanders's cocoa. The honey she used for her tea and random bear cubs was nearly empty. She'd planned to get groceries in the morning.

At least the knocking had stopped.

The child sniffled, wiped her nose on her forearm, leaving a shiny trail up and down her arm

(*urgh*)

and still wouldn't look up.

"Look, it's okay. We'll figure this out—uh, whatever *this* is— and get you home. Wherever home is. And by 'we,' I mean someone in authority. Maybe a bunch of them." She rooted around in a box marked *Who the hell knows? Maybe the living room?*, found a blanket, and draped it over the cowering kiddo. "There's nothing to be scared of." Most likely. But what the hell did she know? Maybe Lilydale was crawling with bear hunters. Maybe it was Shirley Jackson's "The Lottery," only with bears. "It's gonna be okay."

No sooner had she run out of platitudes than she heard the rear porch door *twang* (the hinges were old and stretchy), followed by the sound of wood splintering, followed by the slam of the door against the wall as two kids or a politician or a pizza delivery person or a bear came in without an invitation.

Chapter 3

THERE WAS A SWINGING DOOR BETWEEN THE KITCHEN AND living room, and Lila blessed it. Which was a switch from earlier, when she'd been carrying boxes and mistimed the swing (*"Ow, God damn it!"*).

But now the contrary thing concealed her for a crucial few seconds, and when whoever-it-was pushed at the door and came through, she had the barrel up behind his ear before he was all the way in.

"Jesus, you Domino's guys are persistent," she hissed. "I *told* you. I. Don't. Want. Any. Pizza. Jackass."

"Please. If I was delivering pizza, it'd be Green Mill."

That startled a laugh out of her. She had to give it to him, he didn't sound rattled in the slightest. And he was distractingly good-looking. Not every guy could pull off the classic Caesar haircut. Or had eyes the color of forest moss.

Forest moss? Time to get laid. Not by this guy, though. Most likely.

His looks made up for his clothes: He was wearing scruffy slacks, a shirt he hadn't bothered buttoning up all the way (which revealed the shoulders and abs of a swimmer, which was even more irritating), he didn't have a coat, and...was that blood on his shirt cuff?

"Trespassing," she prompted. "That's you. That's what you're doing for some ungodly reason. Right now. In my house." She started to walk him back into the kitchen. Once he'd kicked the door in, she hadn't heard anything but footsteps, so hopefully her half-assed plan was going to work. She wasn't afraid of him—not exactly—but there was the cub to think about. And he *had* just broken in. But she had no sense of real danger from him, and her gut instinct about people had yet to let her down. Still, precautions had to be taken. "Also, you noticed the gun, right?"

"The one you're aggressively cleaning my ear with?" He tried to move his head away; she followed the movement with the barrel. "Yeah, that didn't escape my attention."

"You want to see aggressive cleaning? Break in again."

He rolled those green, green eyes at her and scoffed. *Scoffed.* She should have been irked but had to give it to him: The guy had some plums. "Aw, c'mon. This is America. This isn't the first time I've had a gun in my face this *month.* Which is a huge problem, by the way. How many hoops did you even have to jump through to get that thing? Not very many, I bet."

Seriously with this? "Yeah, let's leave your personal politics out of it, okay?"

"Plus, it's not loaded—Jesus!"

She used that moment of inattention to drive her toes—clad in her second-favorite pair of steel-toed shoes—straight and hard into his ankle and, when he reflexively bent, Lila dropped the (empty) .380 and shoved him with both hands, hard. He toppled backward through the open basement door

(shouldn't have been in such a rush to get into the living room, pal)

and she slammed it shut. And shot the bolt. It wouldn't hold him for long, which was fine.

She rushed into the living room, intent on her phone, only to pull up short when she realized

"God *damn* it!"

the girl–cub was gone.

Chapter 4

HIS OWN GODDAMNED FAULT. HE'D TAKEN IT EASY ON HER. He'd been too interested in how she looked and smelled to pay attention to business. "I *deserved* to be pitched into a dark spooky basement," Oz Adway announced to the air, then sat up and stifled a groan. "Ass first."

And everything had been going so...so...what was the opposite of "well"?

After he tamped down his suddenly raging hormones and shifted, he'd tracked the cub and the yummy Stable to the wrong house, *of course*, and it was the Curs(ed) House, *of course*, and time wasn't on his side, *of course*, so he had to drop everything (literally—the box of files had landed on his foot in his rush to strip) to rescue the cub and contain the situation.

Plus his shoulder hurt from where she'd clipped him with the ambulance she drove for some reason.

(Also she now smelled like honey and gun oil. Sweet and lethal. She'd take such good care of his cubs! Which wasn't relevant to anything, so you'd think he could *focus on the cub*.)

And he had to do all of it without scaring the Stable in question more than she already was, because Oz would sooner take on a raging werebear than a Stable backed into a corner. When Stables got scared, they thought up A-bombs and poisonous gas and reality TV. (To be fair, if he couldn't shift, he'd probably be scared and grumpy and want to watch terrible people get kicked off a terrible island all the time, too.) So scaring a Stable in general was a terrible idea, never mind one who smelled like high summer in the country.

Needless to say, in keeping with the entire goddamned day,

nothing had gone right from the moment she'd nailed him like roadkill. More alarming/interesting, when he broke in, this particular Stable hadn't been afraid, she'd been pissed. She hadn't lost her head, she'd followed through on her plan. She hadn't run, she'd met him in the doorway with a gun.

Fantastic.

Then he got a closer look at her.

Fantastic. Curves, curls, glasses showcasing blue eyes that were lovely even when they were narrowed into slits. Short-sleeved red T-shirt and black denim shorts, though it was spring. Sharks on her socks. No shoes.

Her curly hair had been his downfall. Not wavy. Curls that if you took one (gently!) and stretched it out (gently!) it would spring right back: *pa-toing!* And he'd been imagining exactly that when she introduced him to her basement. Ass first. With her foot. All he could do was watch the stairwell flip a one-eighty around him and then the cement floor jumped up and slammed into his back, which woke up his bad shoulder that hadn't shut up since.

You should apologize. And ask her out. And sire cubs on her.

Whoa.

What?

He shook off the primitive thought which had come out of nowhere with such force it was like it wasn't his thought at all, more like God yelling at him to hook up and make babies already, and tried to focus. Basement. Ass first. Cub in the wind. Stable in the NRA (probably). His sorta-sister, Annette, would laugh herself into a coronary when she heard. Which was the cherry on the sundae of the crap day that was today.

He bounced to his feet with only the smallest of groans

"Ag."

and limped upstairs, then paused at the door and listened, nostrils flaring as he tried to take in anything but moldy basement. Nothing, which meant she'd fled or was standing really, really still. Waiting. Probably upwind with the gun. Or worse, a lecture. Either way, he couldn't exactly live in her basement, could he? (Nope.) Had to get back to the job at hand, right? (Yep.) Had to earn enough money to buy a good-sized house in the country for their cubs to romp and *what the hell was that now?*

It took longer than he'd thought to break the lock—had to make it look like a Stable broke it—which made sense because it was that kind of day. She and the cub had both left by the time he made it back into the living room.

Of course.

Chapter 5

IN THE END, THERE WAS NOTHING FOR IT BUT TO GO BACK. "Because home is where you go to find solace from the ever-changing chaos, to find love within the confines of a heartless world, and to be reminded that no matter how far you wander, there will always be something waiting when you return."

"Not gonna lie." Lila handed over a backpack bulging with toilet paper and heavy-duty trash bags. "That's some real insight you've got."

"Not mine." Rob blinked rheumy eyes while he pondered. He was slightly built, in a worn sweater, jeans so faded they were gray, and new running shoes. His hair was the color of his jeans, pulled back and secured with twist ties. He shoved up his sleeves, exposing bony wrists. "It's Kendal Rob's."

"Yeah, I don't know who that is. He's right, though. I've gotta go home. Well, technically it's not my home yet. I mean, I only just signed the lease." To the landlord's instant and almost overwhelming delight. Which bore thinking about, but not right this second. "All my underwear's still in boxes." If that wasn't "ever-changing chaos," she didn't know what qualified. "Anyway. Bye."

"Thanks for the stuff."

"Welcome."

Moving: pain in the ass. Figuring out what you can give away: actually enjoyable. It wasn't the first backpack stuffed with essentials she'd handed over to a homeless person, and probably not the last. So the evening hadn't been an entire wash. Just aggravating, stressful, and slightly expensive, like going to a *John Wick* movie.

She'd fled the neighborhood, the wolf, and the guy who'd broken in, then checked into a hotel to give herself space and time. She'd thought about it half the night, pretending to mull her options, but she knew there had been only one, and what she was really doing was laying out the case for herself. Because the truth of it was she couldn't afford to put the time, money, and effort into moving again, and she wouldn't run. Well, she wouldn't run far. And she wouldn't/couldn't call the cops. And it was her home, dammit. Her first house! Technically. As of yesterday.

The stud she'd booted had nothing to do with any of her calculations. Because why would he? The wolf wasn't a factor, either. She certainly wasn't going back because she hoped to see it again, preferably at a safe distance. Or an unsafe one. No: This was about her pride. She wasn't one to be run off.

After Googling closest hotels, she'd booked something called an efficiency room at Hotel 340, whatever the hell that was. When she asked why management didn't just commit to an extra twenty degrees and call it "Hotel 360," she got a funny look.

Turned out efficiency room meant "glorified closet" or, as the hotel called it, "European style!" But she had to admit it was the nicest closet she'd ever slept in. Free Wi-Fi, too, which was vital. She'd also enjoyed some me-time with the shower nozzle, thinking about green eyes and broad shoulders until her knees wanted to give out, and once she was clean and dry she didn't so much fall asleep as pass out.

She made time the next morning to check out the library, which was also vital. Everywhere Lila lived, she immediately located: (1) the nearest ER, (2) the best grocery store, and (3) the library.

She'd also been able to pick up a few necessities and donate merch on her way back to Lilydale. And so the time had come, because that box of faded hipster underwear wasn't going to unpack itself. Nor was the box of cookbooks she never used to cook with.[1]

She pulled up to her rental and eyeballed the place from the

---

1. What? Lots of people collect cookbooks they never use to cook with. It's not weird. Shut up!

driveway. She'd thought it charming pretty much immediately, and that hadn't faded even after an odd night.

The house, built in 1920, was two-storied, slate gray with brown trim, and boasted an agreeably large front porch. (She'd never had a front porch before. Or any porch. Or a house.) The front yard was a typical suburban postage-stamp that probably took the owner all of fifteen minutes to mow, with a larger back-yard that likely took twenty. (She'd never had a yard before, either.) Inside were laughably small bedrooms (she'd never had more than one and often not even that) and a laughably large kitchen (not hyperbole—she'd laughed out loud when she saw it), two baths (one just off the kitchen for some reason, in case you wanted to cook, pee, then cook more), dark hardwood floors, and lots of original woodwork. Too big for one person, but the price had been too good to pass up.

The thing was a hundred years old, so instead of an open plan, it was chopped up into several small rooms, three of which had fireplaces in unlikely spots. (She'd never had three fireplaces before. Or one. Not since she was a kid.) The fireplaces made her nervous, natch, and she couldn't look at one too long before her arms started to itch, but she'd had them checked over pretty thoroughly, made sure they were cleaned and cleared of decades of soot buildup. Off-street parking and a washer–dryer were definite pluses, but the detail that had sealed the deal was the mystery garden in back.

If you went out the back-kitchen door, you'd see the detached garage (gray with brown trim, like the house), a stretch of lawn, and to the right a perfectly maintained smallish garden that she assumed had been lifted from the backyard of a London house way back in 1930. (No other explanation.)

Thick trees crowded right up to the high fence, and there was a charming brick path leading through the lawn and coming to an abrupt halt at the far end of the yard. There was a small brown shed tucked in the corner, probably for rakes and a mower and lawn chairs and whatever else people needed sheds for.

There was a small, black, wrought iron table and two chairs in the middle of the garden, which also had climbing vines and rose-bushes on three sides. There was a small plot that would be perfect for herbs and tomatoes, maybe a salsa garden, and it was all tucked away and impossible to see from anywhere outside the house; the fence was *that* high.

You could sit out there enjoying nature or wondering why tomatoes all ripened on the same hour of the same day, and no one would know what you were doing. You could be by yourself or have company. You could relax in the backyard while a great big wolf rested at your feet, and you'd fix it lamb kebabs. You could grill or just enjoy sickeningly sweet margaritas or flip through a cookbook you'd never use or stream one of the *Scream* movies or all of the above, and they'd have to look *so* hard to find you. And they wouldn't know you were in there minding your own business, you and your wolf friend, unless you wanted them to.

Even better, the landlord straight-up told her that if she liked the place well enough, he'd be amenable to selling. So that was that. Lease, signed. Check, cashed. Boxes, unloaded. Smoke detectors, installed, checked, checked again. Weird bear cub (werecub?) rescued. Cops blissfully unaware of what transpired. Intruder dealt with.

Intruder with merry green eyes and swimmer shoulders dealt with.

And now she was back. But she'd take precautions. Well. *More* precautions.

Home again, home again, jiggity—yeah, she'd never under-stood that one. Home again, then. Best to keep it simple.

Chapter 6

SHE WAS SHE WAS SHE WAS HERE! HERE IN THIS OLD HOUSE that smelled like dust and

(*lemons*)

something sharp, something that would hurt his eyes and nose if he ate it and if she was here and *he* was here then she was safe but the other, the other

(*cub*)

girl, she was out in the world, out of his territory, but maybe maybe she would come to the house of dust and sharp smells and by now he'd prowled around twice and there weren't any predators

(*there's me*)

and the cub might come and then they would both be safe he would keep them safe and then his own cubs would come and he could make everyone safe not like not like

(*the time Before*)

when *he* was a cub, not like when *he* was small so that was that was good she was good and the cub was good and he would keep everyone safe and no one would be hurt and no one would die and leave him leave him alone.

"Boy! Get gone! I might not be able to see you, but I can smell you."

(Mama Mac oh hooray!!!!)

(*oh shit*)

He jumped so high all four paws left the ground and he was grown he was a *big wolf* now and not a cub but he still wanted to run to Mama Mac and run away from Mama Mac because that yell meant trouble and he had to fall back had to slink from sight *and* smell and it was good because Mama Mac would keep her safe inside and he would keep her safe outside and maybe the cub would come and that was good it was all good it was very very very very good.

———————

Lila hadn't been back five minutes when the old-fashioned door-bell rang. It was *really* old-fashioned, the kind where you wound the button like a clock instead of pressing it, and instead of a charming *ding-dong* you got a loud metallic rasp that sounded like the house was giving you a raspberry: *bbbbrrrrraaatttttttt!*

"Let the madness commence," she announced. Or would it recommence? Was that a word? Also, who masterminded the whole "let's make doorbells sound harsh and rude" plan?

Bbbbbbbbbbrrrrrrrrrrrraaaaaaaaatttttttt!

"Jeez, give me thirty seconds to get to the *door*." And on swing-ing it open (even on hinges, the front door was heavy): "Huh."

A tiny woman in purple was beaming at her. She could have been anywhere from her late forties to her early sixties; her face was mostly unlined (save for the network of laugh lines) but her hair was white, she looked delicate but had a firm grip, she had dark brown skin but light blue eyes. Her jeans were dirty at the knees, but her sweater was spotless. She'd chewed off her lipstick, but her purple eye shadow was flawless. She came up to Lila's shoulder, which meant she was slightly taller than a mailbox. A bundle of contradictions, standing on her doorstep.

"Are you here about the stray?" Lila asked.

"Maybe. What kind?"

"A dog, I think." She'd gotten a bare glimpse of a lean canine fading into the shrubbery when she pulled into the driveway. *Dog*, her mind assumed, just like she would assume horse over unicorn. But now she was starting to wonder. The creature had been so fast, she hadn't had time to see if it was limping from, say, being clipped by a decommissioned ambulance. "But maybe not."

"You wouldn't think it, given how close we are to Saint Paul, but there are a few coyotes out in the woods back of your house. They won't hurt you, though."

"Right, right. The old 'they're more scared of you than you are of them' saying."

"No, they just can't be bothered. And before I forget, welcome to the neighborhood!" This while shoving a plastic container at Lila.

"Thanks."

"My name's Meredith Macropi, but everyone calls me Mama Mac."

"My name's Lila Kai, and everybody calls me Lila Kai." She cracked the container and took a peek. "You've brought me piles of…confetti? Thanks. I was out of confetti."

"Fairy bread!"

"I'm sorry?"

"That's what it *is*." The small old (?) woman bustled past Lila, taking back her container

(*oh thank God*)

and heading for the kitchen as if she knew the layout, then putting said fairy bread on the counter.

(*Dammit.*)

"So I just wanted to welcome you, dear…" This while eyeing the large kitchen and looking around at Lila's few boxes. Probably wondering why there weren't more, but too polite to ask. Once upon a time, everything Lila owned could be packed into one of those plastic boxes the post office handed out when you had to pick up a bunch of mail. Once upon a later time, seventy percent of Lila's belongings were books. But last year she'd joined the hordes in the twenty-first century and bought a Kindle, then jammed it with downloads with the money she'd made selling most of her used texts.

"…and see if you need anything," the woman was saying.

"Only confetti. And you fixed that. Thanks again." Lila moved toward the arch that led to the living room and took a step back, as if ushering her out, hoping the other woman would take the hint.

Nope. She wasn't budging from the kitchen. She wasn't asking about the busted screen door, either, though it was barely hanging by part of one hinge, and whenever the breeze picked up, which was constant as it was chilly and windy, you could hear the *whack-thwap!* of it banging against the doorway. What's-his-face from last night was quick *and* strong (though not quick enough), which bore keeping in mind when she saw him again.

If. *If* she saw him again.

She wanted to see him again, which was equal parts worrying and thrilling.

"It's not confetti, dear, it's fairy bread. I told you that. I'm Meredith Macropi—"

"You told me that, too."

"—and—oh, here. Come here."

Lila's feet were obeying before her brain realized it; she instantly decided the elderly (?) woman was no one to mess with. Lila had been ordered around by the best (and the worst), and she'd been able to ignore just about all of them or wear them out. But here she was, crossing the kitchen and accepting a piece of…

"You said this was fairy bread?"

For that, she got an approving nod. Lila felt herself warming to the intrusive creature and took a bite to cover her confusion.

Fairy bread, it happened, was soft white bread generously spread with salted butter, then *drowned* in a rainbow of cupcake sprinkles, which, if you were tired from a long weird night and surprised by yet another mystery visitor, you might confuse with piles of confetti. She would have worried about the sugar content if she could stop devouring the stuff long enough. One of those food combos that shouldn't have worked but did. Like candied bacon. Or chocolate-covered anything.

I'll just gobble down one or four more. Just to be polite. I don't get enough credit for being polite.

"See?" Macropi beamed. "I told you."

"You told me what it was, not that I'd like it," she retorted, lightly spraying the woman with sprinkles. She covered her mouth. "Sorry."

"Never mind," Macropi replied, shaking her head and dislodging sprinkles from her tight white curls. "This is a big hit with the young ones where my folks are from."

"Australia?" Lila guessed.

It earned her another broad smile. "Yes! Hardly anyone picks up on that."

"Really?" Macropi's striking coloring—dark skin, white hair, light eyes—in conjunction with the homemade treat right out of a Buzzfeed listicle ("Top Ten Australian Treats", or "Find out what kind of fairy bread you are!") indicated she could be of aboriginal descent.

"I live just over there," she added, gesturing vaguely. "And I was *so* pleased when I found out the Curs House was being rented again."

"Yours would be the purple house at the end of the block? With the purple birdhouse in front?"

"You're *very* smart," the woman said solemnly, then chuckled. Lila found herself smiling back, which was annoying.

"Naw. Just observant." Lila had no idea what it was like in Australia, but where she came from, you paid attention or you got locked up. Or worse. "Did I hear you call this the cursed house?"

"It's the *Curs* House," she replied, emphasizing the name. "That's who owned it back in the day."

"The landlord's name is Harriss."

"Yes, well. The house changed hands now and again."

"The price was pretty reasonable..." Lila trailed off, inviting gossip.

Macropi didn't disappoint. "It's always something with this place. Oh, don't misunderstand, m'dear! It's a wonderful house, and I'm *so* glad to see someone living here again."

"Yeah?"

"Oh, yes. The Harrisses have been trying to sell it on and off for a decade or so, but every now and again, they'll take it off the market and rent it instead. I can't imagine having to make two mortgage payments, can you?"

Lila, who couldn't imagine making one, shook her head.

"But something always happens, and then they have to clean up and try to sell it again. The tenants will get a new job halfway across the country. Or they'll get a new spouse who doesn't want to live in Lilydale."

"Understandable." Lila started to relax.

"Or murdered."

"Sorry, what?"

"Or the basement floods," Macropi added thoughtfully. "Or there's another fire."

"How many have there been?"

"Or the possums come back."

"Are you serious?"

"Or they have a problem with all the wildlife coming up from the gorge. We're right on a nature preserve, you know. There's all kinds of creatures around."

"Jesus Christ." Then, because little old (?) ladies weren't usually cool with blasphemy, Lila added, "Sorry. You surprised me."

"Don't worry, m'dear. I'm sure *you'll* do fine. You said yourself, the price was right. And it's *so* charming, don't you think? Especially if you like wildlife."

"It's in a river gorge." Plus it had a secret garden in the back. And the trees crowded right up to the fence, protecting everyone in the house. And mysterious hot men tended to show up out of nowhere. "How could I say no?"

Another beam. "Exactly! And big enough for you to fill with a family. You should meet one of my boys. He's an accountant." Macropi paused, considering. "Well, maybe not anymore."

"What, he can't hold a job?"

Macropi ignored the dig. "He would *adore* you."

"That's presumptuous," Lila observed.

"Well, so is he."

Lila laughed before she could catch herself. "How'd you know I don't have a boyfriend?"

"How do you know you won't like my Oz?"

"Who?"

"He has his own money, you know. He doesn't have to work at all. He does, though," Macropi added hastily. "He's not *lazy*."

"Excellent. I certainly don't want to meet anyone who lives below the poverty level in squalid laziness."

"You're teasing, right, dear?" Macropi's smile fell away as she cocked her head to the side like a rabbit listening for dogs. "Oh. I guess I'd better—you've got company."

"Seems about right for this place." She heard the door slam and went to look out the doorway. Her landlord's truck, emblazoned with *Harriss & Son* on the side, had just pulled in. "So I do. Harriss is here, prob'ly about the screen door."

"Screen door?"

Oh, very nice. Macropi did an excellent "golly, I only now noticed that incredibly obvious thing in the room" routine. "Yeah, must've happened while I was staying downtown last night."

"—oh."

The expected follow-up (something along the lines of "why in the world did you sleep somewhere besides your new home last night") didn't come, and Lila was pretty sure she knew why. But by now, Harriss had given a cursory knock on the sagging, swinging screen door, then poked his head inside, also doing an impersonation of a man who has seen nothing strange and isn't being inconvenienced in the slightest. "Morning!"

"It is," Lila agreed. "Do you want some edible confetti? I'd offer you the fairy bread, but it's possible I gobbled it all down."

Harriss wrinkled up his nose, which was broad and almost flat. His small dark eyes peered up at Macropi, as the diminutive fairy bread peddler topped him by two inches. "You *still* handing that stuff around, Mama Mac? Think I still got some sprinkles in my beard from the last time."

"It's hardly my fault your kind are sloppy eaters," Macropi retorted.

Harriss let out a cheerful hoot. "My kind wipes the floor with your kind and has for, oh, as long as the planet's had life? So, millions and millions of years? Yeah." Harriss was short but powerfully built, like a bearded fire hydrant. He was close to bald; the only hair on his head was scattered clumps almost the exact texture of his full black beard.

"Utter nonsense."

Lila let out a discreet cough to refocus the chat. "*Caw-CHAWWWW!* So, the door," she prompted.

"No worries, no worries," he assured her. "I'll have it fixed for you real quick. My son's here to help me."

"How *is* Harry?" Macropi asked with bright-eyed curiosity.

Harriss's friendly expression sagged. "Still living at home."

"Ah. Well. It's…it's nice to have your son so close! He won't always be there, you know."

"Don't tease," he sighed.

"I thought you were going to bribe—" Macropi coughed. "I thought you were going to encourage him to leave home once he got his pilot's license?"

"That was Plan D. We're deeper into the alphabet now."

Lila decided it was time to jump back in. "Well, that's swell. Sorry to inconvenience you first thing in the morning."

Harriss shrugged. "No problem."

"And take you away from the rest of your family."

Harriss shrugged again. "They're sick of my face anyway."

"Understandable," Macropi said with a sniff, then ruined it with a smile.

"It's true!" a male voice, presumably Harry Harriss, bellowed from outside.

"Anything else?" the elder Harriss asked, clearly dying to fix the hell out of anything Lila might name: the door, random cabinets, her juvie record. "Any problems?"

"Aside from my screen door yanked off its hinges my first night?" She paused and realized they were both staring her down, waiting wide-eyed for…what? A confession? A loan? A declaration of intent to vacate the premises? "Nope."

"Oh."

"Great!" This from Harriss, who beamed like someone had just handed him a check instead of a repair bill. He still had that odd odor about him, which she had noticed when he showed her the house. It wasn't unpleasant, just…tangy? Like a pickle. A clean pickle. "I'll get to it, then."

"So you had a…quiet night? Before you left?"

"Soooooo quiet," Lila assured her.

"You didn't see anything unusual?" Macropi persisted.

"Not a thing," she lied with a bland smile. No one—no one on this fucking earth—could lie like Lila. She'd done it to save lives—not just her own—and once she understood the power of conviction paired with conventional good looks paired with a high stress threshold, that was fucking that. There was a time and place for the truth. This wasn't it. "I feel like I could stay here for-*ev*-er."

Take note, friendly weirdos.

Chapter 7

W‍HEN TROUBLE RETURNED, L‍ILA WAS READY.

"Finally," she told the cub–girl. "Been waiting half the day." For the other one—the scruffy hunk she'd booted into the basement—but she wasn't about to tell the kid that. And she certainly wouldn't let the kid know how disappointed she was. Lila figured that was the worst emotion to show a runaway.

She wasn't just disappointed, she realized. She was actually crushed that it was the kid and not the green-eyed stranger. She couldn't get him or the wolf out of her head. If she wasn't so confused, she'd be terrified. *He broke in. He's after a child. You shouldn't be intrigued, you should be scared and disgusted.* And then, the voice of her mother: *Get your head straight.*

"You remember I have a front door, right? And a back door? The screen door's been fixed and everything."

"Uh-huh."

"I only ask because you're hung up in my basement window."

The child grunted and wriggled forward another inch. "I'm mostly all. The way. *Through*," she gasped.

"Is it possible that you were a bear cub a minute earlier and changed back at the worst possible time?"

"I couldn't help it!"

"Couldn't help it? So that…" Lila gestured at her. "That just happens? Anytime? Or during a full moon?"

"What's the moon gotta do with it? Usually I mean for it to happen," she mumbled. "But sometimes I slip."

"Might as well slip down here, then." Lila reached up, caught the kid–cub under her armpits, and pulled with careful pressure.

"Careful!"

"I *am*," she almost-but-not-quite snapped, then carefully lowered the kiddo to the cement floor.

The child blinked up at her in the basement's poor light. "D'you have pizza? Last night you talked about pizza."

"Last night I talked about several things."

"Yeah, but is there pizza?"

There was.

———————————

"So, your leg seems better."

"Mmff? Uh-huh." The girl glanced down at herself. She was barefoot in the clothes she'd tossed into Lila's basement before changing or transforming or warping or whatever the hell were-bears did: jeans that were too big and a sweatshirt she swam in. "Wasn't so bad. S'not like the bone was sticking out or anything."

"No, I think I would have noticed that last night. And you wouldn't be here right now if you had a compound fracture twelve hours ago. You're not even limping."

"Compound fracture, yuck! D'you have to learn that stuff to drive your ambulance?"

"It's not an ambulance. Here, put these on. The bottoms of your feet are coal black. Next time, steal socks, too." Lila, who had liberated clothing from more than one laundromat during her juvie phase, and also three years ago when she drove into Lake Minnetonka, was in no position to judge. So she just handed over a pair of thick red socks. Judging by the unruly mop of black waves, the kid probably should have liberated a brush, too. "And speaking of last night…"

"I know! It's how come I'm here."

"Again," Lila prompted. "It's how come you're here again."

"Well, yeah."

"Are you in trouble? Wait." Stupid question. Bear-Girl was

obviously, clearly, completely in trouble. "How much trouble are you in?"

"I just haveta find my—" She cut herself off, put down the pizza and blushed, hard. It was remarkable to see; one minute you could see the golden undertones in her complexion, and the next she was doing a flawless impersonation of a beefsteak tomato. "Sorry, I just 'membered, I don't know your name."

"Lila Kai."

"I'm Sally Smalls."

"Are you really?" Lila asked, delighted. "That's not a name, that's a mythical elfin creature from an enchanted forest. Or a cartoon character."

"I'm not a cartoon. I like forests, though. Your house goes right up against the woods!"

"Tell me about it. Major selling point as far as I was concerned." A pity the landlord hadn't mentioned the bear cub situation… Perhaps she'd raise that at the next tenant meeting. The thought made her grin. "Okay, so…your folks? You got separated?"

Sally was crunching her way through her third slice. Hadn't even waited for Lila to zap it in the microwave. "Uh-huh. Mommy's been sick, too. So it's really important I get back to them."

"That sucks."

The child nodded. "Uh-huh. Daddy's taking care of her and all, but she doesn't like being sick. She's tired all the time."

"Okay. So you were separated…"

"Well, they had to take a special trip to Boston, but they're late coming back."

"How late?"

"A couple of days," she replied vaguely. "So I need to be ready for when Daddy comes."

"Which is why that guy came looking for you?"

"Uh-huh."

"To take you away? But not in a good way?"

"I need to be ready," the child said again, and the intensity was strange in such a youngster.

"So what's the plan?"

"You're asking me? I'm ten."

Lila sat back in her chair. "Well, *I* don't have a plan. Well, maybe tracking down the guy from last night—except that'd be a dim move, according to every movie in the world."

The girl laughed at her. "You can't track him!"

"Could if I wanted," Lila replied, offended. "Wait, you know who he is? What's his name? Does he live around here? Do you know why he's after you?"

"Uh-huh." She shrugged. "But like I said, you couldn't track him. Anyways, it doesn't matter. He's gonna come here."

"Of course he is," Lila sighed. "That's what my life is now." *And here's the stupid part: I can't wait to see him again. Probably because there's something wrong with me.* How d'you know the guy?"

"Caseworker. A *dumb* one." The child sighed. "Okay, that's kinda mean. It's just, he won't listen to me! About anything!"

"I noticed the same quality. It's why he ended up in my basement."

"Ha! That's right." Sally smirked. "When I heard all the swearing I grabbed my chance."

"Yeah, and next time you suck down all my honey and then dart off into the night, close the front door all the way."

"Oh. Okay." Chastened, Sally added, "Anyways, when he comes back, be careful. If you make him mad, his sister will *eat* you."

Lila, who had been getting up from her kitchen chair, froze mid-rise. "Please tell me that's hyperbole."

"Dunno what that is."

"It means exaggeration."

"Then just say exaggeration."

"Hey!" Lila said sharply. "Did I break into your house and then tell you what words to use?" She didn't bother ducking; the pizza crust sailed past her left shoulder. "Too wide," she observed.

"I didn't break in! I just…came. Into your house. Because of how you were. Last night."

"Because of how I…" Too late, Lila noticed the child's big dark eyes looked bigger and darker because they were filling with tears. "Oh, shit. Don't cry. *Please* don't cry." Lila hated tears, including her own. It was always awkward and weird and terrible, and she never knew what to do with her hands. Pat the weeper on the shoulder? Hug them? Hand over a box of tissues? Or a sandwich? Or just wave goodbye, hoping they'd leave? Or wave at the weeper while *she* left?

Worse, she was still stuck mid-rise. Should she sit back down? Or go to the fridge for more milk? Or stay frozen, adding physical discomfort to an already awkward situation?

It was even worse when the weeper denied they were weeping. Then she had to sit there and pretend everything was normal and that the weeper wasn't leaking like a soft tire. Nine times out of ten, weeping didn't solve anything; it was almost always a waste of time, energy, and saline.

"I'm not crying!" This in a voice thick with tears and pizza.

Lila sat back down. "Well, thank God for that. If you were crying, it'd be super awkward." Like now, for instance. Textbook example of why she hated tears. Should she reach across the table and try to hug a strange child? Who might turn into a tiny bear without warning? Should she pour milk? Or heat milk? Or just call Child Protective Services? And offer *them* milk when they came to get the kid? Actually, she should have called CPS the minute she saw the kid stuck in the basement window. And arguably last night.

But who did you call to report a bear-girl? A cop? A scientist? A Hollywood agent?

And if you *weren't* going to call Someone In Authority, then what?

Did the guy with the Caesar haircut count as Someone In Authority? A caseworker, the kid had said. But not a very good one. Perhaps he had. Um. Other qualities. She'd noted what he didn't have: respect for boundaries or a wedding ring. Maybe those issues were related.

Get the guy out of your head. "I'm sorry I upset you." Lila got up, went to the fridge, and grabbed a bottle of chocolate milk. She handed it off to Sally, who was blotting her tear-stained face and runny nose on a long red napkin, except there weren't any red napkins and it was actually Lila's scarf, *fuck*. "Argh, that'll teach me not to hang it up." Lila pulled it out of Sally's grasp and hung it on one of the pegs on the wall next to the fridge. "How can I help you? You're here for a reason."

"Uh-huh. 'Cuz of you."

"That makes no sense."

"I feel safe here."

"That," Lila said, "makes *less* sense."

"Plus you're not scared of me! Not even a bit!" The child's surprised delight was as warming as it was puzzling. "And you didn't call the bad guys."

"Only because I had no idea which bad guys to call. Or even which good guys. Look, if your folks are missing, shouldn't we call the cops? Or are you the one who's missing? In which case shouldn't we call the cops? Or CPS? Or an agency that's at least CPS adjacent?" Did werebears have their own Child Protective Services? Cub Protective Services? Lila thought about the puzzling call she'd endured last night

I'm afraid we don't deal in cubs. You need to call the IPA.

and thought they probably did. The voice on the other end had been annoying, which she'd expected—what after-hours call to a faceless bureaucrat wasn't annoying? For both parties? The lack of surprise, however, had (irony!) been a surprise. In fact, now that she thought about it, the operator's utter lack of surprise (or any noticeable emotion) while dealing with a woman calling from a Saint Paul suburb to report a bear cub in her house was both unexpected and chilling.

And not even your average bear cub. She'd Googled the cub's interesting coloring last night at the hotel. Sally Smalls was a sun bear, a species out of Southeast Asia. The alternative name was, hilariously, the honey bear. Completely by accident, Lila had picked the perfect snack to calm Sally down.

Sun bears were rare, too…tagged as *Vulnerable* on the list of endangered species.

Or at least, ordinary sun bears were rare.

The IPA. Do you need the number?

Curious. She'd ponder when she had some leisure. For now… "Look, Sally, CPS or the equivalent can at least set you up in a foster—"

Sally nearly choked on her milk. "No, you can't! They'll kill me! They'll tear me to pieces and go after my family and tear them up, too!"

"That's a pretty damning summation of the foster care system. How long have you been on your own, exactly?" Lila had assumed the girl had only recently gotten lost. Or run away. Or been abandoned—*fuck*, she had *no* information here. "Calm down, you don't have to—what are you doing?" The girl had stopped flailing; now her head was cocked sharply to the left and her knuckles whitened around the bottle of chocolate milk. "Are your Bear-Girl senses tingling?"

"Don't call me Bear-Girl. Do I call you Human-Lady?"

"Fair," Lila said, then watched bemused as Sally got up, practically ran to the fridge, then started poking around. "Also, and no judgement here, but what the hell are you doing?"

"Looking for baking soda."

"Sure. Sure. Totally normal thing that strange children do all the time in my kitchen."

"Ha!"

"How did you even know I have that?"

"Everyone has that," was the prompt reply. "And the box is almost always full. And old. This isn't even your baking soda, is it? I bet it belongs to whoever lived here before."

"So you're a werebear and a detective? Do you have an agent? I'm pretty sure you could get your own TV show. And I'd watch that show."

"My folks would be mad. Gotta get through middle school first." Sally fumbled with the box of baking soda, then dropped it, spilling white powder everywhere. "Sorry! I'll fix it."

"That's…" Lila watched in amazement as the child scooped up piles of soda (it had been a big box), rubbed them on her arms and legs, then scooped more. And sprinkled it in her hair, then rubbed it…under her arms? "…not fixing it. What are you *doing*?"

"Sorry. I'm a klutz. Wow, this stuff gets everywhere, huh?"

"Not really." *Laugh? Cry? Take away what's left of the baking soda? Start looking for a new apartment?* No, not that last one. Never that last one. She was in it to win it. Or until she died a terrible death at the hands of whoever was after the kid. Hopefully the former. "Not unless someone's doing it on purpose."

"Don't worry," Sally said and, oddly, Lila was reassured. "He won't dare hurt you." Then she set the near-empty box of soda down on the table, trotted to the basement door and down the steps.

Bbbbbbbbbbbrrrrrrrrrrraaaaaaaaattttttttt!

"Great," Lila said to her empty kitchen. She rose to answer the door, thinking that whoever changed doorbells to the traditional melodic-yet-dull *ding-dongggggg* was an overlooked genius.

Chapter 8

GOD, THAT'S AN IRRITATING DOORBELL. SOUNDS LIKE A ROBOT *yukking it up over a dirty joke.* Oz wound the old-fashioned buzzer again and heard measured footsteps—because of course they were measured, of course they weren't frantically fleet or running in the other direction or frozen in place—straightened from his habitual slouch and controlled the urge to run his fingers through his hair. He looked fine. It was all fine. He was fine.

And not to be crass, but she was, too.

Jesus. I'm sweating. And not because I had to shift back and get dressed in five seconds. What's going on? It was like a crush, if crushes hit with a tsunami of jitters and flop sweat. Who knew crushes

(*not a crush*)

bore such a striking similarity to malaria?

(*again: not a crush*)

Lila Kai peeked through the lace curtain, raised the eyebrow she could see, rolled the eye he could see, unlocked the door, and swung it wide. "No soliciting," she said pleasantly. Her curls were all out for themselves tonight, springing out from the headband she'd slapped on. Her dark blue eyes gleamed. Her pale blue socks read *'fuck off, I'm reading.'*[2]

He smelled the gun oil a fraction of a second before he noticed the pistol at her side. "It's loaded this time," she added in the casually matter-of-fact tone anyone else might use to inform him it was raining. "In case you were wondering."

"I know!" He stared at her, and not just because she looked like a sexy-yet-deranged Orphan Annie. "Because you fully expected me to come back. And…here you are!"

---

2. These exist. I'm wearing them right now!

"Your enthusiasm is off-putting and weird."

"I know!" he cried. "May I come in?"

"Well, there's no way to keep you out," she said, resigned. She pushed her glasses further up and stepped back.

He all but scampered across the threshold. "Thank you. You might not remember—"

"Sure I do. Your name is Ox, and your favorite hobby is trashing screen doors."

He coughed. "It's. Um. Oz, actually." He glanced around the sparsely furnished living room. A couch, an old easy chair, and boxes marked...*eyes*? And *arms*? No photos anywhere—nothing on the walls at all. "So...how's the unpacking going?"

"Nope."

"I'm sorry?"

"Nope to the chitchat. What do you want?"

"To know why you have boxes labeled 'eyes' and 'arms' in your living room."

"Nope."

"A glass of water?"

She sighed. "You know that every building and every house you passed to get here has running water, right?" But she was leading him into the kitchen, thank God. Her back was to him, so he flared his nostrils and tried to parse the cub's scent from everything else. But it was trickier than he'd expected, not least because *her* scent was overwhelming: cotton and blackberries with a smidge of gun oil and something that was just her.

"So how long have you been an EMT?"

"I'm not an EMT." This over her shoulder while she filled a glass.

"But you drive an ambulance."

"That's not an ambulance." She handed him the glass. "And I said no chitchat. What do you want?"

To know what the hell is all over the floor? Oh, and to father cubs on you. Mustn't forget that! "To welcome you to the neighborhood?"

"Nope. Try again."

Oh, Christ. It's baking soda. Nicely done, hot Orphan Annie. He drained the glass because it was time to grab the theoretical bull by the theoretical horns. "Why is there baking soda all over your floor?"

"Oh, that?" Lila looked around, appearing to only now notice the drifts of soda. "Yeah, that's baking soda."

"I know it's baking soda." He also had a pretty good idea about why it was out. "Why's it all over the floor?"

"I use it to brush my teeth."

"You needed all that to brush your teeth?" he asked, dumbfounded. "On the floor and table? In the kitchen? Also, why are you brushing your teeth on the kitchen floor?"

"Well, I also use it for deodorant," she elaborated. "And calluses."

"What?"

"And to clean my bathroom. And to slow down kidney disease."[3]

"Oh my God!" He hadn't smelled a thing! How could he father cubs on her if she had kidney disease? And why was that his big worry right now? "You've got a kidney disease?"

"No. But I'm a huge fan of the Boy Scout motto."

"I don't get it," he admitted.

"That's fine."

"So you're okay? You don't have a kidney disease? You could theoretically be around for years and years?"

She blinked. "Um. What?"

He was staring around at the wreck of her kitchen. "Why's so much of it on the floor?"

"Grease fire."

"You had a…" As far as he could smell, the stove (which, per Mama Mac, replaced the 1972 model that resulted in the Curs House's third kitchen fire) hadn't *ever* been turned on, never mind in the last twenty-four hours.

---

3. Truly a miracle product!

"More water?" she asked with faux brightness. "No? Fully hydrated? Goodbye."

Nothing. Not a whiff of the cub. Just baking soda and blackberries. He turned, following his nose, and then...

"Are you having a stroke, Ox? Your nostrils are flaring all over the place."

...he caught something. A ghost of a whiff on one particular item of clothing, which he snatched up.

"Jesus Christ," she muttered, snatching it back. "What is it with the scarf?"

"She *was* here!" *Now. Now she'll admit it.*

"Nope. Nobody here but us weirdos. Or would that be we weirdos?" Then, abruptly: "What happened to your arm?"

"My arm?" he repeated. He knew he sounded stupid. Couldn't help it. Also, she wasn't supposed to notice. And she wasn't supposed to be the opposite of rattled. Unrattled. De-rattled?

"*Your arm,*" she emphasized, as if speaking to the slow and dim-witted, which he clearly was. "You're obviously a lefty—"

Obviously?

"—but you're favoring it. And..." She reached for him and his heart stopped. Then it got back to work so hard he was momentarily dizzy as she pulled up his right sleeve, exposing the bandage. "...someone bound this up for you."

Mama Mac, in fact. His foster mother had gotten an earful *and* an eyeful last night. And speaking of, there were telltale signs of fairy bread here and there. The Mama Mac Welcome Wagon had clearly been in full swing.

He wrenched his attention back to her observation. "It's just a bad sprain." Truth. Last night, it had been a break. Tomorrow, it'd be a strain. By Friday, it wouldn't hurt anymore. In two weeks, he'd be back to one-armed pull-ups. Theoretically. Who had time for one-armed pull-ups? And now he wanted fairy bread, dammit!

"Did you get that when you fell down the basement stairs?"

He quirked an eyebrow at her. "Fell?" She grinned, which was so distracting he answered without thinking. "No. That was…" *When you nearly ran me over with your ambulance that isn't an ambulance.* "Earlier." He coughed. That sounded natural, right? Like a tickle in his throat instead of a clumsy attempt to get off the subject of his injury? "Listen, Lila, the reason I'm here…"

"Oh, goody. You're finally getting to it."

"…I'm looking for a runaway." Sally Smalls, werebear (subspecies *Helarctos malayanus*), age ten, temporary *parens familia*[4], last seen leading several IPA employees on a merry chase. Well, one IPA employee. He produced a school picture with Sally scowling at the photog. "I've got reason to believe she was here."

"What, you're some kind of social worker?"

"No, I'm some kind of an accountant." *Jesus.* He really should work on his lying. Or his impulse to give her honest answers. Then, compounding his idiocy, he handed her his card.

She examined it. "You've crossed out 'accountant' and written in 'World's Greatest Detective-slash-Juvenile Advocate.' And you wrote out 'slash' instead of putting in a slash."

"What? Oh." He snatched it back. "That's just the prototype."

"For IPA, right? Whatever that is." She paused, but he didn't elaborate. "Macropi was telling me I should meet someone she thought might be an accountant. Must be you."

For the first time in his life, Oz was grateful for Mama Mac's incessant matchmaking. As she bandaged his arm, he had babbled about Lila. A lot. But he didn't have the nerve to ask Mama the vital question. Probably just as well. *Kama-Rupa* was a fairy tale.

"So you're a bum, got it." Before he could defend himself, she added, "This missing girl, what's she done?"

"Nothing," he said. "Her folks passed away a couple of days ago,

---

4. Ward of the Family, a designation unique to Shifters.

and she's having a hard time dealing with it. I've been trying to look after her."

"Is that what you call it?" she asked, so pleasantly it was terrifying. She pointed to his sore arm. "Looking after her?"

Mindful of the gun, he immediately raised his hands. "Hey, I got hurt helping her, not hurting her."

"Oh, sure. That's why you kicked in my door. Because you're *not* one of the bad guys."

"Well, I'm not." *Was that a whine? I think that was a whine.* "I just want Sally to be saaaaaaafe."

"Well, she's not here." Lila shrugged. "So."

So, an obvious lie, which he had expected. Except…

"Anything else?" she asked, just on this side of impatience.

She still wasn't afraid. In fact, he wasn't getting much of anything off her. Last night hadn't been a fluke. She was different, and not just because she was Stable, and he wasn't sure how, and it was intriguing as fuck.

Lock her down before another wolf sniffs her out.

The thought was so sudden and alarming, he started to growl, then loudly cleared his throat to cover.

"Sounds like you need more water."

He shook his head and cleared his throat again. "Listen, I'm not going to hurt you. Or the kid."

"Oh, I know."

"I *mean* you don't need your weapon."

"Not your call. How about you run along while you're still able?"

"Are you threatening me?" he asked, delighted.

"Not if you get off on it. So, to sum up, I don't know anything that can help you and your little runaway isn't here and you need new business cards and you were just leaving, go find a brick-and-mortar stationery store if they still have those, g'bye."

"Ah-*ha*! I never said she was a runaway." Wait, had he? In so many words? Maybe it was inferred. No. Implied. It was hard to remember; she smelled so *good*. "See, you do know something."

"And I never told you my name was Lila."

Shit. Hadn't she? Too late, he realized she hadn't introduced herself. He knew her name because he'd talked to the owner of the Curs(ed) House, who talked to Mama Mac, who talked to him. While she was patching him up after this terrifying crazy-but-cute woman knocked him into her basement and then threw baking soda everywhere. And they didn't talk about *Kama-Rupa*, which definitely wasn't a thing, and since it wasn't a thing, he definitely wasn't in the throes of it. Relief! "I know this looks bad. But Sally needs my help. It's my job to keep her and kids like her safe." Well. Eventually it'd be his job. Depending on how he handled *this* job.

"Then run along and do that. She's. Not. Here."

Oz heard the pounding footsteps half a second before the basement door was slammed open so hard, it bounced off the wall and slammed back shut. The door opened again, slowly, and a familiar face peered out. "I'm not going anywhere!"

"God *damn* it," Lila groaned, rubbing her temples.

"Waste of baking soda," he agreed.

Chapter 9

THE FIRST THING THE LI'L JERK DID AFTER BLOWING BOTH their covers was laugh at her. "What're you gonna do with *that*?" she asked, pointing to Lila's gun.

"Let's not taunt the nice armed lady," Ox cautioned, which was gratifying.

"I'm only one of those things," Lila said. Then, to the kid: "Really? I'm up here lying my ass off—beautifully, I might add, this idiot had no idea—"

"Hey!"

"—only for you to stumble in at the exact wrong time."

"Well, you're talkin' about *me*," the child said pertly. "Doncha wanna know what I think?"

"Not even a little."

"Sally, a whole bunch of people are worried about you," Ox put in. "And what happened to your leg, honey?"

"My leg's good, and you go back to IPA and tell 'em to quit worrying about me," she ordered. "My folks are on the way, and we're gonna go live in California. So you go bug some other kid."

"Sally."

A sniff. "What."

Ox sighed. "Sally…"

Pouting a little. "*What?*"

"Your folks are dead," Ox said gently. "You know this."

"They aren't dead."

"Sally."

"They *aren't*." To Lila: "See? This is the problem."

"I'm lost," Lila confessed. "Also, do I have to be here for this conversation? I feel like I don't need to be here. I also feel the convo doesn't need to be held in my house. If anyone's wondering."

Ox sighed. "Understandable."

"Which part?"

"Look, Lila, I know I'm not exactly an invited guest—"

"Neither of you are," Lila pointed out.

"—but could we just sit down and talk about this?"

"Maybe over pizza?" Sally added hopefully.

"You ate all the pizza." But Lila shooed them both out of the baking soda–laden kitchen and into the living room, and she wasn't sure why. She knew this was idiotic. *Well, I'm intrigued. Sue me.*

Ox and Sally settled on opposite ends of the couch, glaring at each other. Lila stood before them and, from long habit, absently made sure she had a clear shot at the door. "Okay, so, I'm probably wondering why I called you here today."

"He just needs to leave me alone!" Sally burst out, then followed up with an angry forearm wipe to the nose. "I'm not bothering him, I'm not bothering *anybody*."

"That's not true at all," Lila pointed out.

"It's not about bothering," Ox said. "You can't be on your own. You're too young."

"I'm *not* on my own. My parents are *alive*!"

This child, Lila thought, speaks in italics *all* the *time*.

"Sally, I'm sorry to have to say this to you yet again, but the… bodies…"

Wait, a pause? Why is he pausing? Is he about to use a euphemism? Or lie?

"…were identified. There's no doubt. Your parents are dead. Their DNA was all over the… They're gone."

"You wouldn't even let me see the bodies!"

"Of course I wouldn't let you see the bodies!" He shot to his feet, paced a few steps, then plunked back down on the couch.

"I'm not taking you to a crash site hundreds of miles away where you have to wade through loads of debris while trying to get a look at what's left of your poor parents! No one anywhere thinks that's a good idea. You could travel the globe, taking a poll, and every single person would talk about what a terrible idea seeing a crash site is."

Crash site? "Crash site?"

"Their Cessna went down two days ago."

"Oh." To Sally: "I'm sorry."

"You just have to take our word for it, Sally. Why would we lie? D'you think we *want* to haul kids into the system? We don't, I promise. Seeing the bodies, *Jesus.*" Ox sounded equal parts exasperated and horrified. "But my point is, you're not alone. There's a whole system in place to help you."

Sure, your folks are toast and they've forfeited their frequent flier miles and you're all alone in the world, but cheer up—social services exists! Lila began to get an inkling of the dilemma—on both sides.

But at least Ox hadn't simply tried to grab the kid and leave and screw explanations to clueless civilians. So he was either a thoughtful individual who abhorred violence, genuinely cared about Sally, and preferred to talk things out, or he didn't want a bullet in the kneecap. Either way: here they were.

"So…" *He could be really good with our kids. Once he gets in some practice, that is. He'd be a good sire. Tall, smart, quick cubs with green eyes.*

Wait, *what*?

Lila realized they were waiting for her to finish her sentence. "So this 'system in place,' that'd be IPA?" Lila asked.

He did one of those awkward cough things that he could *not* pull off. "I, uh, can't really talk about that to people outside the agency."

"And yet." Lila silently gestured to the three of them, the room, her house…the meeting place. Where they were meeting. Where she, an accountant, and a bear cub were meeting.

And now that she thought about it, in a world with bear cubs masquerading as little girls (or vice versa), having a paranormal social service in place made nothing but sense. It wasn't like you could put Sally in with ordinary children. *Holy shit, no wonder the chick on the phone wanted me to call them! But is that their setup? Any rando can call IPA and report a wayward bear cub? How do they weed out the cranks? And what do they do with the non-bear cub people who call? They've gotta do something, because until last night I had no idea werebears were real. So how far does "the system set in place" go? Do people who find out their secret disappear? Is there a werebear secret police?*

And then, something new: *If there was a fire, he would go in after our babies. He'd never leave them to burn.*

She shook off the alien thought—it felt like a suggestion someone else was trying to download into her brain—and struggled to narrow her focus. "You don't want to talk about IPA, fine, let's talk about *her*." To Sally: "By which I mean you. So you think the accountant's wrong about your folks?"

Sally's dark eyes went wide. "You're an *accountant*?" This was in a tone of someone greatly betrayed. "Not one of my caseworkers? Why are you even chasing me then?"

"Hey, accountants are important! And I'm transitioning departments."

"The accountant," Lila began again, only to be interrupted again.

"My name's Oz," Ox whined.

"He's wrong about your folks," Lila continued. "That's what you're saying, right?"

"Cor-*rect*."

"You know they're alive."

"Yup." This was followed by a vigorous nod.

"Okay, but alive doesn't necessarily mean okay."

Ox cleared his throat. "Lila, we can't indulge the fantasy—"

Lila ignored such obvious madness. "What if your folks are sick? Or hurt? If their plane crashed, they'll have to recover before they can come get you. Maybe *that's* the hold up."

"Oh! Yeah, go ahead. Keep indulging the fantasy," he coaxed.

"Well." Sally frowned and nibbled on her lower lip. "I guess that's possible."

"If they're alive, they'll come for you. Right? You don't have to run. In fact, how will they find you if you're in the wind? Stay put," she coaxed. "Let the system take over, at least temporarily. Let them come to you."

"…maaaaaybe."

"Great!" Ox was on his feet. "Excellent plan."

Not really. But it would suit in the short-term. Even better, it would empty her house. She had a box of eyes to polish and an herb garden to plant and it wouldn't hurt to test all the smoke alarms again and she really should get around to having babies one of these days. Or this month. Sure, because then she wouldn't be too big during the hot summer months or during the worst part of winter. An autumn baby. Which was perfect, because she loved autumn. Maybe she'd even.

Um.

Name it. Autumn?

"Yes? We're all in agreement?" He looked around the room as if Lila actually had a vote. "So that's settled."

"Okay, but I'm not waitin' around too long," Sally warned. Lila doubted the man was listening; he seemed to be all about short-term solutions.

"Great, good. C'mon, honey, we've imposed on Lila long enough."

That, she thought, *was true yesterday. And they're still not out the door. Though the signs of departure look promising. Also, I might be having a series of small strokes.*

"Thanks for the pizza," Sally said, her small hand swallowed in Ox's much larger one. "And for listening to me."

"Sure." Lila couldn't think of anything to thank Sally for, so she kept quiet.

"You're the first one of your kind I've spent any real time with."

"Okay."

"I can't wait to tell my folks!" the child added. "They'll be *so* surprised."

"Okay."

"Great seeing you again," Ox added.

"It was?"

"Yeah, it was. Don't forget to put your gun up."

Lila snorted. Might as well tell her not to forget to breathe.

"Listen, Lila, maybe I'll see you around."

"Don't threaten me," she warned.

"That wasn't—do you think you'd want to get coff—never mind."

"Wait! What? Were you about to—" What was she doing? They were leaving! She must not hinder the leaving! "Never mind."

"Right. Exactly." He nodded. "I'm on the clock. So."

And then they were gone, not quite as abruptly as they came.

Chapter 10

AT THE SHARP KNOCK, LILA STOPPED UNPACKING AND WENT TO the door. "It's upon a midnight dreary," she said to the peephole. "So of course there's someone gently rapping at my chamber door."

From her porch: "It's Oz. From before? Oz Adway?"

Thank goodness he clarified, or she might have gotten him mixed up with the other Oz who'd broken in. She ignored the way her pulse picked up and opened the door. "'Tis some visitor entreating entrance at my chamber door."

He waved like a dork. "Hi!"

"Only this and nothing more."

"Poe?" he guessed.

"Had to memorize the whole thing for speech class my senior year. No matter how much I drink, I can't dislodge it. You can't come in."

He froze halfway across the threshold. "No?"

"It's midnight and you're a bumbling B&E guy I barely know. Of course 'no.'"

"Fair." The foot that had gotten halfway into her house retreated. "I just wanted to check on you."

She ignored the spark of pleasure his words ignited. "At midnight."

"Your light was on."

So he was watching her house now? *Why am I not more alarmed? I should be more alarmed.* "Well, you've checked." She bit her tongue before she could throw (more) caution to the wind and invite him in for a drink. Assuming she could find the box of booze. Perhaps he'd like to come in for tea. If she could find the box of tea.

"I just… I know it's been a long day." He shifted his weight from one foot to another, looked over her shoulder, looked behind him, looked at the floor. "I knew you'd want to know Sally was safe at IPA. And I was in the neighborhood. So."

She raised her eyebrows. She did want to know Sally was safe, but she didn't care for the presumption. "Too bad no one has invented anything that would allow you to pass on news without knocking on my door at midnight. Well, someone will probably think of something. Until then, all we can hope for is a brighter future with cutting edge tech that precludes pop-ins."

He was scrubbing a hand through his short hair, which definitely didn't make her itch to see if the hairs at his nape were as soft as she thought they must be. "Yeah, you're right. Sorry. This was a bad—sorry."

"Do you want to c—ow!"

He leaned forward, clear concern on his face, but respected the threshold, so he looked like he was bowing. "Are you okay?"

"Nit my tongue. *Bit* my tongue, I meant. Why are you really here?"

Seconds crawled by while she waited for an answer, and Lila found she was holding her breath. When he finally spoke

"I don't know."

she was surprised by her lack of surprise. Was that disappointment she felt? Or relief? Or a new emotion as yet unnamed and unknown? "I guess you'd better go, then," she said and preemptively bit her tongue.

He looked at her for a long time, or so it seemed to her. And when he finally spoke, she thought he sounded almost regretful. "Good night, Lila."

"'Night."

He didn't look back as he ambled into the darkness (the neighborhood was seriously lacking in street lights). She knew, because she watched until she couldn't see him anymore.

Oh, oh, oh…hello, darling. Come to Daddy. All that whipped cream, those sexy chocolate curls, there it was, just waiting to be devoured. He hoped there were clean forks, because either way, the pie was going down.

"Ow!"

"You wait," Mama Mac said, implacable. The statue of David would have been easier to move.

"Never! It's not like she'd wait for *me*."

Mama sighed. "Always at it. It's been a decade, aren't you two bored?"

"You just now whapped me on the knuckles with one of your nine thousand wooden spoons. That's as big a cliché as sibling rivalry. And I'm not bored. What I am is hungry."

"There's a box of saltines in the cupboard behind you."

"Or I could just eat a bag of sawdust."

"Sawdust's in the garage," she replied, then ruined her stern mien with a giggle. Oz loved how the girlish giggle made her sound like a fifth-grader huffing helium.

After his late-night porch chat with Lila, he'd headed home, gotten little to no sleep, gave up, got up, showered, took no particular care with his hair or clothes

(*He was wearing an expensive suit because it was comfortable, dammit! Nothing to do with wanting to look good for a stranger!*)

checked on Sally, and then made his way to Lila's.

No. *No.* He'd made his way to Mama Mac's house. Lila was immaterial. Irrelevant. A virtual stranger he barely knew, as she'd reminded him last night. He was still kicking himself for going over there while simultaneously bummed she wouldn't let him in. "Confused as fuck" didn't begin to cover it.

Should I ask Mama Mac? Mama Mac wouldn't laugh at him. Or at least not once she realized he was asking a serious question.

You know the Kama-Rupa *myth? Is it possible it was rooted in reality? Like how the Shroud of Turin exists, but it wasn't necessarily used to wrap up Jesus?*

The fact was, he'd lingered on Lila's porch for too long. Not last night. Earlier, when he left with Sally. And after making sure the cub was buckled in (Shifters were tough, but there was no point to tempting fate), he'd lingered like a loser. A lingering loser. Worse, he hadn't noticed right away. When he'd come back to himself, he realized he'd been staring at the sidewalk leading up to her porch for several seconds, trying to think of a reason to go back in. Thank God for Sally

"Can we gooooooo? Please? I wanna goooooooo!"

or he'd probably still be standing in Lila's driveway.

And then he'd compounded his error by going *back* later that night. What the hell was wrong with him?

His train of thought derailed when he heard the familiar screech of a car driven by a hungry werebear, pounding footsteps, the shriek of the porch door being hauled open, and...

"I came over as soon as I heard about the french silk p—*you.*"

...there was Annette Garsea, tireless IPA employee (except when she needed a nap), loyal foster sister, and singularly ferocious grizzly–polar hybrid (but only when a kid was in peril or if she skipped lunch).

"Finally," he sniped back. He was both relieved and disappointed that Annette had shown up before he could decide whether or not to talk to Mama. "We've been waiting for hours."

"My hirsute butt you've been waiting hours." She bent—Mama Mac was short, and Annette was about five foot ten—and gave the older woman a careless smack on the cheek.

"And I'd like to have one family meeting where we don't talk about your hirsute butt. But here we are!"

"This isn't a family meeting, Oz." Annette all but yanked the deliciously familiar red box away from him. "It's dessert hour.

Other places have happy hours, but we're more ambitious. No, Mama, get the *big* plates."

"I will not. You'll ruin your—"

"Third lunch?" Oz suggested with a smirk. Annette's prodigious appetite was fascinating and not a little frightening. "Ow!"

"Keep it up," Mama Mac warned, brandishing the dreaded spoon. "You're not too old to beat to death." Which was laughable. Meredith Macropi wouldn't raise a serious hand to a kid if you stuck a gun in her ear.

"'I'm pushing thirty, Mama."

"All the more reason. Means time's running out to teach you manners."

"That time," Annette intoned, pouring them glasses of milk, "has passed."

Mama handed out napkins and plates, and the three of them settled around the table in her sunny kitchen. It hadn't changed much in the years since he lived there for 122 days: same worn but clean tablecloth, same citrusy smells. Same cupboards filled with spices and dishes and cereal and other things that made a house a home. Same spotless floor (a good trick when you considered how often muddy Shifter adolescents raced across it), which he knew Mama Mac scrubbed by hand, despite the mops and Swiffers he and Annette had bought over the years.

And speaking of muddy adolescents… "Where are Caro and Dev?"

"School day," Mama replied. "And don't you dare eat the entire pie. I promised them both a slice."

Annette sniffed, which was hilarious because she'd failed to realize she was sporting a whipped cream 'stache. "I fail to see how I'm constrained by your prom—never mind."

Mama lowered the spoon and nodded. "Wise. Now how's that girl doing, Oz?"

Since Caro was safely ensconced in high school, "that girl"

could only be Sally Smalls, recent orphan and current bane of his existence. "Pretty good, considering."

"Pretty good, considering she gave you the slip for a day," Annette said, then added kindly, "I told you the work was going to be tricky."

"Ha! Shows what you know. Sally's not the problem." Oz paused, considering. "Or at least, not the biggest problem." Which was one of the reasons Oz had been happy to hear Annette had been en route. "It gets tricky for a couple of reasons. Big number one…"

"Mama's new Stable neighbor." Annette had just cut herself a slice of pie that was as big as a Stephen King paperback and plopped it on a plate, then slid the box to him. "How could Roy Harriss let that happen?"

"Oh, before I forget." Mama was bustling from the fridge to the counter and back again. "Harry Harriss is back. I guess community college didn't work out."

"Normally I despise gossip, but that's actually fascinating. Harry's—what?" Annette frowned, doing the math. "Twenty-five? And he's lived here all his life, except for a week here or a month there, those little tentative stabs at freedom?"

"And he always comes back, poor lamb." Mama shook her head. "I don't know why Roy doesn't either put his foot down or give up and accept that his son will die in that house."

"Wait, is that the guy who knew he didn't get into college, lied and said he did, and didn't come clean until they were physically on campus, trying to help him move into a dorm room he didn't have? Because that's commitment. That wasn't a little white lie, it was the blackest of deceptions, and Harriss just *flung* himself into it. He packed and everything!"

"That's him. But with all due respect to the Harriss mob, that's not our problem. The Stable is." Annette shook her head. "I still don't understand how Harriss Senior let that happen."

Say, now! Here was a chance for some fun. "Because he's been trying to unload the house for years and beggars can't be choosers?"

Annette shook her head. "He never should have rented to one of them."

Oz felt his eyebrows climb. "You hear yourself, right?"

"I don't have a bigoted bone in my body and you know it," Annette snapped. "It's a safety issue."

He knew what she meant, but he could no more resist the chance to needle her than he could resist thinking about Lila's curls and what they might feel like. Oz took a two-second mental break and reminded himself, again, that *Kama-Rupa* was not happening. It was *so* not happening, in fact, that he'd decided he wouldn't bring it up. For what? The fleeting pleasure of confirming he hadn't gone clinically insane in twenty-four hours? No and no and nope.

He forced his brain back on its accustomed "snark all over Annette" track. "Next you're gonna say property values in the neighborhood are gonna drop like rocks."

"Well, they might, but that's more because of the economic indicators that would—dammit, it's not a race thing!" she nearly shouted. "Or a species thing, rather. I don't have a problem with Stables. In fact—"

"If you say you have a Stable friend, I'm gonna laaaaaaaugh."

"Well, I do. More than one, even! Look, you know me," she whined.

"I *thought* I did."

"Oh my God, I'm going to beat you to death. You know I don't think Shifters are superior. I think we're all—"

"Separate but equal?"

"Dammit!" Annette practically howled.

"*Children*," Mama Mac cut in. "Since there's nothing to be done about Roy's current tenant—"

"I wouldn't say that." From Annette, who'd calmed down and was now staring hopefully at the pie earmarked for Caro and Dev. "They never stay very long, Stables *or* Shifters." She glanced around at the table. "We all know why."

Oz snorted. "Then why are you saying it?"

"That's true, m'dear, but that curly gal's here for—damn, I've forgotten her—"

"It's Lila," Oz broke in at once. "Lila Kai. From Bloomington, Illinois." At their inquiring looks, he elaborated. "Her old address is on the boxes of eyes and arms."

"Boxes, plural?"

"Yep."

"Of *eyes*?"

"And arms."

"Good *God*." Annette shook off the horror—literally shook—and then pushed her bangs out of her eyes. He'd never tell her, but her deep brown waves and white highlights were a striking mess. And no matter how many haircuts she had, she always looked about a month overdue for one, which should've made her look like an unkempt slob but somehow didn't. He and the few who knew her secret—she was probably the only polar–grizzly were in the world—liked knowing her hair was the giveaway, out there for everyone to see if they bothered to pay attention. Multiple deceased bad guys hadn't, Exhibit A for *why* they were deceased.

"All right, let's stay on point," she was saying, because she wasn't just a polar–grizzly hybrid, she was a relentless polar–grizzly hybrid. "Though I have to admit that's a fascinating segue, and we might circle back to it. Boxes of eyes and arms. What do we do about this Lila Kai? If we need to do anything. This could be premature fretting," Annette added, waving her fork to encompass him, Mama Mac, the kitchen, the house, the neighborhood. "She may not know."

"She definitely knows."

"You've got no proof."

"Annette, she one hundred percent knows. This is not a stupid woman. The Vexin kits flagged her down and saw her pick Sally up in the ally. Because *of course* the most curious kits in town happened to be there when this mess started. On a school night, but that's a whole other issue. And before you ask," he added, though neither woman had opened her mouth, "they had no idea the new neighbor was Stable until it was too late."

Annette nodded. "Unfortunate timing, I agree. But Oz, did Lila see Sally shift back?"

"She—she must have."

"Which you're assuming because…"

"She was ready for anything. Both times!" He sighed, remembering. "It was so cool."

"Right. In other words, you've got no idea what she saw. And so the situation may well be salvageable."

"How then?" From Mama Mac, who had gotten up to put the pie back in the fridge, ignoring Annette's pained whimper. "It's not like we can ask her if she knows Sally's a werebear."

Oz laughed. "Yeah, there's no way to slip 'did you see a werebear on your block, where you're surrounded by Shifters, and also everyone in the neighborhood is keeping a wary eye on you, how 'bout some tea' into a conversation."

"The boy's right."

"Almost thirty, Ma."

"And even if we did ask her, she could lie. Roy and I gave her every opportunity to tell us what really happened last night." Mama dimpled as an unwilling grin crossed her face. "She was bland as bread, telling us to our faces that everything was normal. We didn't know what to think."

"And she wasn't scared!" Oz put in.

Mama Mac shook her head. "Not a whit."

"Maybe she's a squib?"

"Or a sociopath," Annette muttered.

"Or both," she and Oz said in accidental unison, because Annette had the misfortune of meeting a sociopathic squib last year. It hadn't been fun. For anyone. It was part of the reason poor Sally Smalls was in such a mess: the dead sociopath had partners.

Oz shifted in his seat. *Now or never. Wait! What happened to NOT bringing it up?* "Listen!" He lowered his voice. "Uh. While you're both here."

After a few seconds, Annette prompted, "Yes?"

That was as far as he'd gotten in his head. The absurdity of what he wanted to ask was almost overwhelming. It was like asking if Santa Claus was a thing. Because the answer was maddening: of course Santa wasn't a thing. Except when he was. It depended how you defined "Santa." And "thing."

"So congratulations on getting engaged to David."

Annette just blinked at him, probably because there had been an announcement months ago. And a party. And a clean-up party because things had gotten a smidge out of hand. (To this day, Oz had no idea how David got all that maple syrup out of his fur.) Since then, wedding plans had proceeded exactly as expected: with Annette protesting all of it and pushing for elopement, Annette's partner Nadia insisting the bride wear a Dior original (and put her bridesmaids in same), Mama Mac insisting they ditch caterers so she could be the one to cook for two hundred people (then changing her mind, then changing it back again), Annette declaring she would kill or die to avoid dealing with two hundred people, and David adding still more Stables to the guest list.

Because that was the other thing. David had Stable friends. A lot of them. Not the kind you sometimes hung out with because they were reasonably cool or had the same taste in movies or played *Halo* online together. Given how outnumbered Shifters were, it was pretty weird if you didn't have at least one Stable pal.

No, Davey-boy grew up with Stables who knew—and kept—the

secret of his other self. His default was to trust them. And his argument was compelling: his friends had had years to burn him and hadn't. So they were true, safe friends. As "safe" as any member of *homo sapiens* could be, at least. Annette had already met a few of them, and they'd guessed her secret pretty much instantly. Give the woman credit, she'd handled it better than he would have. Just thinking about random Stables figuring out his true nature made him sweat…

(implications! change! danger? probably!)

…but it was still less aggravating than talking about *Kama-Rupa*.

"So when did you know David was the one? Probably took a while, right? Since you guys worked together for a couple of—"

"Five days" was the flat response.

"—years—what?"

"I thought you worked together for two years," Mama said.

"Yes, but—not really. He's an investigator, not an IPA employee. An independent contractor. IPA's one of a few clients. So he was in and out all the time. We'd never worked a case together until Caro. We barely knew each other to say hi to."

"Oh."

"So to answer your question, five days. Well. Two years and five days," Annette admitted.

"So it wasn't until he was in your face all the time that you fell for him?" Sweet relief! Maybe lots of Shifters fell for strangers based on nothing but their compatible scent. Maybe he wasn't tumbling into clinical insanity. Or living in the thirteenth century, when *Kama-Rupa* was taken as seriously as ferreting out witches to burn and wondering where the sun went at night. "Oh, man, thank God."

"What?"

"Oz, what are you on about?" Mama asked, puzzled.

"I'm. I'm making a scrapbook." Argh, why was the first thing to pop into his head so terrible? "A bound pile of mementos to commemorate your relationship."

"Good *God*, please don't."

"You haven't seen how cool-yet-touching it's gonna be!" Argh, now he had to make a *good* scrapbook. Were those even a thing anymore? Didn't everyone just use Pinterest?

Just then, the kitchen door was yanked open and in came two bundles of adolescent insanity: Caro Daniels and Dev Devoss. Or as they were more commonly known… "Oh, jeez, here comes trouble squared. Maybe even cubed."

"Back off, Oz!" The tip of Dev's sharp nose was red, like his cheeks. Green eyes gleamed while he shrugged out of his jacket, then grabbed Caro's and hung them up in the mudroom. Well. Flung them in the general direction of the hooks in the mudroom. "Do we come to your house and insult you?"

"You were at my place two weeks ago for game night and you told me my hair was stupid."

This got a snort out of Caro, which was gratifying. Since the sixteen-year-old werewolf rarely vocalized, a snort was as good as a speech. "I have devastating hair and everyone knows it."

"Oh, I agree," Annette said. "We're going by the dictionary definition of devastating, yes? Oof!"

That last because Dev had bounded up to her and nearly strangled her with his enthusiastic hug. She normally towered over him, but when she was seated, the twelve-year-old werefox was half a head taller. "Hi, Net!"

"Ugh, stop, your touch sickens me." This with a smile while returning the hug. "You'd better have passed that geometry test, you multilingual menace. Never think I won't beat you to death."

"Consider it passed, *pasado, chaidh, seachad*. I made that test my bi—um, I got a C."

"Minus," Caro muttered so softly it would have gone unheard anywhere else. She cleared her throat and waited patiently. Which made sense, because Caro Daniels could wait like a champ. She waited two years for rescue, two weeks for bloody, violent vengeance, one week for the truth to come out, and four months to be permanently assigned as Mama Mac's foster cub. And now she was waiting for access to the fridge.

Oh, shit. I'm in the death zone! He moved. Fast. Standing between an adolescent meat-eater and protein... What the hell had he been thinking?

"Maybe we should adjourn," he suggested, trying not to gasp at his near escape.

"Naw, keep talking about Sally." Dev smirked. "We won't hear a thing, promise."

Annette frowned. "Were you eavesdropping again?"

Fair question. Oz wasn't keen on generalizations, but Dev really did seem like a werefox prototype: small and slender, short and spiky reddish-blond hair, wide green eyes, an endless capacity for charming/fooling/frustrating/enraging people, and always always *always* putting his snout in at the worst possible times. He knew that as many times as Annette wanted to give the kit a hug, there were just as many where she'd had to restrain herself from throttling him until his eyes bulged like ping-pong balls.

"Didn't have to eavesdrop. Knew as soon as we saw your cars. What *else* would the three of you be talking about? Politics? Net's love life? Oz's shitty haircut?"

Oz let out a yelp. "Hey!"

Annette sighed. "Good *God*, Dev."

"Nope, none of those, obvi, so it's gotta be work. And *we're* your work." Dev nodded to indicate Caro, too, now bringing the red box o'pie back to the table. "So's Sally."

"You're the living embodiment of 'too smart for your own good,'" Annette said, which she probably hoped sounded stern.

Just as quickly, the kit sobered. "I'm glad you guys got our gal Sal to come back, but you better find her folks pretty quick, or she's gonna be in the wind again."

And if anyone could predict that particular behavior, it'd be

Dev. Back in the day (so, six months ago), prior to living with Mama Mac, the kit ran away as often as most people changed their underwear. Dev's father had done a runner before he was born, his mother was in prison for, among other things, trying to sell her son. As Dev put it after her mother's plea bargain, "It's hard not to take that personally."

"Are you guys listening? Sally'll be gone, *disparu*, *andato*. She's already super pissed that you don't believe her."

"She is? Still? I thought we settled that last night." Since he'd dropped her off at IPA, he hadn't seen her. His job, as he saw it, was done. On to the next cub in trouble! But first, more pie.

"Weren't you wondering why she's not talking?" It was always a bit startling when Caro spoke up. "About anything, including the Stable down the block?"

"Which brings us back to the question: What does this Lila person know?" Annette said. "And how best to find out?"

"No, let's not go back to that, let's deal with this other thing. Why's she mad at *us*?" Oz asked, and he definitely didn't sound hurt. "We're the ones who want her to be safe now that she's an orphan."

Annette just looked at him. He could practically read her thoughts: *I warned you it was a thankless job.*

"That's the problem, duh!" Dev practically yelled. "She doesn't believe you. She's never gonna believe you!"

"Simmer, boy." This from Mama Mac, who was standing over all of them in an unconscious protective pose.

"I understand she doesn't believe us. But what does she think our motive is? Why would we lie about her parents' deaths?" Annette asked.

"She's ten. She has no clue about motive, but the alternative is, y'know, totally unthinkable to her." Dev looked around at the adults. "C'mon! It's obvious. In her mind, her parents can't be dead, ergo they're alive, ergo you guys are lying like you're getting paid. It doesn't matter if it doesn't make sense to *you*."

"So how to make it make sense to a cub in denial?" Mama asked.

"Well, there's the small matter of the crash site and corresponding DNA," Annette pointed out quietly.

"So then." When no one said anything, Caro added impatiently, "*Show* her."

"We can't."

"Maybe we can," Oz said, and everything stopped.

Chapter 11

LILA HAD LOADED THE LAST BOX OF BODY PARTS WHEN SHE glanced up to see Ox and a woman she didn't know striding up her driveway. She mentally rolled her eyes and turned to meet them, squashing the giddy excitement that had risen when she spotted him.

Ox waved like he was on a parade float. He looked unfairly handsome and worriedly cheerful this early in the day. "Hiya, Lila! Hey, that rhymes."

"Barely."

For some reason, her knee-jerk churlishness made his companion smile as she extended a hand. "I'm Annette Garsea. I used to live down the street."

"Lila Kai. I used to go longer than twenty minutes without a pop-in."

This time Garsea laughed out loud, and to her annoyance, Lila found herself warming up to the other woman. Tall—only a few inches shorter than Ox—with a mussed mane of thick, shoulder-length reddish-brown hair with loads of creamy highlights. Her eyes were a startling reddish brown (maybe they only looked reddish because she was wearing a cherry-colored sweater?), as well as pale "oh *God* it's been a long winter" skin and a wide, generous mouth. "Yes, sorry about all that. I've heard you had some excitement and you haven't even been here seventy-two hours."

"My," Lila replied. "What a hotbed of gossip I'm living in."

Garsea didn't demur. "Small towns."

"So anyway," Ox put in brightly, "I was wondering if you wanted to grab lunch. Or dinner."

She blinked. "Why?"

"Y'know…as a thank you."

"For…"

"Well, more as an apology," Ox clarified.

"For…"

"All the trouble Sally put you through," he finished, like this was a sensible neighborhood and he was a sensible man with a sensible plan.

"Oh. That." Lila shrugged. "No biggie."

"That's kind of you," Garsea put in, "but my understanding is she broke into your house."

"No."

Garsea's brow furrowed. "Pardon?"

"She didn't break in."

"Oh."

Silence, glorious silence. Too many people didn't like silence; they'd rush to fill it and trip themselves up. Cops, lawyers, and loan officers banked on it.

Not Lila. Awkward silences could be useful. And she'd long perfected her less-is-more Q&A system. The person peppering her with questions would eventually get impatient (and slip up) or bored (and slip up) or frustrated (and slip up) or hungry (and leave to eat). Nine times out of ten, "yes—no—I dunno" was good for a favorable outcome.

Ox cleared his throat. "So, lunch? Today? C'mon, say yes."

But one in ten was revealed to be a persistent bastard with piercing green eyes and a tailored suit with a black duster that should have made him look like a *Matrix* wannabe but didn't, and here she was already getting distracted, *fuck*.

Incredibly, she heard herself say, "I work in downtown Saint Paul. The Hamm Building. If you wanted to meet there. Or not. I don't care." Even as she heard the words gushing out of her mouth, she couldn't believe she just warmly agreed to lunch with a near stranger and gave that same near stranger her work address. Clearly a week for firsts.

"*Meritage*!" Garsea practically shouted. Lila gave thanks for leaving the Beretta in the bathroom, otherwise Ox's lady friend might have had to deal with a bullet in her knee.

"Sorry?"

Ox leaned in. "Annette was a foodie before 'foodie' was code for 'pretentious jackoff.' She knows every restaurant in town. She's memorized every menu, interviewed every chef, intimidated every maître d', grilled every line cook, and harangued every sommelier."

"Oh, I have not!"

"Grown men weep when she walks through the door. Food critics go to *her* for suggestions. Also, Meritage is a restaurant if that wasn't already clear in context."

Garsea clapped a hand over her eyes. "Good *God*. You're making me sound like someone abnormally, even obsessively, interested in foo—well, that's fair." To Lila: "You've got to try it, their chilled seafood platter is astounding and the profiteroles will make you think you've seen God. But avoid the *salade Niçoise*. Not enough tuna."

Let's zero in a bit, shall we? Because what the hell is happening right now? "So lunch would be on IPA?"

Ox's smile slipped a bit. "Yeah. Business, not personal." A short silence, broken when he added, "So don't worry."

"Whenever someone has told me not to worry, there's been something to worry about. Every single time."

The smile slipped the rest of the way off. "Oh." The big lug's shoulders slumped a little. "Well, if you don't want—"

"Meet you there at noon."

"What?" Up came the shoulders. Like magic! "I mean, great!"

"But I have to go to work now," Lila added, hoping they would notice they were blocking her driveway. She shut the back doors with a decisive slam. "So I'll see you at noon."

"If I may ask," Garsea said, eyeing the vehicle, "are you an EMT?"

"No."

"Oh. But then why…never mind."

Lila couldn't help it; she smiled again. Some people could make you like them. It was a knack, like being able to whistle through your teeth or belch the alphabet. It didn't mean they were good. Just charismatic. Or, in the case of the belching, had great breath control.

"C'mon, Annette."

"You c'mon, Oz. Coming here was my idea. *You* should be following in *my* wake."

Bemused, Lila called after them, "Siblings?"

And, even funnier, Annette replied, "No!" even as Ox answered "Yes!"

Weirdos.

Lunch? But not a date. Who brings their sister to ask someone out?

So: ulterior motive lunch. But why? Nothing to do with Lila's personality, which sparkled like flat, warm Coke. Or Lila's own smashing good looks (she knew she looked like a vaguely dangerous Orphan Annie). Or her riches (after the move, she had $496 in checking and $2,623 in savings). So…

Sally.

Chapter 12

THE HAMM BUILDING IN DOWNTOWN SAINT PAUL WAS positively stuffed with history, among other things, so it was the perfect place to store eyes, mail, and lunch (the latter went into the mini-fridge). Her suite was small, which suited her. The open area in front, a small private restroom on the left, a back room for storage. A desk and worktables, bookshelves and file cabinets, and room to take care of all the shipping, incoming as well as outgoing.

She turned and surveyed the boxes.

Man oh *man*, she loved unpacking, she really did.

In an hour, she had the parts sorted, installed two smoke detectors with fresh batteries, had made a dent in the mail-ins, confirmed her Wi-Fi hookup, and wasn't sweating like a basted turkey, thanks to the building being made of terra-cotta and brick. Old brick, to be sure, and old terra-cotta, but who cared? The place was cool as a tomb and almost as quiet. Late morning on a weekday in downtown Saint Paul, and she couldn't hear a thing from outside. Excellent.

She'd loved the building the moment she checked it out online and discovered its secret and was pleasantly surprised to find the lease wasn't horrifying. She crunched numbers and, after a few weeks of research, decided to make the move. Buh-bye, Minot of the tundra; hello, balmy Saint Paul.

And it wasn't like she'd had to move. She didn't need a fresh start. She wasn't running from a bad breakup (ha) or in hopes of meeting someone new (double ha). She wasn't fleeing from an insurmountable problem or bad career choices. She'd broken no laws (none in the great state of North Dakota, at least). This wasn't that trope; none of that applied. She just liked moving, liked putting down roots (however temporarily) and prowling a new city and figuring out where to eat and scoping the theaters and plotting the best shortcuts and checking out the homeless situation.

Is that what it is? Or do you just miss the excitement of the bad old days?

Irrelevant. The things to focus on were the oddities all over her new neighborhood as well as promoting her business so that when people thought of beloved-yet-destroyed childhood icons, they thought: *Lila Kai!*

(but in a good way)

And maybe Ox's abs.

(uh…no)

And the thing she'd barely stopped herself from buying on the way to work. Which she had put down to sunstroke. Or hypothermia. Something.

Lila nearly swept the boxes off her work table in frustration. It would have been satisfyingly dramatic but also messy, so: pass. Why the hell couldn't she get that guy out of her head? She'd never had a reaction like this to anyone. It made her tween crush on 1980s Al Gore seem like a passing fancy.

"Oh…wow."

And here he was. (Oz. Not '80s Al.) Her lunch appointment, because it definitely wasn't a date, as he'd gone to some trouble to assure her.

"You're early."

Ox was still goggling around her office. "Uh…only by about twenty min—this was a brewery. Like, way back in the day."

"Yep."

"But what is it now?"

"Can't you tell?" she replied, indicating the boxes, the sewing machine, the thread, the stuffing, the balls, the peanuts, the legs, the work table, the standing desk, the laptop. "It's a hospital, complete with triage, operating, and recovery rooms."

Now he was staring at her like she was made of pudding and his sweet tooth was yelling. "We've never had a normal conversation," he said, and it was kind of cool how he made that sound like a desirable outcome. "Not once."

"Give it time," she suggested. "How'd you know which suite was mine? The restaurant's downstairs, and I've been up here a couple hours already. You wouldn't have seen me going back and forth."

"Followed my nose," he replied absently.

Har-har, stalker. Wait. Does that mean I need a shower? Dammit, brick and terra-cotta, you were supposed to keep me cool!

"Plus your name's on the directory on the main level where the security guard is," he added, sidling toward the desk where her mail was stacked while pretending he wasn't.

No, it isn't. Just the name of my company: Bear Down.

"I just need to catalogue this last box and then we can…" She hefted the large Priority Mail box. "Oboy. I recognize that return address." She reached for her drywall knife and slit the package open, wrinkling her nose when she got a whiff of the contents. "Shit."

"What? What?" Oz was looking around and flaring his nostrils. "Are you in trouble?"

"*I'm* not." She withdrew body parts: legs, arm, torso. "Same family! We might have a serial killer on our hands."

"Those are bear parts," he said, staring down at her work table.

"Teddy bear parts," she corrected, logging the package into her system. "But it's all fine. The doctor is in." She looked up at him. "At least his dad didn't run the thing over with the lawn mower this time. *That* took forever to fix."

"Oh, Christ. You scared the hell out of me." Oz poked gingerly at one of the pieces. "This is what you do?"

"This is what I do."

"Not gonna lie, I'm relieved."

"Setting your mind at ease is what I live for."

"This is *so* cool."

She had to laugh. "You're pretty easily impressed."

"Naw," he replied seriously. "Not really. Hungry?"

"Starved," she answered at once, and was surprised to discover it was true. "C'mon, expense account guy. Time to knock my socks off with some comped appetizers."

———————

"So you work in a brewery that doesn't brew and you drive an ambulance that doesn't…"

"Ambulate?"

"And you're a surgeon for teddy bears."

"Stop making it sound out of the ordinary."

That's you in a nutshell, Oz thought. *If I had to pick a phrase that described you without going into your essential hotness: out of the ordinary.*

"Also, you're a snoop."

"It's in the job description," he protested.

"Your job? Show me the part of your hiring package that laid out where you'd have to walk into an office that isn't yours over to a desk that isn't yours to read mail that isn't yours."

Not that she minded. There was nothing on that desk that could hurt her, nothing that could be traced to her past. She'd never shit in her own nest. But still.

The principle of the thing.

Or something.

The waitress's timely arrival put paid to the brewing argument, and Lila briefly considered ignoring Garsea's advice and getting the salad. But who would that punish, exactly? And the red wine–braised duck leg sounded way better than spite salad.

"So kids must really love you, huh?"

Surprised, she almost knocked over her ginger-lime rickey. "Why d'you say that?"

"Well. I mean… You fix up their toys." Oz mimed sewing. Or picking fleas off his napkin…tough to be sure… "And then you give 'em back. You must be like a rock star to them."

"No. I don't meet them or anything. I don't interact. Their folks ship me the remains, I fix 'em and send 'em back. It's just a job."

"Well, Sally sure took a shine to you."

Here we go. "Sally's options that night were limited," she pointed out. "She would have taken a shine to anyone who could have gotten her out of that alley and stuffed her with honey and pizza."

"But still." He was leaning forward now. He'd ditched the *Matrix* coat and was in a crisp white shirt that she just bet was tailor-made. There was a haberdashery in this very building. Lila hadn't known those places still existed. Didn't everyone do everything online?

No tie. Shirt open at the throat, exposing a tanned neck. Black trousers probably tailor-made, too. Pricey-looking loafers. No socks. Even his ankles were tan. Who had a natural tan this time of year? *Gawd, those vivid green eyes are annoying. Oh, shit, he's still talking.*

"…after all, you helped her."

"Yeah, she was a hurt kid in the middle of nowhere. Helping her doesn't mean I get along with all children, it just means I'm not a drooling sociopath. And don't misinterpret this as concern, but how's she doing?"

Ox leaned back and let out a sigh. "She's having some trouble adjusting to her reality."

"Understandable."

"I, uh, can't really get into it."

"You brought her up."

He drummed his fingers on the table and just looked at her. "Mmmm. So why Lilydale?"

"Why *not* Lilydale? Looked like a nice place, rent was decent, office space was decent, reasonably safe from zombie plagues and/or Armageddon."

"What?"

"In the movies, it's always places like New York or D.C. that get destroyed. Aliens don't care about Lilydale. Plus I like seasons. I hear Minnesota has at least two."

He laughed. "I get it. I was in Florida for a few months. A sweaty Santa in shorts and surrounded by palm trees was a real mind-fuck."

Their waitress chose that moment to deposit their orders, then darted off.

Lila took a nibble of duck. It promptly melted in her mouth. "Your sister wasn't kidding. This is pretty sublime. Food this good? Is why I could never be a vegetarian."

Ox shuddered. "Me neither. Listen, thanks for coming out with me."

"Hey, free duck. Who's gonna turn that down?"

"Are you seeing anyone?"

Lila put down her fork. "That's an odd question to ask during a lunch that isn't a date because it's strictly business."

"I'm just trying to get to know you."

"Why?"

"Well, we're neighbors."

"No, we aren't. You've had your own place for years. Don't look surprised. Mama Macropi likes to talk about you. A lot."

His face lit up. "You asked her about me?"

Shit. "No. Like I said. She talks about you."

"Oh. So are you? Seeing anyone?"

"Yes. I've been happily married for some time. Next month is our third anniversary. As the traditional gift is leather, it should be an interesting evening."

"No," he said with aggravating confidence. "You're not married."

"Then why did you ask if I'm seeing anyone? And then lie about *why* you asked?"

Her rising irritation fell apart when she saw his expression: interest, confusion, and a little...fear? "I don't know."

"Oh."

"I'm sorry. We can talk about something else."

"Okay."

"*I'm* not seeing anyone."

"You can't know what a relief that is." The hell of it was, she was only being a little sarcastic.

He leaned in and suddenly her world was a pair of green eyes. "Lila. I didn't ask you that just to fish for info. Something is—I can't even figure out how to explain—okay, ever since we—"

"*Ow!*" Bart Simpson said, because he was a rude cartoon child. *"Quit it. Ow! Quit it."*

Ox almost dropped his fork. "The hell is that?"

"Sorry," Lila said, fishing her phone out of her purse. She'd never hear whatever Ox had been working up to, but now she had something new to fret about. "That's me." She was 95 percent sure what she was going to see, but it was nice to know her paranoia was once again justified. How'd it go again? Is it paranoia when people really are plotting against you? "Oh, look at that."

Oz had fallen to systematically demolishing his tartare, which had been shaped into a thick disc that resembled a raw hamburger sans bun. Which it was, come to think of it. "What? Some poor kiddo accidentally flush their teddy bear?"

"That's only happened twice." Gratifying as it was to be proved right, it pissed her off all the same. As they'd established, this wasn't a date. But her phone had established it wasn't a business lunch, either. "Your sister is breaking into my house."

"Aw, man, you had to fix a toilet bear? That's—what?"

"Garsea." She flipped her phone around to show him. "Is in my house. Which is conveniently empty. Because someone has contrived to keep me fifteen miles away. While his sister breaks into my house. Because he is a sneaky son of a bitch."

His mouth hung open. She took another bite, and she could actually see him working things out: *oh shit she's onto us she'll call the cops why is she just sitting there she knows I can't make a fuss in the restaurant should I talk her out of calling 911 or extract Garsea or go straight to begging forgiveness and offering her $$$$ not to sue my deceitful ass shit shit shit.*

He was halfway to the door when he realized she wasn't behind him. He stopped, turned, saw her calmly plowing through her fingerling potatoes, turned back to the door, stopped again, trotted back.

"Uh. Aren't you going to—shouldn't we be yelling at each other while you call the cops and then I beg you to hear me out and maybe try to bribe you?"

"Our food *just* got here."

"You're worried about your lunch?"

"Typical suit," she sniffed. "'Hang the cost, I'll expense it!' Not okay, pal. Plus you've got somewhere to be."

"I do?"

"The hospital, prob'ly."

Oz frowned, but his phone buzzed before he could reply. He pulled it out, not unlike a man handling an incendiary device, and checked the screen. "Jesus."

"Toldja."

"What did you do?"

"I'll have the waitress put yours in a doggie bag."

"What did you *do*?"

"Goodbye. Waitress?" Lila waved her over. "Could I get a refill on my rickey?"

Chapter 13

"THIS IS FUCKING EMBARRASSING," ANNETTE SNARLED, leaving a trail of blood like an angry snail, which was horrifying because the woman almost never dropped f-bombs. The blood was freaking him out a little, too. When Annette got bloody, corpses tended to pile up in the morgue.

"I'm glad you texted me, Annette, but…jeez, are you okay?"

"What were you thinking?" her fiancé, David Auberon, just about shouted.

"I was thinking *'ow, ow, my hands, who lines their bedroom drawer with blades?'*"

"My, my, my." Mama Mac had hustled Annette over to the sink, snapped on the overhead light, squinted at the slashes, started gently rinsing them. David loomed over Mama's shoulder, glaring down at the narrow, actively bleeding slashes across Annette's index, middle, and ring fingers. "Such a mess."

"The blades were in one drawer? Singular?" Oz asked.

Annette hissed as the water ran. "After the first one, I didn't open any more drawers."

"Why were you in her house to even open *one*? Jesus, Annette, we talked about this!"

Annette had the grace to look abashed. "Not this…precise situation, David. Exactly."

"You said it yourself: Oz has to sink or swim on his own! No matter how he screws up, we've gotta let him make his own mistakes!"

Oz coughed. "Thanks for that, I think."

Then David swung around and locked on (*ulp*) Oz. "This is exactly why you should have stayed in Accounting!"

"Really?" he replied. "This exact reason?"

Caught off guard, David snorted and dropped his gaze, to Oz's relief and disappointment. He'd often wondered which of them would still be standing after a fight. David was stronger, but Oz figured he had the bear beat for speed. *You'd have to go in tight, right under the chin, and hopefully get a chunk of him before he could get a grip and crush…but it'd have to be quick…like, the fastest-you've-ever-moved-in-your-life quick, or he'd claw your eyeballs out of your head and then* really *go to work.*

Worse, David's ire and Annette's blood swirling down the drain weren't his only problems. He had fucked up with Lila, who had every right to assume his only interest in taking her to lunch was to give Annette time to prowl around the Curs(ed) House. There was no coming back from this. There was no nice way to say, *Yeah, I needed you distracted while Annette tossed your place, but I also wanted to be with you because I'm obsessed with your scent and mouth and proficiency with firearms, and I think we should get married and make enough cubs to form our own bowling league.*

Nope. No matter how he explained it, it was gonna sound unhinged.

He couldn't stay away from Lila Kai.

He had to stay away from Lila Kai.

The sound of the screen door being wrenched open punctured his train of thought, which was just as well. "Holy shit, we could smell the blood from the driveway!"

"*Out!*" Annette and David roared in unison.

"Damn," Oz commented, watching the cubs scramble out of sight. "I didn't think either of them could move that fast."

"So the two of you…what? Decided to spy on Stables and be some kind of…I dunno…" David was pacing, and not for the first time, Oz was glad Mama Mac had a big kitchen. "Shifter Neighborhood Watch?"

"Stable," Annette corrected. "Singular."

"I've only seen her porch and her kitchen and the living room—" Oz admitted.

"And the basement," Annette added, smirking.

"Kindly go right to hell, Annette. What was the rest of the place like? I wanted to see more of it late last night, but she wouldn't let me in."

"You went back again?" Mama asked. "Again?"

"No, not really, but, well, yeah," he admitted. "Just tying up loose ends. Stuff like that. IPA stuff like that. Y'know, for the job. Nothing weird about it."

"I don't know what's gotten into you, boy," Mama replied, "but I mean to—"

"Can we focus on how I'm bleeding all over the sink and the floor a bit, too?" Annette asked.

Oz exhaled in no small relief. He'd never wish actual harm on Annette, but at least she was distracting Mama from his runaway mouth.

"You were telling us what the rest of Lila's house was like," he prompted, because he was either clinically nuts or had latent stalker tendencies he'd never dreamed existed before this week.

"It was like *Home Alone* if Macauley Culkin had been raised in a militia. It wasn't just the spring-loaded blades in the drawers. She's got a ScareCrow sprinkler set up in the back garden."

"She has a what?" Mama Mac was tidily laying out what she needed from one of her dozen first aid kits.

"A motion-activated sprinkler. Soaked me before I even got to the door."

"Well, maybe she's one of those lawn fascists," Oz suggested. "The kind who ignore drought warnings and just water their lawn whenever and get super pissy when you point out that they're wasting water."

"This time of year?"

"Point."

"Then when I got into the—"

"How'd you get in? I know you can't pick locks," David interrupted. And when no one answered, he groaned. "Jesus Christ. Which one of you B&E idiots got your paws on her keys?"

"We didn't steal them," Annette said at once. "If you were wondering."

"Besides, if you've got keys, is it really *breaking* and entering?" Oz asked.

"I might still have had one of Roy's sets from when the Weismans were living there and asked me to let the plumber in. Or was it the Johnsons? Two families ago…no, three tenants ago…"

"You just handed them over to Annette so she could let herself into a stranger's house and poke around, breaking any number of laws?" David had stopped pacing, which should have been a relief but wasn't. "*You*, Mama Mac?"

"I have cubs to watch out for," the smaller woman shot back. "I want to know if she's a danger to us. More than the average Stable, I mean."

"So then," Annette jumped in, pulling the focus back to herself to save David from a smack, "no sooner had I crossed the threshold when the air horn went off not five feet from my ears." She grimaced. "I was unaware you could rig air horns with motion sensors. It was an illuminating morning."

David was rubbing his forehead so hard, it was getting red. "And instead of leaving like a smart person who is smart, you blundered further into the house like a dumb person who is dumb."

"Blunder! That's. Um." Annette coughed. "An exaggeration." To Oz: "I could pick up scents here and there, but only Sally's and Lila Kai's. And yours in the basement, of course."

"Shut up," Oz said politely. "I was only down there for thirty seconds." Give or take five minutes. Or ten.

"And I picked up traces of the prior tenants—the Hinds—but that was all."

"And then you came to your senses and left," David said, still clutching his head. "Oh. Wait. You didn't do anything even close to that."

"So by then I thought to take a quick look around in her bedroom—"

Don't think about Lila and her bedroom. Pointless distraction. Yep. Besides, it's not like you'll ever see it after what you put her through. "What was it like?" *Was it a double bed? Queen? Now this is important: did anything in the room give you the impression she sleeps in the nude? This is vital intel for the case!* "I mean—anything weird?"

"Yes. When I walked in, white lights started flashing all around. If I'd been an epileptic I might *still* be seizing."

"Oh, I like this girl," Mama Mac said. She patted Annette's good arm and added, "I feel bad giving you those keys. But you gotta admit, that's a clever cutie down the block."

"Without doubt. And she sews. She had an old-fashioned treadle sewing machine set up in the corner, with the thread all spooled up and ready to go. I think it must be an antique—certainly nothing they make now."

"She's a bear surgeon."

"*What?*"

"Teddy bear," he clarified.

"The box of eyes! That's one mystery solved."

"Great," David managed through gritted teeth. "Now we can get back to the mystery of how the love of my life can be so smart and so dumb at the same time."

"Love of your…oh. That's…oh." Annette looked down and then something terrible happened, and they were all helpless witnesses to the terrible, terrible thing.

"Are you—oh my God—are you blushing right now?" Oz had no idea if he should be pleased or terrified. And who said it couldn't be both? David and Annette hadn't been a couple very long; apparently declarations of love out of nowhere were still novel. "It's cute!"

"I am not blushing!" she snapped. "Or if I am, it's with thwarted rage. To return to my tale of woe, at that point I decided to take a quick look at some personal items, and…" She wiggled her fingers, now wrapped in clean bandages. "Zing."

"Can you describe the zing? And also more of her bedroom?"

"Spring-loaded barbs, rigged to pop out just under the knob. And I think she treated them with something. It wasn't just the shock of being cut—I immediately began to feel nauseated and light-headed. It was at that point," she admitted, "that I came to the vague realization that I might be in over my head."

"Oh, fuck me." David seized Annette (gently) by the elbow and began steering her toward the kitchen door. "On top of everything else, that scary-prepared bitch coated the blades with poison."

"Hey! Lila didn't do anything wrong. And don't call her scary. Only I can do that. But never to her face. Isn't she awesome? I think we should get married."

David ignored Oz's babble, thank God. He hadn't meant to blurt out the bit about getting married. "Hospital. *Now*. And next time, lead with 'she poisoned me.' Don't save it for the end!"

"David." Annette extricated herself. "Stop. Look at me. It was over an hour ago, and I'm fine. Because it wasn't a lethal poison. It was much more clever than that, since whatever-it-was made me immediately stop what I was doing, exit her house, and text you guys."

"Which tipped Lila off," Oz realized. "Damn."

"Damn," Annette agreed.

"Damn!" David fumed.

"But ten minutes later, I felt fine and the bleeding had significantly slowed. And now, I'll…" She raised her wounded hand. "Well, you know. By month's end, you'd never know I was cut."

"Would, too," he muttered, then bent his head and kissed her palm.

"Something else about her bedroom," Annette added. "No pictures. Anywhere. Of any kind: no casual shots, no paintings, no posters, no family photos. We could chalk it up to her having just moved, but it looks like she's unpacked just about all of it. Her bedroom is very like a cell."

"That's a little weird," Oz admitted.

"And believe it or not, my clandestine visit wasn't the strangest part of my day," she added. But before she could elaborate, they all heard it.

"Hellooooooooo? Ox? Garsea? Are you in there?"

"Let me guess," David growled. "That's the scary-prepared bitch on Mama Mac's front porch. Yeah, that's right! I said it."

"What could she want?" Mama Mac asked. She'd begun packing up the first aid kit but stopped and then laid it all out again.

"To finish me off?" Annette asked.

"Is anyone else worried about the fact that instead of calling the cops, she came over? Anyone?" David demanded. "She didn't call the cops on Sally, either. That's not just being easygoing. That's someone who doesn't want to talk to the police under any circumstance."

"Gal after my own heart," Mama murmured.

"Helloooo? Can you hear me in there? Sorry you had to rush away from our lunch so fast, Ox. I hope everything's okay!"

Annette snickered. "Ox?"

Unperturbed by the lack of response, Lila elaborated in a sing-song tone, "I brought ♫♪ your leftovers…♫♪"

"Good *God*, don't let her in. This is clearly a trap."

"Christ, this is ridiculous," David muttered. "We're cowering in here like cubs in a thunderstorm. She's *one* Stable. Dev could take her."

"I also ♫♪ brought Garsea an order of the profiteroles ♫♪…"

"Open the door," Annette said at once.

"And have one of you misplaced a fox?" Lila called. "Because there's a nice little fox out here."

"Oh, fuck," was all Oz had time for before Annette was on the move.

Chapter 14

PROBABLY SHOULD'VE THOUGHT THIS THROUGH, LILA THOUGHT as Garsea charged. The woman's eyes were red, for God's sake. Not reddish-tinged. Not reddish-brown. Red-red. Movie monster–red. Making things worse, the small fox that had begged to be picked up suddenly wriggled, jumped down, and ran to meet the red-eyed wonder racing toward them.

"Stop!" She'd barely gotten the word out before she found herself sprinting forward, snatching up the fox, holding it tight to her chest, and backing away from Garsea, who had pulled up and was staring at Lila with an odd expression. Not rage. Not surprise. Bemusedly thwarted?

"You can be pissed at me," Lila warned, still backing away with the fox, "but don't take it out on the cub. Also, you've got no right to be pissed at me. Pretty sure *I'm* pissed at *you*."

"That's not…uh…that's not why I'm…" Garsea spread her hands helplessly as several other people tumbled out of the house around her. "I think we should all take a step back. And you should *stop* stepping back, you're almost in the street. I won't hurt you. Most likely."

"Jeez," Lila said, eyeing the porch behind them. "You didn't even open the *door*." It was true; the poor battered door was hanging by one hinge. Barely. "Time to call Harriss & Son again."

"Well, hiya." This from Ox, who looked delighted to see her, which couldn't be real. "You said something about leftovers?"

"How's the hand?"

"Fine," Garsea answered at once, then promptly hid her hand

under the table, then caught herself and deliberately picked up her tea cup with her bandaged hand. "No complaints."

"None?" Lila teased. "At all?"

"I can't think of a single thing to complain about." Annette glanced at the ceiling, giving the impression of a woman deep in thought. "Nnnnnn...not one."

"Glad to hear it." Lila sipped her tea. It was something Mama Mac called Buddha's Blend, and it tasted like flowers and springtime. Especially once you added three sugars. "That is excellent news."

"Yes."

"Did you find what you were looking for?" Lila asked. There was a soft rattle as Mama Mac set the plate of cookies down a bit too hard.

Annette coughed. "Looking for?"

"When you broke into my house."

"Um..."

"Happened about an hour ago? You left a trail of blood from my house to this one?"

"I did not," she snapped. "I was very careful not to drip."

Lila smirked into her teacup.

"Hey, Lila can settle this!" Ox said, turning to her with an improbably wide grin. "Is it breaking and entering if you have the spare keys?"

"Yes," Lila said without hesitation.

Ox deflated a little. "It is?"

"It's not about the key. It's about your right to be on the property. It's a misdemeanor, but if you entered with the intent to steal, then it's a felony." She looked around at the group. "You guys work for IPA—which I'm assuming is some kind of branch of child protection—and you don't know this?"

Or maybe they did know and were testing to see what *she* knew.

"You fix stuffed animals, yet you know precisely what is and is not a misdemeanor and what is and is not a felony in the state of Minnesota?"

"Whoa," Garsea's boyfriend said. He'd taken the seat furthest away from Lila and had spent the awkward chat glaring at Garsea, then Lila, then back at Garsea. He was as tall as Ox, but while Ox was all long legs and lean lines, Garsea's boyfriend was a big guy with a blocky, muscular build, a shock of shaggy brown hair, and loads of dark stubble blooming along his jaw. He was wearing— hand to God!—a brown trench coat and took his coffee with a quarter cup of maple syrup. Or at least that's what it looked like when he was slopping it in. When he spoke, his voice was a gruff baritone straight out of Central Casting for *Grizzled P.I.* "Nobody's talking about felonies or jail."

"Well," Lila said, then munched another chocolate oatmeal cookie

(not defiled with raisins, excellent)

swallowed, sipped her milk. The silence got thicker and more awkward as they waited for her to finish chewing. "*I'm* talking about jail. Or are we sticking with the ridiculous fiction that this is all hypothetical?"

"Um…the last one?" Ox asked.

She almost smiled but caught herself. *That's how it is? No problem.* "Well, while we're *not* chitchatting about felonies and prison, it's worth noting that footage of this hypothetical felony streamed to a hypothetical website, which is accessible to a hypothetical group who can view the hypothetical footage whenever they want."

Another awkward silence. Lila's favorite kind. She took another bite. She wasn't especially hungry—she'd finished her lunch at Meritage—but it gave her something to do with her hands so she wouldn't forget herself and fidget.

After a long moment, Garsea spoke up. "We understand if you want to call the police. But I'd respectfully ask that you don't. It'll make an already complicated situation even thornier. And I don't know that you'd like the outcome."

Lila laughed at her. *Since when is "liking the outcome" relevant?* "Jesus Christ, just stop dancing and out with it. What do you want with me? You have questions, I know you do. Just fucking *ask* already."

Ox opened his mouth as if to answer, then closed it and looked at Garsea, who was looking out the kitchen window behind Lila. (Maybe at the fox? It had made itself scarce once Lila had put it down.) Garsea's BF glowered and Mama Mac got up and cleared the cookie plate and napkins.

These people cannot possibly conduct interviews like this for a living. Am I going to have to get this going? Unbelievable.

"You want to talk about Sally?" she prompted. "Because we can talk about Sally. How's she doing? Is she still insisting her folks are alive?"

"Yes," Garsea replied. "That's part of the reason I wanted to talk to you."

"Is that why you set off my sprinkler and air horns and strobe flashes while I wasn't home? So you could talk to me?" She didn't use air quotes for "talk," but assumed her intent came across.

Ox laughed, then shrugged apologetically when Garsea scowled at him.

"Touché," she muttered. "On my way over here, I got a call from my partner. It seems a man identifying himself as Sally's father called IPA."

"Awkward," Lila observed. "Did you tell him he was dead?"

"And," Garsea continued, making a clear attempt to hold her temper, which was hilarious, "Sally must have spoken with him somehow, because…"

"Let me guess: you lost her again." When no one said anything, Lila shook her head. "You guys suck at your jobs. You know that? Nobody gets to give *this* guy—" She jerked her thumb at a surprised Ox. "—any more grief about his job. He's got the excuse of being new. You guys' excuse is that you're all terrible. Let me guess: If I see Sally, I should call IPA or drop back in here—"

"You don't have to find Sally to come visit," Mama Mac put in.

"Absolutely!" Ox added with alarming enthusiasm.

"—or, I dunno, bring her to IPA myself? Maybe that's the best way to go about it. I'll just do it myself, like the saying says." She hoped Google Maps had an inkling of where IPA was. "Way more efficient, doncha think?"

"Ouch," Ox said mildly.

Lila threw up her hands. "Or I could just adopt her. Sure, why not? There'd be loads of paperwork, but in the end, it'd probably be a time-saver."

Nothing. Except for the curious fact that, suddenly, none of them could meet her gaze.

They were stuck, Lila realized. They didn't know what she knew, that was problem number one. They couldn't call the cops—that was problem number two. *She* hadn't done anything wrong; that was problem number three. But a straight-up confrontation was dangerous. Not to mention they knew she had proof of Garsea's illegal shenanigans.

So now a cookie meeting to try and suss out what to do next, but they were still locked in their holding pattern. She figured they were going to observe and circle closer and closer until they thought it was safe, and then…

Pounce.

She rose. "Chickenshits."

"Hey!" From Ox. "If you're gonna call us names, we prefer 'ineffective morons.'"

"He is *not* speaking for the rest of us," Annette said at once.

"Thanks for the cookies and milk, Macropi."

Garsea got up, too, and so did Ox. Garsea's boyfriend didn't move.

"Thank you for the profiteroles," Garsea said with finishing school politeness.

"You're welcome. Thank you for not beating me to death over a random fox. Next time, call first."

Chapter 15

Baking soda. Birdseed. Dish soap. Gummy worms. Bird feeder. Half a dozen lip balms. Baking soda? No, she'd already put that in her basket.

So she was finished. List complete, again—just like when she'd gone to the drugstore before the decoy lunch. She hadn't bought anything, just left. And why not? It's not like she was enduring a birdseed crisis. Or a chapped lip crisis. She had chapped lips, but it wasn't a *crisis*. And did she even need baking soda? Because as a weirdo repellant, it had failed. So maybe she wouldn't buy anything this time, either. She didn't have to. No one could force her to buy drugstore items and associated sundries, dammit!

Anyway.

List, complete. Basket, full.

Time to go up to the cashier.

Time to pay for her things and go home. Because she had finished shopping. Her list had nothing but cross-outs. All done. No further need to remain.

So she dropped the ovulation kit (*Baby4U!*) in her basket and turned and marched up to the clerk and paid for all of it and headed for the parking lot and what was happening to her?

Just...just go home and relax and try to get more than four hours of sleep. Have you considered the idea that a lot of this might be simple fatigue? Or dark sorcery?

"It's *not* dark sorcery," she announced, ignoring the puzzled expressions of her fellow Walgreens shoppers. "I'm pretty sure."

The clock struck 1:00 a.m. (not literally; Lila hadn't unpacked it yet) just as there was a tentative knock on her front door.

Let the wild rumpus start, she thought, and went to the door. As if the person on the other side could hear her approach (unlikely; it was an old house with a thick front door), there was more knocking, followed by a pleasant treble piping up, "Hello? I'm a hapless minor standing on your porch in the middle of the night. Won't you please take me in? It's starting to rain."

It's barely sprinkling.

"Plus I'm cold and frightened."

At least one of those is a lie.

"Match? Anyone in there want to buy a match from an orphan? Well, half an orphan? My mom's still alive. I think."

He'll stay out there and stay out there and talk and talk because nobody ever goes away and other people might notice and I shouldn't let him in but it IS cold and it IS late and I should just go to bed FUCK.

She flipped on the porch light as she opened the door, temporarily blinding whomever-it-was so she had a few seconds to size him up. And there wasn't much to him: a preteen boy bundled into a bulky navy jacket, jeans, tennis shoes. The porch light illuminated his freckles, the spiky dark blond hair, his tentative smile. But his most striking feature was a pair of bright green eyes, exactly like those of the fox cub she'd picked up earlier.

"I don't need any matches," she said.

Grin. Shrug. "Worth a try. C'n I come in anyway?"

She sighed and stood aside. Shoulders hunched, he passed her, then glanced around as she closed and locked the door. He didn't seem tense or frightened. *Shy,* she wanted to say, except he'd hammered on her door in the wee hours and had no qualms about walking into a stranger's house. Embarrassed? No, too strong. Abashed? No, that was a synonym for embarrassed...

"Sorry to wake you," he mumbled to the floor, reinforcing abashed.

"I was awake. I'm a short sleeper."

His head jerked up; bright eyes gleamed. "Four hours or less a night, huh? Bet that's nice."

She smiled. "You're the first non-doctor I haven't had to explain that to."

"I read a lot of books. Lots, *mucho, beaucoup*."

"Clearly."

He unzipped the heavy jacket and pulled out a small, tattered bundle. "Net said you're a teddy bear doctor. D'you think you could fix this? I brought money."

She took the bear, examined it. Loved hard, obviously; lots of matted fur, a missing eye, a third of the stuffing had leaked out a hole in the belly, which someone had then carefully taped with black duct tape. Old, dried stains, but no new stains or so much as a speck of dirt. Loved hard and cared for, then.

It was late.

It was really fucking late and she'd had a long fucking day and no one in this neighborhood understand the concept of business hours or locks and Jesus Christ this was asking too fucking much so he was gonna have to hit the road *now*.

"Sure I can," she heard herself say, and led him to the kitchen.

"Are you a spy?" she asked.

"Are *you*?" he countered, which she had to admit was pretty neat.

Not that she was going to dignify that with an answer. "Or do you just have an aversion to business hours?" she asked. Then she thought about the diffident way he'd handed over the bear. "Or do you not want people to know you care about an old stuffed animal?"

"Yes," he replied.

"Well played," she muttered, and got a giggle out of him. "Who's Net?"

"She's my caseworker, Annette Garsea."

The red-eyed monster who broke through a screen door because she thought I was stealing a fox cub? she thought but didn't say.

"Some of us call her that," the kid continued, "because she's our safety net."

"Mmmm." *That was almost adorable.* She'd brought her emergency surgery kit to the kitchen and was nearly finished; now she was switching out the remaining stuffing for soft, clean polyfill and back-stitching the hole. "Just about done here."

"Great! I'm Dev Devoss, by the way. And I already know your name."

"Because of course you do. Is there a reason that you waited until the witching hour to stop by?"

"There's a bunch of reasons."

I'll bet. "Great. Okay, I think Osa's good to go for now." *Osa...* Pretty sure the kid had named his bear *Bear*, just in a different language. She'd look it up later. "New eyes, new stuffing, a few other details." She'd replaced much of the bear, but not the worn fur, because there was a careful line of demarcation, and it was different for every toy. Cross that line, and you're no longer repairing an old bear, you're making a new one, and then you're dealing with a sad kid and irked parents. "But going forward, here's my advice. If you want it."

He gave her a look patented by mouthy preteens everywhere. "I'm here, aren't I?"

"Osa's fur gets matted like that because you're air-drying her. Does your house have a dryer?"

"Sure, I live with Mama Mac." It wasn't a casually tossed off comment; he'd straightened in the chair and made the declaration with real pride. And he didn't say he lived there, he said lived *with*.

Foster, then. Or adopted. Doesn't take family for granted, or a roof over his head.

"Uh-huh, and she's old-fashioned, and I'll bet she likes to line-dry whatever she can, even this time of year."

"Hoo, yes! I mean, I kind of get it, because the sheets do smell awesome afterward but they're also kind of scratchy. And it takes forever to get wet sheets on the lines; my sister Caro helps, but it's still…yuck. But a guy can't complain about stuff like that without sounding like a wimp, *faible*, *weichei*."

"Yeah, and God forbid anyone call you a *weichei*."

"I've got a rep to worry about," the child replied, absently cuddling his mended teddy bear. "And speaking of reputations, you've got one for—"

"I've lived here for two days," she protested.

"Exactly."

"*Genau, exactamente.*"

His small face lit up. "You speak German? And Spanish?"

"No," she deadpanned. "Was there anything else?"

"I dunno. Was there?"

Lila looked at the boy and thought about the fox. It had come frisking up to her with no signs of aggression, tame as a domesticated dog, running up to her, darting away, then coming back. At one point, it gently rested a white paw on her shin and looked up at her with beseeching eyes, which was when she was totally subsumed by the cuteness and picked it up.

What the hell, I've had my rabies booster. She knew it wasn't actually smiling—she rolled her eyes when people anthropomorphized animals—that it was just the way the fox's mouth tipped up at the corners. Still, the thing was cute AF, its fur coarse and plush at the same time, warm little body wiry but cuddly.

And it got Garsea out of the house in half a heartbeat, so there was that.

Devoss broke through her thoughts. "You *know*, don't you?"

"Sorry?"

"You know what I am," he elaborated in a tone of puzzled

wonder. "You've seen my other self. You *know*. Like you know about Sally. And you're not going to ask. About any of it. You just won't."

Lila shrugged.

"You've gotta be the most incurious Stable I've ever met. I can't tell if that's great or terrible."

That word again. "Or I'm just invested in minding my own business."

"Or *you're* the trap," the child pointed out. "You're, like, luring us into a false sense of whatever so you can pounce."

"*I'm* not the pouncing type."

"See? See? That! What does that mean? Does it mean just what you said, like I shouldn't be reading anything into it, or are you implying that we *are* the pouncing type and you've got secrets?"

She handed him his jacket with one hand and a Target bag with the other, to shield prying eyes from spotting Osa.

Half an orphan.

I live with Mama Mac.

That tattered bear was probably the only thing the kid grabbed when he ran away. Or was removed.

"You're showing me to the front door," he observed.

"Yep. Thanks for stopping by, Google 'business hours' when you get a chance, I'll cover for you if anyone comes around, and remember what I said about using a dryer."

"Wait! I didn't pay you."

"No charge. And if you tell anyone, I'll set Osa on fire."

"Would not. Not after you worked so hard on—o-*kay*, I'm going! Jeez!" And then as she closed the door in his little fox face, he hollered, "Oz really likes you!"

Oh, goody. Because I don't have enough problems.

The teeny thrill she got from Dev's words was annoying.

Chapter 16

"You did *what*?"

"Um…" Oz blinked in the face of the older woman's noisy surprise. "Ate the last piece of pie?"

"Oh. Right. Yes, yes, that—sorry, m'dear, I'm still upset about Dev's walkabout last night."

"If she didn't hurt Sally, she wasn't gonna hurt *me*." Dev's declaration was muffled, possibly because his head was inside a cupboard. School had let out hours ago, and the werefox had been condemned to the gulag archipelago of chores: emptying and scrubbing out every cupboard in Mama Mac's kitchen, then putting everything back neatly and in some semblance of order. The counters, kitchen table, and chairs were groaning beneath the weight of plates and spices and mismatched water bottles and lightbulbs and batteries and candles and matches and notebooks and scores of mechanical pencils that were out of lead. "Which was obvious, *obvio, offensichtlich.*"

"You come down now," Mama Mac ordered as the boy emerged from the cupboard to blink down at her, then sneezed from the dust. Oz obligingly hooked a finger through one of Dev's belt loops and lifted him to the floor. "Supper's ready."

"What, no plate?" Dev asked with grating wide-eyed innocence as she handed him a roast beef sandwich on a paper towel.

"Very funny. You just sit down and—you stand there and eat." Despite her displeasure, Mama Mac had made Dev's sandwich just the way he liked: thick slices of rare roast beef with swiss cheese, paper-thin slices of bermuda onion, heirloom tomatoes, dijon mustard, sea salt, and cracked pepper. In two bites, it was more than half gone. When Oz had wondered aloud if giving naughty kits their favorite foods was a disincentive, Mama had speared him with A Look and explained that nutrition and discipline were entirely unrelated.

He was instantly abashed; he, more than anyone, knew that Mama never punished by withholding food. To her, that wasn't punishment; it was abuse.

And who knew better than he did? Besides his dead sister?

"So tell me, Oz. You find our girl yet?"

"You're gonna have to narrow—"

"Sally!"

Her attitude was to be expected, despite the fact that she'd never met "our girl." Mama was proprietary toward any cub in trouble. Thank God. "It's getting messy," he admitted. "Well. Messier."

"Poor, poor cub," Mama sighed, ignoring Oz's pain.

"There's also the nagging-yet-growing feeling that she's getting help from somewhere." His phone peeped at a pitch too high for Stable ears; he pulled it out and glared at the text. "Annnnnd Annette's butting in again."

"Invite her for dinner," Mama Mac said promptly.

"Pass. Okay, her text says that somebody claiming to be Sally's dad called yesterday, but no one got the message for hours because bureaucracy. Message reads, 'I'm not dead, keep her safe until I get there, you drones.'" Oz looked up. "So Sally's dad wasn't a fan of IPA. Or isn't a fan of IPA. Dammit! Why does everything about this case get progressively weirder? Did he get a message to Sally, too? I think he must have. Isn't that why she ran again?"

"Are you thinking out loud or is this an actual conversation where you want our input?" From Dev, who'd finished his sandwich and was on his third glass of apple cider.

"Both. Maybe. I dunno." Oz rubbed his eyes. "It's 6:00 p.m. on a Tuesday. Why do I feel like it's 2:00 a.m. on a Friday?"

"You need some rest. Stay the night. Or at least long enough for a nice nap."

"Sure," he sighed. "A nap will fix everything."

"Never said it would, boy." This while stabbing a finger in the general direction of Oz's eyeballs. "But you get snappish when you're tired. Eat something and go lie down," she ordered.

"I will, but because *I* want to." He could hear himself whining and sighed. Mama had a point. Everything and everyone around him was pissing him off, and for no good reason. It was just as well Annette and David weren't here; all they could do right now was get on each other's nerves. Besides, maybe Lila would stop by. He'd torpedoed any chance at a relationship with the decoy lunch, but his libido was inconveniently ignoring that. "Thanks, Mama." A true measure of his fatigue: her lumpy sectional sounded more appealing than his own digs, which weren't lumpy at all.

He wasn't lonely, exactly. He had a fine life, and he knew it. But sometimes he wanted to come back home and *stay* home, even if only for an evening. He pondered the dichotomy while brushing his teeth and stripping to his skivvies. Mama always had spare toothbrushes on hand, and Oz kept a couple of changes of clothes at her place, too, for reasons he decided not to examine.

I guess that settles the Kama-Rupa question. Well, it doesn't, but there's no point in speculating any longer; Lila wants nothing to do with any of us with the possible exception of Sally and maybe Dev. Which is sensible for many, many reasons.

He assumed the sleeping position—facedown starfish—and yawned into the upholstery. *I've had that condo for four years, but this crowded chaotic purple house is my home. It felt like that even before I met Lila. There's probably some sort of parable or lesson there, but I'm too wiped to give a shhhhhhhhhhhhhh...*

Chapter 17

LILA SMELLED IT BEFORE SHE HEARD IT, LIKE LAST TIME. AND froze, like last time. An icy hand snaked down her throat and seized her stomach while every hair on her arms came to attention and she thought *everything, it'll take everything.*

She shot out of her office chair and darted to the closet to grab what she needed, went to her bedroom closet and did the same, then walked quickly

(easy…you're no good to anyone if you brain yourself falling down the stairs)

and carefully to her kitchen, snatched the bucket of clean rags beneath the sink, soaked them, grabbed keys, left her home.

She saw it at once—Mama Mac's silly purple house, belching smoke like it was getting paid. She managed to hit 911 and put them on speaker with one hand. "I've got a 10–70. There's a house fire at 1218 Elinor Avenue in Lilydale, Saint Paul. I can see smoke and flames and there's at least one child

(child? is he?)

and one elderly woman in the house. Please roll fire and rescue ASAP."

"Can I g—"

Sorry, dispatch. Lila was flat-out running because her worst fear had become glaring, ugly reality: she could see someone—the kid with the bear?—silhouetted in one of the upstairs windows. She ran right up on the lawn until she was standing below the window, which he now opened

(argh, don't give the fire more oxygen)

(but don't die of smoke inhalation either)

to lean out and call down to her. Instead of the panicked shriek for help, she heard, "Hi! Can you step back, please?"

She cupped her hands and shouted through them. "Listen! I'm tossing up a ladder. You just hook it to the sill and let it unfold and you can scoot right down."

"Um, thanks, but maybe you could just move back a little?"

"Pay attention!"

"You don't have to move back much," he called down. "Like, just a foot or so?"

"I'm throwing it now!" And she pitched the EZ-OUT ladder straight up. It was only six pounds and it was a terrific toss, which is why Devoss watching it fall back to the ground was aggravating. "Okay, don't be scared, I'm gonna throw it again. You have to *catch* it, Devoss!"

"Just step back, *espalda*—" He broke off to cough. "—*retour*!"

"Okay, here it comes!"

"Will you just get out of the way, you silly bitch?" With that, Devoss dived out the second-story window, turned a *goddamned somersault*, and landed right in front of her. Like he'd stepped off a boat and onto a dock. Like he'd hopped down from a SuperCab. NBD.

"Don't call me silly" was all she could manage before grabbing him. "Are you okay? Are you burned?" She felt his shoulders as he coughed, looked at his hands, shoved his sleeves up to look at his arms, glared into his eyes. "Are your eyes okay?"

"Are *yours*?"

"What's—" There was a low, ripping growl behind her, and she turned to face a sight that wasn't as frightening as a house fire, but definitely made her top five. A black wolf the size of a border collie had slouched out of nowhere—well, not nowhere, obviously. But the thing's stark coloring had kept it hidden; the only bits of color were its eyes, glaring at her like baleful lanterns. She straightened and shoved Devoss behind her. "Jesus Christ, this neighborhood."

"I'm okeydokey," Devoss called, peeking around her to address the wolf because of course he was. "Don't scare her. If that's even possible."

"Which one of us are you talking to?" Lila asked.

The wolf crept closer, but at least it wasn't growling anymore. Lila wondered if it was possible to net the thing with the EZ-OUT ladder. *Why did I bring ladders and wet rags to a house fire? Why didn't I bring a shotgun? What an idiot I was!*

Then another wolf came loping out of the dark, this one lean but large, dwarfing the smaller animal; its furred red ears were level with Lila's waist. The only light to see came from the fire (now merrily blazing through at least two rooms) and a lone streetlight, but even so, Lila could make out the tawny fur and the white markings around the muzzle. Greenish-yellow eyes flared as it moved to stand between her and the smaller wolf. She knew it at once: the wolf she had hit with her nonbulance... Had it only been three days ago?

"Whoa." From Devoss, who had stopped trying to peep around her and was trying to stand in front of her. She shoved him behind her as the wolf let out another low growl while the smaller black wolf stood its ground. And while the black one didn't stand down, exactly—its fur was still standing out from ruff to tail—it didn't growl, and it backed up to give the larger wolf more room for...what, exactly? To feast? To run? To huff and puff and blow Macropi's house down?

Just as she had decided the wee hours couldn't get even a bit weirder, she caught movement on her periphery and saw...

No.

No, definitely not. She was seeing things. She had at long last cracked, because while she could handle the bear cub and the fox and the B&E and the trashed screen door and the pop-ins and Ox's distracting cuteness and her sudden urge to forcibly strip the man and make him knock her up and 1:00 a.m. teddy bear surgery and two wolves prowling a suburban lawn while a house fire raged in the background...

...all that, she could take. But the sight of a kangaroo bounding over was, obviously, the most direct way her brain had found to signal her impending insanity. Everything else could be real, but not the Australian marsupial squatting unconcernedly on a front lawn in Lilydale, Minnesota.

"Jesus Christ," she muttered, and she knew that as a response, it was both lacking and overused. But… She had nothing. Nothing. Sure, the big wolf had made the smaller wolf back off. And yes, the kangaroo had bounded closer but wasn't pummeling or kicking her (at the moment). And none of the animals were trying to eat her. Or Devoss, who was still peeking around her and seemed remarkably unconcerned about all of it.

And yeah, she was resigned to nightmares about fires for the rest of the month. Or season. Or year.

But now what? Now…the fuck…what? Because this was problematic even if they *weren't* her neighbors.

Fortunately, the distant wail of sirens snapped her out of her WTF trance. She cleared her throat and said, "You know the fire department will call animal control about two seconds after they get here, right?" But would they? These, um, *people* had their own social services agency. Maybe they also had their own fire and rescue? Maybe if you lived in certain neighborhoods, any call to 911 was re-routed to…what?

Now I know why the Curs(ed) House is almost always vacant. No time to ponder that now; instead, she grabbed Devoss's hand, startling a yelp out of him. "I'm taking Devoss to my place where it's safe, relatively speaking. The first responders are going to want a word with Mama Mac." She made a point of *not* looking at the kangaroo. "So go do your thing—or don't—and come find us when you. Uh. Figure out what you're going to do." Whatever the hell *that* was.

"Don't worry," Devoss reassured her. "They're more scared of you than you are of them."

It sounded like a lie.

Chapter 18

IT WAS 3:00 A.M., AND HER KITCHEN WAS ABSURDLY CROWDED.

"You're not sleeping in Lila's horrible basement, Caro Daniels, and that's an end to it!" There was an awkward pause, and Garsea flushed. "Let me rephrase…"

It was so ridiculous, Lila had to laugh. "No, you're right. My basement *is* horrible. Unfinished, crumbling cement walls, musty, it's always damp though I can never find a leak… It's basically the set of every black-and-white zombie movie you've ever seen."

Garsea cleared her throat. "I only meant…"

"I know what you meant. It's fine."

When Garsea had pounded on her front door, then let herself in before Lila could take one step toward the foyer, Lila had been braced. The woman had come in hot, hair mussier than usual, eyes redder

(eep)

than usual. Daniels had been right on her heels and they both looked relieved when Devoss raised his glass of chocolate milk to them in cheery greeting.

Still, Garsea's eyes had narrowed when she saw Lila leaning against the counter. Which was why Lila let her hand drop to the silverware drawer behind her and thought about her forks and knives and the wicked–sharp fillet knife and corncob holders with their spiky ends.

But there'd been no need for corn accessories; instead, Garsea came right to her and enfolded her in a smothering vanilla-scented hug. "*Thank you*," she murmured intensely, which Lila hadn't thought was possible. She pulled back to scrutinize Lila's face. "You put yourself in danger to save my favorite delinquent. I'll owe you a debt for the rest of my life."

"Not really. He wasn't in any—"

Garsea waved that away. "You couldn't have known. You came for him anyway. And when you thought he was in *more* trouble, you stood your ground. I'll never be able to repay you. Which isn't to say I won't try."

Well. How to respond to that? *"Eh, no biggie"*? That was an insult to Garsea *and* Devoss. But Lila's default was to immediately downplay praise and/or emotionally charged moments. So she just nodded and didn't say anything and tried not to feel (more) awkward. Garsea was acting like Lila had done something above and beyond, which simply wasn't true. Who wouldn't help a kid in trouble?

After that, talk of sleeping arrangements came up, which was when Lila had made her offer, which was when Garsea got hot again. But all the while, Caro Daniels, a gorgeous teen with dark skin with golden undertones, short black hair, and brown eyes, was scribbling something in a battered notebook that clearly went everywhere she did. The girl's pajama top was inside out and spotted with grass stains, but Lila wasn't going to bring that up if no one else was. More worrisome: the girl was too thin and hadn't made a peep since Lila had let her and Garsea in. And though it wasn't relevant, Lila knew plenty of women who shelled out big bucks for highlighter that would give them the same golden undertones Daniels was sporting naturally.

Her eyes, now that Lila was close enough to get a better look without being obvious, also had gold undertones. Or would those be overtones? In the light, they almost look like...

Well. Baleful lamps. Like they'd gleam gold, not brown. Like they'd be the first thing you saw if you were standing on a poorly lit suburban lawn and she came at you out of the dark.

Daniels tore off a sheet and handed her a note; her pen had been flying back and forth so quickly, Lila half-expected the paper to be warm.

Ms. Kai,

Before I lived with Mama Mac, I lived in horrible basements among other places. Net is worried I'll get triggered because she's in full-on protective mode right now. Bear with us. Normal service will resume shortly.

Yours,
Caro Daniels

Lila laughed, and some of the tension in the room dissipated. "Tempting as I'm sure my basement must sound to all of you, it's not necessary. You and Devoss can share the guest room upstairs. My couch folds out into a double bed for Macropi. And someone can sleep on the daybed in my office."

"Oh, no-no-no," Garsea said at once. "We can't let you do that. Good *God*, you just met us."

"Yeah, but such meetings!"

Devoss choked on his milk. "See? That," he cried while Daniels tossed napkins at him. "*That*. What does it mean? Are you saying you know secrets, or are you just being nice?"

"I'm never just being nice. Finish your milk. And it goes in your mouth, not down your chin."

"Picky, picky," he muttered.

And this time, when the door behind her was thrown open, she didn't even jump.

"Are you guys okay?" Ox cried. She turned and saw he was a wreck. Worse than the night they met, and that was saying something. His hair was a mess (and it was hard to muss up a Caesar cut), his smudged dress shirt wasn't buttoned all the way, his suit jacket wasn't buttoned at all, his pants were dirty, he hadn't zipped his fly, and he was sockless while wearing dress shoes (ouch!).

Why, if I didn't know better, I would think earlier tonight he stripped outside, didn't care where his fine clothes landed, prowled around for a bit, did…something…and then rapidly re-dressed and ran over here. At night. During a house fire. In forty-five-degree weather.

"The kids are fine," Garsea assured him. "And you saw Mama for yourself."

His head jerked in what was probably a nod. *Man*, the stress coming off the guy! "Yeah, she'll be over pretty quick—she's talking to the firemen."

Caro held up her pad. *FireFIGHTERS. There's women too.*

"Sure, sure," he replied. "How about you?" he asked Lila, stepping forward. He reached out as if he was going to touch her but settled for raking her up and down with his gaze. "Are you okay? You didn't get singed? Or worse?"

"Don't be a doof," she said but didn't put any venom in it. She wasn't sure if she was flattered or alarmed by his intensity. "I was never in the house." *You know that. You saw me run over there. Or are you wondering how I am after all those wildlife sightings?*

"You weren't, but you certainly came over quick enough. At least, that's what Mama Mac told me when she called," Garsea said. "And you brought ladders."

"*And* wet rags," Devoss added.

"Why are you all staring at me like *I'm* the weirdo? What should I have brought? Fireworks?"

"Damn." Devoss wiped away his milk moustache. "Now I'm kinda bummed you didn't bring fireworks."

"C'mere," Ox said. His hand closed over her elbow and Lila entertained a brief vision of breaking his wrist before shrugging it off and letting him haul her outside. The newly repaired screen door thwacked against the house, then rebounded as he pulled her further into the yard.

"I can appreciate wanting distance for a private chat, but your family's only eight feet away. Pretty sure they can still hear us."

"They *are* my family," he replied absently, sounding pleased, which was strange. "Are you *sure* you're okay?"

She began prying his fingers off her wrist. "Honestly, you seem a lot more rattled than I am."

"Rattled. Yeah. And you're…not."

"Not what? Rattled?"

No response.

"Um. This is really close for a conversation."

Ox had let go of her wrist only to take her gently by the shoulders and was peering at her like a farsighted dentist looking for cavities. "I don't know who you are. Or why you are. But I really, really want to find out. I know I fucked everything up. I know I betrayed your trust. Have dinner with me tomorrow anyway. Please."

"You mean tonight," she corrected, because none of these people ever knew what time it was. "And I can't. I have to put up all new booby traps for Garsea to trip when she comes snooping while we're on our fake date."

From inside: "Obviously I won't repeat the behavior."

From right in front of her: "I'm so, so sorry. But that wasn't a fake date. Not entirely. I really did want to spend time with you. Not a business lunch, not on behalf of IPA. Just you."

She grabbed his wrists with every intention of wrenching them away but then just stood there like a dolt and stared back into his green eyes. She could smell him, and it wasn't at all objectionable: grass, smoke, and something that was just Ox.

"Pretty skeevy trick," she pointed out.

"It was. No excuse. Let me make it up to you."

"Why?"

"You know," he breathed. "I know you do."

The few hairs left on her arms were all trying to stiffen. Fear? Lust? All-consuming irritation? "You'll have to narrow that down, because I know tons of stuff. I know how to pluck a chicken and stuff a teddy bear. I know that custard's just a fancy name for pudding, and I know Dairy Queen makes the best non-ice cream in the world. I know dill and thyme make everything taste better and I know how to train a parakeet to sit on a finger. I know how to change a flat and make a perfect fried egg. I know how to ice fish for walleye and how to de-head shrimp and that real whipped cream is a thousand times better than Cool Whip. I'm a friggin' font of knowledge."

He just looked at her.

"And I know how long it takes the average radius and ulna to knit back together."

He was looking at her with not a little desperation. "What? What?"

She pushed up his unbuttoned sleeve, revealing a sooty—but unharmed—wrist. "Oooh, looky here. You're all better. You went from make-shift cast to bandage to nothing in seventy-two hours."

"Yes! Exactly! *You know this.*"

"Most people don't heal up so quickly after getting hit by a decommissioned ambulance."

"Right!" He sounded so relieved she'd finally put it out there, the Big Unspoken Thing, she (almost) felt bad. "So…"

She took a breath. "So I think there miiiiiiiiiight be something kinda weird going on with your family." Beat. "Maybe."

He let go of her shoulders and let out a tiny yelp of frustration. "That's it? That's all you've got to say?"

From her kitchen: "Take what you can get, Oz!"

Lila snickered. "Devoss has excellent advice for you, Ox."

"Uh. It's Oz."

"Like the wizard?"

"Like the werewolf." Pause. "On *Buffy*?"

She blinked. "Buffy wasn't a werewolf."

She almost whispered that, because he was leaning in again and she could not stop staring at his mouth. (In her defense, it was *right there.*) She felt momentary dizziness, then realized she was holding her breath. She wasn't going to lean in, that wasn't how she played this game, and besides, she didn't have to; he was doing all the leaning. He just needed to lean faster. Much faster. *Much, much faster.*

"Lila, I know my timing sucks, but I haven't been able to get you out of my mmmpphh."

Much better. She ran her tongue across his lower lips and got a tender nip in response, and then she could feel herself stepping closer to him (not that there was much space left between them), could feel herself opening to him. His hand came up to cradle the back of her head and he tasted like salt and smoke and also cookies for some reason, and as far as first kisses went, it was devastating in all the best ways.

"What are you kids doing out here?"

They both jumped apart like guilty teenagers as Macropi came out and held the kitchen door for them. Lila took a second to remind herself that a) she was an adult, b) it was her yard, and c) Macropi was not the boss of her.

She followed Oz inside anyway, already wondering when they might kiss again, which should *not* be her priority right now, which nicely encapsulated the problem.

Never mind the fire and the wildlife. I might be in real *trouble.*

Chapter 19

"You want us to stay with you?"

"Sure."

Maybe it was the (damp) nightgown and robe, her long feet all black with dirt, or the fact that her tight white curls were a disaster, but Macropi looked, for the first time, old and vulnerable. "Really?" she whispered.

"Sure."

She and the kids had just finished drinking their Flanders's cocoas, and Lila was glad to see it had perked them up a bit. The looks on their faces had been worth the effort of making hot chocolate from scratch during the wee hours.

"Wow," Devoss had said when she'd handed him his mug, which had been topped with whipped cream, sprinkled with chocolate shavings, and for a finishing touch, Lila had wedged a vanilla wafer into the cream. "What even is this? It's not a drink, it's a dessert course."

Thanks. The second Caro finished her note, she was again snout deep in her mug.

"It's Flanders's cocoa. You guys watch *The Simpsons*, right?"

"Only the first ten seasons," Devoss replied. "The rest is dreck."

"Yikes. Okay, there's an episode where Ned Flanders makes Homer some hot chocolate, and he goes all out: whole milk, chopped chocolate—not powder—and the works, whipped cream and everything. So I call it Flanders's cocoa."

But now the drinks were done, and Dev in particular looked glassy-eyed. It had prompted Lila's offer, which Macropi was still mulling.

"That would be… I'd—we'd like that. Yes. Thank you." She let out a breath. "We would very much like to take you up on that, m'dear."

"You're *considering* this?" Annette asked, amazed.

"Considered," Lila corrected. "Past tense. Decision's been made, clearly. Try to keep up, Garsea."

"It's absurd!" she protested. "Mama, I'll put all of you up in a hotel. I'd have you over in a nanosecond, but you know my place is still under renovation because, ah, things happened."

Lila couldn't imagine what that meant. "Things" like a bedbug infestation? Or a paranormal creature infestation? A house fire? Or a wrecking ball? A ravaging pack of fox cubs? Or Girl Scouts?

"Out of the question," Garsea continued, because she had deluded herself into thinking it was her decision.

"Now don't you go being stubborn on me, Annette. We'll be fine here."

"It's ludicrous, Mama."

"Jesus Christ," Lila said irritably. "I'm not asking you to fill out a wedding registry. Just crash for a couple of nights until you figure out your next step."

"I trust her," Macropi replied at once. "She's had loads of time to hurt us or worse."

Lila coughed. "I've only had three days to hurt you."

"I'm staying, too," Oz declared. There was a short silence, broken by Caro's scribbling. She held up a note, and whatever she'd written caused him to blush a little and shake his head. "Doesn't matter. I'm staying."

"And now that temporary housing arrangements have been settled…" Lila turned to Devoss. "Go down and tell Sally to just come upstairs already."

"Uh. Okay." The boy glanced at the others, who seemed as nonplussed as he was.

"Oh, please, you've been flaring your nostrils and inching

toward the basement door for a couple of minutes now. You've clearly caught her scent."

"Oh, yes," Garsea said, giving her an odd look. "Clearly."

"Not to mention, you guys would have been far more freaked if you *hadn't* known Sally was lurking in my basement."

"Mmmm," Garsea mmmm'd.

When Devoss was basement-bound, Macropi tugged on Lila's wrist. "I haven't had a chance to thank you for what you did for us tonight."

"This morning. And I didn't do anything. You guys had it all under control. The only reason Devoss might've needed help—which he didn't—was because he went back for his bear."

Oz, who'd shrugged out of his rumpled, stained suit jacket and hung it on the peg next to Lila's scarf, turned back. "How the hell did you know that?"

"It's the only thing he brought." Too late, Lila realized she might have accidentally gotten Devoss busted. She'd promised him she wouldn't say anything about Operation Osa.

"Oh. Right."

She didn't sigh with relief, but it was close. Oz thought she meant "brought out of the fire," and she decided not to disabuse him. But at the first opportunity, Devoss was getting a patented "inanimate things are not worth your life, no matter how precious, never ever go back into a burning house or I will murder you *so much*" lecture. "Right. So we talked about sleeping arrangements before you got here, Macropi. Garsea, I guess you're welcome to stay, too. Just try to refrain from pawing through my underwear drawer."

"Don't worry," she said fervently, waving her lightly bandaged fingers, and while it wasn't especially funny, it eased the tension a bit. "Your offer of shelter is especially considerate given that I... crossed a line earlier."

"That's the euphemism, huh?" But between one heartbeat and

the next, Lila was tired of needling Garsea. She wanted everybody settled and sleeping so she could settle and sleep. Because there was a lot of stuff to do tomorrow, and she'd bet that the others had no idea just what they had to look forward to. Not to mention, she could be a suspect. She *should* be a suspect: new in town, crazy-prepared, ladders and buckets all over the place. If they hadn't gotten that far in their thinking just now, they would soon enough. "Well, if you're not staying, toodle-oo."

Oz, who had been sighing over the state of his clothes, looked up as Garsea headed for the door. "Tomorrow morning?"

"I'll bring the pastry."

"Yeah, but what are you bringing for everyone else?"

"Har-har." But there wasn't any bite to it, and out the door she went.

"Right. Well." He looked up hopefully at Lila. "You never gave me an answer. About dinner."

"Possibly because I mashed my mouth down on yours."

"Oh. Right."

"Jesus. You're blushing."

"The hell I am," he snapped. "Uh. Sorry. Long day. Could I borrow a spare toothbrush? Or even just yours? I'm not picky."

"Yuck. I'll see what I can scrounge up for you and the rest of your wild bunch. I'll dig up some more pillows, too," she added, nodding at the couch.

"Lucky fella," Macropi teased. "Sleeping on two couches in one night."

Oz grinned. "Charmed life, Mama."

Chapter 20

HOT, AND GETTING HOTTER, AND HER EYES HER EYES WERE *streaming and she had no idea how bad the smoke could get and everything was fine five minutes ago and now she couldn't see and couldn't breathe and Mama was going to be SO MAD but maybe she could grab some of the mags, maybe even the little bookshelf just inside the living room that was stuffed with* People *and* US Weekly *and it was worth trying, sure it was, but she couldn't she tried and she lost her grip and when she tried to scoop up the smoldering magazines she was scooping up fire she was holding fire and it felt like a zillion bees were stinging her arms at once and she had to put them out she had to kill the bees every last one and and and*

"Lila?"

and and and and and and

"Time to wake up, Lila."

———————

And there weren't any bees. There was only Oz, the antithesis of bees.

(antithesis of bees? you need more sleep)

Oz was leaning over her, and she swore she could still feel it where he'd taken her by the shoulder to gently shake her awake. It should have been terrifying, waking in a strange place to a strange man looming over her in a darkened bedroom. She should have smelled phantom smoke and assumed her hair was about to catch fire. Instead, she was so relieved to have escaped the nightmare she could have kissed him, and the only thing she could smell was *eau de Oz.*

Which was a terrible idea. Top ten of terrible ideas, right up there with all the record clubs she'd joined as a kid and eating undercooked chicken.

"Are you okay?" he asked in a low voice.

"Relieved and mortified is how I am." She rubbed the imaginary smoke out of her eyes. "Did I wake you?"

"No, I was brushing my teeth and thought—you sounded like—are you sure you're okay?"

She didn't answer.

"Am I freaking you out? I don't want to freak you out."

She sighed. "Hovering over the bed like a hot Vincent Price *is* freaking me out, so sit down already."

He'd half-turned toward the door, but at her words he came back and sat down so hard the bed jostled. And speaking of jostling the bed, Oz dressed in nothing but boxers was just…yum. Which was altogether irrelevant and thus annoying.

She jabbed a finger in his direction. "I have a tragic backstory that I won't be discussing with you."

"Okay. But if you change your mind—"

"Pass. And if you tell anyone about my nightmares, which have been stuck on repeat since I was a kid—"

"So this happens a lot?"

"—you *won't* live to regret it, get it?"

He raised a hand, solemn as a court clerk. "I get it."

"That said." She coughed into her fist. Gratitude was hard. She had a horror of being pitied. "Thanks for coming in."

"Anytime. Really. That's not just me being polite. I'll come in here anytime. Anytime at all." Pause. "Hot Vincent Price?"

"And now we shall never speak of this again."

"Whatever you want," he agreed, rising and backing toward the door. "We established that you're not seeing anyone, right?"

"Nnn." She tried to spit out "no," but her mouth had gone dry so quickly, her tongue stuck to the roof of her mouth. Why? *Why?*

It was more than the thrill of knowing a gorgeous guy seemed to be interested. It was knowing she was single and *he was, too*. Like something could happen. And nothing so easy as a date. Something permanent, like a family. Which was a deeply nutty thought to have about a man she'd just met. "Nuh-uh. I'm not. We established that during the lunch of betrayal."

"Oh," he replied quietly. "That." And then he slipped out, leaving her irritated, glad, and sad, which added up to deeply, *deeply* confused.

"Goddammit," she muttered, and punched her pillow.

"More! Please, please more?"

"Dev, I've got a pound and a half going already."

"Did you read *Oliver Twist*? Please, Mama Mac, some more. Not gruel. Bacon."

"There's loads of it. Heaven's *sake*."

"You can never have too much bacon, Mama."

"Not your call, boy."

"Beg to disag—ow! I can't believe the first thing you did in Lila's kitchen was find her wooden spoons."

"Not the first thing. Go wash up and—" Macropi turned away from the stove to smile at Lila, who was yawning in the doorway. "Oh, good morning, m'dear. Would you give Oz a shake? Eggs are almost up."

"He can sleep through bacon wars?"

"He can sleep through anything." Devoss grinned. "Rallies. Tornados. His own death… It's a pretty long list."

"Good to know," she muttered as she trudged into the living room and beheld a site more terrifying than the woman in Room 217[5]. Oz was…sprawled, there wasn't a better word for it. He

---

5. REDRUM.

filled up her couch by being…everywhere. He was a drooling, snoring tangle of long limbs and blankets. "Jesus. I heard the noise but assumed someone was mowing the garbage cans."

Caro, meanwhile, had come up behind her, given her a nudge, and held up her pad: *A thing of beauty is a joy forever.*

"Ha!" When he didn't stir, she added, "That didn't even make him twitch."

Waking Oz is like an exorcism: You need holy water and a couple of priests, and in the end, you're driven to throw yourself out the window.

Lila laughed. "Damn, you write fast." She reached down, found one of Oz's big toes, tweaked it. "Hey. Wake up. There's bacon and probably, I dunno, work? You've probably got work today? Since it's a weekday?"

Nothing.

Toldja.

"You're like my very own oracle," Lila informed her. "A ridiculously pretty oracle with cheekbones someone could cut themselves on."

Caro ducked her head, flustered, which made her look still younger. Lila had pegged her at around seventeen but decided to recalculate. She thought about the small black wolf she'd faced down the night before, about the fact that Caro was apparently a selective mute, and wondered what horrors the girl had survived.

None of which were her business.

She leaned in and said, "Hey! Deeply unconscious man on my couch! There's bacon, and also, get up!"

"Whuh? Bacon? I'll have some. Can I have some?" He blinked up at her, smiling sleepily. "Hey. I'm still dreamin' 'bout you. Are we gonna—" He ran his fingers through his rumpled hair. "Finish? Is this round two? Which I'm." He stared past her at Caro. "Fine with." Looked back at her. Around the room. Caro. Then he sat up and yanked the blanket more securely over himself, doubtless shielding Caro's tender eyeballs from his morning wood. "This is real."

"Yep."

"This is *so real*."

"Real as rain. By the way, it's raining." Caro was already walking away, giggling. "I know this because I looked outside and not at my phone, because Macropi has a huge deal—"

"No!" From the kitchen. "I refuse to look at a *telephone* for a weather report when I'm in front of a *window*."

"Okay, Macropi."

"Not to mention it's all of six steps to go outside! You don't need your phone to tell you what the weather's like ten feet from where you're standing! I am desperately tired of having this conversation!"

"—about using phones as the Weather Channel," Lila finished.

"Annnnnd that proves it. That was way too realistic. None of it was a dream," he groaned, sitting up and scrubbing his face with his hands. "The fire. Everyone staying here. Sally's dad. Your nightmare, of which we must never speak…"

"Yep."

"…your couch, which smells like oranges."

"I might've spilled some juice. Or lost an orange in the cushions."

"Fuck."

"Shush. Tender ears and all that."

"They've heard worse." Then, hopefully: "The bacon part was real, right?"

———————

Just as Lila was unfolding an extra chair, there was a Sally-shaped blur as the child emerged from somewhere and jumped straight into Macropi's arms, causing the older woman to stagger a bit before regaining her balance. "I know you! You're Dev's foster."

"So I am, m'dear." Macropi gave the little girl a squeeze and a smile. "And I'm glad to meet you, and so happy to see you're all right. But you've caused my older kids no end of trouble with all this running away nonsense."

Sally scrunched down and tucked her face into Macropi's neck. "I know. But I had to listen to my daddy."

"And we're going to talk about that, but first you're going to eat. Now back up and sit down over there. I don't want you getting hit with bacon grease."

"Hi, Lila!"

"Hi, Sally." Lila guzzled a glass of chocolate milk. "How'd you sleep?" Devoss had gone to fetch her out of the basement so she could sleep in an actual bed, but Sally had made herself a nest beneath the basement stairs and was sound asleep, which Lila would have found charming except Sally used her three best blankets, *fuck*.

"Dunno." Sally shrugged. "I closed my eyes and then it was morning. So, I guess…good? Even though it seems like I only slept for one second?"

"Gotta love REM sleep. Which I'll explain to you after breakfast. Eat."

She did. They all did, and Lila had real appreciation for Macropi's bacon: crispy but not burned, as opposed to limp on the fork. She had less appreciation for the scrambled eggs, which had been desecrated with onions. Ketchup smothered the taste nicely.

"Annette's on her way over," Mama Mac informed everyone over a table that looked like it had endured a tsunami.

"Boo," Oz replied, but there was no heat in it.

"And you." Mama pointed her—well, Lila's—spatula at him. "You should get dressed. We've got a long day and it's already seven."

"Gosh, half the day's gone."

"That's right!"

So he wouldn't have to eat bacon and scrambled eggs in his

underwear (not that she would have objected…exactly…), Lila had lent him her robe, a knee-length thing that was once blue but was now a ratty gray. Repeated washings had left it softer than velvet. She'd been half-kidding, but he immediately shrugged into it and then walked around sniffing the lapels and smiling, which was equal parts endearing and off-putting.

Get laid, get focused, get whatever you need to GET IT TOGETHER. And stop finding Oz endearing when he's shuffling around in your robe. A shorty robe and hairy knees should not be erotic. Neither should the memory of betrayal.

"Net's here," Devoss announced. "Who's gonna break the bad news?"

Before anyone could answer, there was a quick knock at the kitchen door, followed by "Good *God*, something smells heavenly."

"Smelled," Devoss said. "Past tense. Okay, not really. But you're not smelling actual bacon. You're smelling ghost bacon."

"All gone," Sally said mournfully.

"Oh."

Garsea's shoulders bowed, and she looked like someone stomped on her puppy. While it was eating the last of the bacon.

"Easy," Lila said, rising and going to the counter. She hit the Open button on the microwave and extracted a plate with half a dozen slices, which she handed over to Garsea. "Crisis averted."

"Well, *now* it is. Ummm. Thank you!"

"I *thought* that last platter looked a little light," Macropi mused.

"When'd you even do that?" Oz asked.

"The second I realized Garsea was coming."

"Thanks again," Garsea mumbled, chewing. "And look how easily fooled you all were!"

"I don't know if it was easily," Lila said. "You guys might have great sniffers, but apparently you can't tell the diff between ghost bacon and actual bacon."

And just like that, the fun was sucked out of the room.

"That. That!" From Devoss, who'd dropped his fork. "Are you saying you know we have preternatural smelling abilities—"

"Olfactory capabilities," Garsea corrected.

"—sure, whatever, that we smell good? Or are you just generalizing us as ordinary people who *don't* smell good? Wait, I said that wrong…"

"We went over this last night," Lila said mildly as she sat at the head of the kitchen table because it was her table and her kitchen, thanks very much. "Oz will tell you."

They all looked at Oz so quickly Lila fancied she could hear their eyeballs click.

"Uh…" Oz cleared his throat. "She reluctantly and vaguely acknowledged that maybe we were a little weird. On occasion. And she emphasized maybe."

"That? That was the Big Talk?" Devoss asked. "The Confrontation?"

"Wow," Lila marveled. "I can actually hear the capital letters."

"No way," the boy insisted. "That wasn't it. It doesn't settle anything! We still have questions!"

"Calm down," Lila advised him. "We've got more important things to talk about."

"We really don't," Devoss grumbled, but after a warning glare from Garsea and a raised eyebrow from Macropi, he ducked his head.

"Okay, so," Oz said with forced breeziness. "Lots to talk about. But after, I gotta run home for clean clothes and toothbrush because my *God*, Lila, when the bristles are that raggedy you're supposed to buy a new one!"

"Don't you toothbrush-shame me."

"But on my way back, any of you guys want me to pick up some of your stuff?"

"Macropi already went over."

The older woman turned to look at her. "And how d'you know that, m'dear?"

"Are you kidding? Look at you. You're wearing clothes that fit you perfectly but aren't new, so are Daniels and Devoss. You went back, probably while I was in the shower. You also raided your kitchen, which I deduced when I remembered I didn't have three dozen eggs and four pounds of bacon when I went to sleep last night."

"Lucky it was a chilly night," Macropi said. "Everything in my fridge and freezer was still okay."

"Glad you were able to stock up. So I'm betting I shouldn't open *my* freezer, right? Unless I want to risk getting crushed beneath the weight of all the meat you stuffed into it?"

"I'd never tell you what to do in your own house, m'dear, but… that's right."

Sally had finished eating first and had wandered into the living room a couple of minutes earlier. Lila had shown her how to work the On Demand and she was watching classic *Simpsons*, which was why they were all listening to the citizens of Springfield singing about the coming monorail.

Oz took advantage of the little girl's absence to lower his voice. "Did the firem—the firefighters have any updates this morning?"

"I hear those things are awfully loud."

"No, just that it started upstairs, and they're researching the accelerants," Macropi replied.

"It glides as softly as a cloud!"

"Oh, excellent." At their stares, Garsea elaborated. "Well, there were all those candles and matches lying around because Dev had to scrub out the cupboards…"

"I didn't do it!" he yelped. "I'd never, *jamais, nunca*!"

"Not on purpose. C'mere." Devoss got up like he was on springs and nearly lunged at Macropi, who hugged him while leveling a death glare at Garsea, who just stared with her mouth open until Lila kicked her under the table.

"Ouch!" Garsea recovered and added, "Dev, I'm sorry. I said that all wrong."

"I just *got* here," the boy practically shouted. "There, I mean. I'd never burn up a house I wanted to be in!"

"Of course you'd never do anything to hurt us or Mama's home." Garsea spread her hands. "I thought that with the house being so old and matches and candles and paper being all over the kitchen, that a spontaneous combustion of sorts may have been the culprit. Not that you were the spontaneous culprit—never you. I expressed myself poorly, and I'm very sorry."

An elegant and sincere apology. Didn't know she had it in her. "Hey." Lila cleared her throat. "Devoss. Nobody who's spent more than five minutes with you would think that. You're so smart and sneaky, you could've killed everyone in that house ten times over by now. You wouldn't *need* to set a fire."

There was a muffled sniff and the kid's head came up. "Really?"

"Oh, definitely. Ten times over...maybe fifteen times over. Macropi, Garsea, Oz... They'd all be *long* dead if you were bent that way. No question."

"Okay."

"Wait. *That* made you feel better?"

Devoss ignored Oz's surprised squawk and pulled back from Macropi with the self-conscious air of a child embarrassed to be seen acting like a child. "Um. Sorry. I guess I didn't sleep very well. And there's all the stuff with Sally, so."

"Speaking of Sally," Lila said briskly, "is anyone wondering if the fire was an attempt to either harm her or shunt the rest of you away from her?"

Devoss, clearly relieved that Lila had deliberately moved the group's focus away from his outburst, nodded. Garsea exchanged glances with Oz and Macropi, then replied, "The thought had crossed our minds."

"Leaving us with the possibility that *my* house is now at risk. So what's the plan? Does your IPA have some kind of protocol here that you have to follow?"

"Uh. Lila. It's beyond decent of you to take us in—"

"I took Daniels, Macropi, Smalls, and Devoss in, but don't let that get in the way of your revisionist history."

"What's 'shunt'?" From Devoss, who then read the quick note Caro scribbled and nodded. "Oh. Thanks, Caro, I never heard that word before."

"—but this really isn't your problem."

She just looked at him. Orphaned bear cubs who might not be orphaned. A dead father calling his kid. Spontaneous house fire, possibly to harm the aforementioned orphan who might not be an orphan. Devoss sound asleep in the guest room with a stranglehold on his stuffed bear. Macropi staring out the living room window and still there at 2:00 a.m. and 2:30 a.m. and 3:00 a.m. Oz on her couch for the foreseeable future, too tired and worried to take five minutes to unfold the thing into a vague approximation of a bed before lapsing into a snore coma.

"Were you gonna say something?" Devoss asked. "You're just sort of staring intently at Oz."

"I'm in," she replied. "I'm helping you well-meaning but possibly incompetent dopes with this until Sally's safe and we know what started the fire so the neighborhood is safe and you can all go back to your lives and my house is no longer at risk so I can go back to my herb garden and that's how it's going to be, so just be resigned."

"But—"

"That shit *isn't funny*, Oz. Kids could've died."

Garsea spoke up. "No one here thinks arson is funny."

"Excellent, glad we're all on the same page." *For a change.* "So what now? Wait for Sally's dead dad to call again?"

Monorail! Monorail!

"Turn it down, please," Macropi called.

"*Monoraillllllll!*"

"Not exactly." Garsea excused herself, then returned to the

kitchen with Smalls in tow. "We need to talk about that phone call from your father again, Sally."

"Which?"

"Wait, what?" From Oz. "How many have you gotten?"

"And why," Lila asked sweetly, "are you guys only now asking that?"

"Hey!" he replied sharply. "Do we come over to your house and tell you how to—never mind, I just heard myself."

"I *told* you." Sally sounded as put-upon as any child hauled away from the television. "Daddy called and we talked about Lila—"

Lila blinked. "Uh, what?"

"—and Daddy said he was coming, but it would take time, so watch out for Maggie."

Caro scribbled: *Well, at least that doesn't sound incredibly ominous.*

"You don't even need a sarcasm font," Lila observed.

Oz was frowning. "When you say you and your dad talked about Lila, what does that mean?"

"Well. Daddy wanted me safe. But not with CPA."

"Unless you're talking about accountants, which we shouldn't rule out," Oz continued, "you mean IPA, right, hon?"

She nodded. "He said I had to stay in Switzerland until he could come. But not *really* Switzerland, just—a place that—that doesn't pick sides? Where I could be safe? But IPA couldn't be that."

"So, instead a stranger?" Macropi asked. Then to Lila, "No offense, dear."

"None taken."

"Daddy said it was okay once I told him about the Stable who found me. You tried to help me, even 'cuz you thought I was a wild animal. And when I wasn't, when you knew I was a Shifter, you kept my secret. And you didn't kick me out when I came back."

"So you're all in my house because I'm not enough of a heartless wench?" Lila snorted. "Noted."

"*Anyways.* Daddy said to go to you. And I figured he was right. 'Cuz it's not just that you don't have a side. It's that you don't care!" The girl beamed like she'd been given a grand gift. "At all!"

"So you're all in my house because I'm not enough of an *indifferent* heartless wench. Got it."

"Lila, you're the first one of your kind I've spent any real time with," Sally added.

"Yeah, you told me that."

"I can't wait to tell my folks! They'll be *so* surprised."

"Sally, did he give you any kind of time line? Did he tell you how long you'd have to stay? Or where he was? Or what happened?" Macropi leaned forward, almost vibrating in protective urgency. "And what about your mother? Was she—"

"Whoa, back up." Oz held up his hands like he was being mugged at gunpoint. Which was tempting to contemplate and she might try it later. "Sorry, Mama, but I think we're getting ahead of ourselves."

"Agreed." From Garsea. "How did you even know it was your dad?"

"Because." At the silence, she added impatiently, "He's my *dad*. I know his voice."

"Even if it was someone pretending?"

"But why would someone pre—oh." Small shoulders slumped. "You still think he's dead-for-real, not just playing."

Garsea and Oz exchanged glances, and then Oz gently said, "We're just trying to put the puzzle together."

Sure. The puzzle analogy. Except they were trying to put it together in the dark with half the pieces missing and an arsonist waiting in the wings to torch it the moment they made even the smallest amount of progress.

Sally, meanwhile, had sidled over to Lila's chair. Like any child trying to get out of an unpleasant conversation, she was anxious to change the subject. "Dev told me you're a teddy bear doctor. Cubs send you their broken bears, and you get to fix them?"

Get to, not *have to*. As it happened, Lila felt the same way. "Yeah, I do."

"You prob'ly like it."

"I do. I set my own hours and the pay's adequate and I hardly ever have to deal with people because it's all mostly done through the mail."

"You don't like people?"

"We're getting far afield."

"Dunno what that means."

"It means, Sally, that other than his voice, did your dad say anything while you were talking, something that proved he was who he said he was?"

"He called me Possum. That's our joke because when I was little I used to play dead to get out of chores. I don't, um, actually turn into a possum."

When you were little? Because you're now the ripe old age of ten?

"Oh. Well, that makes sense." Lila settled back, figuring Garsea and Oz would want to pick up the questioning, but they just looked at her. It took an embarrassing amount of time for her to realize they wanted her to keep going. Which was nuts, except Sally did seem more inclined to answer questions when Lila posed them.

"Okay, he used a family nickname, that answers that. Did your dad say what had happened?"

"He said their plane crashed and that he was hurt but was coming."

"And your mom?"

Nothing. Nothing for a full twenty seconds… Lila kept half an eye on the kitchen clock.

"I think…they *must* be together. I think that's the other reason he's so late." Sally's anxious glance was skittering all over: Lila, Macropi, the tabletop, Oz. She cast another longing look toward the room with the TV, then added, "Because Daddy wouldn't have left Mama. He couldn't."

"Because she's been sick," Lila guessed. "And still is, maybe?"

Oz straightened so suddenly, he nearly fell out of his chair. "What was that?"

Lila thought back to the night Sally had come back on her own. *Mommy's been sick, too… It's really important I get back to them. Daddy's taking care of her and all… She's tired all the time.*

Sally's chin wobbled. Lila pretended not to notice. If hugs were required, Garsea and Macropi had the requisite comforting arms and bosoms. "Mommy's got some kind of cancer thing. We only found out a few weeks ago. He wouldn't have left her."

"And you think that's what's delaying him."

"Sure."

"*How* did you talk to him, exactly?" Lila asked. "Do you have a cell phone?"

"No." This with a scowl. "Dad says I'm too little to have one, which is wrong and dumb."

"Okay…"

"Do you have to go to school to be a teddy bear surgeon?"

"Yes, for at least fifteen years. Sally, did you borrow someone's cell phone?"

"Fifteen y—oh. No. Those're private. And people don't want to borrow them to kids anyway."

"Lend them," Garsea interjected, because she couldn't help herself.

"Right," Lila continued. "So if you don't have a cell, and you didn't borrow one, how were you able to talk to your dad?"

Sally shrugged and was suddenly interested in her feet.

"Did you have help?" Dumb question. The kid was ten and (temporarily) alone in the world. Of course she had help. "Are you trying to keep someone from getting into trouble?"

"…no."

"You know I don't give a shit either way, right?" Lila leaned back and shrugged. "For me, it's more like a crossword puzzle.

Something to do, but it's not the end of the world if I don't finish it. You are the Fourteen Down of my crossword, Sally. And I'm not gonna give whoever helped you a hard time." *Damn right. Let the IPA flunkies handle it.*

"You don't have any fur in the game," Sally said, which was one of the strangest things to come out of the kid's mouth. "Okay, so. The thing is, they said not to lie but not to volunteer, either."

They? Lila started to laugh.

"I'm lost," Oz confessed.

Garsea looked unamused. "Sally, who helped you speak with your father and how did they do so?"

Cornered (finally!), Sally sighed and flicked a glance at Lila, who said, "Better go get it."

"Be right back."

"Get *what*?" From Oz, who seemed torn between annoyance and amusement as Sally rushed out of the room.

"She's got a secret stash in my basement where she keeps a couple of things."

"Which you know about because…"

Because I used to be ten and on the run. "Because why wouldn't she? Don't look at me like I'm a weirdo. Everybody builds blanket nests and keeps secret stashes in the basements of strangers they only met three days ago."

"I can't tell if you're joking," Macropi mused, then turned to look as Sally pounded up the stairs and reappeared with a folded sheet of paper, which she handed to Lila.

"Oh. Thanks. Gosh, I'm so nervous! And the winner is…" She unfolded the thing and took a look, then handed it to Oz.

"Huh. These are instructions on how to get an outside line to make long distance calls on the IPA WATS line. *Really* clear instructions. The kind a child could follow. And they're in Caro's handwriting." He looked up. "And I'm betting that Dev, who treats the IPA offices like his own personal vacation home, tracked you down there once I dropped you off and gave 'em to you. So you were able to return your dad's call and get your marching orders without anyone noticing because we *really* need to hire more staff."

"And install a more complex phone system," Lila added, trying not to smirk.

Garsea was making an odd noise, and it took Lila a few seconds to realize the woman was grinding her teeth. "Oh, you troublesome cubs…" This was growled at two empty chairs, as Dev and Caro had slipped away a few minutes earlier.

"Annnnnd of course they're gone," Lila observed. "On the upside, mystery solved. Well. One mystery. Jesus, Garsea, you're gonna crack a molar."

Chapter 21

SHE'D NOTICED CARO AND DEV LEAVING, OF COURSE, BUT hadn't made a point of calling it out. It was, after all, IPA business, and the werewolf and werefox were minors with no official role. In fact, "no official role" should be their official motto. And did she really just think *werewolf and werefox* like it was an ordinary day? Like this was her life now?

Well. It apparently *was* an ordinary day. At least in this neighborhood. As to whether it would be her life, who knew?

"Later for them," Garsea vowed. "Mighty will be my wrath!"

"Don't worry," Lila soothed. "You don't sound like a cartoon villain at all."

"Okay, so the wretches are colluding, fine, we should have realized. And it would seem there's now a good chance Sam and Sue Smalls are alive."

"Oh my God." Lila rubbed her head. "Sam and Sue Smalls named their baby Sally? I bet they thought it'd be cute. I bet they thought it would be downright adorable. And I bet they were sorry about a month in."

"We'll deal with the cubs later. Right now, we need to reach Sam Smalls—or the person impersonating him. And we must 'watch out for Maggie' as well." Garsea was pacing back and forth from the living room (where Sally had retreated after giving up the older kids) to the kitchen. "And the first step toward any of it would be—oh." Garsea stopped, went to the front door, let in a firefighter before he could knock. "Hello, we're all in the kitchen. Mostly."

"Yep," Lila said. "Here we all are. In my kitchen. Mostly."

The firefighter, who had been trudging behind Garsea,

straightened up when he saw Lila. He was a bullish man of about six feet who looked even bulkier in his heavy coat and boots. He had bushy, short dark hair and chocolate-brown eyes, with shoulders he could probably use to hold up the Hollywood Sign, and his head was a block. He smelled like smoke and sweat and smoke, and there was a long silence while he looked her up and down, nostrils flaring, forehead furrowing, finally coming out with "…huh." Then he turned to Macropi. "Definitely on purpose."

"Well, hell, Benny," she sighed. "That's nothing I wanted to hear."

"Accelerant was avgas."

"You know that already?" Lila asked. "Your lab must be humming twenty-four-seven. That was *so* fast."

She got another long stare, followed by a laconic "Lab'll hopefully narrow it down."

The lab, your preternatural senses, toe-may-toe, toe-mah-toe. Is it me or does this guy look like a great big chocolate lab?

Oz spoke up. "I'm just gonna ask. What the hell is avgas?"

Benny blinked mournful smoke-reddened eyes. "Aviation fuel."

"That's unusual, right?" Oz replied. "It's not like people keep a can or two of aviation fuel in their garages."

"Not this time of year," Lila deadpanned.

"I'll talk to the chief, get more info. Insurance guys're gonna be poking around later this morning. Cops'll be looking, too."

Oh, goody. I can't wait for them to let themselves in whenever the mood hits.

"Thank you, Benny. You should go on home and rest, you were up half the night."

"Paperwork," he replied, which was apparently how he bade farewell, because he left.

"Aviation fuel," Garsea said, puzzled.

"Good thing this case isn't getting weirder by the hour," Oz sighed.

Before they could speculate further, there was a knock at the back-kitchen door. Cop? Insurance adjuster? Avgas salesman?

"Wait!" she hissed as Garsea presumptuously went to answer. The other woman froze in mid-step.

"What is it?"

"Just…wait." Another knock and another long silence. And after yet another long moment, there came yet another knock, this time on the front door.

Lila all but ran into the living room, dropped to her knees, smirked to hear Oz's sharp intake of breath behind her, crawled over to the window facing the driveway, peeked. "See?" Garsea, Oz, and Macropi had all knelt behind her, which was more than a little amusing. "See what he's doing?"

"He's…leaving. Getting ready to leave, anyway. Nice rental car, though," Oz added.

"If by 'nice,' you mean idiotic," Lila replied, staring at the blue Ford Mustang convertible.

"Naw, by nice I meant nice."

"Pfftt. He'll be lucky if he doesn't get frostbite. And look! He's getting ready to leave! To go work on his frostbite!"

"Lila, why are you so—"

"You don't understand. He knocked on *one* door. Then he knocked on the *other* door. And now he's leaving. And why? Because I didn't answer the door! Either door! Don't you see how revolutionary this is?"

"Oh, for the love…"

"This is the first time this has happened in all the days I've lived here!" Lila hissed triumphantly. "You could learn a lot from this guy, gang. This, *this* is how you call on people you don't know."

"A revelation," Garsea said sourly. "But he *is* still leaving. Shouldn't we find out what he wants? Now that we have to watch for an arsonist, we shouldn't let anyone just slip in and out as they like."

"Excellent point," Lila replied, standing. To Oz: "Well, don't just stand there. Go get him, tiger." And slapped him on the ass for emphasis.

"Right!" Oz did exactly that, rushing out the door and straight to the convertible.

Macropi and Garsea rose to their feet, and Garsea's grin was positively gleeful. "I like how you chased him out of here before he remembered he's wearing your shorty robe."

Chapter 22

"You're telling me that my friends are dead but perhaps not and while you try to determine which, someone tried to burn my goddaughter alive?"

As a summation, Lila thought, *it is devastating in its accuracy.*

"Unacceptable!" This in a roar. An actual roar; Magnus Berne was one of those people who filled every room they were in, like Churchill and Lady Gaga and the Phillie Phanatic. He towered over all of them, even Oz, though she thought Oz might be able to give him a run for his money. Oz's wolf, she'd decided last night, was nothing to be fucked with.

But Magnus made even the bulky firefighters look like wraiths: He looked to be in his mid-thirties, was well over six feet, with thick brown hair that had an odd violet tint. Shoulders like cement blocks, fists like bowling balls made out of cement blocks. He sported a deep tan, dark slacks, a navy-blue sweater with epaulets, and sturdy shoes. He'd flung his tan trench coat over his shoulders when they followed him to the site of the fire, and every time he moved quickly, the coat flared. Lila couldn't decide if the man was naturally theatrical or playing a part or was some kind of superhero (or villain).

"Are you kidding me with this ridiculous bullshit?" he roared.

Naturally theatrical. Most likely. Can't rule out super villain.

Oz had brought Berne into Lila's house, where the man curtly introduced himself, listened to Oz and Garsea's explanation, then turned without a word and marched over to Macropi's still-smoking house. All the rest of them could do was look at each other, shrug, and follow. And in Oz's case, frantically change back into yesterday's clothes, *then* follow.

"What?" he snapped as someone whacked the bathroom door. It wasn't a knock; it sounded more like someone irritably slapped at it. *Oh, God, I hope I didn't just snap at Lila.*

Someone slid a piece of paper underneath the door. Oz had no trouble reading it, despite the fact that he was standing; the letters were as long as his fingers.

WTF, Oz?????

Oh.

That.

Good timing, at least; he'd finished buttoning his shirt. He opened the door and surprised Caro in mid-scribble. "Yeah, about last night. Sorry. Put it down to stress. Or low blood sugar. Or how I wasn't actually growling at you, it was Dev. Or how it was a garbage truck, not you. A midnight garbage truck."

You shifted and looked like you were ready to throw down!!!

So did you, he wanted to say, but it would have been a lie. Last night, Caro had been cautious with good reason—her foster mother's house was on fire and there was a strange Stable in the yard in close proximity to her foster brother. But aside from the time she ripped a child-trafficker's arm from the socket, she'd never attacked anyone, Shifter or otherwise.

"I overreacted," he admitted. "I'm sorry."

I get that. WHY, tho?

"I can't explain it." He could feel the hairs on his nape trying to come to attention simply because they were talking about last night. "I just—I saw you sizing up Lila and I didn't like it."

WHY, tho?

Good question. And she deserved an answer. Too bad he had no idea what it was.

"Sorry again, Caro."

She just looked at him, then shrugged and walked away while he finished tying his tie.

"Mr. Berne, I can assure you, we'll have everything under control."

Berne's rebuttal: "Ridiculous bullshit!"

"Well, I did use the future tense," Garsea admitted. "I never intimated everything was under control right this second."

And didn't Berne mean bear? Lila made a mental note to look it up later, because if his surname did mean bear, she could only assume these guys weren't even trying. It wasn't the first time she wondered if her life's triumphs weren't due to the fact that she was exceptionally smart but because the people around her were exceptionally stupid. (This theory did not go over well with her eleventh-grade guidance counselor.)

"And why is there a noncommissioned ambulance in the driveway?"

"Because I don't like parking on the street."

She was on board with tagging along wherever this leg of the journey led, right up until the moment Berne walked into the burned house, which was when she stopped short so suddenly Oz ran into her, apologized, then walked around her. Then he stopped short (again) and looked back. "Oh. Uh. Lila? You coming in?"

"I'm good," she replied, and her voice wasn't thin and high at all, but Oz immediately walked back to her side anyway. Which she didn't need him to do. And didn't care that he did.

"That's okay," he said, which was unnecessary. "I don't need to go in, either."

"Go in if you want to go in. I just don't need to go in right this second. But you go. I mean, just because I don't want to go in doesn't mean you need to stay out here. You could go in." Was she saying 'go in' too much? "Go in if you want to go in." Definitely not.

"Naw." Then he looked at her, really looked. She felt like she'd stumbled under a microscope and simultaneously loved and hated the sensation. It was nice, being the object of Oz's intense focus. Just…not right this second. "What did you lose?"

None of your business. It's not important. Her brain ran through the litany: *It was a long time ago. I didn't even like that house. What are you even talking about?* "Everything."

"I'm so sorry." He reached and took her hand in his. "That must have been a nightmare."

"I didn't even like that house," she replied on auto-pilot. "Sorry. Force of habit."

"I can't think of a single thing you need to apologize for. So. Magnus Berne," he said, and she was so grateful he'd changed the subject she almost kissed him. She might kiss him anyway. No, no… "D'you think his friends call him Maggie?"

That had been her first thought when the man introduced himself: Sally's father (if that's who had been on the phone) had specifically warned her: *watch out for Maggie.* "And you've gotta admit, that's an interesting coincidence."

"Yep."

"And if you and I thought of it—"

"Yeah, Annette's in there politely giving him the third degree. Bet on it."

"If he's willing, you could bring him back to my house. If he's been traveling—do we know how he got here? Or where he came from?—he might want a break. It's still early, but he's bright-eyed and neatly dressed, so I'm thinking he pulled an all-nighter on the way here. So he might want a drink or what-have-you. He might say something he wouldn't, normally. Or he'll totally clear himself."

"And Sally should see him," Oz added. "She might know if he's the real deal. And if he's the Maggie she was warned about."

"I'm aware this is the question of the week, but where *is* Sally?"

"Still watching *Simpsons.* I caught Dev skulking outside on my way here, so I told him to get his sneaky butt in the house and keep

an eye on her until we got back, on pain of violent dismember-
ment if he disobeyed."

"All that, while you were simultaneously changing your
clothes," she teased. "Impressive."

"I fucking love your robe," he replied with off-putting intensity.

"Uh. Okay."

"Have dinner with me."

"Try to stay focused."

"I dunno who this is." Sally was blinking up at Maggie-the-giant.
"But it's nice to meet you?"

Berne threw back his head and laughed. After they went back to
Lila's place, Magnus Berne had wasted no time introducing himself to Sally. "We've met, darling, but I don't expect you'd remember... It was two years ago. You were just a wee thing."

And wasn't *that* convenient: the goddaughter hadn't seen her
godfather, but oh, sure, they'd definitely met, and he was definitely
a friend of the family, so there was definitely no need to worry further on that account. Or ask any more questions.

Sure.

Macropi hadn't come back to Lila's, preferring to remain and
sift through some of the wreckage. She promised/threatened to
bring more clothes and food to Lila's and insisted they make "poor
Mr. Berne" comfortable, and at her insistence, they left her to it.

"Magnus was just telling us that he flew here in his own plane,"
Oz said with an impressive lack of *ah-ha!* in his tone. "He lives in
Scotland and has his own Cessna."

"Fascinating. I didn't know you could make that flight in a
single-engine plane," Lila said.

"Y'can, lass, but takes some planning, I can tell you. And my
island is in Lake Minnetonka. And you... Miss Lila, is it?"

"You're half right."

"How d'you know my goddaughter?"

"I found her in an alley, took her home, gave her honey, and my life unraveled from there."

"Hey!"

Lila smiled and took Sally's hand. "'Unraveled' in a good way."

Berne's broad face was furrowing, which wasn't unlike watching a cliff frown. "When ye say 'found her,' she was. Ah. Her other self?"

"She was Sally," Lila replied, piling on the "why, whatever could you be getting at?" attitude. "She's always Sally."

She could actually see Magnus Berne working it out: Sally was a werebear + the others were also shapeshifters + Lila wasn't = what the hell is going on?

Oz cleared his throat. "We're. Uh. All working together on this one. Lila's been a big help."

"That's a lie," she replied. "But a sweet one."

"Nobody's really talking about it," Sally told Berne. "I dunno why. Dev says it's a cat-and-mouse thing but with wolves and bears."

Berne swooped down into a squat, which the kid probably appreciated though he was still a head taller. "Sally, darling, what were you doing in that alley all by yourself?"

"Bleeding. I'm better now. I didn't even need animal control!"

"Animal control?"

"Yeah. Don't be mad at her. It's not her fault she thought I was a *wild* bear." This in a tone of pure disdain, the way Lila talked about cold Pop-Tarts.

Berne straightened. "Can you run along, darling?"

"How come? It's my kitchen!" Lila protested, and got a frown for her pains.

"Not you, lass." To Sally: "*You*, lass. Run along and play, there's a darling."

Sally immediately darted for the kitchen door. "Don't forget the bag," Lila said, and the child swerved to scoop up said bag on her way out.

"What new ridiculous bullshit have we here?" This to everyone except Lila. "Are ye wasting time by dancing? Lives are at stake."

"We're not wasting time, we're being careful. This sequence of events has never happened to anyone in this room," Annette admitted. "Possibly anyone anywhere. It's not like there's an official protocol to follow. We've trod lightly."

"Yep," Lila confirmed. "Lots of trodding, but it was all light. Why? Do you want to address the elephant in the room? Which isn't an elephant?"

Berne scowled and sighed at the same time, which was a sight to see. Then he gave Lila his full (ulp) attention. "You're an apex predator—"

"Thanks!"

"—your species, I mean. But you're not at the top. We are. Shifters. Because we can change our shape. You, poor lass, are Stable. You're locked into a bipedal form all your life."

"Oh."

"My condolences."

"Thanks." The hell of it was, Berne sounded genuinely sorrowful at Lila's bad luck of not being born to werebears. "But I think 'apex' is in the eye of the beholder. Drop a bear in the ocean, a great white or a tiger shark moves up the scale, don't you think?"

Berne ignored her devastating logic and continued. "Our world runs parallel to yours—"

"And now I'm not sure you know what parallel means."

"—but as your kind vastly outnumbers mine, it's just been easier for us to keep off the radar."

"That's what you think this is?" Lila made a gesture encompassing the room, the block, the world. "Because that's hilarious."

More frowning. More lecturing. "The few people who find

out about Shifters are either natural allies, eventual allies, or aren't credible. They get dismissed as loony conspiracy theorists or someone struggling with mental illness. But why are ye here? That's what I canna figure. Why are you involved in any of it?"

"Because I'm not a gutless sociopath?"

"Well, you're definitely not gutless," Garsea muttered, earning a smirk from Lila.

"I never thought otherwise, lass—at least, not on short acquaintance. But most Stables would have immediately left town."

"That *is* what usually happens," Oz admitted while Annette nodded.

"Or have a nervous breakdown—"

"That also happens."

"—try to tell the world what's happening, get ignored or laughed at, and then leave town."

So that's why it was the Curs(ed) House. In a neighborhood teeming with Shifters, the rare Stable would come along and see something and get freaked out and vacate. Lila was willing to bet nobody overtly harassed the hapless Stable. But the neighborhood would only come together to help *Shifter* renters. And when something would inevitably go wrong, the Shifters had a built-in support system. The Stable was on their own.

She was willing to give Macropi and her landlord the benefit of the doubt: that they weren't actively driving away Stables by sabotaging appliances and trapping then loosing squirrels in the attic.

For now.

"T'me, lass, it sounds like your time here has been—"

"Ridiculous bullshit? I really like that phrase, by the way. It applies so *many* ways."

"—stressful. So why not step away?"

"Because someone wants your goddaughter badly enough to set a fire that could have killed people. So they *can't have her*." Lila crossed her arms over her chest. "I'm also abiding by her dad's wishes—he wanted Sally here, not at IPA or with an IPA…" How to label Macropi's purpose in the system? "…ally? So she's here for the duration, God help me. But yeah—mostly because half the neighborhood could have roasted, so fuck them, and they can't have her."

"Protective spite?" Oz sounded delighted.

Berne seemed satisfied as well. "So what happens next? Lila? Ms. Garsea?"

Oz coughed. "It's technically my case."

"O'course," Berne assured them. "But I'm asking all of you, since you apparently do things by committee."

"We've got some more questions," Oz replied. "And we wanted to talk to you about the plane crash."

"Ach." Berne's shoulders slumped. "I'll answer anything you want, but I hate the thought—it was my plane, y'see. Sue got her pilot's license years ago, so I let her borrow it. The little Cessna I flew here isna mine." At their stares, he elaborated. "I'm a ferry pilot."

He probably thought that cleared things up.

"How unfortunate," Annette said.

Oh, this just gets better and better. "Macropi's not the only one dealing with insurance guys this week, huh, Berne?"

Oz was already on his feet. "I know you've had a long morning so far, but could we get you to come to IPA? We've got some paperwork for you to look over, as Sally's closest known guardian, and we could answer your questions, too. The more we find out, the better chance we have of helping Sally."

"O'course."

"I'll get you the address… Meet you there in two hours?"

"Aye, that'll give me a chance to clean up a bit. Two hours and then—" Berne cut himself off and grimaced. "Paperwork."

Lila had a pretty good idea what "paperwork" meant, and it wasn't forms. Berne was going to have to look at something much less pleasant (though forms were horrible, too). She almost felt bad for him.

Well, no. She didn't. Not really.

———————

Just when she thought she'd gotten rid of a few of them for the morning, there was a rap at her bedroom door. She let out a groan that was a bit exaggerated; she wanted a quick break from unpacking. A brief (brief!) distraction was welcome, especially since her Berne = Bear research had only taken sixty seconds. Armed with Berne's business card, she found that Berne didn't mean bear, but *Bern* did. In German, at least. She assumed the man's family had dropped the 'e', though they needn't have bothered. Even with the 'e', it was pretty on the nose.

The knob turned, and Oz poked his head inside. "I'm interpreting that groan as 'come in.' Okay?"

"Interpret it any way you like. Don't you have somewhere to be?"

"In two hours, yeah."

"IPA must be pretty flexible. I mean, it's a weekday, and you're starting a new job…"

"You get time off when someone tries to burn out your foster mother."

"Excellent. You guys must have a great union. Are you coming all the way in or are you going to keep hovering in my doorway?"

He came in and held out a small bundle of…green dusty garbage? "Did you—is this yours? D'you want it back?"

She looked at it and realized it was a bundle of artificial mistletoe, the cheap kind they sold in drugstores in September, October, November, and the first half of December, at which point they began selling valentines. The previous tenants must have put it up for the holidays, then forgotten to take it down before they were transferred. Or were run out of the neighborhood by a concerted possum attack. Or voles. Or a plumbing explosion. Or a short in the kitchen wiring. Or a double homicide.

She shook her head. "I don't want it back. Where'd you even find it?"

He was looking at her like *she* was the weirdo walking around with fake mistletoe after crashing (uninvited) on the Curs(ed) couch. "It was under my pillow. I found it while I was folding up the blankets."

"How tidy of you." *WTF?* "Well, thanks, I guess."

"So you didn't plant the mistletoe?"

"Is that a pun?"

"Not on purpose," he admitted.

"The only way to pun is accidentally," she agreed. "But now that we've got that out of the—uh, you're standing really close."

He was peering down at her like a sexy scientist scrutinizing a slide of something weird and great. (Not her best metaphor. It was hard to think when he was standing so close and looking at her so intently and smelling so terrific. What was that cologne? *Eau de Jump Me*?) "So you didn't leave it for me?"

She blinked up at him. "You think I wander the house stuffing fake plants under your pillow in the desperate hope that you'll find them and come see me?"

"…no?"

She snorted at the obvious lie, and the inelegant sound made him smile. In another couple of seconds, she was leaning on him and they were both giggling like sleep-deprived morons. It wasn't funny, and yet it was hilarious. Punch-drunk, she figured, only without the punch. She reached up and grabbed him by the ears, pulled him down, and gave him a sound kiss, smack on the mouth. It was the least romantic kiss she'd ever given—and maybe that he'd ever gotten—but what the hell. He'd earned it, even if he had lied about expecting it.

She gave him a gentle shove. "Go away, I've got more unpacking to half-heartedly get back to. And give me that." She snatched the plastic mistletoe from his grasp.

He went to the door, then turned back, looking not a little hopeful. "Should I look under my pillow again tonight?"

"You can if you want, but it'll be a waste of time. I'm burning this unholy talisman, no doubt the product of some sorcerer's lair…" She squinted at the label. "…made in China."

Well, no. She couldn't burn it—she and fire didn't always get along. Maybe she'd bury it in the backyard like a dog. If she left it lying around, one of the kids might bury it for her.

"Bye, Lila."

"Take your time coming back," she called. "Seriously. No rush. No rush at all."

"But I will come back," he replied, and she grinned in spite of herself.

Chapter 23

"Christ, lad!"

"I'm sorry," Oz replied. "I did warn you."

They were in IPA's terrible break room because Berne hadn't eaten yet (and after the pics, might not for a while), and Annette generally kept two or three courses in the fridge.

The break room was less terrible than it had been six months ago. It was a windowless room about half the size of an elementary school classroom, and it took up the middle of the floor like Mount Doom with a microwave.

Which was fine, or at least bearable. But then Nadia Faulkner's lunch escaped, mated within the walls, and produced more than Nadia—even five Nadias—could gulp down. The carpet had never been cleaned. Nor the area beneath the sink. Nor the area above the sink. The room's history, plus Nadia's lunch teeming everywhere, brought out the apathy in everyone.

All that could be managed, if not for the fact that IPA was staffed with savages.

("Wait, we have a garbage disposal? Here I've been flushing my shrimp shells in the ladies' room like an idiot!")

And teaching the savages basic break room courtesy had taken forever.

("Wait, shrimp shells clogged the disposal? What, I should throw the shells out the window? That's littering!")

Then, and only then, had Oz dipped into his private funds and had the place thoroughly cleaned, the fridge and microwave replaced, the old carpet torn out, and converted it from "vile cesspool" to "passable break room if everyone just does their fair share."

And who better to decide what everyone's fair share was and call out those who were slacking? Nadia Faulkner, whose escaped lunch had set the whole disgusting business in motion.

Annette, while grateful, had also warned him, because she lived to harsh his buzz. "This was really generous. But your money isn't going to solve all your problems here."

"But it'll solve some of 'em. Frozen Swiss Roll? Only the deeply uncouth eat them at room temperature."

"Why, yes. I'll have four. Thank you."

All this to say they were in the break room, showing Magnus Berne pictures of the plane crash while Nadia was scorching the ears of the poor idiot who threw his half-empty Coke can into the recycling bin.

This was almost welcome, because Oz had been replaying the mistletoe scene in his head on a near constant loop for the last two hours. Her eyes. Her snort. Her gentle touch as she seized his ears and dragged his mouth down to hers.

"And I am shocked, *shocked*, that I need remind you of such basic recycling etiquette," Nadia shrilled. "You need to think of others, you wretch!"

Bob Links cowered away from her. "You're on us to recycle. I friggin' recycled!"

"Making a sticky Coke soup that congeals on the bottom of the bin is *not* recycling," Nadia snapped. "Well. Technically it is. But it's disgusting and makes everyone's job harder and it is *quite* unacceptable and you will cease this behavior immediately."

"You remember how I'm your boss, right?"

"Irrelevant!"

The hell of it was, Nadia was right. Bob Links was one of the IPA directors, and thus was *all* their bosses (except David, who was an independent contractor). But it didn't matter because Links was also a jaded bureaucrat who preferred to keep his head down. (That wasn't figurative; he'd been caught dozing at his desk more than once.) And he let his staff get away with everything up to murder (and maybe even that—no one had tested that theory so far) as long as their numbers made his quarterly reports look good.

"And stop stealing sugar to sweeten the vile brew you think is coffee," Nadia added, towering over Links, a good trick since he was taller.

"Using break room sugar packets isn't stealing!"

"Those packets belong to me, Robert Links! Stop absconding with them. I have counted them and shall know in an instant if you've disobeyed me."

"Ridiculous bullshit," Magnus muttered as Bob made himself scarce. Then, louder, "Should we be doing this somewhere else?"

"Probably," Annette muttered.

"Not at all." Nadia turned to give Magnus an appreciative once-over, and Bob used the chance to lunge for escape. "I don't believe we've met."

"No, you started t'introduce yourself, then saw the state of the recycling bin. Magnus Berne."

"Nadia Faulkner. No relation to the writer, I'm much more clever." Nadia showed her teeth and extended a tiny hand. She was dressed neck to knee in sapphire blue, which exactly matched her eyes and made her fair skin seem even paler. Nadia probably went about ninety-five soaking wet, and men underestimated her to their peril. She was Annette's partner, but as far as Oz could tell, Annette did most of the heavy lifting, leaving all the paperwork and most of the snark to Nadia. "No need to compliment me on my charming accent, either, Mr. Berne."

"Thank you, lass, I'll cross that off my to-do list."

"As for yours...let me guess—Edinburgh?"

"As good as. Currie."

"I regret meeting under these circumstances. You're Sally's uncle, yes?"

"Godfather."

"Ah. Terribly sorry to hear about your friends."

"Might not be anything to be terribly sorry about." Magnus quirked an eyebrow. "Reports vary."

Before Oz could elaborate, David Auberon, Annette's fiancé, walked in, looking over his shoulder. "Damn. Bob just scuttled past me like someone singed his ear hair." He spotted Nadia. "Which, I just realized, makes sense. Is he still throwing half-full cans of Coke into recycling?"

"Perhaps not." Nadia folded her fingers into small fists, then cracked her knuckles. "Time will tell."

David fixed himself a cup of coffee, dumped a glug of maple syrup into it, then walked behind Annette's chair and dropped a hand to her shoulder while he sucked down his homemade caffeine sugar bomb. She reached back and squeezed it (his hand, not the bomb) without looking, still skimming files, and Oz smiled and looked away. Once David and Annette stopped with the "we're not into each other at all oh wait maybe we are" bullshit, they went from colleagues to live-in mates pretty quickly. Like, speed of sound quickly. Now it was hard to picture either of them as single, for all it was only six months ago.

Where will Lila and I be in six months?

Nowhere, dumbass. The thing you're worried is happening? Isn't happening. Old wives' tale. Not to mention—stop me if you've already heard this—you betrayed her! It's weird that I have to keep reminding you.

He shook off the distracting thoughts to refocus on the case. "This is David Auberon. He's an investigator who works with IPA, usually tracking down kids."

"Nice t'meet you, lad," Magnus said automatically, with the polite air of a man who wanted to be somewhere else.

"We were just bringing Mr. Berne up to speed," Oz added, indicating the files on the table.

"Magnus, please."

"Oh, look at you with your first case, Oz. Adorable!" Nadia beamed and turned to Magnus: "Oz comes to us from the accounting floor, the one that hums at all hours with the sound of keyboard strokes and spreadsheet shuffling and all the occupants suffer from an abundance of paper cuts and never see the sun."

"Only two of those are true, Nadia. Let's get back to it." Oz tapped the picture of the crash scene for emphasis. "Magnus, as you probably know, Sally's family moved to Saint Paul last month."

"Aye, from Boston."

"Given that her mother had a terminal illness, it's a safe assumption that they wanted to be close to United's oncology specialists while having the option of the Mayo Clinic. It's only a two-and-a-half-hour drive from here. And for some reason last week, they needed a plane, so they…?"

"Reached out t'me," Magnus replied promptly. "Told me they had a project needed looking into. I told 'em they could have whatever they needed."

"So you just handed over the keys?" Oz prompted. "Or whatever?"

"Aye, lad, Cessnas have keys, and yes, I handed them over. Sue and I've known each other since Shakopee. She c'n have anything she wants."

Oz took a few seconds to digest that. "The SAS thing? You guys were there?"

"Aye."

"I loathe that acronym. Call them what they truly are," Nadia sniffed. "Unattractive, racist, species-ist imbeciles who want to destroy every Stable they see, don't know how to dress, and don't care to learn. Why are master race–types so often cursed with unfortunate facial features?"

"A mystery for another day." *Shakopee. Huh.* That was interesting, and it explained why Magnus was Sally's godfather: he and Smalls had been through war together. Or, as some liked to describe Shakopee, a pathetic coup sprung by reactive morons who got what they deserved. "Oz had been a teenager when it happened, but Mama Mac had plenty to say about it at the time. This week was the tenth anniversary of the debacle."

"So your friends borrowed your plane, which crashed."

"In the interest of full disclosure, while I considered Sue to be a sister, Sam and I were never friends."

"Fair enough. So they borrowed your plane and it crashed. And then?"

"When they didn't land, I reached out. Turns out they dropped off the radar just before crossing the Iowa–Minnesota border. Took a couple of days for them to find the plane. I was told there were no witnesses to the crash, only the wreckage. No one saw it go down."

"Is that normal?"

Magnus nodded. "Unfortunately. Even when you know a plane went down and roughly where, you can't always find the crash site. It's not like when a semi goes missing. A plane can end up anywhere. There are wrecks all over the world that simply rust away. Sue and Sam went down in a field just outside the Albert Lea/ Scarville area. The woman who owns the property uses the farmhouse and buildings but rents out her fields. She was showing the land to a prospective tenant when they found the crash."

"Are we assuming pilot error?" Annette asked.

"I think assuming has been enough of a hindrance to this investigation. But, Nadia, would you mind following up with Rochester International?"

"Of course I would, Oz, but I will anyway."

"Thanks." Oz had been scribbling like mad. "Okay, so you knew the plane went down, and you came to town to check on your goddaughter, who was…"

"Well, like you said, they were new in town, but one of Sally's school friends is a werewolf. Sue told me they'd asked if they would take their wee lass overnight while she and Sam were out of town."

"Yeah, the…" Oz pawed through the file. "Bauers. They called us when Sue and Sam didn't come back to get Sally. That's when we started a file, which landed on my desk. I went to break the news and bring Sally back to IPA. And she wasn't here two hours before…"

"The adorable, maddening troublemaker had fled for the greener pastures of Lilydale for some reason. *Lilydale*," Nadia added with an eye roll.

Annette groaned. "There's nothing wrong with Lilydale, you sharp-tongued snob!"

"Darling, if I have to *explain* to you all that is wrong with Lilydale, there's simply no point. You will never get it. But why did she run that first time? And why to Lilydale?"

"Well, she was adamant from the beginning that her folks were alive. So I'm guessing her father called her and/or she ran into Dev Devoss."

"And who," Magnus demanded, "is Dev Devoss?"

"A plague upon the whole of mankind, Shifters *and* Stables," Nadia said brightly, while Annette suddenly looked like the Before picture in a headache commercial.

"He's kind of the agency mascot," Oz said, aware of how intensely lame (yet true) that sounded.

"If mascots were multilingual and bent on world destruction," Nadia added.

"The children in our charge nearly always side with each other," Annette explained. "Many of them have learned the hard way that adults will invariably let them down. Dev spends almost as much time here as he does at home. So when he saw a cub in trouble who didn't trust anyone here, his default was to help her the best way he knew how."

"Which, naturally, was also the most felonious way he knew how," Nadia added.

"I was right behind her," Oz said, "but she scraped herself badly on a low fence, and that's when Lila found her, and then I tracked them both to her house."

"Your Stable?"

"Uh. She's a Stable, yeah. Not mine. She doesn't, y'know, belong to me or anything. She's not my property. She's not any-one's property. I mean, I would love it if she *was* mine… Well, now I'm getting a little ahead of myself. Anyway, it's not like that. She's her own person. So she's *her* Stable, is how you could put it? Not mine? I guess? But I don't think of her like that. Just as a Stable, I mean. She's Lila. Is it getting warm in here?"

David chuckled while Nadia's bright blue eyes had gotten still brighter. "Oh. My. Goodness."

"Settle y'self, lad. She's independent and you admire the hell out of her, we get it. Must be formidable, given all her disadvan-tages. So this fine, competent lass—"

"That's not what I—"

"So this Lila lass, she found Sally and took her in. And then *you* found *her*. You all did. And Lila knows about your true natures. How long have you known her?"

"What day is today? Uh…four days. No, five."

Magnus's eyebrows arched. "Is that normal in this part of the world?"

Fair question. And a complicated one. Shifters lived and worked parallel to Stables when it was unavoidable (e.g., when you had to visit the DMV). But in general, they preferred to keep to The Beneath. Which, generally, worked fine and should as long as they were in the minority. There were only about sixteen million Shifters in America, less than half of one percent of the population.

But while all-Shifter agencies like IPA existed, there really wasn't a group whose job it was to figure out which Stables knew about which Shifters, and then decide what to do about it and act accordingly. No clandestine black ops teams ran around the country executing random Stables because they Knew Too Much. Shifters didn't have a central government (though Minnesota's current lieutenant governor, as well as two Cabinet members, were Shifters).

So when something like Lila happened—well, not really, she was one of a kind—when a Stable figured out Shifter secrets, it was on the individual Shifter to deal with it. Or not. Depending on the circumstances.

Of course, on the rare occasion a *lot* of Stables figured out a *lot* of Shifters…well, then you ended up with the Salem witch trials and Shakopee, but the former was centuries ago, the latter a decade ago, and there hadn't been a flare-up since. Or at least, not one he'd heard about.

Magnus, meanwhile, had picked up the photo that triggered his initial outburst, and sighed. "Oz, were ye sayin' you were going to show these pictures to my goddaughter?"

"That was one option," he admitted. "I thought it might help her come to terms with her parents' deaths. Because she simply wouldn't believe me or any of us."

"Possibly, only *possibly* because her deceased father kept calling."

"Nadia…"

"Terribly sorry to interrupt, Oz. Go ahead. You're doing *wonderfully*."

"What with one thing and another," he continued, "we haven't had a chance to show her this part of the file. But as you're here, can you tell us if that looks like your plane?"

"Oh, aye." Magnus picked up another photo. "You can even make out some of the tail number here…and here."

Oz had been intrigued to find out that actual plane crashes didn't look like what he'd seen in the movies. The wide scattering of papers was the first surprise; it was like a giant had thrown a confetti party in the muddy field. Who knew there were so many papers in a small plane? And that they were the first thing you could see when you looked at the site? How well some parts of the plane had held together on impact, while other parts looked like they'd been run through a metal shredder had been another surprise. An armrest was intact, while one of the doors looked like someone had balled it up and tossed it out.

And in the upper left part of two pictures, what looked, very obviously, like remains. Some inside the plane, and some...not.

"I don't think these would have convinced Sally," Annette observed. "Not to be crude, Mr. Berne, but that could be anyone. Your friends—"

"Friend."

Oz looked up. "Sorry?"

A finger the size of a bratwurst stabbed at one of the pictures. "I see one friend. Sue. I don't see Sam anywhere."

"Wouldn't he be in the cockpit? Er...most of him, that is?" Nadia asked with unusual tentativeness.

"I certainly hope not, lass. Sue's the pilot, not Sam." A short, difficult pause. "Was the pilot."

"But the body we can see..."

Tattered blouse, a small, feminine arm...

"And she wasn't buckled in," Annette observed. "And she didn't shift to her other self. She didn't even put her coat back on."

"But that doesn't make any... What about the black box?"

"Too many movies, lad," Magnus said, kindly enough. "Smaller aircraft aren't required to have them. They're heavy, besides, and not as helpful as the movies make 'em seem."

Why did she leave the cockpit? And why wasn't she belted in? And where's Sam? How could he possibly have survived the crash that killed his mate?

"Magnus, what's a ferry pilot?"

The man blinked at what he probably thought was a subject change. "You live in Duluth or Dublin or wherever and buy a plane. I'm the one who flies it to you."

"Huh." From Annette. "I had that all wrong. I thought an actual ferry was involved."

"And they haven't cleared the crash site yet, right, Annette?"

"No. Only the cor—they've removed the remains and taped it off." She looked across the table at Magnus. "Which I imagine is the other reason you're here. To identify your friend."

He nodded. "I'm to be at the ME's office in an hour."

"How about after?" Oz asked. "Feel like taking another trip?"

Chapter 24

HELP! WE'RE COWERING IN YOUR SHED AND NET WILL MURDER US SO MUCH so we live here now! Send snacks! And maybe Flanders's cocoa!

That was the note Lila had found in her mailbox earlier. At the time, she'd packed a bag o'snacks and dispatched Sally with it while everyone was talking to Magnus Berne, who had popped up out of nowhere, was big and mildly terrifying, had a cool accent, but probably wasn't the villain because it was never the first suspect. Except when it was.

Also: *I have a shed?*

Oh. Right. Her very first shed, in fact. The small brown building was tucked in the corner of the backyard against the fence, partially hidden by trees that should have been trimmed but never were. It was at the furthest point you could be on the property while still being on the property.

Once the IPA gang had left with Berne and Macropi went to chat with insurance adjusters, Lila had reorganized her OR schedule for the week—the Harrington kid's teddy bear could wait, the Opitz twins' Raggedy Ann and Andy, not so much—then went out to confront the vermin problem in her shed.

She looked to her left, even though it was dumb—you couldn't see Macropi's burned house from here, but she fancied she could still smell smoke. And there was no way to know if it was real. She'd smelled smoke on and off for over a year after…after what happened. Couldn't even abide being around lit candles for the longest time. She fully expected the night terrors to return shortly, which was a bore. The nice thing about *new* trauma is that you got a break from your brain's reruns.

She knocked. "Kids? You guys okay? Or are you planning more mayhem? I don't care, I'm just trying to plan my day."

Nothing.

Another rap. "Are you in there?"

She heard muffled shuffling, and then a note slid beneath the door.

No!!!!!

"This note is a lie, Daniels."

And here came another one. *No it's not. There's nobody in here. We swear!*

"Then you won't mind if I come in."

Dammit.

She opened the door and greeted them with "You guys suck at stealth."

"Ha! Only because we *want* you to think that."

She blinked at them in the gloom. Like the Pevensies' wardrobe, the shed seemed bigger on the inside. The shed had a cement floor, which had been swept clean and the broom had been placed neatly in the corner. The windows had been washed and the workbench had been tidied, then stacked with the snacks Sally had brought. Ritz Crackers, cans of smoked oysters and packets of tuna, dry cereal, dried fruit, two boxes of beef jerky. A bag of miniature marshmallows. A case of Coke and half a dozen bottles of Snapple. Two water bottles. The kids had been at Macropi's larder except she just now realized the Little Debbie Swiss Rolls and the bag of miniature Milky Ways were from her own kitchen, *fuck*.

Two flashlights, extra batteries. Textbooks on the shelf just below one of the windows. An iPad and cords plugged into nothing.

There were also sleeping bags set up on lawn loungers that had been made to fold flat; Caro was stretched out on one, intent on a graphic novel. Sally was on the other, curled up like a shrimp and snoring lightly.

"Huh. You weren't kidding when you said you lived here now. And hey, I have lawn chairs!"

"That's not all." Devoss hopped up and scampered—there was no other word for it, though she'd never tell him how adorable it was—to the far left of the workbench, showing her the back wall. "Check it!"

With that, Devoss gripped the back wall and…flipped it up. Lila realized that there was a small secret door set on hinges. When you pushed in the right spot, the door swung out and up, leading to…

She bent for a closer look. The doorway led to a path through the trees that grew right up to her fence, which you could follow through the woods, probably all the way to Pickerel Lake.

"Huh. That's nifty." She stepped back and straightened as Dev swung the doorway closed. "Let me guess—escape hatch for… what'd you call yourselves? Shifters?"

"Escape hatch for anybody, really."

"Sure, sure. Totally normal. Everyone's shed has a cleverly concealed escape hatch." That might actually be true. This was her first shed, after all. "And I get why you guys are hiding, but you gotta know the adults know exactly where you are, right?"

"We're huge believers in the 'out of sight, out of mind' axiom."

Lila thought that over, then said, "I'm sure everything will work out just fine, Devoss."

"Y'know, you could turn this into a She Shed."

"Never while I live, Devoss."

"Whatcha got against She Sheds?" the boy asked, sounding not unlike Oliver Twist asking for more.

"The silly-ass name, for starters."

"Well, that's fair. How about…" Devoss squinted up at her. "What's your last name again?"

"Kai," Lila replied.

"Kai's Korner?"

"No."

"The Kai Kubby?"

"Absolutely not. I'll commit homicide all over you if you so much as try."

"My point," Devoss replied, and it was hilarious that *he* sounded exasperated with *her*, "is you could fix this up and it'd be super nice."

"But why?"

He spread his arms to encompass the small dark building. "To have a sweet little den that nobody knows about."

"It's a shed, Devoss."

Again with the arm spreading. "So? Look at it! It won't be hard to fix up."

"It's dark."

"Low lighting," Devoss corrected.

"Crowded."

"Cozy," Devoss insisted.

"It smells like grass and dirt."

"True," he admitted. "But my point stands, it'd be easy, *einfach*, *facile*. You wouldn't even know you were sleeping in a shed! Or if you had people over, you wouldn't have to have them inside bugging you. They could just hang out here."

Wow. She didn't want to think why the kids were so excited at the prospect of out of sight, out of mind in a stranger's shed, possibly indefinitely. Why they felt *lucky* to be in such conditions. She *would* think about it, of course. She just didn't want to.

Daniels, she just realized, had been engrossed in *Elfquest* Volume Two during the entirety of the She Shed chitchat. She must have felt Lila staring because she looked up, grabbed her pad, scribbled.

These are great #!#??# books.

"Huh. You swear like a cartoon character."

She'd seen the teenager flipping through them—Lila had her

books out of boxes in the living room, but not yet on shelves—and had tucked a couple of volumes into Sally's shopping bag. And it was nice to see a teen reading an actual paper book. Lila loved her Kindle while acknowledging it had spoiled her. Last week she tapped an unfamiliar word (*diffident*, which she always confused with *indifference*), and when the definition didn't obligingly pop up, tossed the book aside and sulked. Five seconds later, she realized it was a paperback.

"I'll think about the shed thing," Lila promised. "But you guys know this is a stopgap measure at best, right? Sooner or later, you'll have to face the combined wrath of Macropi, Garsea, and Oz.[6] I wouldn't wish that on my worst enemy. Which you might end up being; we've only known each other a few days."

"How come you call everyone by their last names except Oz?"

She blinked. "I…don't know." Huh. Was that something she should worry about? Was it ponder-worthy? Was there some sort of hidden meaning in her unconscious need to call Oz *Oz*?

Naw.

"He's into you," Devoss added. "Just so y'know."

"You mentioned that."

"Are you guys going out?"

"No." And why did saying that make her chest hurt? Actual, physical pain, like someone had slugged her in the sternum? "And no to this."

"This?"

"Whatever this convo leads to. We're not in some TV show where the precociously adorable kids overstep with the matchmaking. This is real life, where grown women don't discuss their love life with random kiddos."

"You think we're precociously adorable?"

"It's kind of annoying how that's the only part you picked up

---

6. Is it me, or does Macropi, Garsea, and Oz sound like a personal injury law firm?

on." Then, because she was a moron who couldn't help herself, she undid what she had just declared. "Why would you even ask that?"

"Because he's acting weird." Daniels was shaking her head at Devoss, who ignored the warning. "Even for Oz."

Lila blinked as she considered his words. "I don't have a baseline for him, so I'll just have to take your word for it."

"Yeah, we figured."

"We"? Leave me out of this, Dev. Leave yourself out of it, too!

"That's good advice, Daniels," Lila said. "And even if he's 'acting weird,' why would I discuss any of this with you two?"

"We don't have a baseline, either," Devoss replied pertly. "So how can we answer that?"

"Are you aware of the phrase 'too clever by half'? And speaking of too clever, did you guys find some fake mistletoe when you were rooting around?" Their perfectly blank expressions (and silence) were all the answer she needed. "I don't even want to know why your first instinct after finding fake mistletoe was to plant it under Oz's pillow."

"Why did you buy an ovulation kit?"

She clenched her teeth so hard, she almost bit her tongue. Because of course he'd found it. And she couldn't even accuse him of snooping. She hadn't wanted to wonder what it meant, this sudden urge out of nowhere, multiple trips to the drugstore where she struggled not to buy the thing, finally giving in, and then the fire happened, so it had all gone right out of her head. Small wonder—she'd determinedly not thought about what she had done and what it could mean. So her subconscious obliged and let her bury it.

She hadn't even really hidden it. Just stuffed it beneath the bathroom sink along with her tampons, extra toilet paper, and an EZ-OUT ladder.

IDIOT

"Well put," Lila said dryly as Daniels smacked him on the shoulder with her notepad.

"Well, I'm in for it now, so I might as well go all the way," Devoss said, because he was stubborn and maybe a demon. "You *just* bought it. The receipt was in the bathroom garbage can. I'll bet you didn't care about ovulating before this week."

"Nope. Not doing this."

SERIOUSLY STOP NOW, DEV

"Okay, okay. It's just, we're here if you want to talk."

DEV ISN'T SPEAKING FOR ME I AM NOT HERE IF YOU WANT TO TALK

Lila snickered. "Your frantic efforts to distance yourself have been noted. Now. Change of subject."

"Okay." Dev sulked for half a second before his default sunny disposition rebooted. "You said we'll eventually have to deal with Net and Mama, and you're right. We'll show throat eventually. But we're gonna try and put it off. That whole 'get something unpleasant out of the way ASAP' sounds like a trick grown-ups use to get kids to cop to their shit right away."

"How are you naïve and cynical at the same time?"

"Dunno. Anyways, with Magnus Berne in town and everyone running around looking for Sally's dad, they'll probably forget all about us."

"There is no way in hell this crew is *ever* going to forget all about you."

Dev beamed like he'd won the lottery. "Yeah. They wouldn't. We're gonna try and sleep out here anyway. So if they ask, would you tell 'em that we seemed super sad and contrite?"

"I could, but then they'd laugh themselves into hernias."

"Maybe it'll work anyway. Mama Mac's a big fan of letting kids sleep uninterrupted. Sometimes she'll put off a lecture if she thinks you're asleep."

"Uh-huh. I'm sure no one's tried that before and she's totally oblivious to your sophisticated mind games." That earned her a raspberry from Daniels, which Lila was far too mature to return.

She looked down at sleeping Sally, who hadn't so much as twitched during their chat. Who knew werebears could hibernate for two-hour stretches? "I'm not sure it's a good idea for her to spend the night out here, though."

"She could do it. But Mama Mac won't have it. She's got this nutty idea that if she's not watching Sally, the cub'll just up and vanish."

"What a fanciful notion!"

Devoss grinned, showing his sharp little teeth. Not for the first time, Lila thought he'd make a formidable adult. "She won't run anymore. She's like me: Why would she leave the place she wants to be? They'll put up with us hiding for a bit, but ultimately, bed-time is bedtime."

"Bedtime *is* bedtime," Lila replied. "Can't argue that."

"I can't tell if you're making fun of me."

"You should always assume I am," she admitted.

"Besides, Sally's just a kid. She needs, y'know, stability and a warm bed and a house n'stuff. A shed's not so great for that."

"No, it is not," she agreed. "I've got some hand warmers in a box somewhere. I'll squirrel them out to you later."

There was a thwap as Daniels finished scribbling and whacked Lila in the shin with her sketch pad.

"Ow! Jesus."

Squirrel's not a verb. Don't make it one.

"What I do and do not turn into verbs is no concern of yours, sunshine. And have you guys thought this through? You'll be chilly," she warned. "Temp's supposed to drop to forty tonight annnnnnd you're both giving me 'are you stupid' looks because I just remembered you can grow your own fur coats at will, fine, forget I said anything. Also, isn't this a school night?"

"You don't have to go to school the day after someone tries to burn you up," Devoss said, and the hell of it was he sounded genu-inely serious. "It's a rule. And tomorrow's Saturday, so."

"Fair enough. Now that we're done with the post-awkward conversation chitchat, I have to go polish some eyeballs."

Before she could get away, Caro's hand shot out quicker than thought and snagged the cuff on Lila's jeans. "Gah! I mean, can I help you?"

Daniels was looking up at her; Lila couldn't imagine what she'd seen in her brief life with those big brown peepers and didn't want to. "Thank you," she said in a soft, low voice. "For everything you're doing for us."

"It's just a shed," she said, and left.

Chapter 25

"A life well-lived and at the end, you're pieces of meat on a slab." Magnus shook his head. "Poor lass, you always did tell me you'd go first. But I never thought it would be so soon."

"You're certain this is Susan Smalls?" the ME asked. He was short and muscular, about five foot five with a shaved head and deep-set brown eyes behind rimless glasses. In his scrubs, he looked like a green fire hydrant.

"Aye, and no mistake. Look here." Magnus stepped closer to the table and pointed to a mangled wrist. But not, on closer inspection, mangled in the crash. "She almost lost her hand at Shakopee. I got a tourniquet on it and we ran…oh, five kilometers at the least. To the nearest Shift-safe hospital."

"I had wondered at that." The ME, Dr. Gulo, was eyeballing Magnus with no small amount of interest. Oz figured he knew why. Like Annette explained when they were kids, werebears are rare bears. And she'd know. "You were both Shakopee survivors?"

"Barely."

"I only ask because it's on my mind—the tenth anniversary of that glorious mess," Gulo added.

"Glorious?" Nadia asked. "What an altogether ridiculous word. It could have been a bloodbath. That's not hyperbole, so many would have died, we would have been bathing in their blood. Would have been, if some of those idiots hadn't come to their senses in time."

"I meant 'glorious' in the literal sense: worthy of fame. Or infamy, in this case." Dr. Gulo shrugged. "Ancient history. If you count a decade as ancient."

"Ridiculous bullshit! I can't even think of Shakopee without embarrassment. So that's quite enough o'that." Magnus stopped staring down at all that was left of Sue Smalls. "This was all you found?"

Dr. Gulo inclined his head. "We were lucky to get what we did, given that the crash site is on land owned by a Stable."

"Lucky," he replied, and shook his head.

"I have to say, Dr. Gulo, this is the most immaculate morgue I have ever seen. Not that I've seen any particularly dirty morgues, mind you." Nadia looked the way she did when she got advance notice of a Macy's sale: delighted and a little surprised. "It's quite, *quite* something."

Gulo smiled. "I find it easier to concentrate when surrounded by order as opposed to chaos."

"Really? Sounds dreadfully dull." Nadia was doing the wide-eyed simper thing, which was all to the good. Oz had long gotten over his surprise at how easily a sharp-dressed woman with a cut-glass British accent could get people to open up to her. "Speaking only for myself, I thrive on chaos."

Gulo nearly shuddered. "That would be difficult for me."

There were autopsy kits (for lack of a better word; this wasn't Oz's field), and all the scalpels were perfectly lined up. So were all the scissors, the chisels

(what the hell are those for?)

and the retractors. There wasn't a speck of dust anywhere. All the chrome and steel gleamed; so did the floors. The light bulbs weren't even dirty, and the lights themselves were almost blinding. There weren't any smudge marks on the light switches, despite all the fingers that flipped them back and forth every day. The bio-hazard bins looked like a biohazard had never been allowed near them. The bottles in the recycling bin looked like someone had sterilized them first. The carts looked like you could operate on them. For all he knew, that's exactly what Gulo did with them.

Gulo had apparently recovered from the revulsion at the

thought of working with a dusty scalpel. "But we were discussing the crash site and the remains. For now, it's sealed off. But it seems an obvious accident to me."

"Really? Because it doesn't t'me."

Dr. Gulo bristled; you could almost hear his hackles going up. No surprise. Bears and wolverines, what could you do? "Please elaborate."

Berne obligingly started ticking off his points: "Sue was an excellent pilot, I take meticulous care of my property, and her little girl is in the center of something increasingly sinister. I wouldn't be so quick to rule out foul play, lad."

"Lad?" Gulo replied. "You're not much older than me."

"It's slang," Annette broke in. "Like man or dude. He doesn't think you're a child."

That earned her glares from both men, possibly for the—uh—well, mansplaining was a thing. What could this be? Slangsplaining? Scotsplaining?

Gulo had folded his arms across his chest and took a step closer. "Are you suggesting that someone murdered her on the way to that field? And then fled the scene?"

"I'm suggesting that some shithead messed with my plane, which pisses me off to no small extent," Magnus replied. "And I've no idea why, which pisses me off even more."

Gulo shrugged again. "That's not my purview, obviously. I'll be submitting my report when the labs are back."

"And when will that be?" Magnus asked.

"When the labs are back."

"Thank you for your time, Doctor," Annette put in hastily. She'd been so quiet, Oz had almost forgotten she was there. He wasn't sure if he was relieved or anxious that she meant what she said: it was his case; her role was strictly advisory. "We'll leave you to it, if that's okay with Oz."

Was it? Yeah, that actually worked. There wasn't much more to be learned here, and he wanted to put his idea in motion. Oz cleared his throat. "D'you have a card, Dr. Gulo?"

"Fresh out."

Oz took one last look around the morgue, then followed Magnus and Annette back out to the sitting area, where Nadia and David were waiting.

Oz had been surprised yet again at how *un*like the movies it was. There was no dramatic reveal, no whipping away the sheet to suddenly reveal a corpse. There wasn't a sheet at all. And they wouldn't have been in the morgue proper in the first place—a crisis counselor had met them in a small, comfortable, almost parlor-like room, with discreet photos of what was left of Sue Smalls—if Annette hadn't pulled a little weight. So David and Nadia stayed with the grief counselor, talking about who knew what, while Oz, Annette, and Magnus went deeper into the building.

Even inside, it didn't look like a gigantic operating room, all cold and sterile and shiny. Depending on what part of the morgue you were looking at, it could have been an ordinary office.

Television has lied to me. For years!

"All sorted, then?" Nadia asked as David put his phone away.

"No," Magnus said shortly. "I hope we're on the same page, lad. And if we are, I should be headed north right this minute."

"And then south." Oz turned to Annette. "If *Game of Thrones* and every graphic novel in the world have taught me anything, it's that unless we see the body, we can't assume they're dead. And sometimes even if you do see the body."

"I don't think basing your casework on *Game of Thrones* is a good idea."

"We need to get a look at the crash site."

She arched her brows, considering. "In a perfect world, yes. But you know our boss will never okay the paperwork. Our mandate allows investigation to a point, but there's no way he'll sign off on a trip so social workers with no lawful authority can visit the site. Bob will tell us to leave it to the local cops."

"Local Stable cops," he reminded her. "No Shifters in the Lake Mills PD down there."

"It's still out of our purview. I hate to admit it, but Bob might be right."

"Not our table," Nadia chimed in. Then, almost to herself, "I cannot pull that off. I am officially declaring 'not our table' to be overused and off-putting."

"Fuck Bob. I'll pay for it myself." To Magnus: "Will you take us? Today?"

Magnus grinned, showing so many teeth Oz felt his hackles rise in response. "So we *are* on the same page. You know I will, lad."

"When can we leave?"

"Twenty-five minutes after I get to the airport. I'll see you there."

"Exit Magnus, and oh my. I don't like bears," Nadia murmured as the man marched out to the parking lot. "All that hair. Ech."

"Two werebears are still in the room with you." David coughed.

"And their bulky shoulders remind me of bison," she continued. "Not yours, Annette. Your bulky shoulders are really quite feminine. The shaggy hair, too."

"Good *God*," Annette sighed.

"Bears are altogether too much to reliably handle." Nadia was still staring in the direction Magnus had left. "But occasionally, exceptions might be made. He has his own island, didn't one of you tell me that?"

"Nadia, jeez. The near-drooling is shit timing. The guy just lost his friends, maybe. One for sure."

"Yes." Nadia turned and fixed him with her bright blue gaze. She'd worked with Annette for years, he'd met her dozens of times, and still, her steady gaze was disconcerting. "His friend is dead. And that is a tragedy. Sally's mother is dead, and the child is perhaps an orphan. Another tragedy."

"Your point?" The worst part of whatever-this-was? She didn't sound like Classic Nadia at all: smug and condescending and razor-sharp teasing. She sounded sad and sorry...for *him*.

"And you will likely meet a new orphan tomorrow, and the day after, and next month, and next year. In this job, you will always meet people undergoing the worst phase of their lives. Set your watch by it, Oz. It is disagreeably stressful, and it is your new reality. Find a way to deal, or you'll be swallowed like prey."

"And lusting after random weres is the way you deal?"

"That, and loads of Glenfiddich," she confessed, which cracked him up.

Chapter 26

"This is gonna sound nuts—" Oz panted.

"Yes," Lila agreed.

"—but will you come—"

Lila hid a smile. "Uh-huh."

"—to a field just outside Scarville, Iowa—"

"Ready when you are." She paused. "Wait, Scarville? Seriously?"

"Yeah, it's a little town just outside Albert Lea. Anyway, will you come with us to see if we can figure out what happened? That's…" Oz, who'd burst into her house and skidded to a halt in front of her, was staring at her. More than usual, even. "You're not surprised. Not to see me, not to be invited."

She shrugged. "It was only a matter of time before you guys actually got down to business and *did* something. And I told you: I'm in."

Oz's mouth opened and closed like a trout on a dock, until he finally came out with "You are *terrifying.*" Which would have been annoying, save for the admiration in the man's tone.

"And you're late. I'll bet Berne is champing at the bit to get into the air or the Shifter equivalent."

"Gnawing at the bone," he replied absently. "Oh. Hi, Mama."

"Nice of you to notice, boy," Macropi replied dryly. "Seein' as how I've been standing four feet away this whole time."

"Magnus is going to fly us to the crash site. We'll be gone a few hours."

"No worries, then. I'll watch the cubs. And the fire chief told me there'd always be someone in the neighborhood to keep half an eye on this place until we catch who set the fire."

Random fire fighters hang out to house-sit? Must be a Shifter thing.

"Thank you," Lila replied. "Also, stay out of my shed. For no particular reason."

This earned her a snort. "Foolish cubs. Oh, I might rearrange your cupboards a little."

"Touch *nothing*, Macropi."

Oz jumped back in. "Gotta go gotta go gotta go-go-go."

"Touch nothinggggggg!" she hollered as Oz hauled her out of the house and over to his pretty, pretty car. He slid her bag off her shoulder, then tossed it into the backseat. "Hey! For all you know, I packed a dozen jars in the hopes we'd find a beehive."

"If that's what you packed, they deserve to get smashed. Because that's just insane. C'mon, it's only fifteen minutes to the airport from here." Oz started the car, then pulled out of the drive the second she closed the passenger door.

"Your grille looks like a pair of kidneys."

"Huh? Okay." Oz seemed entirely focused on getting them to the airport ASAP. Lila could count on one hand (one finger, actually) how often she'd ridden in a BMW SUV, so she decided to settle back and enjoy the ride. "Orange, huh? Did you just fall in love with the floor model and snatch it up? Or do you really, really like orange?"

"Sunset metallic," he corrected. "What's wrong with the color?"

"Nothing. I love riding around in a huge metal pumpkin."

He snorted. "Y'know, anyone else would wonder why we were going to the airport."

"Why? Seems obvious. You want to get a look for yourself. Or a smell for yourself… That's it, isn't it? You want to prowl and smell and solve the mystery. You can't expose Sally to such a sight, but you can expose yourself. Uh. I'll rephrase…"

"All those things. And we should go out again."

"Let's see how things go in the field. And why me?"

"Are you kidding? You're all I think about."

"That's disconcerting, especially given your new line of work. Maybe spare some thought for Sally?"

"You're eighty-five percent of all I think about."

"Better." Then, in a low voice, "Really? Not that I care. ButIthinkaboutyoutoo."

"So come out with me later," he coaxed. "I promise to grovel. If you want revenge, you can break into my condo and rummage through all my drawers."

"Tempting," she admitted. "But we're getting off track. Why aren't you bringing Garsea and Auberon instead of me?"

"You said it yourself. You're in until Sally's safe. Inviting you along is easier than trying to keep you out of it."

"How wise of you to know it." She was glad but more than a little surprised. Auberon and Garsea were more qualified for the airborne ride-along. Was Oz just naturally this inclusive and accommodating or was he trying to score points?

Why does it have to be one or the other?

"Besides," he continued, "you're letting us live in your house, for God's sake."

"Not you, Oz. Everyone *but* you. I feel like I can't emphasize that enough. I also noticed your huge suitcase in the back when you were trying to break my jars."

"I need more clothes, obviously. I can't wear your robe *all* the time. As for the others, Bob—that's our boss—heroically reminded Annette that she has her own caseload to worry about. And by 'heroically,' I mean he sent her a text and then locked himself in his office."

"Amateur. Garsea can get through a locked door."

"Uh. Yeah. About that… She felt bad before—"

"She would have felt worse if she'd kept opening more of my drawers. She thought the bottom one was bad? Just wait."

"—but now that we know you better, she feels *really* bad. Also, at the risk of repeating myself, we should go out again. A pretense-less lunch. Or any kind of lunch you like." He glanced away from the road to look her right in the eyes. *Green eyes green eyes ohthosebeautifuleyes.* "It's so fucking decent of you to help me," he added, squeezing her hand.

"No."

He dropped her hand. "What?"

"I'm not helping you. I'm helping Sally. You should probably keep that straight in your head. She's the priority, not you or Garsea or Macropi. Also Macropi's arsonist. They're my other priority. If I empty a shotgun into someone's face, d'you think you could look the other way?"

"Depends on the face."

She laughed. "That's cold. Almost as cold as me."

"Cold is the last adjective I'd use to describe you."

"Chilly."

He shook his head. "No."

"Frosty"

"Nope."

"Icy."

"Nope."

"Frigid?"

"Christ, I hope not."

"And here I've been giving Delta all my frequent miles like a sucker."

Berne chuckled. "Keep with them, lass. I've got no plans to put any major carrier out of business."

They were mounting the steps to the plane while Berne finished his preflight check. Lila had been surprised to see Oz skip the Minneapolis–Saint Paul International Airport for a vastly smaller airfield just outside Lakeville. They'd been directed to the right gate (one of five possibilities), and then Oz took her outside, where Berne was prowling around his plane like an overprotective…well. Bear. No TSA, no pat down, no wildly over-priced bad coffee.

The Cessna was a small white plane with long navy blue stripes along the body and belly. She could see three windows in addition to the cockpit, and then she and Oz were ducking their heads to enter the cabin and take their seats. It wasn't her first ride on a single-engine high-wing plane, though it had been about five years. One and done, in fact.

Meanwhile, Berne was explaining that preflight checklists saved lives. Specifically, they would have saved a Gulfstream crash in 2014, and several other crashes the man rattled off because he thought talking about plane crashes would calm his passengers.

"And not just twenty-fourteen! D'you know that the NBAA[7] found only partial preflight checks on fifteen percent of all flights? Fifteen percent! Even though they've been recommended since the thirties! It's a bloody miracle there haven't been *more* crashes."

"Um," Lila began, because the color was falling out of Oz's face, making his eyes seem that much greener. Which should have been sexy but wasn't.

"Back then, the gust locks something and then they something-something. Leave it to those buggers at Boeing, eh? And not only that, but something else and then another something else, so of course something-something. Everyone died, poor bastards. All right, buckle in, we're cleared."

"Oz," she murmured, which might have been a waste of time. Did werebears have super hearing? Could Berne hear her over the engine? "Are you okay?"

"Fine. I'm totally fine. Everything's fine." This while he cinched his seatbelt tight enough to obstruct his breathing. "Totally, completely—hurrk!—fine."

Sure, pal. She raised her voice in an attempt to turn the chitchat

---

7. National Business Aviation Association.

away from crashes. "So, Berne, is this a super-duper secret Shifter-only airport? I've never heard of it, but I've only lived here a couple of days."

"No, lass, it's a reliever airport. When MSP gets overloaded, they shift flights here. Now pipe down your chatter, they don't have an air traffic control tower here."

Ack! Lila instantly piped down the chatter.

"Not a very long flight," she said quietly as they taxied. "So that's nice."

"Grrtt." Oz forced that out through gritted teeth, probably "great." Or "grate," which made less sense and would be weird, but she shouldn't rule out the possibility.

There were two kinds of nervous flyers: ones who liked to be talked to, and ones who absolutely *hated* being talked to. "So about this make-up lunch…" What could she say? In this moment, he was pitiful. So why not offer a pity lunch, which was bound to be an improvement over a decoy lunch.

"Mmmmm?"

"Maybe you know a few good places?"

"Mmm."

"I'm pretty easy. Just don't serve it to me in something deliberately weird, that's all I ask."

"Mmmm?"

"Oh, you know. Because it's *whimsical* or whatever-the-hell. 'Here's your daiquiri in a bag!' 'Here's your ice cream served on a block of ice.' 'Here's your white chocolate truffles served in a flip-flop.' 'Here's your appetizer served on a two-by-four and wrapped with sandpaper!'[8] Just give me the damned shrimp cocktail already."

"Ha!"

Lila jumped; she couldn't help it. That laugh had *exploded* out of him. She glanced down and saw white knuckles.

---

8. Only one of those is made up. The others were actually served in restaurants. That's the world we're living in.

"Mm fnnn."

"Of course you're fine. I never thought otherwise. You are radiating fine. If I were to grab a dictionary to look up 'fine,' your grinning mug would take up half the page."

"Ha!"

"And since you're totally fine with what's happening at the moment, maybe you should buy your own plane. Berne could fly it to you. You're rich, you could probably buy two. One to keep at the airport, and the other to annoy me by parking it in my driveway."

"Ha!" Oz turned his head to look at her. "Well. I am. Rich, I mean. But how'd you know?"

"Seriously? Let's count the ways. The suit. You were still in yesterday's clothes and while *you* were a rumpled mess, the suit held up beautifully. So did your shoes. And now you're wearing a different suit, and this one's high quality, too. That's top-notch tailoring, probably from Heimie's. And Byredo Eleventh Hour aftershave isn't cheap. And don't forget your giant metallic pumpkin. And the Louis Vuitton you threw into the backseat of your giant metallic pumpkin. And the breakroom."

"How'd you even know about the—"

"Macropi and Garsea found it gossip-worthy." She began prying his fingers from their death-lock on the armrest, then took his hands in hers. "Here's the thing I can't figure: you hate flying—"

"I don't hate it. I'm just terrified because we're hurtling through the air in a narrow tube thousands of feet off the ground and there's nowhere to go, and I can't get out unless Magnus *lets* me out. But I'm not scared."

"Gotcha. But this was your idea."

"Yeah, well." Oz was facing front again. She could see the muscles in his jaw work as he clenched his teeth, then consciously tried to stop. "I have to do everything in my power to make Sally feel safe again. And this is part of it. You like flying?"

"It's okay. It's better than jumping."

"Y'mean parachuting?"

"No, I meant hurdles." When he blinked, she added, "Sorry, sometimes I'm on auto-snark. Yes, I meant parachuting. I did it a few years ago."

"For fun?"

"No, I lost a bet. That's not snark. It was a real bet."

"What was it?"

Chapter 27

IT WAS THE HOT SMELL OF PLANE FUEL AND THE COLD BLAST of wind. It was the dizzying euphoria of free fall and the surge of adrenaline that made her mouth taste like she'd been sucking on a roll of pennies. It was getting out of your seat so you could jump out of a plane while ignoring your brain's panicked demands that you sit your ass back down. It was standing by an open plane door and intellectually knowing the static line was in place to help while your gut was positive it was a hindrance.

It was putting your trust in canvas and rope and nylon. It was feeling the greedy earth use terminal velocity to snatch you back, back, all the way down.

And then the shock in your knees when gravity reminds you: You belong to the earth again. It's letting the big muscle groups soak up and spread out the impact, the way Kevlar soaked up bullets: you lived, but it still hurt. All that kinetic energy had to go somewhere.

She'd done her research. Over three million jumps every year, just in the US.

Millions of people hurtling toward Earth at terminal velocity. Every single year.

It was…too much. Too chaotic, too much free fall, too inherently unstable. That had struck her first thing during her research: "The deployment process is inherently chaotic."

Nutshell.

So once was enough. Because she only had to jump once and she knew: you could go high and you could go far; you could jump three million times a year, but the earth always got you back, one way or the other.

Chapter 28

"No, Lila, I meant, what was the bet?"

"Oh. In that case, sorry about the flashback."

"You've got an empty Subway bag in your purse."

"That was an abrupt segue." She picked up her purse, opened it, found the bag with her used napkins. She'd been in such a rush at the airport, she'd just stuffed it in her purse to be dealt with later. "Here you go. So no more jump stories?"

"If you're brave enough—hurrrk!—to do it, I'm brave enough to listen."

"Good to know."

"Excuse me."

"That's a shame about your breakfast," she said as he yarked into the bag. "Well, Macropi will fix you more bacon, I'm sure. I've also got some wet wipes in my purse, if you're interested."

"Thanks," he said hollowly, which made the bag puff, which she swore to herself wouldn't make her laugh (out loud). "You and the Boy Scouts."

"Always prepared," she agreed, then waited until he tied the bag off, and held his hand the rest of the way.

Chapter 29

"Well, there it is," Lila observed. "This is definitely a field. Where a plane definitely crashed."

Berne had landed on a gravel road that, from the air, looked miles long and deserted, and also walking distance to the crash. It was almost ridiculously convenient, but she wasn't about to complain. She'd braced herself for gore, but the powers-that-be in charge of such things (IPA? A different agency? Local cops? Local Shifter cops?) had apparently scooped up all there remained of Sue and Sam Smalls and bore them away. Dr. Gulo had been right about that much, at least.

I'll bet they were awake all the way down. And terrified and scared for Sally. Christ, what an end.

This time of year, the field was an acre of mud, and the wind brought the smell of dirt and scorched metal right to them. If *she* had no trouble smelling it, the men must have found it almost unbearable. The debris was spread out and the crime scene tape (if it *was* a crime) was doing a shit job of keeping the small stuff in place. But unless Shifters had perfected the science of creating protective domes over crime scenes, there was nothing to be done about it.

Despite the damage, it was instantly apparent that this was the graveyard for a small plane. Metal had been wrenched into impossible shapes, along with all sorts of other debris: blackened plastic, wiring, mangled seats, and a thousand shattered pieces of equipment she didn't recognize. The nose of the plane looked like a giant had seized it and squeezed, and one of the wings had cracked into thirds; the other was almost completely untouched.

She was worried they hadn't found all of Sue Smalls or missed pieces of Sam Smalls, but she couldn't see or smell anything like a corpse, which was an immense relief.

"All right, this is sad and awful. But you didn't need me along to tell you that. So why—"

"You're the lookout, lass."

"People have said that to me so many times, the words have lost all meaning."

"Seriously, Lila…" Oz paused while reaching for his top shirt button. "Do you mind?"

"Nope." What else could she say? Magnus and Oz were already disrobing. She wasn't sure if she was in a horror movie, a rom-com, or a porn. Or a sick combo that would sound lame but most people would watch anyway for the curiosity factor if nothing else.

She politely turned her back, which took *so much willpower* because at quick glance, both men appeared to have the bodies of Olympic athletes. Not a fake sport, like race walking. Something hard, like boxing. She got a quick glimpse of profoundly terrific abs and then stared at a tree.

A lot of people wore tailored suits to fix figure flaws.

Oz Adway was not one of them.

Stupid, ab-less trees.

She could hear…something. Rustling as they dropped their clothes. (Damned good thing Oz had money, because he was hell on his suits. Guy needed a pair of denim overalls in the worst way.) Then sounds like the noise your body makes when you stand and streeeeeetch. The sharp retort of cracking knuckles. A *lot* of knuckles. Thirty or more. And then more shifting around, sharper cracks, some low, pained grunting, and then a cold nose was nuzzling her palm

"Ack!"

which wasn't startling *at all*. She spun and there was Oz looking up at her.

As she was in a field of mud in the middle of the day, she got a much better look than she had the night before in Macropi's yard. His head came up to her waist, his ears were longer than her middle finger and tipped with red fur, and he was lean all over with sleek muscles that rippled beneath sand-colored fur. His ears twitched forward as she squatted and held out her hand, palm up. "Gimme."

The wolf blinked at her.

"Your right forepaw, please." There was a short pause, and then Oz complied.

"No, your *other* right forepaw." He obliged and she gently palpated the fur. She'd done a little research; she knew wolves used their claws for digging and traction, not fighting, but she was mindful of the claws anyway; they were dull black, tipped under, and nearly an inch long.

And his paw was perfect, as far as she could tell without a degree in veterinary medicine. "I guess you're all healed up from the other day." She released his paw, smiled, stood. "I'm glad."

She heard a low rumble behind her and turned. Oh. Right. The werebear. She didn't really care if *his* forepaw hurt, which was good because she had zero interest in getting closer. Berne was massive, there was no other word that fit so well. He would have looked like a common brown bear save for his size; on all fours, he was over two yards long and must have weighed well over one thousand pounds.

Even if his size hadn't set him apart, his dark brown fur had a violet tint, just like Berne's human hair. *Aww, cute! I think.* She'd never heard of a bear with fur that color; maybe they were native to Scotland? What if it wasn't a natural color? If a Shifter dyed their hair purple, was their fur purple, too? So many questions.

"I'm done gaping now, fellas, thanks for indulging me. Do your—go do your thing. Sniff or scavenge or whatever." She looked around the mess one last time. "I'm gonna go stand over there where it's slightly less muddy, which is still pretty muddy, and keep out of your way." And look out, apparently. But for what?

If a van full of state troopers suddenly roared up to the crash site, what was she supposed to do about it?

Too late to worry about that now. She watched as they prowled the crash site, noses down, and it took a minute for her to realize they were working the field in a grid. Oz in particular seemed determine to sniff and paw at everything; she couldn't imagine the number and depth of scents he was taking in.

They're not wild; they're not dumb animals. They're self-aware apex predators who have avoided detection for millennia. Which is very, very important to keep in mind, pretty much every hour of every day.

It was nuts, but she had no sense of personal danger. She figured Macropi's gang had had ample opportunity to eat her if that had been the goal. And maybe she was kidding herself, but they all seemed to like her. Or, in Auberon and Berne's case, tolerate her. Either way, endangered or not, who else in the world was spending their day the way she was?

She could have watched for hours, but it turned out that wasn't an option. And ironically, given that she was the lookout, Oz and Berne spotted (smelled?) the trouble before she did. It took her a few seconds to realize she hadn't been ditched, and a few more to realize she had company.

Worst. Lookout. Ever.

Chapter 30

THE HELL OF IT WAS, THINGS HAD KINDA BEEN PICKING UP. SHE
was able to replace the truck's muffler on her own (no burns this
time). Winter had been fought to a draw and was panting in the
corner, thinking about a final rush. It was too early for mosquitos.
And too late for blizzards. And she'd finally talked her wife into
selling the north field, which had been nothing but an unprofit-
able mud pit for over a decade.

Then: an unbelievable ruckus from—where else?—the north
field. Goddamned plane came down like an arrow fired from God:
BOOM!

Except it was more like *BOOM!*

Wendy, who had bought the farmhouse from her folks when
they moved to Arizona ("Fuck shoveling" was how her dad broke
the news), heard it like it was happening in the next room, not a
mile from the house. She'd rushed off

(now what the holy old hell is this?)

found the mess, found the

(aw jeez poor thing urrgghh here comes my lunch)

body, called the cops and asked them to send an ambulance,
which turned out to be waaaay too optimistic.

There'd been nothing but trouble since. Needless to say, poten-
tial buyers weren't keen on the wreckage. Assurances that such a
thing had never happened before—and what were the odds of a
repeat performance?—were shrugged off. Worse, the cops had
told her the whole thing would be sealed off for a bit, probably just
long enough for spring buyers to peter out.

But then what? Wendy didn't even know who to call. Was her
field a crime scene, or just an accident site? Was there a business

that specialized in plane crash cleanup in rural Iowa? (Though her wife would say "rural Iowa" was redundant. But Kelly could be a snob and a half. Thought getting a degree from the U of M meant she was a city gal.)

So all week, she'd taken the path around the back of the house that led to the edge of the field, staring at the morbid mess and wondering if she could just rent a bulldozer and raze it all, damn the law and the consequences, just raze it and then bury it deep and stick the FOR SALE sign back up.

Today, someone beat her to the field. As she approached, she was waved at by a young woman with a mop of butter-colored curls and eyes the color of the sky. Not today's sky. A random sky in June when the forecast was for pure sunshine. She was wearing jeans, a red sweatshirt (*It's a beautiful day to leave me alone*), muddy sneakers, and glasses.

"Well, hi there!"

"Uh. Hello. Is that a plane behind you?"

"It's *two* planes behind me."

Wendy shook her head. "No, I meant the one that isn't all smashed up."

"Yes. The plane behind me is also a plane. Can I help you?"

"I think that's supposed to be my line." She came a bit closer, more curious than nervous. "This is private property. Mine, I mean."

"Oh! I'm sorry. As soon as my pilot gets back we'll take off. Heh."

"Where's your pilot?"

"His amoebic dysentery came back, so." At Wendy's wince, she added, "Don't worry, he promised not to diarrhea downwind this time. I'm sure we're perfectly safe. Well. I am. Have you had all your shots? No judgement, especially if you're an anti-vaxxer."

"Anti-vaxxers are gonna kill us all," she said automatically, because Kelly had had plenty to say about *that* as well. "So you're not from the county? Were you maybe interested in the land? Is that why you're here?"

"Why else would I be here? There's simply no other explanation for this conversation. So yes, obviously, verrrrrrrry interested. Does all the crash debris come with it, or will you be charging extra for that?"

"I don't know." Wendy felt desperate but hoped it didn't show. "I've been trying to figure out how to get rid of it. Unless you want it. In which case I'll throw it in for free."

"Good to know. I'll tell my client. Pilot, I mean. My pilot-client. My client who happens to be a pilot."

"You're a Realtor?"

"Number one in Fargo."

"But this isn't Fargo. It's not even North Dakota."

"That's why I moved. There were no real estate challenges left for me in Fargo. Or North Dakota." She spread her hands. "So. Here I am. Ta-dah!"

"Okay." Wendy couldn't tell if she was overtired (sleep had been in short supply since the crash) or if the woman was wacko. And there was always the chance that both things were true. "D'you have a card?"

"I threw them all down the garbage disposal."

Don't ask. Just don't. "Why?"

"I was having a career crisis."

Toldja not to ask. "So you're not a Realtor anymore?"

"Well, the crisis ended. So, yes, I'm still a Realtor. Why else would I be standing in a muddy field by myself? I mean, with a client?"

"Beats me. So…I guess I'll leave you to it? Are you sure your pilot's coming back?"

"He has to, I stole the keys to his airplane."

Sure. Totally normal. People do that every day. Yep. "Oh. Well, if you have any questions, I'll be just down the road in the farmhouse next to the big willow."

"Thanks!"

"And you're welcome to bring any other buyers out here, too."

"Thanks!"

"Okay, well. Bye."

Wendy went back the same way she came and couldn't shake the idea that there was more going on than she knew. Not just because of the vague-yet-specific weirdo; she felt *watched*. Had felt like that all week, to tell the truth, and was it any wonder? Part of her wanted to go back and talk to blondie some more, but there was a more urgent voice in the bottom of her brain that was telling her to get gone in a hurry. One she obeyed. And the closer to the house she got, the fainter that warning voice got. Half an hour later, when she ventured a look outside, the plane was gone.

Chapter 31

"I KNOW I WAS THERE AND SAW THE WHOLE THING, BUT WILL you please tell the tale of Magnus Berne's amoebic dysentery again?"

"We're never speaking of it again," Berne commanded. "Couldna think of something less graphic, lass?"

"That's not what you brought me along for. You brought me along to be a terrible lookout. Which I nailed, FYI."

The crash site was five minutes behind them; once the farmer had left, Oz and Berne wasted no time shifting back and taking off.

"And before I forget, here." Oz stuck his hand out.

"What?"

"It's my 'other right' forepaw." He wiggled his wrist back and forth. "Good as new. But you don't have to look for excuses to hold my hand. You can hold it whenever you want."

"Sure, Oz. Because that was at the forefront of my mind all this time. Not the crash or running interference with a random farmer or Sally or her dad who's maybe not dead…it was all about your other right."

"As long as we're clear."

"I have to hand it to you, lass, y'kept your cool."

"Nonsensical babbling is an underrated camouflage technique."

"Ha! Well put."

"Not just that," Berne insisted. "When you got a look at my other self. Weren't you surprised at all?"

"Nope. Don't even try," Oz advised. "She doesn't surprise. She lives in a constant zone of not-surprised. And if she ever *is* surprised, she'd die before showing it. I honestly believe that. She. Would. Die."

"Jesus, Oz. Dial it back."

Berne let out a snort. "Is that how it is, Lila? Or was it something else? Oz here didn't warn you ahead of time?"

"*Berne.*" It was so rare to hear Oz use such a sharp tone, she almost did a double-take. "I'm not an outer. Your other self is your own business."

Berne seemed a little taken aback, too. It didn't help that they were all using raised voices; the Cessna's engine, while not deafening, necessitated speaking louder than normal. "All right, lad, I meant no offense. I was just wonderin'."

So is it a personal choice kind of thing? Who a Shifter tells about their true nature is generally frowned upon but ultimately up to the individual? Note to self: "Outing" is a major faux pas.

Regardless, time to straighten Berne out. "You're the one who told me."

"Wi' respect, I did no such thing."

"Your last name is *Berne*, for God's sake. At some level, I've gotta assume your entire family wants people to know."

For that she got a dry chuckle. "Ach, no. I'm the last Berne."

"Oh." *Poachers? Or something more mundane? Because if it was poachers, maybe look into changing your name. If it's not too late. Sounds like it might be too late.* "Sorry. I'm the last Kai, if it's any consolation."

"Now why should that console me?"

Oh, I dunno...because my kind outnumbers yours thousands to one? More?

"Doesn't console me, either," Oz added. "I'm sorry. It sucks to be the last. For anyone, I think."

"Careful, you're showing depth," she teased.

"Sorry. Won't happen again."

"Are you *sure* you didn't know about Shifters until this week, lass? Because you're taking insane risks with your own safety."

"Why? Are you a shitty pilot?"

"I'm an incredible pilot. But weren't you wurred? Even a bit?"

"Oh, please. Nothing to be wurred about. You've all had ample opps to devour me. Besides, you took precautions." Berne had politely asked that she keep her phone in her purse, and her purse in the plane, which she respected, and not just because he'd been polite about it. "You didn't have to worry about my purse, though—I left my .380 at home."

"You didn't bring a gun? I couldn't tell, but I thought you…"

Excellent. Lila, two nights ago, had emptied her purse, grimaced at the inevitable detritus

(When did I have oyster crackers? Or soup?)

cleaned it, cut the lining, sprinkled a tablespoon of baking soda into it, sewed the lining shut, and went back to business as usual.

"Oh, you couldn't smell anything? No idea I hadn't brought a handgun?" she asked, giving off wide-eyed Orphan Annie innocence.

"Not even the shotgun," Oz replied cheerfully, which was silly. Where would she have put it?

"Good Lord, Berne. Why would I bring a gun to an airport? I've got enough to do this week. I don't have time for a body cavity search followed by a stint in lockup."

"You are terrifying."

"Why do people keep telling me that?"

"Because you're terrifying?" Oz guessed.

"Not like regular Stables are terrifying," Berne added. "You're terrifying in an entirely unique way."

"Thanks! Wait. I have the feeling that wasn't a compliment. Let's table my penchant for terrorizing random citizens around me and talk about the site—did you guys pick anything up?"

"No."

"Which is a problem," Oz added.

Lila waited, but Oz had apparently finished. "So…should I guess? Maybe play a round of charades? What?"

"Sam wasn't there."

Berne's sentence hit like a dull thud. "You didn't…find his body? Or you didn't—"

"No body. No scent. No tracks—not that I think he could have survived. Two people went up," Oz said, "but only one came down."

It sounded impossible, so she sounded it out to be sure she had it right. "Sally's parents boarded and took off together, they didn't make any stops to refuel, but somewhere between D.C. and a muddy field in Iowa, Sam Smalls got off that plane."

"Nailed it."

"That's correct, lass."

"Did—was there a flight plan? Is there a rule about that?"

"You don't have to file a flight plan," Berne explained, "but Sue was meticulous. Two on board, no cargo, straight shot to MSP."

"Well. Shit."

"Succinctly put, lass."

Chapter 32

"YOU KNOW WHO FAKED THEIR DEATH?"

"You mean besides Jesus?"

Oz groaned. "Lila, please tell me you've never gone to church and sprung that theory on anyone."

"It's a perfectly legitimate—wait, how do you know about church? Are Shifters religious?"

"Why wouldn't I know about churches?" Oz replied, bewildered. "Or religion?"

"Hey, I don't make the rules. I just want to know what they are."

It was late afternoon and they'd just gotten back from the airport. Berne had landed, taxied, given them cordial goodbyes, then pulled Oz aside just as he and Lila were about to head for the parking lot.

"Sure you don't want to come with us, Magnus? Mama Mac's turkey chili will make you cry and cry and then feel great but sleepy the rest of the day."

"I need about twenty hours of sleep *now*, lad. And I need to think about what we know, and about what we've yet to know. I also need a shower. Badly. But that young lady...the Stable. Be careful."

He wanted to bristle; Berne was acting like an overbearing big brother, which was Annette's job.

"You've only known her a couple of days."

"I've known you for *one* day."

Magnus shrugged that off. "She flew to Iowa in the company of two men she's just met, men she knew could overpower and kill her—not that we would've, but *she* didna know that, and she still wasna worried. So she's stupid, or dangerous. And I dinna think she's stupid."

Almost against his will, Oz turned to look at Lila, like a flower following the sun.

(*Following the sun? Jesus.*)

"No," he replied slowly, watching her hop on the escalator. "She's not stupid."

"Hey! Are we going, or what? If you're inviting him to move in with me," Lila called, "I don't have the room! I am not a Motel 6!"

Berne let out a snort. "Good luck, lad."

"In general, or with the case, or with her?"

"Which d'ya think? It's obvious you find her intriguing beyond the boundaries of your case."

Shit. That obvious? "It—that's not relevant."

"Trust me, lad. She likes you. She barely glanced at me, which I can honestly say has never happened to me before." "Peeved" was a new look for Magnus Berne. Oz decided, quite irrationally, that he liked it.

"Hey!" From the escalator. "You want a ride?"

"Ha!" To Magnus: "Finally a bluff I can call. She can't leave without me."

"Er…lad…"

Oz could tell what had happened from Berne's expression; there was no need to look. He looked anyway; Lila was waving his car keys at him from the escalator. *Oh, who am I kidding? She probably knows how to hot wire anything with an engine. Probably could have taken the plane, too.*

"Like I said, lad: Good luck."

With that, Oz collected his keys and his dignity, then drove them back to Lilydale while Lila played with his radio and mocked his taste in music. He poked her back because (1) it was clear neither of them were ready to talk about what they hadn't found in Iowa, and (2) anyone who liked Katy Perry that much deserved mockery.

But now, in her kitchen, the subject needed to be broached, and not just because Annette was there.

"That's the new theory?" she asked, hanging up her raincoat on one of the pegs by the door.

"Huh." Lila was giving the slicker a critical once-over. "I didn't take you for a fan of salmon pink, Garsea."

"No one is more surprised than I am. Well. Maybe Nadia. But the color has grown on me. Like lichen! You see, about six months ago—"[9]

"I don't actually need the backstory on why you wear a pink raincoat when it's not raining. Plus, laundry."

Annette, Oz was glad to see, was also surprised by Lila's abrupt segues. "It's your laundry day?"

"No."

"Okaaaaaay." Then, as Lila left to...*not* do her laundry? "So tell me."

Oz sighed. "You're not gonna like it."

"I have no doubt."

"Sometime between takeoff and Iowa, Sam Smalls got off that plane."

"Well, hell." Garsea sat at the table and nibbled her lip.

"Why did I think that trip would clear anything up?" he groaned, slumping into the chair opposite her. "Why do I think anything I've done on this case will clear anything up?"

He braced himself for "I told you so" and was pleasantly flabbergasted when Annette flashed him a sympathetic smile. "Some cases are like that. You've heard me make the same complaint."

"I dunno, you complain all the time. Sometimes it's hard to narrow 'em down."

"Har, har. All I'm saying is I know our work can be problematic. You dig and dig but all you raise are more questions. You think you'll never figure it out or, worse, you *will* figure it out, but nothing can be done to help the cubs in question. If David was here, he'd tell you the same thing."

---

9. The gory details can be found in *Bears Behaving Badly*.

Is she talking about Opal? Because once upon a time, IPA had discovered neglect and abuse, but not in time to save Opal Adway. Only her brother. And there had been many dark days (several spent in the purple house up the street) when he doubted he *had* been saved.

"You kick over rock after rock," she continued. "You reread your files until the letters don't make sense anymore and kick more rocks. But sometimes, when you can't see anything besides your mistakes, when the night is darkest, you stumble over the right rock, and now I hear it, I'm mixing my metaphors when all I meant to say was hang tough."

While she spoke, Annette had casually risen, casually sidled over to the stove, casually eyeballed the big black pot simmering away, casually reached for the small spoon

"Ouch!"

and casually got her knuckles rapped.

"Sorry." From Lila. "Macropi made me promise to keep you out of it 'til suppertime."

"When is that?" Annette whined.

"I've no idea. Macropi didn't tell me when supper would be served in my kitchen."

Oz cleared his throat. He was having trouble figuring out if Lila was genuinely aggrieved, or fake-aggrieved to cover her concern. "I called her from the car so we could talk about Iowa."

"You're both uninvited pains in my ass," Lila pointed out. "And you'd better stay for supper, because Macropi made ten gallons of chili for some reason."

"And two pans of corn bread," the lady in question added, coming in through the kitchen door while lugging…something. She gave Annette an awkward one-armed hug. "Where's David, m'girl?"

"Case. I'll fill him in when I go home. What're the cubs up to?"

"They're back in Lila's shed, hoping I've forgotten about them.

They've fixed it up nicely, Lila, and I assume that's partly your doing?"

"It's a shed," Lila replied. "Why would I give a shit?"

Which wasn't an answer, but Oz decided to keep that observation to himself.

"And look what I found!"

"Perfect. We can hang it right there," Annette said, gesturing to the blank expanse of wall opposite the kitchen table. "There's still a nail left from the last tenants."

"Why have you dragged a whiteboard into my kitchen? And why do you think you're going to hang the whiteboard you dragged into my kitchen? And where did you find a whiteboard to drag into my kitchen?"

"Your shed," Mama Mac replied, in a tone that implied it would have been strange to *not* find a whiteboard there.

"Oh. Of course. My shed. The shed I should have inventoried, definitely. You found a whiteboard and hauled it in, just like people do every day because it's perfectly normal and not weird at all."

"Trust me, it will help." From Annette, who retrieved her purse, dug around, then set half a dozen dry-erase markers on the table. "As will these."

"Yep. Also totally normal. Who *doesn't* walk around with dry-erase markers just in case someone produces a random whiteboard? Again, why would you need—oh." Oz had grabbed the black marker and started scribbling a rough Smalls family time line on the now-hung whiteboard. "So you guys work for IPA but don't actually...y'know. Work *at* IPA?"

Oz had no idea how to answer that, so he kept scribbling. Because the truth was tricky. They were brainstorming in the Curs(ed) House's kitchen for the same reason that Annette occasionally wore salmon: because cub trafficking.

The kitchen screen door twanged open again. "Hi, Lila! Hi, the rest of you guys!"

"You know all our names, Sally," Annette pointed out kindly.

"Uh-huh. So when's dinner? For everybody, including the big kids who only wanted to help me so really they didn't do anything wrong so they're not really in trouble I bet?"

"I'm still thinking about that," Mama Mac replied.

"Which part?" Lila asked.

"How much trouble they're in." To Sally: "And dinner is right after you go wash up."

"I'm clean, though," the cub protested as she was gently shoved toward the kitchen sink.

"You've been playing in a shed all afternoon, m'girl. You'll be taking a shower tonight, too."

"But it's Friday!"

"And everyone knows Friday showers are absolutely forbidden," Lila added. "Minnesota state law. Or is it a federal law? I haven't kept up on the legislation."

"You go wash up, too," Mama ordered.

"I'm going, but not because you told me to. After wandering around in a field half the day, I need a shower. I'll be quick, I promise."

"Don't rush," Macropi told her. "This is your home. We'll wait for you."

Annette let out a groan they all ignored.

"I'll hurry. And toss *Baby4U*. Or at least hide it properly."

Oz, who'd been hunched over scribbling, suddenly straightened. "Baby for what now?"

Mama rolled right over him. "Sally, go tell the others that supper's in half an hour," she said, blotting the girl's clean hands dry. "Scoot, now."

As Sally scooted, Oz turned to watch Lila head upstairs.

———————————

"Shit!"

Lila knew it was going to happen; why was she cursed with a half-second of foresight? The bathroom counter was agreeably long—the room was shaped like a lowercase "l"—and her pro tem house guests had spread out their sundries. Macropi had placed a glass jar full of cotton balls beside their toothbrushes, and Lila had knocked it over when she was reaching for the lotion. Stupid.

"Are you okay?" Oz, from the other side of the door. Damn. The guy went through two rooms, up the stairs, and to the end of the hall in the half second between the crash and her yell.

"I'm—"

There was a sharp *crack*, and the door opened with a crash.

"—fine." She took in a wild-eyed Oz while tightening her sagging towel. It wasn't her modesty she was worried about so much as the scarring. "Do you want to sit down? You look like you're about to stroke out."

"*Don't.*" This as she had taken a tentative half-step toward him, mindful of the glass.

"Oz, I can't just live in the bathrooooooo—whoa!" Faster than thought, he'd navigated the glass and scooped her into his arms, pivoted, and they were back on glassless carpet. It had been so quick and efficiently graceful, it was almost like a dance. "And again: whoa."

He'd handled her like she weighed no more than a shoebox, then set her back on her feet while she grabbed his shoulder and clutched her towel—thank goodness it was one of the big ones. "Unnecessary," she managed, annoyed at how breathless she sounded. "But thanks."

He hadn't let go of her waist. "Are you sure you're okay? No cuts?"

"No cuts, just a case of the stupids. I'll sweep it up once I get wet. Dry! Once I dry off."

Oz shook his head, adorably assuming he had any say in who performed Curs(ed) household tasks. "I'll do it."

"Don't be a dope." He still had her by the waist, so she kept clutching his shoulder. Damned if she was going to be the first one to break off. And she was amazed to realize there was no need to worry about him seeing her scars; his gaze hadn't ever left her face. "I'm almost positive I know where the broom is."

"You're doing too much already," he murmured. Murmured? Yes. He was practically whispering in her ear. His mouth was… very close. Very close to *her* mouth, to be perfectly mouth. Frank! "Let us help you with some of the load."

"Load, sure, uh-huh," she replied, not really listening because— just as an objective fact—Oz's mouth was kissing close. If this was a love story, there'd be a passionate embrace right about now, his mouth would slant over hers and she'd grab both shoulders and they'd cling to each other and her towel would artfully slip and it would be passionate and terrific.

"Lila, dear, I'll call Harriss & Son to come fix the bathroom door. You get dry right now and put some clothes on before you catch pneumonia." Mama Mac, from the other end of the hall. "I can see your butt!"

But this was a sitcom, so none of those things were going to happen.

"My butt is none of your concern, Macropi!"

There was a short silence, followed by laughter drifting up from the kitchen. Lila had to bite her lip, hard, not to add to it. Focusing on Oz's abashed expression and reddening face helped. "Why is this my life now?" she asked.

"The main theories are that you're hospitality personified or that you lost a bet with God," he replied.

"It's not the former."

Oz spread his hands and shrugged. "Then I guess God's a gambling man."

Well, yeah. Anybody who ever read a history book knew that.

Oz made his way blindly down the stairs, trying to get his focus back and hoping he wouldn't trip and brain himself on the bannister. Damp, warm, freshly shampooed Lila was a goddamned menace. Putting her back down and going downstairs was so anathema to what he wanted, his teeth ached.

"If you're wondering where the broom is," Annette said when he came back to the kitchen, "I've got no idea."

Oz waved that away—the reason Mama had seen Lila's delectable butt was because she'd found the broom and was determined to sweep—and said in a low voice, "I'm worried about Lila."

"Don't fret, I'm sure she's covering her butt."

"Hilarious. But that's not what I meant."

"I knew what you meant. And yes, you're right to worry. Lila may yet cause complications. I believe she cares about Sally—she never smells aggressive or angry around her—but who can predict how she'll deal with the rest of us, knowing what she knows? As she herself reminds us, we don't know her terribly well."

"I feel like I'm getting there, though." Kind of. A little. Maybe?

"But even if her intentions are benign," Annette continued, "she could unwittingly jeopardize any one of us."

"Uh. Sure. All that stuff. Everything you just said, I'm worried about. Mostly. But she had a house fire, too. A bad one. And now she's taken us in."

"Us?"

"Shut up. You saw how she wouldn't go into Mama's house after the fire was out, right? This house has two fireplaces and they're both spotless. She hasn't stocked anything to make fires with, either. And it might be because she's still unpacking, but I doubt it."

Annette raised her eyebrows. "And?"

"I'm just worried. I don't want to churn up bad memories."

"Too late, I suspect."

"And I noticed you left out how *we* could unwittingly endanger *her*. Whoever set the fire didn't care if anyone, including Mama, got hurt," he said. "Now she's taken us in—"

"Again: us?"

"Again, shut your pie-maw. I'm saying she might have a target on her back now, just like Sally."

"Fair point," Annette admitted. "But you're assuming whoever has done these things wants to hurt Sally. What if the opposite proves true?"

"Jesus." Oz had a little trouble digesting that one. "Anyone who commits arson to 'help' an orphaned cub is not someone I want to hang around with."

"Nor should Sally," Mama added, coming back into the kitchen. "Or anyone."

Annette opened her mouth to add something, then hesitated. That was so out of character, Oz immediately gave her his full attention. "What?"

"It's a bit off topic. Mama…are you sure letting Caro and Dev make their own den is wise? I'm not talking about how they're trying to avoid the consequences of teaching a child to circumvent the entirety of IPA's phone network. But given Caro's history…"

Given Caro's history, she had an affinity for small, dark spaces. Given Caro's history, after being kidnapped and kept in a cage for two years, she tended to think the roughest, most basic necessities—a roof, regular meals, clothing—were vast luxuries often out of her reach.

In short, given Caro's history, she likely thought the shed was as good as a luxury suite at the Waldorf.

"I see why you're concerned, m'girl. But I know you've also seen Caro's progress in the last six months… Remember how long it took me to get her to stop sleeping in the basement? And if she prefers her own small dark den—or at least the illusion of one—maybe that's not something we should try to take away from her just now. She sees her therapist every week, she's an absolute darling when she's not being an absolute pain, and as everyone in this room knows, it takes time to get back the equilibrium other people stole."

Annette didn't say anything, just inclined her head. She had a master's in social development, but it wasn't the first time she'd deferred to Mama's judgement when it came to traumatized cubs.

"Besides, Caro knows someone set her new home on fire. If denning in a shed thirty feet back from *this* house makes her feel more in control, for now, we should leave her to it. Now hush, Sally's coming back."

"They're sleeping," the cub announced. "Really hard. They're just izzossted."

"Exhausted," Annette corrected. "And my ass they are. Sorry, Mama."

"No, 'ass' seems appropriate. Well, let them stay out a bit longer." Mama found some Tupperware, then began ladling chili into it.

"You don't have to do that," Annette said. "You can just ladle it directly into my mouth."

"No one wants to see that, dear," Mama Mac said mildly. "Lila! I've got what you asked for!"

"Oh my God with the yelling," Lila commented, fully dressed and walking past them with an armful of blankets. Impressive speed for a Stable. Her hair was still damp; Oz wanted to touch it, then rub his face in it.

Hmm, better not.

"Sally, grab the door for me, wouldja?"

"Okay, Lila!" The cub complied, Lila went out, the cub followed, and Oz watched it all, bemused, then picked up a dry-erase marker and turned to the whiteboard. *Focus. Vulnerable cub who may or may not be an orphan should be your focus.*

Mama Mac started pulling bowls out of the cupboard. "Annette, m'dear, would you check that drawer for silverware? Then we can—ah, thanks. Napkins? There they are…"

Annette cleared her throat. "Ah. Oz?"

"Yeah?"

"You just wrote *sabotage fake death Kama-Rupa Kama-Rupa pilot error K-R.*"

"The hell I—oh." As he straightened and stood back from the board, he could see it. *Deny or embrace?* "It's a brainstorming session, isn't it? That means everything's on the table." *Embracing has never failed me!*

"Oz, what in God's name is going on with you?"

Except in this instance.

"Brainstorming! That's what's going on. Here's what you can't deal with, Annette." He jabbed the dry erase marker in her direction to punctuate his words. "I'm so open-minded, so ready to discuss any possibility, that it—it creates storms. In my brain!" That sounded nice and normal, right?

"You do understand that's nothing at all to do with what happened to Sam and Sue Smalls, yes? Oh, and that *Kama-Rupa* is not real?" Annette asked with the slow care of addressing someone who wasn't entirely sane. "That modern-day Shifters aren't drawn to a mate who is the physical and spiritual manifestation of their fondest wish and greatest desire? Drawn to that perfect person so when they die, their animal spirits live on together forever? It is deeply odd that I find myself explaining this to you."

"Of course I know it's not real," he snapped. "I'm not a child. That'd be like—like—" He tried to think of a parallel, but there was nothing in the tank.

"Like saying everything found in Song of Songs is a modern blueprint for finding a soul mate. Or God taking a rib from Adam to make Eve, his spiritual and physical mate, and they were together forever despite earning the Big Guy's wrath. They're ancient stories that don't carry over into this century."

"Or *Romeo and Juliet.*"

"No, Mama."

"*A Midsummer Night's Dream*?"

"No."

"Rhett Butler and Scarlett O'Hara?"

"…well, they were made for each other, but there wasn't anything spiritual about it."

"*Anyway.*" Oz turned back to the board and made frantic adjustments with the eraser. "Brainstorming, remember? Let's get back to it."

Chapter 33

"Sally, get that door open, would you?"

"Okay!"

With the girl's help, Lila brought in blankets and the small bucket of chili, still steaming because after covering it tightly, she had wrapped it in one of the blankets. There were already paper plates and plastic cutlery in the shed, which weren't green, but throwing them all out to facilitate buying metal versions wasn't green, either.

And now what was this?

It's not every day I see a fox curled up with a black wolf. It's not even every month. The kids had shifted, probably because the temp was dropping.

"Don't worry, it's not Macropi." Lila immediately realized what a dumb comment that was; the kids had probably known it was her before she knocked. This was brought home to her when Caro cracked open an eye, rolled it, then appeared to go back to sleep. "Also, constantly throwing shade without saying a word might be your superpower."

Behind her, Sally let out a belated giggle, and half a second later, a plump bear cub was clambering up on the cot and curling up behind Dev.

"Y'know, given that you guys are constantly flinging your clothes all over the place, I'd think you'd take better care of them. Wow, that sounded really curmudgeonly out loud. You kids stay off my lawn! There, now I've gone full curmudgeon." She shook out two of the blankets and draped it over them, then neatly stacked the others at the end of the sleeping bag. "Chili's on the shelf. Try to eat some before it gets cold. And the thermos is full of hot chocolate. Okay? Helloooooo? Grunt once for yes, twice for no."

"Nnnnnffff."

"No idea which of you did that, but okay." Lila couldn't help smiling at the picture the kids made, curled up nose to tail to conserve heat. She was reminded again of Sally's unusual coloring, the reddish-orange fur contrasting the black, the cream-colored claws, and that got her thinking about Garsea's coloring.

Now that she better understood the nature of those in Macropi's care, she realized that the white tips weren't artificial highlights but her natural hair color, just like Berne's natural color was deep brown with a violet tint. What animal had deep brown fur with white tips? She'd have to look it up.

Not that she cared. She was being neighborly, which wasn't the same thing. Right? Right. Her interest was purely scientific. *And* for the purpose of self-preservation. It paid to find out everything you could about the people around you. Especially Oz. In particular, Oz. That wasn't compassion, it was common sense. And a need to run her fingers through his Caesar haircut. And over his abs. And the abs of his ass. But mostly it was all about the common sense.

Chapter 34

LILA CAME BACK INSIDE TO CATCH THE TAIL END OF AN argument between Garsea and Oz.

"No, *you* use the green one."

"What difference does it make, you clown?"

"The kids are snuggled down and have eaten," she announced. "I am officially washing my hands of them. And of you, too. Also, you know you've misspelled *syndicate*, right?"

"It's purposeful," Garsea replied.

The whiteboard was a mash of loopy scribbles. In addition to *Sindicate*, Oz had written several names and places, with arrows connecting some of them and circles grouping others together. *Caro* and *Sindicate* were in the same bubble; *Dev*'s bubble intersected it. The name *Lund* was connected to *Sindicate*; someone named *Wapiti* was, too. *Magnus Berne* was in *Sally*'s circle along with her parents. There was even a sketch of a little plane, with arrows pointing to *sabotage?*, *forced to land?*, *parachute?*, *only Sam faked death? WHY???*, and *pilot error?* And something had been erased in big sloppy swoops; all she could make out was a *k* and part of an *r*.

"We're trying to think of motives someone would have to steal, hurt, and/or kill the Smalls family."

Lila found the names and arrows all over the board disquieting and reacted with a dumb joke instead of processing in silence like an adult. "Is cuteness a factor? Because Sally's loaded with all the cute. And her coloring is pretty striking. Sun bear, right? I looked them up. They're rare. Tagged as Vulnerable by people who keep track of stuff like that." She was very much afraid she was babbling but couldn't stop. "Maybe someone wanted her because she's an exotic catch?"

When no one replied, she added, "Well, maybe only actual sun bears are in trouble. Not weresunbears. Weresuns?"

More silence. But not like they were judging her, or patiently waiting for her to stop babbling. More like she'd stumbled over something. *No, no. Couldn't be right.*

"What? Oh, come on. I was kidding! Why would someone want a little kid just because she's got cool-looking fur?"

She saw Garsea and Oz trade glances, and then Oz said, "We have to tell you something."

"Ohhhhhhh boy."

"Something you need to keep to yourself."

"Is there booze? One of the boxes in the kitchen has booze. I feel like I might need booze."

Oz walked over and gently guided her toward one of the kitchen chairs. She could actually feel her body temperature trying to climb, and he was barely touching her. She squashed the warring impulses to snuggle closer and shove him away. "And the only reason we're telling you this is because you put yourself in danger to help Sally and Dev, which might've made you a target."

"Vodka, beer, alcoholic seltzer, mead, mouthwash… I'm not picky."

"Six months ago, Annette and David exposed a syndicate that had been making money off of child trafficking."

She paused to digest that. "Okay. That's completely fucking horrible, but it happens."

Oz was now pacing back and forth in front of the whiteboard. "Yep. However, *these* completely fucking horrible people weren't just targeting juveniles. They were targeting a particular sect of Shifter kits: the runaways, the addicts, the orphans shuffling through the foster system. The homeless, the sick and injured Shifters…"

"There are homeless Shifter kids? Kits, I mean?" Lila wasn't sure why she was shocked. Being able to grow fur didn't guarantee a roof over your head. How very fucking depressing.

"Yeah, unfortunately. Anyway, these guys would zero in on at-risk cubs."

"Like Caro."

"Exactly like Caro," he said, tapping the circle intersecting Caro and the name Lund. "This guy, Lund, was managing the day-to-day stuff—picking the cubs, breaking them, arranging for some of them to be shipped overseas, juggling the money... He hid the profits in twenty-two bank accounts and eleven shell corporations. He was in charge of all the ops. Like an office manager for Satan."

"Please tell me Lund was cut into a thousand pieces and those pieces were then set on fire and the fire was doused with battery acid."

"No, he was shot to death in his own apartment. Bled out in minutes."

"Too quick."

"Damned right," Garsea muttered.

"Anyway, he had a warehouse down by the river where they'd break the cubs, then sell them as exotic pets."

Must have a drink. Right now. "Did you say *pets*?"

"Yeah."

"We speculated it was their twisted version of, say, tropical fish." Garsea was apparently on board with Team Booze, because she'd fixed herself something, then set an orange drink in front of Lila that she prayed had at least an inch of vodka. "Or a potbellied pig."

She sipped. *Two inches! Excellent.* "That must have been horrible. Stumbling across that must have been truly horrible. I'm sorry. But I'm glad you got them."

"It was Annette's case; she's the one who figured it all out."

"With Oz's help," Garsea put in quickly. "He's the one who figured out about the overseas accounts and the shell corps."

Oz ducked his head a little, clearly pleased Garsea had given credit where it was due. In that moment, he looked like a shy boy happy to get his big sister's praise. "But, Lila, that's not the worst of it."

"Jesus. Hit me."

"The worst of it was, Lund wasn't breaking Shifter juveniles just to be a humongous dickcheese. He was breaking them—*house*-breaking them—for syndicate members who wanted their very own pet Shifters. But also..."

He trailed off and they both looked at her and she didn't want to finish the sentence but she had to finish the sentence because the end of the sentence was perfectly, horribly obvious: "But also Stables. This Lund guy, he was selling werebears and werewolves and—and werefoxes and werelabradors and wereroos, he was selling them to people like me."

"*Not* people like you," Oz said firmly.

"People who know about werewolves and keep quiet, but only because they want to own one for their very own. Like slaves."

"Told you it was bad."

"But you got him." She pointed at the Lund circle, which should be in red and scribbled over with great big loops of black. "He's dead, you saved Caro. So why would you...d'you think some are still out there?"

"We're very nearly positive," Garsea replied as Lila drained half her glass. "Because it was never just Lund. He was simply—how'd you put it? Satan's office manager. We had a mole at IPA. She would help Lund target vulnerable weres. Not to worry," she added, anticipating Lila's next question. "I killed her and ate her." She smiled with a great many teeth, and Lila felt every hair on the back of her neck come to attention as she recalled an earlier conversation in that very room.

Be careful! If you make Oz mad, his sister will eat you.

Please tell me that's hyperbole.

"Okay. Now I know why you work for IPA but don't want to work *at* IPA. Because where there was one, there could be another.

You're pretty sure work is a safe place to do this stuff, but not a hundred percent. Am I getting that right?" She couldn't imagine what it was like to find out a colleague—someone whose job description meant they had to be on your side—was complicit in the trafficking of *children*. "So Lund is dead, and the Sindicate member at IPA, she's dead. And not just dead. Devoured, even. So, super-duper dead."

"As well as a few SAS foot soldiers," Garsea added.

"SAS?"

Garsea looked away while Oz rolled his eyes and replied, "They're a fucking embarrassment. The Shifter version of the Ku Klux Klan."

"Oh, charming." But it wasn't a surprise once she thought about it. Garsea and Oz and Auberon and probably Sally could all take her in a fight. They were faster, stronger, and at least one of them didn't mind eating people. No surprise there were some supremacists in the mix. "Was there a war, like there was just before the KKK was founded? A reaction to, what would you call it—changing social mores?"

"Not a war," Oz replied. And was he having trouble meeting her gaze? "More like a few lame skirmishes that most people never noticed."

"Given the sudden lack of eye contact from you both, I'm pretty sure you're downplaying."

"It's embarrassing," Oz admitted. "Ten years ago, there was an attempted takeover. A bunch of SAS assholes and their allies staged a takeover attempt in Shakopee, which was gonna be the starting off point for a worldwide coup. They disguised it as a protest against climate change."

"Are you talking about the Kiyuska thing?"

"Unfortunately," Garsea replied sourly.

"But that really *was* about climate change. It made national news. It's why they picked Shakopee, the town was built near the

Mdewakanton Sioux burial mounds. I read about it when I was researching whether or not to move here."

"That's not the only reason the SAS picked Shakopee."

"Well, sure. They also wanted to push a specific narrative: 'We nearly wiped out this entire tribe, and P.S. we're also destroying the planet, so pay attention and fix everything right n—'"

She cut herself off. Because there was something odd about that protest. It didn't make national news solely because of the violence, or the unprecedented number of fatal casualties. There was something about the police response. They'd been essentially ineffective, because…

Her brain found the fact, grabbed it. "Their tear gas didn't work. None of their crowd control stuff had much of an effect."

"The Shakopee Mdewakanton Sioux are part of a sub-tribe called Kiyuska. And Kiyuska means 'rule breaker,'" Oz said. "Want to guess how they came by it? Or why the settlers coming west wanted to kill them all so badly?"

"It wasn't just Native Americans vs. encroaching Europeans, which was horrifying enough," Lila said slowly. "It was also about Shifters." Three hundred years ago, natives who could change into wolves and bears and possums would have been interpreted by Europeans as the basest of sorcerers practicing all manner of witchcraft. An evil not to be borne, monsters who had to be wiped out to the last man, woman, and child.

"Indigenous Shifters," Garsea clarified. "Nearly all of whom were wiped out. And so Shakopee was to be a staging area for the ultimate Shifter takeover. It didn't work," she added, anticipating the question, "because sanity prevailed."

"After a bunch of them died," Oz pointed out. "It took a while for sanity to get the upper hand."

"Enough of us—well, not 'us,' we were all teenagers at the time, and kids like Sally hadn't been whelped yet—but enough Shifters found out and put a stop to it."

"Why?"

Garsea stared at her. "I'm sorry, Lila, did you just ask me why Shifters didn't let reactionary racists with delusions of superiority attempt the bloodiest of coups, which ultimately would have resulted in a six-figure body count *at best*?"

"But you guys *are* superior. And we *are* ruining the planet."

"But that isn't the way, Lila." Garsea sounded equal parts exasperated and sad. "Obviously that's not the way. Even if they had only killed half the Stables in the world, it's still billions dead. So we put a stop to it before the movement could catch fire and spread all over the world. It wouldn't have been a coup. With the population so reduced, it would have been Armageddon."

"Huh. Well, on behalf of my species, thanks."

"On behalf of mine, you're welcome."

"And I've got a bunch of questions about Shakopee for later." So much to research; the mere thought made her giddy. Were there Shifter libraries? Shifter databases? There had to be. "Thanks for indulging my curiosity. But getting back to the point, Shakopee was the jumping off point, and if it had gone as planned, there were SAS sleeper cells all over the world ready to do the same thing, so long Stables, all hail furry Shifters? Right?"

Oz nodded. "Nutshell."

"Nobody would ever 'hail furry Shifters,' but I see your point."

"But that's kind of what you're dealing with right now, don't you think? You got the Sindicate clerks, but not the boss. Or bosses."

"Precisely our fear," Garsea replied. "All we did was shut down the cell in Minneapolis. That was all we *could* do. But the Sindicate could be anywhere. Everywhere. That isn't a misspelling, by the way—it's how Caro refers to them."

Jesus. Lila had, for a minute, forgotten about Caro's involvement. *House-training? Breaking kids to be pets? How long did they have her? How did she get away? No wonder she never talks and loves tool sheds and constantly throws silent snark!*

She stomped on the questions before they could escape her big mouth. That was Caro's business, just like the destruction of Lila's first home was hers.

"It's only been six months," Oz said, picking up the narrative. "Maybe their remaining membership decided they've laid low long enough. Maybe they need more product. There's also a good possibility they're hard up for money. We were able to freeze millions in Lund's funds."

"So the Sindicate came out of hiding and targeted Sally? Because she checks a lot of their boxes—rare, vulnerable, almost an orphan?"

"It's one theory," Garsea admitted.

"But think about all the things that must've happened for that to be true. For starters, Sally's only lived in Minnesota...what? Couple of weeks?" When Garsea and Oz nodded, Lila continued. "So they would have *just* spotted her. And they were going to grab her...how? By sabotaging Berne's plane five hundred miles from here, when the Smalls family didn't even know they were going to need it until a day or two before the crash?

"And then Sam got off the plane somehow, didn't die, called Sally at IPA and told her to...hang out with me? Why? Did he know about the Sindicate? If he did, why did he and his wife leave Sally to fly east? And where the hell *is* he?"

"Those are all good—"

"And where does Berne fit in? Is he in on it? Or just a bystander? And why try to burn Macropi's house down? How does that help them get their claws on Sally? All it did was piss us off and put everyone on their guard."

"And wreck my carpets and some of the drapes," Macropi added. "And my houseplants!"

"And now there are fire inspectors and insurance guys running around the neighborhood, and trust me, your neighbors are all gawking, too. Nothing brings out the lookie-loos like a house fire. So why draw that kind of attention?"

"As I said." Garsea, who'd gotten up to freshen their drinks, handed her another screwdriver. "It's a theory."

"Look, I'm not trying to run you down…"

"Oh, we're aware." Garsea smirked. "If that's what you were doing, I doubt there'd be any confusion on our end."

"Touché. All I'm saying is, sometimes it's not a great big conspiracy. Sometimes it's bad luck and pilot error. Sally's mom was sick—maybe that ties in somehow."

"True," Garsea agreed. "And I have to wonder if we're missing the obvious. Perhaps Sam Smalls parachuted out of that plane?"

The shocked laugh was out before Lila could lock it back. "Sorry. But if he jumped, he's dead. Simple as that. You can't just shrug into a parachute pack and jump out of a random plane. It has to be specially modified, there are too many snag points. Your momentum is the same as the airplane's when you jump, which is problematic for all sorts of reasons… When I was researching it a few years ago, I ran across a story where a crash in Finland killed eight skydivers. A parachute isn't a magic wand."

"You really like to research," Garsea observed.

"I fucking love to research."

"Yeah, those are all good points," Oz admitted. "Nadia did check on Sally's pilot qualifications. She got her license years ago, just after flight school but before she got out of the Twopers."

"Flight school? And troopers? You guys have your own military?"

"Twopers. Slang for the Two Percenters," Annette explained. "Which isn't even accurate, it's arguably four percent. And it's nothing so organized. More like a militia whose primary function is more about protecting the community and our territory than going on the offense."

Two percenters? Or four? Does it indicate the Shifter population? "Okay. So maybe not pilot error. But maybe not sabotage, either."

Annette shrugged. "It's what we have so far. We'll keep at it."

"Good." They were using her, Lila realized, letting her bounce ideas off them to (hopefully) inspire cognition that would lead to an answer. "And I hate to admit it, but it looks like the whiteboard was a good idea. Right, Macropi?" Lila turned around. "Macropi? She was here two seconds ago."

"Yeah, operative word *was*. First, she was tense since we're sharing deep dark secrets with you. Then when you were appropriately grossed out and horrified by the Sindicate, she was relieved and approving. And then she got upset all over again about what Caro went through, so she slipped out to check on the cubs she knows are perfectly snug and safe. And when she comes in, she's gonna overcompensate for all of it because she hates the thought of the Sindicate and of any of us being in danger. So she's probably gonna b—"

The kitchen door twanged. "Who wants apple pie?"

"Me," they all said at once. And Oz gave her such a warm smile, Lila couldn't help grinning back.

Chapter 35

"Thanks for coming out with me."

"No biggie. I needed some fresh air after spending the afternoon in a field."

Oz chuckled and swung into the parking garage. After pie, after Annette left for home and the cubs were settled, he'd asked Lila if she wanted to go for a drive or grab a coffee, expecting a polite "under no circumstances." For whatever reason, she not only said yes, but packed a tote and practically dragged him to his car. From there, she directed him to the Hamm Building for reasons unknown, and they'd made the drive in no time thanks to zero traffic at such an hour.

He had no idea why she'd wanted to come.

He wasn't dumb enough to question it.

She wanted to go back to the Hamm Building, where her office was? Okay. To check on her "patients" and/or perform more stuffed animal surgery? No problem, to the Hamm Building they would go. He'd take her to the Empire State Building. The Golden Gate Bridge. The Goderich Salt Mine. Pripyat. Wherever she wanted.

Lila slung her tote over one shoulder and fell into step with him as they left the car and took the elevator to the offices. "I just wanna check my intakes and then show you somethin'."

"Sure." She was a bit tipsy, which was to be expected after she'd sucked down two of Annette's notoriously vodka-heavy screwdrivers. ("It should not taste like a breakfast drink," Annette had explained. "It should taste like something that will knock you on your ass and also oranges.")

She brought him to her office suite on the second floor,

humming as she unlocked it and disabled the security system. It took him a few seconds to realize she was humming the theme from *Psycho*. Not the bit from the shower scene. The first movement by Herrmann, which *The Simpsons* used in one of their "Treehouse of Horrors" episodes.

She had quite a few Priority Mail boxes waiting for her, which she quickly shuffled through, then stacked indifferently on the nearest table. "Nothing that can't wait until Monday," she said. "And two of them are repeat offenders! If you don't want your manic toddler to tear the head off his stuffed snakes, stop giving him stuffed snakes."

"These kids today," Oz sighed, because he couldn't help it.

"I'm gonna lock up and then take you upstairs, if that's—"

"Okay." Upstairs, downstairs, the roof, a parking garage, a closet: it made no difference. Never in life had he wanted to follow someone while not caring about the destination. It was exhilarating and a little frightening. "I need to hit the Men's, and I'll find you."

"Okay. See you in a couple. Think you'll like this."

He was sure he would. Drinks? A second chili-less dinner? A moonlit walk on the roof with a biting wind and the wind chill hovering at twenty degrees? Baling hay? A tonsillectomy? He was up for whatever the curly-haired devil/darling had in mind.

First, the loo. He washed his hands, looked up at the mirror, then swallowed a groan of horror. He liked to think that going without sleep, skipping meals, and obsessing over *Kama-Rupa* when not obsessing over the Smalls made him look lean and dangerous, but the dark circles under his eyes made him look like an addled raccoon. Nothing to be done about it, so he walked to the end of the hall, went up a flight, took a left and another flight, and there she was, obligingly holding half of a double door open when she spotted him at the end of the hall. "You didn't know where I was going. How'd you find me up here?"

Oz tapped the side of his nose.

"Oh. You're saying I smell."

He was so appalled, he nearly fell down the stairs he'd just climbed. "What? No! You don't smell! I mean, you do smell. We all smell. Everybody smells. Including you. But it's okay! You smell wonderful. Not that I've been going around smelling you. Because I haven't. That would be weird. I can't help smelling you, though. I mean, I can, but not…oh thank God you're fucking with me."

She giggled. "Sorry. It's just so easy. You get all stammer-y, like Hugh Grant on Benadryl. C'mere, look at this."

He obliged, stepping into the low-lit room as the door shut behind them.

Whoa. "This is amazing," he said, goggling like a yokel.

"Right?"

"I mean, it's a big building, but *that* big?"

"I know."

"But why is it here?"

She was just standing there, hands on hips, grinning. Delighted by his amazement. "Because the Hamm Building used to show movies."

"It was a movie theater?"

"Movie *palace*," she corrected with relish. "And not just any movie palace. Back in the day, it was a palace that held the largest, most expensive, dazzling, amazing super-cool breathtaking huge movie theater in the entire Midwest."

"You're *really* excited about this."

"The new owners decided to open up a brewery and other offices, and they always meant to do something with the theater, but they ran out of money. And all the subzagent—subsequent— owners, they could never figure out if they wanted it all torn out or fixed up. So fast forward seventy-five years, we get this."

This was a movie theater spread out in front of him that could easily seat hundreds, in the big old-fashioned velvet chairs from the 1920s that could accommodate the widest of bottoms. There were close to a dozen rows to a section, forty-odd seats to a row, and three sections of seats: closest to the stage, the middle, and the nosebleed seats. The door she'd brought them through was in the middle. He stepped forward and looked behind him; the projectionist booth looked big enough to be a living room. He felt small; it wasn't unlike standing in an empty stadium.

"Jesus. This isn't a theater, it's a temple."

"Yes! Can't you picture it? The intense awesomeness of it all?" He was amazed; this was as animated as he'd ever seen her, and she was a goddamned vision, practically vibrating with excitement, anticipation, and vodka. "Just *thinking* about all the films they showed makes me want a big Coke with lots of crushed ice. And popcorn. But not just any popcorn. Stale movie popcorn that only gets switched out every week or so."

"You want a Coke with crushed ice? I'll get you a Coke with crushed ice." He wasn't sure he could find stale popcorn on short notice, but he could crush ice, by God…

"Fuck ice." She pulled a thermos and a couple of bottles of Coke out of her tote. "Rum will be fine."

"On top of the screwdrivers?"

"Oh, is that what they were? I thought Garsea gave me glasses of vodka with a tablespoon of orange juice for color."

"What can I say? She's got the constitution of a horse. Never, ever tell her I compared her to a horse."

She snickered. "I'll take your horse-shaming to my grave." She opened one of the Cokes, took a couple of swigs, then filled it back up with rum. "You've probably deduced by now that you are the designated driver this evening."

"I had a feeling."

Twenty minutes later, they were watching her laptop, which she'd carefully set on the ledge between the front and center sections. Their choices had been *Cabin in the Woods*, *It*, *Roxanne*, *Black Panther*, *John Wick: Chapter 2*, *The Sixth Sense*, *Finding Dory*, season one of *Salt Fat Acid Heat*, *It Chapter Two*, *Maleficent*, and every *Toy Story* movie.

"God, you're eclectic."

Lila looked oddly pleased. "Thank you. D'you know the best part of *It Chapter Two*?" she asked out of nowhere. "It's that Mike Hanlon gets to live in a library. We're supposed to feel sorry for him because he was the Loser the turtle decided to leave behind as a night watchman, for almost three decades. We're supposed to feel he got cheated because his other friends went on to found their own companies or make it big in the arts and got rich. Right?"

"Right."

"But Mike gets. To live. In a library!"

"I never thought about it like that," Oz admitted.

"Yeah, well, my hidden genius helps me spot stuff like that. You're welcome."

"And you like the *Toy Story* franchise?"

"Obviously. The best part is when the Fixer makes Woody like-new again."

"You're the only person who watches the *Toy Story* franchise for a glimpse of the geezer who fixes dolls," he declared.

"That's enough ageism from you, pal."

They settled in for the latest *Toy Story* movie. Lila concentrated on drinking, and Oz concentrated on regulating his breathing when she let her head rest on his shoulder. He supposed they could have watched the movie on her laptop in her office downstairs—or anywhere, really; that was the beauty of laptops and Netflix—but he was glad she'd brought him to the theater. He felt like she'd cracked the door to herself a bit, letting him have a glimpse. The trick was to stay put and be patient and hope she opened the door wider.

"I've lived here all my life and I had no idea," he marveled. "No idea this was here."

"Yeah? Well, the device you use for social media? It has a search engine, too."

"Seriously," he said, shaking his head. "I can't get over it."

"Oh, goody, you're one of those people who talks through movies."

"Sorry," he replied, and shut up.

Thirty seconds later: "Are there really Shifter homeless kids?"

"Well." Oz shifted his weight, hoping she wouldn't think he was subtly trying to shrug off her head. "Yeah."

"Well," she began, then paused for so long he was sure that part of the conversation was over. "I guess that's not…all bad. If anything, Shifter kids are better equipped to be on the street, right? Even if they're country kids, and there's not a street to be out on?"

How the hell to answer that? "That's…a good point. Uh. But I think we can agree being homeless sucks regardless."

"Exactly!" She sat up and smacked his chest with her fist for emphasis. "It can happen to anybody. And it's not like it's the kid's fault."

"No, of course not."

She settled back. "Except now I'm thinking about all those times people thought they found a wolf or a dog or whatever and didn't know it was a *person*. Can you imagine some poor Shifter kid locked up at a pet shelter? Imagine the freak-out when they changed back!"

"The freak-out would be colossal," he agreed. "Or maybe not. You handled it pretty well."

"High stress threshold. Comes from having an eventful adolescence."

I'll bet. He was torn: on one hand, he was dying to know what

Lila had lived through that left her ready to rescue cubs, face down werewolves, prep for anything from natural disasters to arson, casually pack heat depending on the occasion, and fly to an Iowa field in the company of a werebear and the aforementioned werewolf, all while demonstrating an unshakeable calm.

On the other hand, he was sure the answers would infuriate him and make him want to track down and grievously injure anyone who had ever messed with the *Kama* to his *Rupa*.

Except she wasn't. Because Annette had been annoying *and* right: Lila Kai was not the physical and spiritual embodiment of his fondest desire that his soul cried out for so they could be together for all eternity. Even thinking about it made it sound

(*true*)

ridiculous.

"Garsea told me werebears are rare bears. She said it jus' like that, like a chant, almost. But I gotta say, for a rare subspecies—that's what you call 'em, right?—there are a lot of 'em."

"Four is not a lot."

"*Obviously* there's more than four. I'm just sayin'."

"It's actually kind of ironic." He finished his Coke and reached down for another one, moving the thermos of rum to one side. The half-empty thermos of rum. Add something new to Lila's list of attributes: she could put it away like a lumberjack. "Lots of Shifters go their whole lives without meeting another werebear, but you saw one your first night here. Bad luck."

She shrugged. "Or good. Depends on who you're talking to. But listen—since meeting you guys, I've been thinking about history."

"Me, too," he admitted.

"So, for instance, were the Salem burnings about witches or Shifters? Because I can see some poor werepossum or whatever being accused and then getting burned up."

"There have been…misunderstandings." *Gah. Stop being cryptic.* "And there's no such thing as werepossums. I'm pretty sure." Werecoyotes, yep. Wereroos, check. Werewolverines, yup. Werepossums, wereraccoons, werevoles, nope.

"Yeah, well. Misunderstandings can happen to anybody."

Oz took a breath and plunged. "How long were you homeless?"

She just looked at him with those blue eyes. She'd left the glasses at home. He wasn't sure if that meant she was starting to trust him or was just tired of wearing them. Her mouth moved, almost like she was tasting her response. "Thirteen months, seventeen days."

"After the fire."

"Yeah."

"I'm sorry."

"Why? Did you set the fire?"

"No. But I'll be happy to track and crack the person who did."

"Then you'll have to crack me, Oz." At his stunned silence, she added, "The tracking part you've already got down."

Chapter 36

"OH, BOY. THE LOOK ON YOUR FACE."

"My face is fine."

"Yeah, it is," Lila muttered. "Annoyingly so. Look, I can see you're about to burst with questions, so here's the CliffsNotes version. I never knew my dad, but given my mom's terrible taste, I can only assume he was an asshole. My mom worked shit jobs to support us and in her spare time—and there wasn't much of it—was a hoarder. You probably didn't know that someone who doesn't make much money can also be a hoarder, but I'm here to tell you they can."

She's sharing intimate details with me! "Okay." *Calm down. Be cool. Don't smile.*

"It was March and we were living in a little house in North Dakota. Up by the border, y'know? Bottineau. Home of the Winter Park and Tommy the Turtle."

"Seriously?"

"Very, *very* cold. The living room had an old fireplace and I decided to get a fire going. I forgot to put the screen back, and there were tons of magazines and newspapers in the living room. Everything went up."

"Jesus. Were you hurt?"

"Barely. It was way worse for my mom. She just…fell apart. She never recovered. Our relationship is—what's the word? Strained. Or is it estranged? It's whatever word fits best when I'm not semi-drunk."

Semi-drunk? What does she consider all-the-way drunk? She's got the constitution of…well…me! "She must have been terrified. You both could have been killed."

"Terrified?" Lila chuckled, and there was no humor in it at all. "She was mad because I burned up all her stuff, Oz. She's still mad."

He sat and stared and tried to process. And he would sit still and concentrate for however long it took, because this was a delicate subject and he didn't want to say the wrong thing except nope, his brain was ignoring the *process this weird shit before you open your big mouth* command. "Well, your mom's a worthless idiot who doesn't know the true value of anything. Oh, shit." He rubbed his forehead. "I shouldn't say that about anyone with a mental illness, much less your mother."

"It's fine." And apparently it was; Lila seemed more amused than anything else.

"So you were on your own?"

"Yeah."

"For thirteen months and seventeen days."

"Yeah."

"You couldn't—I mean, your mom didn't—"

"She didn't want to look at me. Like I said—I burned up all her stuff. So I slept on a lot of couches. And parks, when it got nicer. It *does* get nicer in Bottineau. Y'know, eventually. Then some cousins stepped in. I bounced around for a bit—my rep as a vengeful firebug prob'ly preceded me—and then I was eighteen. I still bounced, but by then it was by choice. And I bounced here. It was all apartments, before. This house, where I am now? It's the next step. Curs will sell it to me eventually. If I stick it out."

Oz hardly heard her. "Homeless by fire. Then essentially orphaned. On your own for years, and…"

"Ask, Oz. You know you want to. Why d'you think I decided to suck down half my weight in booze tonight? I knew I was going to show you things." She waved a hand, indicating the palace. "Tell you things. And I promised myself I'd answer anything you asked. I don't know why. Don't ask me why."

"Are you—do you feel compelled to do that? To share things with me? Like you didn't have a choice?"

"Huh?"

"Do you believe in love at first sight?"

She laughed and shook her head. "No, Oz. Lust at first sight, sure. But love takes time. I oughta know—I'm pushing thirty and haven't found it."

"Yes. Right. I—I agree. But how could you protect yourself with no cover? And no den? Home, I mean. Did anyone ever... when you were on the streets, did some people ask—or make—" He cut himself off and met her impatient gaze.

"What do *you* think?" she asked with bitter humor. "It's not like they were interested in conversation." She thumped his chest again. "It doesn't matter now."

"Lila. Of course it matters."

"No, it *doesn't*. It's done, it's over. I have a home now. *Mine*. And nobody chases me away from it. If I leave, if I move on again, it's because *I* say so. But I won't. I planted fucking basil and dill, Oz. So it doesn't *matter* if werebears go through my underwear drawer or Magnus fucking Berne—or some other jackass from their shared past—did something to Sally's folks. I'm staying. So internalize that. Make it a fact in your mind, like two plus two equals four. Get it?"

"Yes, ma'am." And now a new emotion was penetrating his shock

(*oh my God she just wanted to be warm and her mom BLAMED HER*)

and dismay

(*if anyone forced her I will find them and eat their hearts*)

and this new emotion was delight. Which was wrong, probably. Nothing about this should please him. (In fact, hearing her dismiss love at first sight was depressing beyond belief.) But everything about Lila *did*. He'd wondered—they all had—how she could be so calm. Why she didn't call the cops that first night. And why she always came back to the Curs(ed) House. Now he had his answer. She remade herself after the fire took everything: material goods and her mother's fractured, distracted love. She was a woman with enormous pride in her self-sufficiency who was wary of cops.

Or the short version: she planted basil and dill.

He caught her fist before she could thump him again, held it gently. "Thank you for telling me this, Lila."

"Thanks for being horrified, but only on my behalf." Her gaze slid away. "I was wondering how you'd take the news that you're squatting with a firebug."

"You're *not* a firebug." Then: "Squatting?"

"Again: I never invited *you*. Just the others. *Ergo*, you're a squatter."

He carefully unclenched her fingers and held her hand. She let him. She was staring owlishly at their entwined fingers, but she wasn't reaching for a weapon, which he took as an encouraging sign.

"Lila? What are we doing?"

"You're asking *me*?" She was still staring at their entwined fingers. "Whatever this is, it's terrifying."

"*This* scares you?" He almost laughed. "Not the fire or the Shifters or plane crashes that may or may not have been engineered? Romance is the real danger?" *Romance might be a strong word. Mutual like-liking?*

She met his gaze. "It never works out for me. Not once. They're too weird, or I am. They don't get me, or I don't care about them. And I never stay. Sometimes it's a race to see who lunges for the door first."

"Then you've only ever been with absolute morons who didn't deserve you."

"Careful. You might end up on that list."

He laughed, which was when she leaned in and kissed him.

And it was a fucking lovely kiss; she tasted like rum and Coke and Lila, and he clenched his fists so he wouldn't grab her tight, tighter, and even before their second kiss was finished, Oz was already wondering when they'd have their third. And ninth. And thousandth.

And then she pulled back. Teasing and flirting one minute, distant the next. That far, no farther. Which was just as well. The kiss had caught him by surprise. He couldn't in good conscience allow another one until she'd sobered up. Which would take sooooo fucking looooong. Not for the first time, he thought a Stable metabolism must be a huge pain in the ass.

"Sorry, Oz. I don't fuck on the first date. Or the second—if that's what this is. I still haven't decided if the distraction lunch counts as a date." Then, anticipating his unspoken question, she added: "The seventeenth date. That's when I go for broke."

He laughed. "I wasn't looking for a fuck." *Wouldn't say no to more kisses, though. Later.* "But thanks for the heads-up."

"I really like you. Even in the beginning when you were just some thug I had to throw into my basement."

"Not to sound corny, but that's when I fell in love with you. Well, no. I think I fell for you when you almost ran me over in your ambulance-that-isn't that first night."

She giggled. "Love? Ha! You're funny."

"Thank you for showing me this." He gestured to the auditorium. "I'd love to come back. Anytime you say."

"It's a date. Or whatever we're going to call it. I gotta pee. And we should probably get going."

"Only when you're ready."

"I won't be. Not for a couple more days." She met his gaze again, took his hand again. There was an expression on her face he couldn't name at first, because he'd never thought to see it there: vulnerability. "It smells like smoke now. My lovely new-old house. Even when it doesn't."

"I can fix that."

"Really?" Instant perk-up. "Okay."

"Okay."

"Still gotta pee, though."

"Well, one thing at a time."

Chapter 37

After snoring all the way to Lilydale, Lila was

"Five mmrrr minutes."

disinclined to move under her own power. So he slung her tote (full of empty bottles thudding against the near-empty thermos) over his shoulder, got the passenger door open, unbuckled her, scooped her up

"Your car's gotta elevator? Cool."

kicked the car door closed, and started up the sidewalk. Mama Mac must have heard him pull in, because by the time he got to the kitchen door she was holding it open for him.

"The lady likes rum," she said, smiling at them both.

"The lady fugging—fucking—loves rummmmm," Lila slurred, snuggling into Oz's chest. "Sorry 'bout the fucking."

Mama's eyebrows arched, and Oz rushed to fill the gap: "Not actual fucking. That's not what we—it was a movie. In a palace! And Cokes with a tiny bit of alcohol, but no fucking. She's apologizing for the swearing."

"I gathered, Oz. One of these days when you fall over yourself explaining the obvious, you're gonna have a nervous breakdown." Mama went to the fridge, pulled out a bottle of water, came back, dropped it in Lila's tote.

"Thanks, Mama."

"No problem, m'boy. Get to bed, it's late."

"You, too."

"By and by," she replied, and he knew she was staying up to check on the cubs a few more times. She stroked Lila's curls away from her forehead. "Good night, darling."

"Yr chili wuz good."

"Thank you."

Up, up, up the stairs, where Lila's bedroom door was open, thank God. He carefully laid her on the bed, and while he set the bottle of water on her nightstand, she yawned and sat up, fumbling with her turtleneck.

"Ugh, it's a million billion degrees in here. How can you stand it? I can't mmmf mmffff mmmelp!"

He hastily moved and helped her pull her sweater off, revealing a navy-blue tank top. "There you go, hon."

"You saved me! Don't call me hon. Makes me think of Attila."

"Got it. I…oh, Jesus. Lila." He stared at her, saw—and felt— the burn scars; there was plenty of light from the hallway. He gently grasped her hands and turned them wrists up and saw the patches of burn scars on the tender underside of her arms, too. Her hands were surprisingly clear, except the underside of one palm. "You said you weren't hurt."

"Said I was barely hurt. Which is mathematically fac…fact-shul…true. Eleven percent burns is barely cuz thirteen isn't sixty or eighty or ninety-five. It's not as good as zero percent, though, which is what my mom got."

"Lila…" He held her wrists and stroked the scars he could reach. How had he not noticed this when she was in his arms dressed in nothing but a towel? he asked himself.

And answered himself: because he hadn't been thinking with his *big* head, plain and simple. The flesh was rough, ragged, but she shivered a little—still some nerve function, then. He realized for the first time that he had always seen her in sweaters or long sleeves. Even her sleeping shirt had long sleeves. He'd assumed it was the weather. And he'd always taken her right hand, not the one with the scarred palm and wrist. Pure luck. And when she had reached out for him

(oh GOD I want her to reach out for me)

it was always with her right hand.

"It was dumb. I was dumb. Tried to grab some of Mom's stuff so she wouldn't be so mad." Lila shrugged. "Didn't work."

Didn't work as in "I was unable to grasp the items in question" or didn't work as in "My mother was not appreciative of my efforts"? He had a horrid feeling he knew which it was.

She was fully prepared to go into Mama's house for Dev.

"Your mother," he managed through gritted teeth, "is a worthless twat."

"Whoa! Well, that's fair. Y'know what? It doesn't smell so much like smoke in here now."

"Said I'd fix it, didn't I?" How, he had no idea. But he would. Somehow. *How do you fight phantom smoke?* "I'll do anything you want. Anytime."

"Won't work," she sighed, lying down and rolling over to her side, pulling her pillow in close and snuggling up to it. "Never does with me. And thass okay, I expect it. I just wanted to let you know what you were up 'gainst."

He draped the blanket over her. "Good night, Lila."

"G'night, Oz."

"I love that you call me by my first name."

"Gotta raise that bar higher, Oz."

And before he could come up with a response, she was out.

Chapter 38

SHE WAS GOING TO KILL, UTTERLY MURDER THE BASTARD WHO was playing the bongos in her brain. How did the bongos guy even get *in* her brain? And where'd he get bongos?

She cracked an eye open and everything was blurry except the water bottle, which glowed and seemed twice its size, like a Dasani oasis in the driest of deserts. Eight seconds later, it was an empty oasis. She lay back and pressed the heels of her palms to her eyes. She could feel her heartbeat in her head, in time with the throbbing in her temples; her pulse was annoyingly loud and strong this morning. She was craving a glass of V8, but the mere thought of it made her stomach threaten a walkout.

Gah, even her soul was hungover.

She had vague memories of the movie palace and *Toy Story* and Oz being sweet and seeing her…

Oh, fuck. Seeing her ugly arms.

Well, so what? Her burns were nothing to be ashamed of, except for how they were definitely something to be ashamed of. A therapist from her eventful adolescence tried to point out that her scars could be considered badges of honor. She'd laughed so hard the therapist's fixed smile vanished, never to return. It was downhill from there; she couldn't respect a therapist she knew was an idiot. A *nice* idiot, but still.

So, yeah. Oz saw them. Which changed everything, and none of it for the better. Because it wasn't a vanity issue for her, dammit, it *wasn't*. It was the fact that fun, hot, slightly loopy Oz was now going to be sympathetic, hot, boring Oz. And almost as annoying?

"She's awake now."

"So let's go talk to her."

"Mama might get mad."

"Why?"

The hissed conversation taking place in the hallway. "Oh my Gaaaaaawd," she groaned. "Either come in here or take your convo somewhere else, the suspense is killing me."

She was resigned to inconvenience and constantly sniffing the air to test for fire and a return of the nightmares where she beat at imaginary flames so hard she woke herself up. But furtive whispering outside her bedroom while her temples beat "La Copa de la Vida"? That's where she clawed the line.

"Uh. Hi?" Sally poked her head in. "Are you okay? You smell kinda bad."

Lila could imagine. A Shifter disadvantage: the kid could smell all the stale alcohol pouring from her pores. "Matches my mood. What d'you want?"

"D'you want something to eat?"

"God, no. So, yeah."

Sally tiptoed closer. "Mr. Berne is gonna call you and Mama Mac says there's bacon left if you want some and are you sick? You smell sick."

"Not surprised. About any of it." Her phone chirped at her. "Ah. That'll be Berne. The prophecy has been fulfilled." She groped for her phone, almost dropped it, took the call. "Yeah?"

"And a good morning t'you as well, Ms. Kai."

"Ugh."

There was a bemused silence (at least, she thought it was bemused), followed by "I wanted tae stop by and see my god-daughter and get any updates. Perhaps an hour from now?"

"You want to come to my house, so you are calling me and asking to come to my house."

"Aye. Problem?"

"Not at all. How'd you get this number?"

"Ms. Macropi."

"How'd *she* get my number?"

"I dinna know, lass, but I trust that was all right."

"I've got no idea. But I've gotta admit, Berne, what with how you haven't broken into my house or subjected me to a pop-in, you're growing on me."

"Naturally," he replied, and disconnected.

Lila flopped back. Berne. Bacon. They meant the same thing: getting out of bed was an inevitable nightmare, like wearing shoes you bought without trying them on first. Getting dressed wasn't going to be fun, either. If she took it slow and easy, she might not die.

"He's coming?" Sally asked.

"Yep."

"What's it mean?"

"It means that you'll be his problem now."

"I'm your problem?"

Shit. "Um. No?" Lila finally picked up on Sally's anxiety, but her big mouth had already done some damage. The kid had been bounced around like the cutest of ping-pong balls for the last several days. Naturally, anything new made her apprehensive.

"Why'd you even help me?" she burst out. "You don't even *like* kids!"

"Argh. Softly, please. And it's not that I don't like kids. I don't know kids. I don't…" She spread her hands in a helpless gesture, which made her head hurt more. Everything did. Blinking. Breathing. Mitosis. "I don't know anyone, really. That's…how it is with me." She paused, then corrected herself. "How I've made it be with me."

"Oh." Sally sniffed. "So you don't like me, but you don't dislike me, either."

"Well. Depends on the day."

"Hey!"

"Ow! I deserved that." She rubbed her forehead and seriously considered the prospect of an Advil smoothie. "But listen, Sally.

I'm not Mary Poppins. I think it's important for you to take that to heart."

"Why? Who cares about Mary Poppins?"

"I'm trying to tell you I'm not gonna show up out of nowhere and take care of you and magically solve all your problems."

"You've only done two of those things."

"Just so we're on the same page."

Lila heard new footsteps on the stairs, on the bedroom carpet, and then Caro was looming over her. "Now what fresh hell is this?" The girl was waving a pad of paper in her face. "Oh my God. You're gonna make me read a handwritten note in low light." Click. "AAAGGGHHHHHH!"

When her eyes had half-heartedly adjusted to the light and she was reasonably certain her head wasn't going to implode as she simultaneously shat her pants, Lila read Caro's note.

They told you.

"Yeah. But it's not like they lost a bet or something. They were legit worried I might be in danger." She squinted up at Caro, who either had a halo or her eyes were still adjusting to the blast of light after Sally hit the switch. "Don't worry, I'll never discuss it with anyone else. I've got a strict 'your business is your business' policy, which I implemented when I turned twelve."

More scribbling, which was just fine. Write a paragraph. A page. Write goddamned *Moby Dick*, if it meant she could stay in bed another few minutes.

They told you…but you're treating me the same.

"Uh. Yeah. That's…how I work." She listened to herself blink. "D'you want me to treat you different now?"

For that, she got a patented Caro Daniels eye roll and more scribbling.

About that ovulation kit—Dev only thinks it's Kama-Rupa because he's too young to get that it's just a fairy tale.

"Kama what? What are we talking about? And can we stop?

Because I'm dying, Daniels. The angel of death is ready to tap dance my soul to Hell."

For that she got another eye roll and, even better, the room to herself, as the girls, having done their best to destroy her, departed.

"Oh, God, oh, God, this is fresh-squeezed orange juice, oh, God." Lila drained the glass, almost shuddering at how good and sweet it was. Then she nearly Frenched Macropi, who was holding out two Advil. "Not enough," Lila told her, "but a good start." She shook two more out of the bottle, then gulped them down with more juice. "Ahhhhhh. I may yet live. Can't remember the last time I got that loaded."

"One-on-one time with Oz will do that to a girl." This from a smirking stranger who was one of the most striking women Lila had ever seen. She was petite and slim—maybe 110 pounds?—with raven hair and crystal blue eyes. Her ruby-red suit set off her pale skin to terrific effect; against the mundane backdrop of Lila's kitchen, the woman practically glowed. Like Snow White, if Snow White had a perma-smirk and a crisp British accent. "You must be Lila."

"I must."

"I am Nadia Faulkner. Annette would be lost without me."

"I don't doubt it. I've seen her in the field."

"Yes! With all your cunning little bear traps, with which you were able to thoroughly subdue her." Nadia gurgled laughter. "Tell me what I must do to get a copy of that security cam footage. Name your price, my dearest, because if I must sell everything I own, except for my Anne Klein suits, that ought to go without saying, then I will, because I must, *must* have that footage."

"You don't have to sell a thing. Gimme an email address and it's yours."

"You didn't destroy it?" Garsea asked, and she had the nerve to sound appalled.

"Why the *hell* would I destroy it, Garsea?"

"Wishful thinking?" Macropi guessed, busy at the stove. Lila couldn't smell bacon, but she *could* smell... *Oh my God, waffles!*

"I wasn't thoroughly subdued," Garsea whined. "Just taken by surprise. Several times. In a shockingly short time. David was furious. With me," she clarified. "Not you, Lila."

"Where *is* David?" Macropi asked. "There's plenty for him."

"Case," Garsea replied. "Don't worry, I'll gladly devour his share."

"I don't care about anything you two are discussing," Nadia declared. Then to Lila: "I give you full marks for ingenuity. But how did you come to have everything set up to decimate Annette, dear, *dear* Lila?"

"I wasn't decimated!"

"I just Googled 'bear repellant.' I'm bummed the Bear-B-Gone is on backorder. I was dying to try it out."

Nadia sidled closer and took a barely audible whiff. "It's true, and no mistake...you *are* Stable."

"Depends on who you ask. And don't sniff me, it's rude."

Nadia turned to Macropi. "Oh, I like this one. Can't you do something to abort the inevitable household catastrophe that always leads to the tenant's swift departure?" To Lila: "You *have* heard this house is rumored to be cursed, yes?"

"It's not like I'm doing any of it on purpose, Nadia," Macropi replied, exasperated. "Besides, Lila's tough. It'll take more than a squirrel coup—"

"Or a stove fire," Garsea added.

"—or asbestos in the attic—"

"—or a vole invasion—"

"I'm not going anywhere," Lila said, cutting them off before she had to hear about more Curs(ed) catastrophes.

"It looks like she's talking to you," Garsea told Faulkner, "but she's really talking about everyone in the room. She's not subtle."

"Says the woman who got cut while she pawed through my underwear drawer."

"Finefaulkner@comcast.net, Lila. And if you could oblige me by sending the footage today, I could make it the focus of movie night tomorrow." Faulkner actually hugged herself in delight. "Hang the new *Fast & Furious* movie, we'll watch Annette instead."

"You like the *F&F* franchise?" It seemed incongruous. Lila would have pictured Nadia somewhere fancy, like a tea room or a restaurant that served salad at the end of the meal, watching a black-and-white movie that tried too hard to mean nothing and ended with *fin*. Not sitting through movies with dialogue like "You know we're crazy, right?" and ex-wrestlers driving 90 miles per hour in reverse.

"My tastes occasionally run along the plebian," Nadia admitted. "It's why I'm so fond of Chicken McNuggets."

"If I may ask—wait. Of course I may ask. This is my house. Why are you here?"

"I have updates for Annette—she'll claim we're partners, when the reality is that I'm her keeper—and the delicious Magnus Berne will be in attendance. After what the poor man has been through, he deserves the chance to drink me in again."

"I really like your confidence."

"I really like how you set traps for Annette, all of which she tripped," she said lightly and smiled. "Of course, if she had been seriously hurt I would have had to pluck your eyes out of your skull."

"And I respect that." What kind of Shifter, then, was Nadia? Something with claws and sharp teeth, no question. Not a bear, because werebears were rare, even though she'd met three in less than a week. A wolf, like Oz? A hyena? A posh bobcat? "So I guess the gang's all here." Lila glanced around, pretending to just realize something she'd noticed the second she walked into the room. "Except not really. Where's—?"

A sonorous snore came from the living room.

"Never mind. Hey, Macropi, you want me to boot him out of bed? Out of couch, technically."

"Would you, dear? Mr. Berne will be here soon, and I want that boy to eat something first."

"I'm reasonably certain 'that boy' is older than everyone but you, Mama," Garsea pointed out.

"And it's lovely to see you up and around," Macropi continued, ignoring Garsea, which was right and good.

"It wasn't my idea. At all." Though the shower had helped. She now felt like she might not die. She'd probably only have a violent aneurysm and languish in a hospital for weeks while her brain knitted itself back together.

"And Nadia, I expect you to eat some breakfast."

"I would love to, Mama, but I have not kept such an admirable figure by partaking in your gooey buttery waffles. I will simply smell Annette's plate."

"I hate when you do that," Garsea grumbled.

Lila stifled a giggle and went into the next room, and there he was, sprawled and sexy

(*Jesus, those legs go on forever, don't they? It's not a cliché! They are endless!*)

and deliciously rumpled and snoring like an asthmatic orangutan.

She reached down and grabbed his big toe. Oz was not a believer in pajamas, but he was rocking those boxer briefs just fine.

Rocking those boxer briefs? Time to find your box of vibrators, doncha think? Well, maybe not. How good IS their hearing, anyway? Awful, awful thought.

She cleared her throat. "Wakey wakey, something that rhymes with wakey."

He cracked an eye open, then sat up with a big smile. "Hey! Hi!"

"Hi, yourself." She hadn't decided if Oz being a morning person was a plus or minus. "Macropi's cracking the breakfast whip, there will be waffles, and Berne's on his way over like a civilized creature who calls first."

The smile disappeared. "Good. I've got more questions." Then, as she sat beside him on the couch: "Are you okay? Because, and I say this with total admiration, you put away enough rum and vodka to incapacitate several NFL quarterbacks."

"Pshaw. You should see me on my birthday." She reached out in a futile attempt to straighten his Caesar-cut hair. "I swear, you're the only guy who can pull this—oh."

"Oh" because he had flinched back and was now scrambling off the couch while she sat there, blinking. "I'd better. Um. Get dressed. And. Y'know. Okay, bye."

She watched him take the steps two at a time and would not would not *would not* cry, because she'd known him less than a week and there was absolutely nothing to cry over.

Your arms. You've got a long-sleeved T-shirt on, but he remembered what's under your shirt and so that's that.

Over, then. Before it even got started. No follow-up dates at the movie palace. No nothing anywhere.

Bright side, though? Oz's new attitude would, at the least, save time. They could skip the relationship part and go right to the awkwardly avoiding each other part.

Hoo-fucking-ray.

Chapter 39

"I was meanin' to ask you lot last time...who's driving the decommissioned ambulance?"

"It's not a—oh. Sorry, Berne. Force of habit. Yes, it *is* a decommissioned ambulance and thank you for asking. It's me, by the way. I'm the one driving it. Not right this second, though."

"But why?" Oz burst out, like he'd been dying to ask the question.

"Because it's big enough to be a portable hospital and the mileage isn't horrible. All I had to do was remove the forward emergency lights and strip off the EMS logos. Piece of cake." And when all she got back were bemused looks, she added, "Why are the people who grow fur and run around on all fours during the full moon staring at me like *I'm* the weirdo?"

This prompted snickers as Garsea cleared her throat. "Contrary to legend, phase-shifters are rare. Most of us can shift whenever the urge hits."

"Oh. Good to know. The urge isn't hitting now, is it? In the middle of my living room?"

"We'll try t'give you ample warning, lass."

"Mr. Berne!" From the kitchen. "Something to drink?"

"Nae, I'm fine."

"Come see me if you change your mind!"

Before Berne could reply, there was a minor ruckus outside, and then the kids burst through the front door.

"There's my possum," Berne boomed. Sally came right over and he scooped her up; she looked like a doll in his arms. "Glad t'see you're staying in one place, darling."

"For now," she replied pertly, and though she was probably

kidding, Lila shuddered at the thought of the kid going on walk-about again.

"Hi, I'm Dev Devoss. This is my sister, C—" Except Caro had taken the opportunity to slip upstairs. "Was my sister, Caro. She's not cool with strangers." Devoss had planted himself in front of Berne, like a stop sign in front of Mount Everest. "Do you really have your own island?"

"I do, lad."

"How big?"

"Big enough. About thirty thousand square feet. There's room for my house and garage and a studio, and that's it."

"Sounds horribly cramped," Garsea said with a straight face.

"Her studio's an old grain silo," Devoss said, jerking his thumb at Garsea. "And her house is beautiful, *bella, bonita*. And big!"

"*Grande*," Lila added helpfully. "*Gros*."

"So she has room for guests. And it's out in the country, with woods all around." Devoss waved spindly arms to indicate acres of space. "Lots of room to run."

"Did you get your Realtor's license while I was asleep?" Lila asked, honestly curious.

"Dev." From Annette, and the warning was unmistakable.

"All I'm saying is that Sally's covered, Mr. Berne."

"*Dev.*"

"C'mon, Net, you gotta know why he's here."

"Oh?" Berne set Sally down, whispered in her ear, and shooed her toward the kitchen (given the speed of her departure, she probably smelled the apple crisp that went into the oven five minutes ago), then gave Devoss his full attention. "Why am I here, lad?"

"Either to tell Sally you can't take care of her or to tell Sally you don't know anything about kids but you'll take her away where she'll be stuck on an island without any other cubs around." Devoss took a deep breath and let it out. "But the thing is, Mr. Berne, you don't have to even worry."

"I don't, eh?"

"We want her to stay."

Lila put her hand up. "Could I hear your definition of 'we'?"

As Berne opened his mouth, Devoss rushed ahead. "You don't have to do anything! You can go home. We've got it covered. That's all I'm saying."

"Dev." Annette rubbed her temples like she had a sudden urge for a pallet of Advil. "That's not how IPA does it."

"Sure it is!" Devoss spread his arms. "Just look around. Just ask Caro!"

"Come here."

Devoss dropped his arms and went to stand in front of Garsea, who took his hand. "I know it probably seemed like an easy fix to you, how you and Caro are safe with Mama now, but the reality was it took months of paperwork, and if Judge Gomph hadn't expedited the process, your status wouldn't be finalized by now. You can't just plunk yourself or someone else into a home and declare it's an IPA-sanctioned foster home, boom, all fixed."

"You could do it, Net. You could push everything through. Everybody follows your lead…your boss, the phone company, David, Nadia…"

A gasp, followed by a squawked "Oh I *do* beg your pardon, Devin Devoss!"

"Sorry, Nadia. But everything else I said is true, Net. Your boss is scared of you."

"And do you think that's a help or a hindrance? And he's not scared of me. He's just, uh, nonconfrontational."

Nadia let out an elegant snort, proving that anything that came out of a posh Brit sounded classy.

"I'm not taking her away right this minute, lad," Berne said kindly. "And perhaps not at all. And I'm not going anywhere soon, either."

"Your boss won't get mad? Make you come back?"

Berne laughed. "No one makes me do a damned thing, lad. And since I'm the boss, I won't get into trouble."

"Oh. Okay." Devoss's expression of relief was nearly unmistakable. "Hey, while I'm gettin' info, why is everyone rich besides us? Mr. Berne has an island, Oz has the car and the suits—"

"Don't forget about Garsea's grain silo," Lila added with a snicker.

"—and Lila sets her own hours."

"I'm not rich," Lila replied at once. "I'm just a careful budgeter. To a near-pathological degree. And I have a weird niche job so I can set my own hours and prices."

"And you don't want to get rich the way I did," Oz added.

At that, Devoss's small face went the color of a July tomato, so quickly Lila wondered for a panicky second if the kid was stroking out. "Oh, shit. I'm sorry, Oz. I forgot. Just—forget I said anything. I'll go play with Sally, keep her out of your fur."

There was a short silence, as Devoss practically sprinted from the room, broken by Lila. "Well. At least that didn't make me incredibly curious about Oz's money and wonder if it'd be rude to ask about it."

"Kids died," Oz replied shortly. "And I almost did. Lawsuits made the guilty parties pay up."

"Got it."

"Anything else?"

Which kids? When? And what were they to you? Is that why you had to live with Annette and Mama when you were a kid? Is that why you want to get out of accounting so badly? Is it why I'm drawn to you—because you're someone who nearly died when their life imploded?

"…nope."

"Liar," he replied, kindly enough, so she chanced a smile and was relieved to get one back.

Chapter 40

"Now! What have you lot got for me?"

"All *sorts* of exciting things," Nadia said. "By which I mean the coroner's report and more distressing photographs."

"Lovely. Er…" Berne made a point of looking around Lila's humble living room. "Are ye sure this is the best place to meet? Shouldn't we be at IPA?"

"I think you're gonna be glad we're meeting here, Magnus," Oz replied, sounding terribly serious, which wasn't sexy at all, except it was, so *fuck*.

Berne turned a friendly gaze on Lila. Gah, the guy was so big he was blocking the sunlight from the window. "And you're here for this meeting, too, lass?"

"It's *my house*, Berne." Why were none of them getting this? She was starting to think it was pathological.

"O'course, o'course. It's kind of you t'offer it up. I havna said so and I'm remiss—I'm grateful for all you've done for Sally. Especially since you're not. Ah."

Lila didn't say anything, so they could all feel the enormity of the elephant in the room. Fifteen. Excruciating. Seconds. Went. By.

"Right," Oz said, and you could almost hear the collective gasp as everyone started breathing again. "So, updates. First, thanks again for flying us to the crash site." He had riffled through Nadia's file of photos, found what he was looking for, put it on the vintage trunk Lila used as a coffee table. She hoped to be buried in it someday. (Roomy!) "D'you mind telling me what this is?"

They all leaned forward to look down at the pic, which was kind of funny, given that at least three people in the room had already seen the photograph. To Lila's eyes, it was just another pic of twisted metal and torn cloth, with something that looked like a mangled backpack, all smooshed and flattened at the edge of the frame.

Wait. Not a backpack.

"That's a parachute," Berne said, staring fixedly at the picture.

"Uh-huh. A parachute in your plane. The plane you lent to the Smalls."

Berne was still staring.

"Do you often carry parachutes on your planes?"

Ten. Excruciating. Seconds. Went. By.

"Magnus?"

"As a matter of fact." Berne looked up. "Yes."

"More than one?"

"Usually two."

Oz took a few seconds to digest that. "Why?"

"In addition to being a ferry pilot, I take people jumping."

"Wait, *what*?" Lila could have bitten her tongue; the filter in her brain hadn't engaged quickly enough. But Oz just looked at her expectantly. *Keep going* was (probably) written in his body language. Or *Keep out*. She sometimes got those mixed up.

"Lila? Something to add?"

He's looking at me like he's giving me a cue. Like I'm part of the IPA team. Or an aviation expert. Which is deeply nuts. "It's just. When I heard Sally's parents went down in a single engine, that's the first thing I wondered about. But it doesn't fly, no pun intended. An unmodified Cessna? Going down? That's a terrible plane to jump out of. And a terrible altitude. There probably wouldn't be enough time for the chute to deploy." She looked around the room full of people giving her 100 percent of their attention. It was gratifying and nerve-wracking at the same time. "And depending on what was wrong with the plane, it was probably safer to stay on board. Planes are designed to glide even if the engine quits. It's a much safer bet to stay put."

"Because a parachute is not a magic wand," Oz prompted.

"Well. Yeah."

"For Stables," Berne said, and Lila cursed herself for overlooking that rather large fact.

"You think a Shifter with no experience could have gotten into a parachute and jumped out of an unmodified plane at low altitude and lived to tell the tale? Of course you do," Lila realized. "Because you think Sam's out there somewhere, calling ISA and being sneaky."

"That does explain a few things," Annette observed.

"So why didn't you say anything?" Oz asked Berne.

"A fine question! What's that phrase of yours, Mr. Berne? The one you love to shout when you don't care for a data set?" Nadia asked sweetly. "Ridiculous...? I forget."

"Bullshit," everyone said in unison.

"Ah! There it is."

Berne straightened to his full height and looked Oz square in the eye. "Am I officially a suspect, lad?"

Oz held his ground. "Well, let's see. You lent the Smalls a plane that crashed. Someone set Mama Mac's house on fire with avgas. You didn't volunteer any info about why there would be one parachute in the ruins. I even said it on the trip back: two people went up but only one came down. You still didn't say anything."

"One might argue that's not my job, lad."

"One might argue you'd do everything you can to help your friends, including questions you know the answers to, even if they haven't been asked. Oh. Sorry... As you made clear, Sam wasn't your friend. Sue was. And Sam knew it, too—he warned his daughter to watch out for you."

Berne raised his eyebrows. "Is that what he did?"

"Did you and Sue used to go out?" Lila asked.

"How—not that it's anyone's business, lass, but how did you know?" For the first time, Berne looked really worried. "Did Sally say something?"

"You think a kid is up on her mom's ex-boyfriends?" Devoss, maybe. Not Sally. "Nobody told me. It's just a theory that answers all the questions."

"All what questions?"

"Well, you've repeatedly emphasized that Sue was your friend, not Sam. And loaning someone a plane is a pretty big favor. She was obviously special to you. And it explains why you only visited once or twice since Sally was born. Because who wants to make nice with the guy who got your girl? Who wants to look at their ex-girlfriend's kid and wonder, 'What if she hadn't broken up with me?'"

"For your information, lass, *I* broke up with *her*. Nobody 'got' Sue, she was always her own woman."

"Okay." *Whatever you need to tell yourself, Berne.*

"Clever, clever girl." Berne's tone was low and quiet. He wasn't scowling, he wasn't getting red, he wasn't clenching his cabbage-sized fists or pacing. Lila couldn't tell if he was pissed or dogged or mildly curious. Which was horrifying, frankly. "And I'll ask you lot again: Am I a suspect?"

Oz shrugged. "Even if you were, we're not cops. We've got no lawful authority to make arrests and don't get me started on the jurisdictional issues."

"But I simply adore getting you started on the jurisdictional issues," Nadia protested.

Oz didn't miss a beat. "We're technically not supposed to be investigating the crash at all, just figuring out the best custody arrangements for the cub. IPA gives us more leeway than the Stable foster system, but our authority is still limited."

"A lot of words to avoid answering my question, lad."

"What cops *are* investigating?" Lila broke in. Did Shifters have their own police force? Or was it like their military, the Twopers: nothing official or, as Garsea described it, "nothing so organized." "Iowa staties? The Scarville police? Or is it a federal issue?"

"Funny you should ask, darling." Nadia waved another folder. "The Lake Mills Police Department, who tirelessly guard the safety of Scarville citizens both Stable and Shifter, has written off the recent unpleasantness as pilot error, though it's absurdly early to do so. So no homicide investigation. And Dr. Gulo—he's the coroner, Lila, you haven't yet had the pleasure, you lucky, lucky girl—has come to the conclusion that Sam *did* go down in that plane. In what must be a triumph of forensic science, he's now claiming he found enough of Sam's DNA to back that supposition."

"Wait, *what*?" Lila looked at Oz and Berne, who looked just as surprised as she felt.

"Isn't that marvelous? Doesn't that just solve everything and tie it in a big garish bow?" Nadia tossed the folder on the coffee table. "Now Sally can go live on Berne's island, Oz can move on to his next case, and Annette can finally get a haircut."

"Nadia…"

"Your split ends, darling. It physically hurts me to be around them."

"Well." Lila cleared her throat. "Either Oz and Berne's preternatural senses of smell aren't good for shit…"

"They *are* good for shit," Oz insisted.

"Or Gulo's lying," Berne breathed. "Goddamned wolverines, I *knew* it."

"But why would Gulo lie about—oh." It was starting to look like the Sindicate *was* involved. IPA knew they hadn't caught everyone. It's why there was a whiteboard in her kitchen right this minute. Also, what did *goddamned wolverines* mean? She'd ask Oz later. It sounded like a generalization, which could be problematic. "He's lying because he doesn't know we went to the crash site. You said it yourself—you're not even supposed to be investigating it. He's counting on no one checking—why would they? Like Nadia said, case closed."

Nadia smirked. "A consummate hostess *and* you pay attention, just wonderful."

"I'm no kind of hostess, but thanks anyway. But what I don't get is why would the coroner lie about that particular crash? That particular family? What the hell is so special about the Smalls?"

"Well." From Garsea, who was on her feet and ~~smiling~~ showing her teeth. "Let's go ask him."

Chapter 41

MACROPI WAS CRYING QUIETLY ON THE PORCH.

Lila made sure her red scarf, recently paroled from the dryer after Sally had again used it for a Kleenex, was tucked safely out of sight, then went out to the porch.

"This is where making an onion pie gets you," Lila observed. "How many did you have to peel? Plus you made it up.[10] You must've. Onion pie? Yeerrggh."

Without turning, Macropi wiped away her tears with her palms like a little kid would, and Lila felt her heart turn over in a spasm

(ow!)

of empathy.

"You want me to leave you alone? I can leave you alone. I can leave you alone like you wouldn't believe. It'll be the gold medal standard of leaving you alone. Just say the word."

"Not necessary, m'dear." She sighed and looked down at her feet. "You didn't go with them to confront that doctor?"

"No, it struck me as IPA-only. Well, IPA-only plus Berne. And I don't want to overstep. Also Oz told me to stay put and then ran away." That had stung, but only a little. He'd been incredibly generous and inclusive, especially considering it was his first case. But maybe that was why he'd been so inclusive, wanted her to go to Iowa with him, bounced ideas off her. Maybe he just didn't know any better.

Not that it mattered. They were done. Done before they started. Which was good. Yep.

"I'm glad you stayed behind."

---

10. Alas. Onion pie is a thing.

"Well. Was left behind. But okay."

"I wanted to talk to you, anyway." She sighed, turned around, dropped her hands.

"Agh! I mean, were you at your house? Touching things? Touching things that were recently on fire? And then touching your face? And hair? And neck? Because you've got soot all over your…everywhere. C'mere." She grabbed Macropi by a bony wrist and led her into the kitchen, where she ran a paper towel under the tap. The older woman's face and hair were dusted with soot particles; against her white curls, it looked like someone had decided Macropi didn't have enough seasoning and vigorously peppered her.

"That's better." Lila tossed the now-black paper towel in the garbage. "Now you don't look like you tried to beat up a chimney sweep."

"A great relief. And yes, I was at the house. I went out to check on the cubs first. They're amusing themselves in your shed."

"Sure, sure. Little weres have moved into my shed, which happens in backyards all over the world every single day, totally normal."

"And then I went up the street to my house. I don't know why," she confessed. "I knew what I'd find. I knew what was damaged, and even better, what wasn't."

"Okay."

Macropi turned to look out the kitchen window over the sink. "And I know I should be grateful. Most of it's fixable. I already got a check from the insurance company, and there's more coming. I can hire carpenters and buy new curtains and pull up the old rugs. There are entire rooms that weren't damaged at all."

That *was* fortunate. Lila decided not to point out that a homeowner was often better off if the entire place went up. Depending on the severity of the fire, it could take ages before the smoke and water damage was fixed; it was often quicker to just build a new house from the foundation. People assumed most of the damage was caused by the fire itself. They discounted what happened after firefighters spent half an hour spraying water into their living room at three hundred gallons per minute.

"Like I said," Macropi continued, "I know I'm lucky. No one was hurt, thank God, and nothing irreplaceable was lost. But I feel so—it's such a—"

"Violation."

"Yes."

"I know," Lila said. "I had to learn, too. The weirdest thing for me was that over a year later, we still hadn't replaced everything. You think you've got it all back and ten months later you want to make Christmas cookies and realize you don't have a rolling pin. Or a toilet plunger. Those two things aren't related, FYI. And what do you buy to fill a junk drawer? They make themselves, they're practically organic. Which mug should you buy to store all the pens that don't work? Where do you get an old clamshell to keep spare change and the odd safety pin?"

"That's it," Macropi said. "That's exactly it." She straightened; one moment she'd looked small and defeated, the next brisk and no-nonsense. "Thank you for listening, m'dear. I do feel better. I don't want to talk to the cubs about it, their lives have been chaotic enough. And my Honey Bear would just worry about me."

"Oh my God. Please tell me you just let slip Garsea's embarrassing childhood nickname."

"I deny everything. Now don't you go teasing—"

"Ha! I have not yet begun to tease!" Lila was almost giddy; it was Christmas and her birthday rolled into one. "And I don't care if you beat me to death with every wooden spoon in the house, I *will* make use of this incredible tidbit you've dropped. Is it too late to order her a vanity plate? H0NEYB5AR? D'you think that's taken?"

"Oh, no-no-no-no-no. Don't ask me. In fact, leave me out

altogether," she insisted. But she looked loads happier than she had five minutes ago. So that was all right.

"Tell you what, I've got a deal for you. You answer some questions for me and I'll only use Honey Bear as a greeting for the next five years, and I'll only buy five hundred 'HONK 4 HONEY BEAR' bumper stickers."

"Oh dear God."

"Yeah, I drive a hard bargain."

"I heard you asking Oz if Shifters are religious."

Lila blinked. "That came out of nowhere, but okay."

"We're like Stables in that regard. Some of us are, some aren't. Some of us try to nurture our spiritual side and some don't even think they have a spiritual side."

"Okay."

"There's an ancient story among our kind," Macropi went on, because now she wanted to talk about Shifter religion for some reason. "Like the Adam and Eve story. Here's how it was told to me."

Once there was a man born to loneliness. This man called himself *Kama,* and he had no memory of his family, of his village, of anything but his travels. His world was the road in front of him, and always he walked alone. If he met a man or woman or child on the world his road, they could not see him, though he dogged their footsteps and shouted and cried. And so he continued, always a solitary creature.

Soon he stopped eating, for what good was it to know the world if he was only ever alone? But even now he could not stop seeking, so he walked and his hunger grew, as did his thirst, because when he decided to stop eating, he stopped filling his waterskin. And his only comfort was the knowledge that he would soon lie down and be dead, and perhaps he could escape his loneliness in death. Death would see him and know him, surely.

And not long after, he came upon the widest river he had ever seen, so broad that he had to squint to see to the far bank. And on that far bank stood a woman, who beheld him and raised a hand in greeting. Her name was *Rupa*, though he did not yet know that.

The man was shocked. In all his long life, no other creature had acknowledged his existence. He waved back and, though terribly weak from hunger, began to wade into the river, only to see the woman wave back. As her motions became more frantic, his determination to cross increased. Even if she no longer wished to see him, he had to speak with her, if only to thank her for her courtesy, the first ever shown him in his long, long life. And it was only when the water reached his chest that he understood her warning, because the greedy current snatched him away. He stretched his hands out to her, and she ran. In despair, he prepared to give himself to the river. But then he saw she wasn't running away, but running alongside the river bank, keeping pace with him even as the current played with him like a lion with a brace of hares.

And when the river finally tired of him, he was so exhausted he would have sunk beneath the water save for the woman who had kept pace with him all the day, and now swam out to him and took him in her arms and tugged him back to shore.

After his ordeal, the man fell into an exhausted sleep, and when he awoke, he feared the woman had been a fever dream. But she was still there and smiled at him. And he looked at her and knew her, as she knew him, and they were together for all of their lives and raised many fine strong cubs together, for he was a good hunter, having hunted for himself all his life, and she was a fierce mother and gave him fearless cubs.

And when death finally came for them, it came as a swift, sweet river, but these waters were gentle and bore them away together, and wherever the river brought them, they are still there, together.

"Well! That was…" Lila trailed off. "I'm not sure what you want from me right now."

"I just think it's interesting that every culture has legends about soul mates. And that's our version."

"Okay."

"But there's another version where the man is a Shifter, and the woman he sees across the river is a Stable. And he swims to her and they become the Adam and Eve of Shifters, with all the fine qualities of both. If they hadn't mingled the bloodlines, both their species would have died out."

"Uh-huh."

"Which is silly. Obviously we're simply a different branch of evolution."

"Like *Homo erectus* and Neanderthals," she suggested.

"Right. It's just a story. But sometimes you meet someone and you instantly connect with them, don't you know? And it's overwhelming and strange and wonderful all at once."

"I'm desperately afraid to ask where you're going with this."

Macropi spread her hands. "I'm just saying that it happens, whether you call it a crush or a soul mate or *Kama-Rupa*. Sometimes you meet the exact right person at the exact right time. Even if you don't know it, the universe does."

Lila (barely) held back her snort. "I'm not swimming the widest river Oz has ever seen—which would be the Mississippi, I'm assuming—no matter how attracted I am to him. That's all it is, y'know. You're talking about soul mates and connections and crushes, but you left lust off that list. Which, ninety-nine times out of one hundred, is what it is."

"Oh, yes," Macropi agreed. "But you're one in one hundred, Lila. And so is my Oz. All I'm saying is, sometimes strangers are brought together for reasons even they don't understand. Both versions of *Kama-Rupa* are about lonely people who will die alone if they don't find their physical and spiritual counterpart."

"Jesus Christ."

Macropi brightened. "But in the second version, meeting the right person didn't just save their lives, it birthed an entirely new dominant species. So you have to ask yourself, 'What am I missing in my life? What's the thing that is slowly killing me that *Kama-Rupa* is trying to fix?'"

"Again: Jesus Christ! Look, this has been weird and interesting, like every other thing this week, and I guess butting in is your prerogative as the neighborhood mother figure, but I'm not Oz's *Kama*, or his *Rupa*, or his *Karma Chameleon*, or whatever you want to call it."

Macropi shrugged and smiled. "As you like, dear."

"So to get alllllllll the way back to what I wanted to talk to you about in the first place, in return for me not taunting Garsea *too* often about her Honey Bear nickname, you were gonna tell me about Shakopee."

Macropi's smile disappeared. "Oh."

"That killed all the fun in the room, didn't it?"

"Just a bit, yes. But." She spread her hands. "A deal's a deal." She leaned against the counter, folded her arms across her chest. "What do you want to know?"

"Were you there?"

"No, thank heavens. I found out afterward, like most of us."

"And you guys kept it out of the news, positioned it as a climate change protest turned violent, one-time only, such a tragedy, thoughts and prayers…like that?"

"It seemed safest at the time. You understand how vastly outnumbered we are."

"There are a crap ton of Stables crawling all over the world," Lila admitted.

"Yes. So our standard response is always geared toward staying hidden. It trumps every other consideration. But it also gives rise to that tired 'separate but equal' canard. That's how you get the Klan and imbeciles like SAS. Lila, dear, are you all right? You look like someone clipped you with a brick."

"Is that what it is?" Lila breathed. Everything had disappeared as her brain followed the trail that had suddenly lit up like a fireworks display. Macropi, the kitchen, the state of Minnesota, the northern hemisphere all faded away while she followed her train of thought.

You're the first one of your kind I've spent any real time with. And Sally didn't just say that once. It wasn't an offhand comment. It made enough of an impression that she pointed it out twice.

"Is that the connection?" Lila knew she was breathing, but still felt like she wasn't getting enough air. "*That's* what makes Team Smalls so special?"

"Lila?"

"How."

"What?"

"How! How'd the protest—the coup attempt—how did you guys—Garsea said sanity prevailed. How?"

Macropi looked taken aback but answered readily. "There was a mole among the SAS. Or a traitor, depending on who you're talking to."

"So a few disaffected Shifters lost because it was a numbers game."

"It's almost always a numbers game," Macropi replied. "As anyone who's read a history book knows."

"Right. So it was already going to be difficult. For their power grab to have even a prayer of working, they needed *every* Shifter to go all in on their national tantrum. But it sounds like they didn't have every Shifter on their side, there at the very beginning. Because of the mole."

"Yes. My understanding is that whoever he or she was—I

never got all the details—they were in the SAS but realized at the last minute that they didn't want it to go that far. Or they were a spy and notified their handlers. Whatever the motive, he or she sounded the alarm and non-SAS Shifters got to Shakopee in time."

"So with two groups, each with a different agenda…"

"Rather than a power grab from one apex predator to another, it looked like the groups facing off were just two sides of the climate change debate. The 'everything's fine, knock it off' group and the 'you're killing the planet and dooming us all' group. And in the middle of all that, the police came and added to the chaos, and someone set fire to downtown, or more than one someone, and when the smoke cleared, the dead were in the streets or locked up, and the movement was in ruins."

"You hope."

"Well." Macropi shrugged. "Nothing's happened. If there were other blocks of SAS scattered about, waiting for their cue, or even to start their own revolutions, they haven't done anything in ten years. Exactly ten years, now that I think about it. You wouldn't know this, Lila, but this weekend is the tenth anniversary of the Shakopee riot."

"Wait, what? *What?*"

"Yes. That's why it's been on everyone's mind. It's—"

"Now? This weekend? Right now? *Now* now?"

"Yes. Oh, but don't worry, dear! You must know we would never let anything happen to you. There's no one under my roof who would hurt you, and we would never, ever allow anyone to—"

"I'm not the one they want to hurt! Jesus Christ, why didn't anyone tell me?" She had to call. Or run. Or drive. Because it was never about Sally Smalls. It was always about her parents.

And Magnus Berne, of course.

Chapter 42

"WHAT DO YOU MEAN, GONE? LUNCH? HE DIED? WHAT?"

"Dr. Gulo gave notice last Thursday." This from Debbie, Dr. Gulo's assistant, a curvy brunette with incongruously small wrists and ankles who probably got carded for R-rated movies. "Sorry you missed him."

"Last week? How fortuitous!" Nadia exclaimed. To Oz: "The day after the plane crash."

"I *know*, Nadia." He was getting a distinct herbivore scent from Debbie, who was so short her head didn't even come up to his shoulder. Weredeer, probably. Maybe wereantelope?

"Touchy, touchy." Nadia turned back to the assistant. "And here you are, poor darling, trapped like a fly in honey, stuck with the grunt work. So typical of upper management."

Gulo's assistant waved her hand to indicate semipacked boxes, the desk, the room. "Yeah, needless to say, we're running a little behind. Most of this we'll have to ship to his new job."

"Which is…?"

She frowned. "I don't know. He keeps telling me he'll zap me his forwarding address, but…" She shrugged. "Like I said. We're all running behind."

"What about his open cases?" Oz asked. "Did they get reassigned, or…"

"He doesn't have any."

"Really?" From Annette. "Is that common?" (Trick question; Annette knew damned well it wasn't common.)

"No, actually, but it's Dr. Gulo, so." Debbie shrugged again. "He practically lives here. Anyway, he closed them all. The Smalls case—the one you were asking about—was the last."

"Gosh, efficient *and* timely," Nadia chirped.

"Ridiculous bullshit!"

Oz nearly jumped through the wall. Berne had some lungs when he wanted 'em. "Calm down, Magnus."

Magnus put his hands behind his back, possibly so he wouldn't pick Debbie up and shake her like a maraca. "We require answers, lass, d'you understand? Lives are at stake!"

"And you. Um. You got them. The answers." All the color had fallen out of Debbie's face as she shrank from a grumpy, shout-y Magnus. "He's not here. I mean…maybe he'll stop by on Monday to get the rest of his stuff. I could." She stopped, coughed. Swallowed. "I could give him a message."

"He won't be stopping by," Oz said. He turned to Magnus and raised his eyebrows. *Apologize, would you?* "He's long gone from here."

"I'm sorry, lass, I didna mean to bark."

"It's okay," Debbie said, visibly relieved. "Dr. Gulo's been on edge, too, what with trying to close all those cases in time for him to take a new job. And that put everyone else on edge."

Oz doubted job stress was responsible for Gulo's mood this week. And he was pretty sure the guy was suffering from OCD. Which might work in their favor—Gulo clearly couldn't leave any of his work unfinished; his disorder wouldn't let him. Even if it meant fabricating evidence. Nadia was already busy with her phone, doubtless requesting any additional records about Gulo, his cases, and his background that she could get her talons on.

"Plus, it's hard for him, leaving his family behind in Shakopee. Guess he wanted a new start." Debbie looked down at some of the pictures she'd been packing up. Gulo with family. Gulo with more family. Gulo in front of a car that had been washed and waxed so thoroughly, if you even looked at it you'd slide off. "I don't know… We were all surprised when he gave notice. I thought he loved it here."

Oz could actually hear the tendons in his jaw creak as his mouth fell open. "Gulo lives in Shakopee."

Debbie looked up. "Yeah. His whole family does. He's fifth or sixth generation, I think it is. His family's descended from the Native Americans down there, what d'you call them? Cherokees?"

"Shakopee Mdewakanton Sioux," Annette prompted, looking as poleaxed as Oz felt.

"Yeah, them."

Yeah, them. Debbie, like Dev and Caro, was too young to grasp the seriousness of the riot, then and now, and the centuries of bloodshed underlying the ongoing tragedy. To them, the Shakopee "protest" seemed as distant as the California Gold Rush or Prohibition.

Debbie cleared her throat, totally unaware that she'd dropped a bombshell, and likely to be horrified if she found out. "So, um, if I've answered all your questions, I haveta get back to this. Dr. Gulo might've quit, but he'll still be super mad if I don't get this done. Okay? You guys?" She was addressing her remarks to the group, but only looking at Magnus, clearly wondering if another roar was forthcoming. "Okay?"

"O'course, lass." Magnus had recovered quickly. Almost too quickly; Oz had a niggling suspicion that Magnus Berne was keeping something back. "Again, I'm verra sorry. I lost a friend—Sue Smalls—but I didna mean to take it out on you."

"A friend? I mean, I know you ID'd her, but…" Debbie looked startled, opened her mouth like she was going to say something else, then closed it. Then tried again and said to her feet, "Oh. That's okay. I'm sorry about your. Uh. Your friend."

"Never mind him," Nadia said, sidling closer to Debbie, who kept twitching her nose like she couldn't make up her mind to fight or flight. "He's just a large dim cantankerous idiotic noisy uncouth *bear*."

"It's true," Annette said with a straight face. "Bears are the worst."

"I don't know why anyone puts up with them. Can't they hibernate longer?" Oz added, sidling out of Annette's kicking range.

"You poor thing, I'll bet Dr. Gulo was short with you, too." Nadia was nearly vibrating with commiseration. "Under all that pressure to close—he must have snapped at you more than once."

"It's—yeah. I mean…he's *so* uptight. But it's gotten worse." Debbie had stopped talking to her shoes, which was a relief. "And it's funny—I shouldn't say this. I really have to finish the packing."

"We'll help! Say whatever you need to say. Pretend we're not here." Annette looked around, grabbed a half-empty box, and emptied the entirety of the in-bin tray into it.

"Um, Annette, I think you just packed Debbie's bin."

"Shut up, Oz."

"Oh, go on, darling. Our lips are…" Nadia mimed buttoning her lips closed, because she thought zippers were for lazy people. "You don't fool me, sweetie. I know you're dying to tell. Think how satisfying it will be."

"Okay. After you guys left last time, after Mr. Berne identified the remains of his friend? Dr. Gulo said Mrs. Smalls didn't *have* any friends. He said she did when she was younger, but not anymore. Which was weird, because he'd never gotten personal about a body before. It's not like he knew her."

Except he did know her. His family is Kiyuska.

"I just figured it was the stress of switching jobs and moving. And now I really have to get back to it," Debbie said, which was a relief, because Annette was still "helping" by packing up more of Debbie's workspace. "The only reason I told you guys this stuff is because Gulo's gone."

Not if we can catch him.

"And the quicker I get him packed up," Debbie added, "the truer that's gonna be."

Cling to that hope, Debbie.

"We'll see ourselves out," Oz told her, and Debbie's relief was palpable.

"Sneaky, clever, wretched little man," Nadia hissed on their way back to their cars. To Oz: "And that, darling, is why you must always, *always* be nice to your assistants. In their hands lie the power to destroy your life, your lunch orders, and possibly your dry cleaning."

"Noted."

"And slow *down*, damn you. These shoes cost nearly as much as one of your suits."

Oz realized he was practically jogging toward the cars. "Sorry. Okay, so I'm betting Gulo wasn't personally involved with Shakopee ten years ago—too young. He's...what? Mid- to late-twenties? But I'd bet every pair of shoes Nadia has—"

"I *beg* your pardon!"

"—that his family was. They might've masterminded the whole thing. And why wouldn't they? They'd been soaking up resentment and rage—"

"To which they're entitled," Annette pointed out.

"No one's arguing that," Oz agreed. "But they're not entitled to start riots and murder every Stable and Shifter who gets in their way. They had a plan. Obviously. And when it went wrong, the survivors would have asked themselves why."

"Exactly," Annette replied. "They would have realized someone talked. They would have been wild to find out who blew up their little power grab. But it's not enough."

"What?" From Berne, who'd been shockingly quiet. "It's more than enough to find that Gulo and pull out his guts."

"How is that enough?" Oz asked. Because here was something else Annette had warned him about. *You're going to find out the worst of people. You'll come to realize that what happened to you and your sister happens all the time, all over the world. And there will be times when you won't be able to do anything about it. Our work is primarily custodial.* "The cops have closed it—and they're Stables, anyway. Gulo has signed off. We can't raise much of an alarm. You know why."

And there it was: every Shifter's priority, all the time. Oz was glad David wasn't here just then, because it was a major (and justified) peeve of his.

We went through this when we were tracking the Sindicate, he thought, while they stood in the parking lot and looked at each other and pondered what came next, since the obvious options weren't actually options. *David was right then, and he's right now. It cuts us off at the knees at every turn. So we fumble around on our own and pull back the moment we get close. We prioritize getting the children to safety, but then we step off when anyone else could call a cop or go see the DA.*

How much evil will I have to look away from? What will get overlooked—who will get overlooked—because our bosses figure the devil we know—ourselves—is better than the devil we don't?

"What, then?" Berne was asking. "All we know is that his family is from Shakopee."

"We don't even know that," Annette pointed out. "If you want to get technical, all we know is that Debbie *said* his family was from Shakopee."

"What, then?" Magnus asked again. "What can we do? Say it and I will. Anything. She was my friend. Her mate was a good man. And I have a responsibility to their little lass."

"We can dig around quite a lot more," Nadia said. She held up a shipping label with the address of a self-storage company. "Starting with where Gulo is keeping his pristine belongings while he transitions."

Oz broke into a delighted smile. "So *that's* why Annette keeps you around."

"That, and my impeccable fashion sense."

"No," Annette replied. "Just the first thing."

Chapter 43

"I DON'T KNOW WHAT'S SCARIER, THE CACHE OF AUTOMATIC weapons or the fact that you could eat off the floor in here."

"You don't have to choose, Annette," Oz said. "They're both pretty damned scary."

Nadia had gone off to track down more files, so Berne had driven his rental and Oz and Annette had taken the *other* love of Oz's life to the Burnsville address for ShiftStuff.

Oz and Berne made quick work of the lock, and now they were examining the most immaculate storage space in the history of storage spaces. Annette was still frowning at the paper with the address Nadia had procured. "ShiftStuff? That doesn't even make sense unless you're a Shifter. And their company motto is just as insipid. 'Need to Shift your stuff? We can help!!!' A single exclamation point is more than sufficient."

"That all sounds bad," Oz agreed, "but could we maybe focus on what the hell we're looking at?"

"War." Berne sounded grimmer than usual, which was disconcerting. "That's what we're looking at."

If it was an exaggeration, it wasn't much of one. Because there were boxes marked *kitchen* and *bathroom*, but there were also boxes marked *ammo* and *9mm* and *reloading presses* and *casings* and *gunpowder*. And yes, it was an ordinary storage space, but it was climate-controlled, and someone had put in extensive, expensive shelving, and those shelves were jammed with boxes of rifles. And instead of a standard ten-by-fifteen-inch slot, Gulo had taken down the wall and doubled his storage space.

"And what's this?" Annette said, walking over to the bench in the corner, nostrils flared while she tried to parse the jumble of scents.

"Reloading bench," Berne replied. "Dr. Gulo likes to make his own ammo."

"I'm flummoxed," Annette admitted. "This is odd and off-putting."

Oz could relate. Most Shifters avoided guns, and he'd never known one who loved guns enough to make his own ammunition. And then there were the weapons, enough to be the envy of the prop guy from an R-rated movie about cops and gangsters. Boxes and boxes of rifles, pistols, shotguns.

"He's not violating the 'No food, no drinks, no fireworks, no propane, no chemicals' policy, at least."

"Jeez, Annette. We're in a bad guy's super-duper secret weapons storage chamber and you're still reading the brochure?"

Annette ignored his excellent point. "But this firepower definitely breaks the 'nothing worth more than $5,000' rule. And the boxes are all precisely four inches from the wall. I'm serious, does anyone have a ruler? I swear they're all exactly four inches. It's amazing."

"Sounds exhausting," Oz replied. "Not amazing."

"This is damning," Berne observed after walking around the death room. "I'd think Gulo would be more careful."

"Naw," Oz replied. "It actually makes sense that he'd use a place like this. After spending what had to be three months of his life sterilizing it, I mean. There are thousands of storage spots just like this all over the Twin Cities and millions in the Midwest. Without the address, you'd never find it. Plus, if cops are looking for any of this, they can't come in here without a warrant. So anything they found would be inadmissible."

"But padlocks? To protect all this?"

"It's got to look normal from the outside. If he put up a fancy electronic lock or security grid or what-have-you, it would draw exactly the attention Gulo wants to avoid. 'Gosh, what's in there that he wants to protect so badly? Let's look and see!' But who's gonna case a place like this and think, 'I'll pick that random stor-age space on the very off chance that it has $100,000 worth of new weapons and ammo in it'?"

Annette was groping the wall next to the bench. "Besides, if someone wants in badly enough, they'll get in. So he—or they—didn't waste money on locks, it was spent on space, climate con-trol, and ease of access. Thus the elevators," she added, because holy shit, there was an elevator behind the reloading bench. You had to push the bench aside to access it, which was why Oz hadn't seen it; Annette had found it because she wanted a closer look. Not to mention…

"The lighting in here is for shit. Gulo must hate it—did you notice how bright the lights were in the morgue?"

"This is all puzzling and probably terrible, but it's not helping me figure out Gulo's connection to the Smalls and the genocide his family may or may not have planned. And we'll need to figure out who else is involved."

"D'you suspect Debbie, lad?"

"A wereroe who nearly passed out when you raised your voice? Gulo wouldn't have any use for her. He wants fighters. Resentful fighters who feel disenfranchised and pissy."

"SAS members," Berne sighed, resigned.

"Such a stickler for details, Oz," Annette teased. "I've only seen you apply that to your wardrobe."

"Ugh. Even your compliments sound bitchy." Oz's complaint was pure reflex—he and Annette had been sniping at each other for over a decade—because he was beginning to realize the impli-cations of a reloading bench and crates of new weapons. The smell of gun oil was sharp and earthy and got stronger when Berne pried open one of the crates; even in poor light, the blue-black barrels gleamed. "Fucking guns, the irony isn't as clever as they think it is. Just hypocritical."

"What d'you mean?"

Berne looked up from the crate and Oz was startled at the man's haunted expression. "SAS is trying another takeover. Or something just as bad. There are too many guns in a storage space rented by a coroner who falsified evidence for it to be anything else."

"It's the anniversary weekend," Annette said dully. Oz could practically read her mind: *What a waste, what a waste, and now a new bunch of people are going to die. And for what?* "And what better way than to use Stable weapons against them?"

"Point," he agreed. Shifters tended to look at guns as crutches and the people who wielded them as dangerous small-minded adolescents. Annette was the only Shifter he knew who even owned a gun, and it stayed locked up in her closet 99 percent of the time. Which was sensible, because whenever she took it out of the closet, people died. Was there a metaphor in there somewhere? Lila would know. He couldn't *wait* to tell her about all this. Given her ease with firearms, she'd probably pick up on things he'd miss. He loved her fierce protective instincts, all the more admirable because she was new to…well. Everything. The neighborhood, Shifters, his nutty extended family, house fires—

No, not house fires.

Maybe he shouldn't say anything. She'd been pulled into Shifter madness, into his family's chaos on top of all *her* chaos. If he really cared about her, he'd leave her the hell alone and fuck *Kama-Rupa*, which wasn't the lovely soul mate fable he'd been told as a kid but just an adult rationale for why Shifters got crushes on strange Stables they scented from a distance.

Focus. Guns. Murder. Impending doom. Remember?

He turned back to Berne and Annette. "Gulo and Co. might think guns are the tools of primitive adolescents, but they learned from their mistake a decade ago. If you're going to try to take power from billions, you'll need more than teeth and claws. The worst of it is, it probably won't work. But a lot of people are gonna get shot before SAS figures that out."

"Lad, I have t'tell you something," Berne said dully, just as they heard the hum of the elevator and saw the doors start to slide open.

"Hold that thought, Magnus." Oz was happy to see Annette and Berne stay put, despite the imminent arrival of bad guys. Bolting wasn't an option with all that was at stake, but that didn't mean it wasn't tempting.

"It will work," Dr. Gulo said.

"Rude," Annette observed. "No one was talking to you."

Gulo glared and started to shout something, then got hold of himself. He pushed the reloading bench away from the elevator doors and stepped out. "It'll work because you said it yourself—we learned from our mistakes."

Oz and Annette laughed. Berne looked at them, surprised, then grinned and shook his head.

"No," Oz replied. "Shitheads like you never do. Are you going to shoot us in here? You don't have any plastic on the floors." He kicked at the glossy floor, which was so clean the toe of his shoe squeaked. "It's so slick! The blood's gonna run everywhere. It'll be the scene with the bloody elevators from *The Shining* in reverse."

"What a slippery mess we'll make," Annette promised. "I plan to thrash around as much as I can for maximum grossness as I exsanguinate."

Maximum grossness! Finally, a title for my autobiography.

"Nobody's dying." This from one of the two men who had come out of the elevator behind Gulo. The one who spoke, a muscular redhead of medium height, was dressed in jeans and a black turtleneck, which was kind of funny. *Why is that funny? Is it the gun? Gun + turtleneck = weird?* "Wait, I'll clarify. Nobody's dying in this storage space," he added, making a shooing motion with his gun. "Time for a ride, you three."

Gulo nearly sagged in relief. Oz was torn; on one hand, he was thrilled that they were (hopefully) taking them to whatever bullshit was going on in Shakopee. On the other, he loved the idea of desecrating Gulo's sterile space with any number of bodily fluids.

"And y'think we're going with you why?" Berne asked mildly.

"Besides saving Gulo's obsessively waxed floor?" Annette asked.

Turtleneck McPistol waved his gun again. "Do you know what this is?"

"A really off-putting turtleneck?" Oz squinted. "An off-putting navy-blue turtleneck?"

"It's a 9mm pistol, wiseass. Fifteen bullets to a clip, one for the chamber, and if I empty it into your brainpan, your weekend will be fucked."

"That *would* put a crimp in date night tomorrow," Annette admitted.

"All three of you are coming with us right now. If any one of you resists, I'll murder your sister."

"Foster sister," Annette corrected.

"Colleague, really. And not even my favorite colleague." Oz shrugged. "Sorry, Annette."

"But I'm ahead of *Nadia*, at least. Right, Oz?"

Oz didn't need the reminder but appreciated it anyway. "You're two slots ahead of Nadia."

"Oh, thank God. Wait. Two? Who's—"

Oz raised his voice. "Our point, boys, is that there's no blood tie."

Turtleneck's rebuttal was to fire his gun a couple of inches from Annette's left foot. The bullet plowed into the cement floor and didn't ricochet, thank God.

"Hey!" Annette snapped. "You're making a terrible impression. Just be aware!"

"Do you get it now?" Turtleneck said, attempting a Tough Guy expression but coming off as Constipated Guy, while beside him, Gulo gasped and dropped to his knees to inspect the gouge the bullet made. "Do you?"

"Big sound," Berne said. "Go bang. Which you're proud of for some reason. Yes. We get it." Then he shrugged and turned to face the third man, the one who was keeping his ears open and his mouth closed. "Have we met? I've the nagging feeling I've seen ye before."

When there was no response, Oz stepped forward. "You want us to come with, we'll come with. Look, I'm cooperating. I'm gonna cooperate all over you guys." Oz started for the door, side-stepping Gulo, who was still examining the hole.

"It's okay. It's fine. I can fix this. Won't take long to fill. And then I can paint it over. Nine or ten coats ought to do it." He shot to his feet, and Oz was completely unprepared for the hard shove. "Keep to yourself," Gulo snapped. "You stink like a Stable."

"Hey, thanks!" He and Lila could never be, but it was kind of cool that some of her scent was on him. Yet another benefit of sleeping on her couch. "Oh. You prob'ly thought that was an insult."

"You piece of shit," Annette said in a low voice. She didn't normally swear, so…*whoa*. "Don't touch him again."

Oz flipped to his feet. "Don't make her angry. You wouldn't like her when she's angry. I'm fine, Annette, don't sweat it. So are we going? We should be going."[11]

"It's not going to work out for you," Gulo said. "I'm sure you morons think you have a plan, or that you're pretending to cooperate because you're expecting a nick-of-time rescue, but it won't happen."

"So, then." Annette shrugged. "You've got nothing to worry about."

"Phones." This from the third man, who been watching like it was the best tennis game ever. He had gray-flecked brown hair in the de rigueur villain buzz cut. And either he and the redhead shopped at the same store or got the same memo, because he was wearing jeans and a turtleneck, too.

---

11. *Hulk* shout-out!

Wait… That's a mock turtleneck. Which is slightly less silly. Why? Why is it less silly than the full-on turtleneck? I don't know, it just is.

"Phones out! Right now," Mock Turtleneck ordered. "Take them out and drop them on the floor."

They complied; Oz was actually surprised it took Gulo and the Turtlenecks so long to get around to a crucial step in managing hostages. He couldn't help wincing when they hit the floor. Magnus, by contrast, looked so preoccupied he didn't even look when his phone hit the cement floor with a *crack!*

"See? This is what I'm talking about." Pissy Gulo wasn't as annoying as smug Gulo, though it was a close race. "You're done. No way to call for help. And I'm sure you noticed there's no Wi-Fi in here. Part of the design."

Yep. It was one of the reasons why Annette had emphasized Nadia's name.

I really, really hope Nadia isn't the one to save us. Ideally, we save ourselves and foil the bad guys. Death is almost preferable to Nadia swooping in. She'll ride that story for the rest of our lives.

"I won't lie," Gulo continued, which was hilarious coming from the guy who falsified evidence. "I'm sorry your Stable girlfriend isn't here. I wanted to see what a .357 Magnum carbine does to her torso."

She's not my girlfriend; more's the fucking pity. And never would be. Lila had been through so much as a kid, she deserved some stability. Instead, she was reliving her childhood fire trauma and stuck with a houseful of weres. He was going to solve this, he was going to get Sally squared away and find out who tried to burn Sally and Mama out. And then Lila would be safe, and if she smelled smoke, it would be dream-smoke. Nothing real.

And if that meant distancing himself once the mysteries had been solved so she could have the uneventful arson-free life she deserved, then that's what he would do. And Annette might tease him and call him a "noble knight errant," but it wasn't about that. It was about being decent and putting his heart ahead of his cock.

Something like that, anyway.

Meanwhile, there was still *this* dill weed to deal with. "Is that my cue to lose my mind and take a swing at you? Lila can take care of herself." And in a perfect world, Oz would get to see what Lila could do to Gulo. But all bullshit aside: He was very, very glad she was at the Curs(ed) House, and out of danger.

Chapter 44

HOT, AND GETTING HOTTER, AND HER EYES HER EYES WERE streaming and she had no idea how bad the smoke could get and everything was fine five minutes ago and now she couldn't see and couldn't breathe and Mama was going to be SO MAD but maybe she could grab some of the mags, maybe even the little bookshelf just inside the living room that was stuffed with People *and* US Weekly *and it was worth trying, sure it was, but she couldn't she tried and she lost her grip and when she tried to scoop up the smoldering magazines she was scooping up fire she was holding fire and it felt like a zillion bees were stinging her arms at once and she had to put them out she had to kill the bees every last one and and and and and and*

Lila woke with a gasp. She'd slapped herself awake. No surprise, but Christ, that was a vivid one. She could still smell the smoke. She'd never been a lucid dreamer; no matter how ridiculous or fanciful the dream. She could dream she was elected POTUS and declared all Mondays to be Chocolate Pudding Day, she could dream she was a NASCAR driver who only raced horse and buggies, she could dream she was Anne Boleyn chopping off Henry VIII's head, it all seemed perfectly real until she woke up. Small wonder she thought she smelled smoke.

It's just the remnants of a dream, the oldest and worst dream. Calm down. Nothing's on fire. Look at your arms, see? No fresh scars. You haven't had a burn graft in years. So just calm your ass down and tell yourself that **holy shit I can still smell smoke!**

She sat up and flung the blankets off. Only then did she

remember that Sally was napping beside her with Osa tucked under one arm. After she'd left three urgent voice mails for Oz, she'd realized there was nothing more to do. She had no idea where Oz was, and it was unlikely that Berne would go on an Oz-murdering rampage to protect his secret. She'd catch him up when she saw him for their next not-date.

Except she wouldn't, because they were done not-dating.

Mama Mac and Daniels had gone shopping—new wooden spoons, no doubt, and several reams of paper for Daniels—and she'd gotten drowsy. (Busy week.) She was almost asleep when Sally crept in beside her.

That had been over an hour ago. At least her nightmare thrashing hadn't disturbed the kiddo. Lila stumbled out of bed—naps always left her feeling like she was moving through wet polyester—and went to the door. She felt the doorknob, listened, and then

"Jeez, a guy can't even take a shower, *ducha*, *douche*, without the place going up in smoke. That's literal, by the way!"

opened the door. Devoss was standing just outside the bath-room, stripped to the waist and looking scrawny and vulnerable. His shoulder blades stood out like…well, blades. Behind him, the shower was running, and to her left, smoke billowed and rose from downstairs.

"Get your shirt back on and get in here," she barked, and to the kid's credit, he wasted no time. "Sally, time to get up." She closed her bedroom door, went to the closet, pulled out the EZ-OUT ladder. "Devoss, open the window. Punch out the screen if you have to." She went to her top dresser drawer and pulled out two pairs of thick socks. "Put these on, both of you. No time for boots."

She picked Sally up, swung her around until the girl was sitting on Lila's lap, and tugged on her socks. "What is it?" the child whispered, scrunching into Lila to get small.

Devoss hadn't punched out the screen, he'd bent it, then pushed it out the window. "What else? Bad guys set *this* house on fire, too."

Lila bit her lip; she'd never felt such pride and sorrow at the same time. Devoss's words were fearless, but his assessment was heart-breaking. *Matter-of-fact becomes jaded so quickly. Can't anyone just be a kid anymore?*

"We don't know that. It might just be a grease fire or something." Technically true. But she wasn't a big believer in coincidences. Not a single one of her smoke alarms had gone off. "Up. Window."

Devoss hooked the EZ-OUT to the windowsill, then watched as the thing unfolded itself down the outside of the house. "Hey! You weren't exaggerating the other day. This ladder *is* quick to install."

"We'll make sure to send them an appreciative email later."

"Ugh. Nobody sends emails anymore. Well, maybe grandmas."

"Listen. Both of you." She put her hands on Sally's shoulders. "You're going to climb down this ladder *carefully*. Just like the jungle gym at school."

"I think 'jungle gym' is offensive to people who live in actual jungles," Devoss said, because he was smart and brave and also a pain in the ass.

"Devoss will be right behind you. I'll come last."

"No!"

"Sally, you'll be fi—"

"What if the bad guys come up after we're out and you're in here all by yourself? You need us!" Sally pointed to Lila's fingers with their short, blunt nails. "Your claws are pitiful!"

"You are wonderful now get your ass out that window. *Move.*" And then, as Sally's tip-tilted eyes filled with tears, Lila added, "I will be fine. You've seen me work."

"C'mon, Sally." Devoss picked her up, and Lila helped him ease the child out the window until her arms were on the sill and she was standing on the ladder, small face pinched with anxiety. "Think how pissed Caro's gonna be that she missed this. I'm right behind you."

"O—okay."

"Watch her," she told Devoss, then went to her closet.

"Yes, ma'am."

"When she's just a couple of steps from the bottom, you go."

"Wouldn't dream of arguing with you."

"Wise."

"Even though you have firsthand knowledge that I don't need a ladder to get to the ground."

Lila broke a major-ass gun rule, then joined Devoss at the window. "Here. Turn around." She stuffed Osa down the back of his jeans

"Ack!"

and then he was climbing out the window. "I'm going, jeez!" he said before she could open her mouth. She poked her head out and saw Sally standing on the ground, cupping her elbows and looking up at them, her face a pale, frightened oval.

"Fuck," Lila said, went back to the door, listened

(*good—if weird—that I still don't hear anything*)

checked it for heat again

(*cool it's cool that's excellent there's time*)

and then went to her closet, grabbed one of the few boxes left to unpack, and went back to the window. Devoss was standing next to Sally, both of them squinting up at her.

"Heads up!" She pitched the box of sweaters, took one last glance around the room, and started down the ladder. *Next, what next? I left my phone in the kitchen like a moron… Find a way to call 911, try and figure out where the fire is and how bad. Keep the kids safe. In the opposite order.* "Open the box and put on sweaters!"

Mama Mac and Daniels and Oz (and presumably Garsea) were safe, that was something. She and Oz weren't non-dating anymore, they would never be a thing, just two ships passing in, et cetera, and BTW, if Berne hurt him, he could kiss his patellas goodbye.

But Oz was off somewhere working his case, getting on Garsea's nerves and probably confronting evil, and not just when he sassed Faulkner. So that was a relief.

Chapter 45

ANNETTE LET OUT ANOTHER YELP. "STOP TORTURING ME WITH torture, you torturous scumbags!"

"Jesus Christ," Turtleneck hissed. "Will you stop?"

"Will *you*? That's all I'm asking."

"No! We're not stopping at McDonald's or Wendy's or KFC—"

"Not even for some gravy?"

"—or Sonic or Subway or Culver's or DQ or Sakura or any of the dozen steak houses or sushi bars you've been babbling out!"

"This stall technique is pathetic," Gulo put in.

"She's not stalling," Oz said, slumped back in his seat and staring up at the van's skylight. "It's not part of a carefully thought out subterfuge to get you guys to drop you guard. This is just Annette Garsea." *You poor bastards.* "Enjoy."

"Would stopping for a Peanut Buster Parfait be *that* detrimental to your time line? *Honestly.*"

They'd piled into Gulo's gray cargo van

"Nice rape van, Gulo. Not creepy at all."

and were Shakopee-bound. Mock had a gun on Annette, and Magnus was in the passenger seat with Turtleneck right behind him, pointing the gun at the back of his head. Magnus didn't seem to notice; he was staring out the windshield and hadn't said a word since they got in the car.

"This is the second time this week I've had a gun in my face," Oz commented.

Annette snorted. "Welcome to social work."

"I liked it better when Lila did it," he admitted.

"No doubt. Since we have some time to kill, did you want to explain that odd *Kama-Rupa* outburst on the whiteboard?"

"Annette, please!" Oz yelped. "Not in front of the turtlenecks."

"Our murders are imminent," she reminded him. "So if not now, when?"

She's got a point. "Nothing to explain. We're not a couple, never were, never will be."

"Does she feel the same way?"

"She," he replied firmly, "has enough of her own traumas and troubles. I won't add to them."

"Oh, God, Oz. Not you, too. Don't do that."

"Do what? Be considerate?"

"Be an overbearing man–jackass hybrid. A manass. Don't do something for her own good while leaving her out of the conversation. It's condescending *and* tacky."

"How is being consid—"

"All right!" Gulo shouted from the driver's seat. "Jesus, it's like you *want* to get shot in the face. Now pay attention, I'm going to explain what's about to happen."

Oz sighed. "You're going to kill us, then leave our bodies somewhere that will make people think we were killed in your New and Improved Race War, because you're boring and don't have an original thought in your obsessively scrubbed head."

"Species war," Gulo snapped. "And it's typical that you sheep would misunderstand."

"I like how Dr. Gulo instantly proved your point," Annette said.

Oz laughed. "Yeah, that was a nice bonus."

"This is an act of survival! You species traitors are worse than the Stables. But starting today, we're going to—"

"Nobody wants to hear your B movie villain monologue," Oz said, stifling a yawn. "So just go ahead and do what you're gonna do and spare us the chatter."

"It's for—"

"Revenge. Or profit. Or spite. You're mad because your ancestors were disenfranchised. Or because you weren't breastfed.

Or because you've gone crazy from close contact with too many cleaning products. What-the-fuck-ever. Just do it already."

Turtleneck shook his head. "You're begging for a bullet in the throat."

"Not in the van!" Gulo yelped.

"You can't, can you? Kill us? Not yet."

Annette raised her hand like they were in a mobile classroom. "Quick question, gentlemen. I think I understand the insanity behind all your nonsense, as much as a sane person can. But why set fire to Meredith Macropi's house? Intimidation? A warning?"

"What the hell are you talking about?" Mock asked. "Who's Macropi?"

Oz straightened in his seat. "So that wasn't you guys?"

Gulo was shaking his head; the other two hench-turtlenecks looked equally mystified.

He exchanged a glance with Annette, then said what they were both thinking. "Then who the hell tried to burn Mama's house down?"

Chapter 46

"Both of you shift," Lila ordered. "Right now. And wait here. Do *not* leave this spot. I'll be back in a sec."

She'd never get used to how quickly these guys could get out of their clothes. Fabric tore, and she was glad they were following instructions even if telling them to put on her sweaters was dumb in retrospect because now they were getting torn to shit, *fuck*.

She walked softly and steadily around the side of the house, hoping whomever set the fire was still there. It wasn't likely—arsonists who hung around their own fires tended to go to prison—but she had to check anyway.

The kitchen porch door was open. Was the firebug still inside the house? Was he a suicidal firebug? Even more interesting, there was a familiar truck in her driveway: Harriss & Son.

Which made perfect sense once you looked at the clues. Too bad he had to set another fire before she caught on to the fact that he set fires.

She ran back to the kids, went to her knees, stared straight into Devoss's furry fox face. "You both get to the shed and get out the hidden door, and you hide in the woods until me or Net or Oz or Macropi call for you. If not for yourself, then to keep Sally safe." She picked up Devoss by his scruff and tossed him gently in the direction of the shed to get him moving. "*Now*." Sally hesitated, then scampered after Devoss, her roly-poly body making her look like a moving medicine ball.

Then Lila turned back to confront the dumbass who thought he could burn out someone who planted dill. It was broad daylight, which seemed wrong. Surely such terrors came by night? When the hour was darkest, when the body's circadian rhythms were at their lowest? When, if you were still awake, you felt like the only person on earth? Even though she knew that was childish nonsense—the fire that consumed her mother's possessions had been started at 3:00 p.m., Sue and Sam's plane crashed around lunchtime, she sat through M. Night's *The Happening* at 4:00 p.m.—it still seemed strange to confront horror in daylight.

There was a crash as someone shoved open the kitchen door and stumbled out into the yard, smoke pouring out behind him. "*You.*"

"Me," she agreed. "You disconnected my smoke detectors, you arsonous douchenozzle." That was a word, right? Arsonous?[12] "Macropi called your dad to fix her screen door, but you showed up instead." And when he was done with the door, she realized, he saw a window of time when the Curs(ed) House was empty and made his move.

"Why didn't you take a fucking hint?"

"Perfect question," she told Harry Harriss, son of the owner of the Curs(ed) House. "There were enough clues, I should've confronted you two days ago."

Macropi: *I thought you were going to encourage him to leave home once he got his pilot's license?*

"You don't know what you're talking about."

"You had access to avgas, and I'll bet your handy-dandy repair truck is full of stuff you used to sabotage the place until whoever-it-is moves out. How long have you been doing this? Never mind. Whatever the answer, it's pathetic."

It's not like I'm doing any of it on purpose. And Macropi hadn't been. It was all on Harry Harriss.

"You think this is bad?" Harry asked, pointing at the smoke.

"Well, yeah."

"That's just from the fireplace. Wait 'til I get some wood in there."

---

12. Yep. Spellcheck disagreed, but the dictionary insisted.

Lila laughed at him, relief making her giddy. "That's what you did? You tried to burn my house—"

"*Our* house, the Harriss house, you fucking ape."

"—by starting a fire in the fireplace?" That explained why there was smoke, but she couldn't hear or feel any flames. "What kind of arsonist doesn't know about fireplace flues?"

"Who rents a house with fireplaces but doesn't keep anything on hand to make a fire?"

"So it's been a frustrating week for both of us."

"Week's not over yet," he snarled.

"True." *Wow, he's really going to stand there and confess to felonies in broad daylight. Awesome.* "But why torch Macropi's place?"

"It was supposed to teach her a lesson! Whenever anyone moves in, Shifter *or* Stable, she's always on the front stoop with fairy bread or some other bullshit. And she's always bummed when they move out! Even the Stables!" He threw his hands in the air, exasperated by the fact that Macropi wasn't a drooling sociopath. "She's just like my dad." Harriss was a stockier version of his father, with tufts of black hair valiantly battling male pattern baldness, and beard stubble that looked so coarse it could be mistaken for steel wool. And what the hell was he, anyway? What was his other self?

He was also chock full of grievances this afternoon. But on the upside, it sounded like Harriss Sr. had no idea what his idiot son had been up to these last few years. "They both need to be way more discerning," he finished contemptuously.

"Is that why you've never moved out? Is that why your dad has to bribe you to get you to leave? So you can hang out here and purify the neighborhood with your assholery?"

"They *told* you that?"

Wow, he looks more upset about that than he did about getting caught. "What can I say? People love to gossip about the pitiful."

"I shoulda taught her a lesson about sticking with her own kind years ago."

"You would have loved all those separate-but-equal lunch counters in the 1950s, I bet."

Harriss ignored her history burn. "But what does she do? Huh? After the fire? She moves in…with the Stable! And takes her cubs, too!"

"Yeah, it's a real bummer when you go to the trouble of committing arson and it doesn't work out exactly the way you planned. Plus, that just made it harder to make mischief, didn't it? Whenever you tried to arrange another accident or vole invasion, even if Macropi wasn't there, Oz and Garsea were always around." *Huh. Never thought I'd be happy about all the squatting.* "You disabled my smoke detectors a couple of days ago, but only came back today… why?" Even as she asked, Lila knew the answer and snapped her fingers. "To fix the bathroom lock that Oz demolished. And when you got here, you saw—"

"It's just *you* here right now. You and some cubs. And it was the perfect day."

"The tenth anniversary of what happened at Shakopee."

Harriss went pale under his stubble. His eyes were so wide they were showing the whites all around, like a horse about to kick down a barn door. "You know about that? Those fucking species traitors, they *told* you about that?"

"Yeah, it's weirdly relevant this week. Now get the hell off my lawn." *I've always wanted to say that.* "Or I'll *make* you get off. Yuck, I'll rephrase…"

"Get out of my way," he snarled, and she saw him pull a jug out of the back of his truck and realized what he'd gone back for. *Avgas belongs in planes, dammit. Planes! Not in my house! Or Macropi's!* "Move!"

"You first," she replied, then reached back and pulled her handgun out of the waistband of her jeans, a ginormous no-no where gun safety was concerned, but necessity was a mother. Or something.

"Typical ape," he sneered, and the guy was, what? Twenty-two, twenty-three? Yet looking at a near-stranger with nothing but contempt. And by-the-by, what kind of a Shifter was he? Was she going to have a tiger on her hands? A rare bear? A wolf, like Oz?

No. There weren't any wolves like Oz.

"Harriss, you dumbass, what are you doing? You're not getting away with any of it, and you're making it worse for yourself right now. I know they say that a lot in cop shows, but you really are."

Harriss kept coming. "Your little toy doesn't scare—oh fuck *that hurts*!"

"Nine left in the clip," she said helpfully, as Harriss staggered back, clutching his bloody knee. "And by my count you've got one knee, two elbows, and two ankles left. And a forehead. Or you could lie facedown on the ground like a good boy and wait for the cops."

"Fuck you!"

Before she could form an appropriate rebuttal, she heard a screech, and then Macropi's Outback was roaring up the lawn

"My hydrangeas!"

and was still moving when Caro Daniels opened her door and jumped out, shouting so hard she was spitting. *"You leave her alone!"*

"I'd listen," Lila advised an increasingly shocked and pain-riddled Harriss. "While we're killing time, you wouldn't have any fertilizer in that truck, would you? The soil here's a little too sandy. I want great big hydrangea flowers, big as my head. What? Why is the racist deadbeat arsonist looking at me like *I'm* the freak? Oh, no. No-no-no. Keep your clothes on. This has all been surreal enough without a naked Harry Harriss thrown into the mix and you're totally ignoring me and now you're naked and what *are* you?"

There was squirming and writhing as Harry's other self fought to get free of his overalls, and then there was a squat beast with black fur with a splash of white fur running across its chest, a thick tail, and small, roundish ears with pink insides. Harriss had long whiskers where you'd expect whiskers to be, and also on the top of his head for some reason. Now the size of a big fat basset hound, he scream-growled and tried to run at her, remembered he'd been shot, and then hunched in on himself, probably to look fierce. Instead, he looked like he was taking the mother of all dumps, which was anything but frightening.

"Okay, I—now this is just sad." Lila lowered her gun. "You've made me sad for you. I don't want to be sad for the guy who thinks setting fires means he's the good guy, dammit!"

"Careful, m'girl." Macropi had rushed to her side while Daniels loomed over Harriss like an avenging angel in her *A wise man once said NOTHING* sweatshirt. "His bite force is ridiculous. See the disproportionately large head?"

"No, I was distracted by the fat tail. And the whole turning into whatever he is."

"Tasmanian devil." Macropi looked down at him and tsked. "*Sarcophilus harrisii*. Caro, you come away from him now."

"Really?" Lila inspected the bulky beast from a safe distance. "The *Looney Tunes* cartoons made them seem a lot more intimidating. Shouldn't he be a whirl of flailing limbs and teeth?"

"He can crush bone. Don't you try it, Harry Harriss! You just sit there and think about what you've done until we get someone to tend to you! Oh, what your father will say, I just can't imagine." Then Macropi's hands landed on Lila's shoulders as she pulled her in for a close look.

"That's a terrible idea when I'm holding a gun, Macropi."

Nose to nose, anxious blue eyes searched her face. "Are you okay, dear?"

"Sure. And don't worry, the kids are back of the shed, hiding in the woods until I give the all—"

"Here we are!"

"Goddammit."

Sally had stopped long enough to put on one of Lila's old sweatshirts, which fell to her knees. Devoss had put his jeans back on and nothing else, then rushed to tell Daniels what she'd missed.

Sally darted straight for Lila, who had to pick her up or be bowled over. "You were wrong," she said, and kissed Lila's cheek with a loud smack. "You *are* Mary Poppins."

"Oh, ugh," she replied, then looked away so they wouldn't see how much that pleased her.

Chapter 47

"Your new revolution starts in the *Reflections Dance Academy*?"

"Bold," Annette added.

"This benighted studio was built over the burial mounds of our people," Gulo declared.

"No, it wasn't," Annette scoffed. "The burial mounds are in the historical district down by the Minnesota River. Note my use of the present tense, because *they're still there*. You could walk out the door we just came in and find them in ten minutes. This is another reason why your Genocide 2.0 is doomed to fail. You can't be bothered to do your research."

"That doesn't matter!" Gulo snapped. Despite the Closed sign, they'd been able to walk right in. Gulo was leaning on the reception desk and none of them seemed to be in a hurry to go anywhere. Waiting for a signal, then. Or reinforcements. "This dance studio is a symbol of Stable tyranny and complacence."

"And also a great way to stay in shape," Oz added.

"I know our lives are in danger," Annette said, "but I really feel like we're nailing some of these asides."

"Oh, yeah." Some people went on roller coasters to get a rush; he and Annette faced down insecure grumps with guns and riffed. If he hadn't cared deeply for her since they were teenagers under Mama's roof, he would've loved her for that alone. "We're on fire! That's not an invitation to set us on fire, by the way."

Mock lashed out, quicker than thought, and the gun sight split the skin just above Annette's left eyebrow. Blood trickled, then streamed. Oz knew any wound on the face or head bled so much it looked worse than it was, knew that a week from now it would be nearly healed, but that didn't stifle the urge to break out Mock's teeth and shove them up his ass.

Annette grinned a red grin, seized a startled Gulo by his coat lapels, and kissed him on the mouth. The resulting scream was shrill and satisfying. "For someone so fastidious," she said, releasing him as she licked blood from her teeth, "it's odd to me that you're neck deep in a plot that will guarantee major messiness and a number of corpses."

"Stables brought this on themselves," Gulo insisted. "They're greedy and destructive and they breed like they're getting paid. They've endangered the entire *planet*, don't you understand? They've had years to get on top of climate change and what've they done? Had meetings. Took to the streets in protest, then *more* meetings. And when an administration puts environmental protections in place, the next guy comes along and un-does them. They're children smashing a toy, then crying after the damage is done, with no clue how to fix it."

All this while he was frantically scrubbing his face with his hands, then rubbing his hands on his slacks, then seeing the bloody streaks on his pants and rubbing his face some more. He was generating amazing friction; if his hands were two sticks, he'd be on fire by now.

"Your thug lashed out because he didn't like what we were saying, but Stables are children?" Annette asked as blood dripped down her jaw. "And speaking of smashing, what'd you do to Magnus's plane?"

"Ridiculous bullshit!"

Am I ever not *going to jump when he does that?*

"*That's* where I've seen you," Magnus continued, turning to glare. "Logan Airport."

Mock grinned. "Was wondering when you'd put it together."

Berne growled. "This…" (The pause was hilarious.) "…person used to be on the ground crew in Boston. Which is where I'd berthed my plane for a bit."

"Until Sue Smalls called to ask a favor," Oz guessed.

"Aye."

"Because somehow, she'd gotten wind of Team Genocide's plan for a do-over the weekend of the tenth anniversary. Or she was in on it."

Now Berne was glaring at Oz. "Of course she wasn't in on it. Don't be daft. We learned, even if they didn't." He pointed at the Turtleneck Gang, his contempt plain. "She wasn't sure what was happening, just that she'd heard some things and wanted to check them out. She told me she also wanted to see her GP to get another referral for the Mayo. I didn't think much of it at the time, to my everlasting regret."

"But why were *you* there?" Oz asked Mock.

"Keeping tabs," Magnus said heavily.

"On Sue?"

"On both."

Annette blinked. The bleeding had stopped, for which Oz was thankful, but she could have been gushing by the gallon and wouldn't have noticed, not when she had that look, like she had hold of a rope but wasn't sure where it would lead her. "I'm missing something," she admitted. "I feel like it's right in front of my face." She wiped her jaw, then flicked her fingers in Gulo's direction, who flinched back so hard he nearly fell down. How the hell did that guy do his job without having a nervous breakdown?

"You might as well talk about it, Magnus," Oz said. "I assume it won't be Murder O'Clock until Team Race War's reinforcements show up."

"Species war," Turtleneck snapped. "Do we have to carve it into your forehead?"

"It'll kill some time," Oz finished. "So why not?"

Annette's eyes widened in comprehension. "Magnus, what side were you on? At Shakopee?"

"You already know, lass, or you wouldn't be askin'."

He'd said, *Can't even think of it without being embarrassed.*

He'd said, *Sue and I've known each other since Shakopee. She c'n have anything she wants.*

He'd said, *You're not at the top. We are. Shifters. Because we can change our shape. You, poor lass, are Stable. You're locked into a bipedal form all your life.*

And then he'd said, *My condolences.*

Annette sighed. "This is disappointing, Magnus."

"Aye, lass. And you haven't heard the worst of it."

Chapter 48

Then.

THEY'D GONE TO THE MEETINGS, THEY'D LISTENED TO THE rhetoric, they'd agreed that the Stables couldn't be trusted with the planet's well-being any longer. It wasn't a superiority thing. It was a survival thing. Not just their survival. Everyone's. Seven billion everyones.

But this?

"If SAS had a brochure, this wouldn't have been mentioned. Like how they don't give you all the details of the timeshare until you've signed," Sue Smalls whispered. She had to whisper; they were in the back of the Shakopee Ballroom, listening to City Councilman Ben Wapiti exhort them to shed blood. There were angry Shifters on all sides, and too many of them sounded like they were one hundred percent on board with Team Mass Murder. "Should have guessed when they planned to start at nine p.m. Who starts something like this at nine o'clock at night? And doesn't invite the press?"

"So it's true," he replied in a low voice. "They're going to kill every Stable who crosses them 'for the greater good.'"

"Anyone who says that, I just automatically assume they're a sociopath. I can't believe it, Sam was right!"

Jealousy flared, burned a line down his throat and into his chest. "I thought you guys were done."

"And I thought he was full of shit and apathetic, two things I pretty much can't stand." Sue was counting heads while they whispered to each other and inched toward the doors. "We need to find him."

"Why?"

"So we don't die, Maggie."

He grimaced. Sue Smalls was the only woman in the world who could use that nickname without incurring his wrath. She knew and took full advantage.

"We can just leave. Right now. You said it yourself, this was never our intent. So we'll go. Together."

Sue quirked an eyebrow at him and half-smiled. "You think it'll be that easy?"

Chapter 49

Now.

"Pussies back then," Mock sneered. "Pussies now."

Berne ignored the critique of his narrative flow. As far as Magnus Berne was concerned, he had an audience of two, neither of whom were wearing turtlenecks. "I followed Sue," he said simply. "Always. She really was a believer. She genuinely feared for billions if Stables kept up their headlong rush into making the planet uninhabitable. Al Gore's *An Inconvenient Truth* had just come out, people were starting to grasp how real—and huge—the problem was."

"I should have known they'd never let a werewolf become president." Annette shook her head. "I know that sounds like an unhinged conspiracy theory, but Gore was clearly and repeatedly discredited. It's no coincidence he was considered a national joke for years."

"My point is, anything Sue was that passionate about, I wanted in. Y'see how it was?"

"In the lady's defense," Oz admitted, "she had a point."

"Aye. But by and by, we learned more about their long-term goals. By then, I was with SAS of my own accord. Even if Sue had left, I'd have stayed, because the movement was about more than reassuring ourselves we were the superior species."

"It was?" Annette asked, earning a trio of glares.

Why are they letting Magnus narrate?

"SAS favored exposure to the wider world. In my stupidity, I didn't realize that their idea of 'coming out' wasn't at all the same as mine."

The exposure question. Again. Weres like David Auberon thought it was long overdue, but then Davey-boy grew up with Stable pals who knew—and kept—the secret of his other self. His default was to trust them, but he was in the minority of a minority. There were plenty of Shifters in the world who would eat glass before trusting a Stable. There were an equal number who told their cubs boogeyman stories about Stables. And when you're *that* afraid of a group, how do you overcome it?

"Our long-range goals—mine and SAS's—were the same, we just differed greatly on the short-term policies that would get us to that goal. And it was...nice, at first," he admitted. "Better than nice. Exciting, even. It was great to talk to so many weres who favored coming out and showing the planet what we could do if given the reins. In Scotland, there aren't nearly as many, and no bears at all save for my family. It's not the issue it is over here. Here, I knew there were millions who thought the way I did. It's easy to feel alone in Scotland. It's impossible here. Or so I told myself."

"So then what?"

"Then it got verra bloody verra fast."

Chapter 50

Then.

"**What the hell are you doing here?**" **Sam Smalls** hissed. "I told you to stay away, Sue! This day of *all* days!"

"And it was adorable that you thought you could direct anything I do. You remember Magnus."

"Obviously." Sam shoved his glasses further up his nose and fixed Magnus with an unfriendly look. "Where you are, he follows."

"They say the qualities you dislike most in others are qualities y'have yourself," Magnus replied pleasantly. "Otherwise, why are *you* here?"

"Not to hang around a female. Is this why you moved here from Scotland, Maggie? To widen the dating pool?"

"Can you two out-asshole each other some other time?" Sue hissed. "If you haven't noticed, we're in big-time trouble."

"Of course I noticed! You're out here with me, right?"

They were. Sam had somehow scented Sue through the hundreds of other weres and all but dragged her outside. Berne had followed, because that's what he did now, apparently.

He'd never know what Sue saw in the boy. Sam Smalls was short and wiry, with the eyesight of an aging vole; his other self barely topped 175 pounds. In a fight for dominance, the best Sam could hope for was immediate evisceration. And he was smart. To be fair, he was one of the smartest people Berne had ever met, probably the smartest on campus, but Sam Smalls needed everyone to know it, all the time. And he was majoring in English lit, for God's sake. With a minor in media arts. *Jesus wept.*

Which was why it drove him crazy that Sue actually favored

the worm over the Scot. Magnus hoped any kid Sam and Sue had (God fucking forbid) took after her side.

"Look, you have to leave," Sam insisted. It was nearly dark and the temp was dropping. The three of them had left their coats inside, and Berne doubted they were going back for them. "Right now. You should, too, Maggie. Don't look so shocked. I wouldn't wish what's coming on my worst enemy."

"Didn't know you cared," Magnus drawled.

"It's bad," Sam said simply. "I don't want to see anyone hurt, even you. None of us should be here."

"So why are you?" Magnus asked, thinking, *Oh, aye, it's bad all right. If Sam Smalls, who wouldn't spit on me if I was on fire, thinks I should leave, then we're in trouble.*

"It's my job. You think no one notices when a group of weres with an agenda start mobilizing? People are coming."

"Isn't that the point?"

"God, you're thick!" Sam hissed, then smacked Magnus in the chest with the back of his hand. If Sue hadn't been standing there, Magnus would have pulled it off at the shoulder, then beat Sam to death with it. "*They're coming.* This revolution or whatever it is will not get off the ground. Everything's going to happen here, tonight. Everything's going to *end* here, get it? There won't be a worldwide chain reaction. When the smoke clears, the status quo will still be the status quo."

"But…" Sue looked stricken. "Some of them are our friends. Yours, too."

"They were never my friends."

"You're not a bear," Magnus told him. "You're a vole."

"I can be both," he replied, and pushed his glasses up again. "And better a vole than a mass murderer."

"Barely."

Chapter 51

Now.

"FUCKING TRAITOR IS WHAT HE WAS," GULO SAID. "IT WAS A pleasure to pronounce him dead."

"Um. Gulo? Saying he's dead doesn't actually mean he's dead. You get that, right?"

Gulo waved away the piddling detail of falsifying evidence in a homicide investigation. "He bailed on Sue. And I don't mean figuratively. If he didn't die in the crash, then where is he? It's been days. If he lived, he crawled off somewhere to die like a tabby cat hiding under someone's porch. Some Stable who thinks shooting herbivores means they're a Big Bad Hunter will find his bones in a few years and that will be fucking that for Smalls. Both of them." Gulo smiled at Berne. "I haven't seen Sue in years. She looked pretty good on my table, all in pieces. What little there was of her."

"That's your cue to swing at him," Oz volunteered, "because, again, Gulo doesn't do original thoughts. Or subtlety."

"Aye, lad, I'm aware. Sam wasn't my favorite person, but he wanted to save lives. And not just ours. It's not traitorous to stop people from jumping off a cliff."

"Spoken like the guy who ducked and ran."

"Yes," Magnus replied, and Oz had to give it to the guy, he positively radiated dignity. "SAS wasn't what I thought it was. And when I began to suspect, I should have trusted my instincts and acted right then. Instead, I dithered and hoped our other selves would reveal our *better* selves. That was a mistake, and people died."

"So SAS started out fairly benign, then slowly evolved into

a thing of unmitigated evil, feeding on itself and growing ever darker." Annette paused expectantly.

"Go ahead," Oz sighed. "You know you want to."

"Just like the Republican party! Wait. Too political? Just like the DMV! Better?"

"For God's sake," Mock muttered.

Magnus didn't even crack a smile.

"I ran to save us. I ran because I finally realized I never had any business being there. I couldn't set the clock back, there was no way to make it right, but I could learn. O'course, a couple of buildings had to catch fire before I came to that realization."

"Isn't that the way it always is?" Annette asked wryly.

Chapter 52

Then.

THEY WERE STILL ARGUING WHEN THE INCENDIARY DEVICE blew. They'd had no warning, there'd been no smell of gasoline or chemicals to tip them off. They hadn't heard ominous ticking that induced them to flee. One minute Sam was exhorting them to get gone, the next a terrific blast and the air was full of projectiles, many of which were on fire. Sue screamed as Magnus lurched toward her, only to get knocked off his feet as Sam threw his ridiculously small body at him.

He rolled to his feet and saw Sam had shoved him out of the way for a reason; the wall where he'd been standing was riddled with holes and smoldering. He'd been so focused on Sue, he'd ignored his own peril. Sue had dropped to her knees, clutching her arm above the wrist; her hand dangled by tendons and bones and not much else.

"Christ, lass!"

"Go!" Sam urged. "There's more, and—" They all stiffened as the sound of sirens permeated. A lot of them. "It's not just Shakopee Fire and Rescue. It's the feds, it's my bosses, *you can't be here.*"

"You come, too," Sue said tearfully.

"Aye, lad. All three of us need t'go. If the SAS finds out who you're with, they'll kill ye."

"Who, me? Teeny tiny Sam Smalls, whose last name is an accurate joke? I'd never have the brass balls for anything like that. Ask anyone." He grinned and there was another blast; across the street, another blaze had begun. "By the time they figure it all out, the mess will be swept up, the story will be quashed, and I'll be safe. So you be safe, too." He pushed his glasses back up; Magnus had decided it was a tic, since the man's glasses never seemed to need adjusting. "I know your intentions were good. Both of you. I know you weren't on board with SAS's real plan. This doesn't have to follow you for the rest of your lives."

"Ridiculous bullshit," he snarled, because he had a feeling it *would* follow them. Worse, now he was indebted to the bespectacled bastard.

That brought a smile to Sam's face, the first one Magnus had seen that day. "You need a better catch phrase."

"I hate you."

"Better." The grin widened. "Get her out of here."

"I fucking adore it when men talk like I'm not in the room." This while Sam ripped up part of his shirt and fastened a crude bandage for her wrist. "Cut it out—*fuck* that hurts!—before I pull my hand the rest of the way off and shove it down your throat."

Magnus picked her up, thought about all the times he'd wanted to hold her like this, and had new respect for the "be careful what you wish for" cliché.

"Maggie." He could have smiled at the pure exasperation in her tone. "My legs work fine."

The sirens were getting ever closer, and people were suddenly everywhere, pouring out all the entrances to the dance academy, darting here and there in the confusion. To say 'chaos reigned' was to say hurricanes were windy.

How could they have thought this would work? This isn't a plan, this is anarchy. And I endorsed it, if only by being here.

"Keep y'self safe," he told Sam. "I mean to repay this debt."

"Deal." He leaned down, kissed Sue on her grimy forehead. They were all grimy, smoke-smudged and worse to come, no doubt. "Get better."

"That's the plan, Sam," she replied, and then they were gone.

Chapter 53

Now.

"SCUTTLED OFF TO SAVE YOURSELVES, I KNEW IT," GULO snapped. "My father died that night. My big brother. And you ran off and left them."

So that's why they're letting Berne narrate. They want to know what happened, too, not just the stuff that made the papers, or the theories the survivors spun to explain what happened. Sam and his mysterious bosses managed to keep the AP and national press out of it by spinning it as a simple protest that turned violent. So for ten years, SAS has been wondering about the rest of the story.

"We knew there were traitors, we just didn't know how many," Gulo continued. "And it wasn't safe to go after the ones we could identify. Not then. So we waited. We had to, most of the leaders were dead. We had to build ourselves back up in a way that wouldn't attract attention until it was too late. All because you turned on your own kind."

"How?" Berne challenged.

Gulo blinked. "What?"

"How did they die? Your family? Your leaders? In glorious battle against the oppressors? A hand-to-hand brawl they heroically fought despite being outnumbered?"

Gulo glowered but stayed quiet.

"No. They died in the explosion," Berne continued. "The one *they* set. They blew themselves up out of pure piss ignorance, because your family had a shit plan they didn't think through. And in the chaos, more people died. The *only* saving grace that day came from the first responders, Stable and Shifter, and you were all too stupid to see it."

"Oh, please." Turtleneck rolled his eyes. "Not the 'only by coming together can we mend our differences' speech. If you're a fireman and you don't know the guy driving the truck is a Shifter, it doesn't count as peaceful interspecies cooperation. It just proves that hiding our natures is stupid."

"You want the story?" Magnus snapped. "You'll hear it to the end. The firefighters and paramedics didn't give a shite what your agenda was, they just wanted to save as many as they could. You lot, though? You tapped into your entitlement and assumed everything would work out simply because you wanted it to. Your plan wasn't noble or for the greater good, you just wanted to sow bedlam. Well, ye did."

"A little preachy," Oz said. "But dead on."

"And you're meaning to again, and for what? Because it's the anniversary and you feel you've got tae do something? To waste more time, money, and lives?"

"It's not just about a date on the calendar," Mock said. Oz hoped he would warm to the subject, maybe get distracted. From the moment he'd stepped out of the elevator, he and Turtleneck always had a gun trained on two of the three of them. If he or Annette or Magnus made a move, at least one of them would end up with a bullet in their frontal lobe. At the least, they were more formidable than Gulo, who always seemed on the verge of, or in the middle of, or recovering from, a tantrum. "This has been in the works for years." Mock swung around to point at Annette. "And that's your fault."

"Me?" Annette replied, startled. "What'd I do? Don't get me wrong, I'm delighted that my actions inconvenienced you, but which ones?"

"You shut down our funding!"

"What are you bloviating about now? How could I have—oh."

Magnus had been watching Oz and Annette, and at their expressions, asked, "What? What did ye do?"

"The Sindicate," Annette sighed. Then she brightened. "Just so you know, Oz helped. He's part of the reason your time line was adversely affected."

"Thanks, Annette, but you barely needed me. I just moved in at the end to help with the clean-up."

"That's not true, Oz. You figured out what all their fake shell companies were for, you figured out what the warehouse was for, and you stuck by us when you knew it was dangerous. And when we had to fight for our lives, you were there for that, too."

"No, no." Oz made a show of pooh-poohing the praise. "I wouldn't say I was a hero, but *you* can say I was a hero."

"Jesus, shut the fuck up, you two!" This from an aggrieved Mock. "You're gonna break bones patting yourselves on the back. And if you don't, I will."

Magnus spread his hands. "I'm still lost."

"There was a cub trafficking ring," Oz explained. "A sick, disgusting, pathetic, shitty trafficking ring run by sick, disgusting, pathetic, shitty people, and yeah, I'm looking at all three of you scumbags. We found out about it a few months ago. Magnus, you remember Caro? We rescued her. Well. *She* rescued her. We were late to the party." To Gulo: "That's what the Sindicate was for, wasn't it? Not just so sickos could get off on abusing cubs. Not just so Stables could have pet werewolves."

"*What?*"

"I know, it's fucking awful. Pets for Stables who knew their true nature. Pray you never see the files, Magnus, or the pictures, they're that bad. And a perfect measure of how we're *not* superior to Stables. When we're inclined, we savage our young just like they do. Often for profit."

"What are ye saying? That SAS evolved into this syndicate or whatever it was?"

"Or the reverse." Mock shrugged. "Who gives a shit?"

"Spoken like a true student of history," Annette muttered.

"Point is, at this time last year, there was plenty of money. We were getting ready to move again, we had the means to watch the traitors, and we could indirectly punish some of them. Direct punishment would come after we had control."

"Indirect." That rang a dim bell, and he thought of Lila, who had diligently researched sun bears and then asked the crucial question about Sally: *Maybe someone wanted her because she's an exotic catch?*

"Some of the cubs you targeted…they were the offspring of SAS members who let you down?" Saliva spurted into Oz's mouth as that awful, gut-clenching feeling when you know you're going to throw up washed over him. "Their cubs? Who never did anything to hurt you?"

"Everything was going fine and better than fine," Mock continued, because his idea of "fine" was twisted. "And then those happy assholes at IPA blundered around and accidentally shut off the money faucet. And like that." Mock attempted a finger snap, which he couldn't pull off. "We had no funds and no options and more of us were dead. But SAS didn't want to change the time line, the symmetry of doing it on the tenth anniversary was too perfect."

"So the Smalls family was targeted," Annette realized. "Sally for sale and her parents for punishment as species traitors."

"You weren't there," Mock snapped. "Are you telling this or are we?"

Oz couldn't believe they hadn't caught on yet, were still chatting like everything was going according to plan but was grateful regardless. "I like when Annette tells it."

"They moved," Annette said, rubbing her forehead. "The Smalls family. They packed up and moved halfway across the country, and you thought they'd gotten wind of your newest, nastiest plan. And maybe they did—Sue told Magnus she'd heard some upsetting rumors. She was going to get to the bottom of it, wasn't she? She and Sam. I'm sure he stayed in touch with his bosses—I never found out who they were. No one did. So you guys panicked. I'll bet you had no idea she had a terminal illness."

"The feeling when you cheer for cancer," Gulo sneered. "We know now, but you're right…not then. But we needed the money we'd get for Sally, so it was perfect."

Perfect? Any number of things could go wrong—and did. And if they'd succeeded in getting their hands on Sally? She was still only one cub. They would need millions (wars were expensive), while the anniversary got closer and closer.

"Oh my God with all the bullshit," Oz groaned. "It was about punishment, pure and simple. SAS is going with today's date and you were always going to. The Smalls family—that was for fun. You didn't have the money, you *don't* have the money, and you went after them anyway. That way, you could tell yourselves that regardless of how today went, you showed your enemies you're not to be fucked with. Can you hear how absolutely shortsighted and stupid you are? Gulo, how the fuck did you get through medical school?"

Magnus was staring at the ceiling as if hoping for a roof collapse to put everyone out of their misery. "That should be SAS's motto: shortsighted and stupid."

"Oh, spare us the righteous crap, Berne. Nobody stuck a gun in your back and made you join. You were on board with us until you saw it was gonna be messy."

"Messy." Magnus seemed to taste the word, savor it. "Is that what you call it?"

"Can you say, right now, that if SAS could pull off a bloodless coup and we could be running the planet without any casualties, you wouldn't join?"

"No," he said quietly. "I can't say that."

"See?" Gulo looked triumphant. "You're not so high and mighty."

"I never said otherwise. Not once."

"But that's the start of the slope. 'No casualties, sure, sign me up.' Then it's 'Well, a couple of people got hurt.' 'Okay, sign me up anyway.' Then it's a dozen. Then a hundred. So when is it unacceptable, Moral Majority? What's the magic number?"

Berne, now staring out the window showing the street, didn't bother answering. (Assuming there really was an actual number and not a rhetorical.) "Which one of you called for an ambulance? I mean, you'll all need one—you in particular, Gulo—but I didn't see any of you make a phone call."

"Now you're fucked," Mock said smugly. "Took 'em long enough."

"What are you grinning about? Those aren't your reinforcements," Oz said. "They're ours."

And then the world that was the Reflections Dance Academy caved in.

Chapter 54

LILA HAD SEEN CARS CRASHING INTO STOREFRONTS ON TV and assumed that it wasn't so easy in real life. There were bricks and cement and steel and aggregate and concrete blocks to get through. She figured in real life, a car would destroy itself when crashing into a storefront, or the Reflections Dance Academy.

Wrong.

Also, she wasn't driving a car.

Lila had followed the directions all the way to Shakopee, stopping as instructed a mile inside the city limits. She pulled over her nonbulance and waited for something weird.

She wasn't disappointed. Not two minutes later, a hawk—eagle?—some kind of bird of prey swooped down and alighted on the mailbox she'd parked beside. The street was quiet, probably because school hadn't let out yet. The large, fierce-looking bird of prey looked especially incongruous with a suburban neighborhood as a backdrop. She could see a McDonald's from her parking spot.

Curious, but not too strange, I guess. Maybe it nests around here. The river's close, so are the bluffs. Lots of prey.

And then it stared at her. Not a glance, a stare. An intense, fixed glare.

Okay, that's unsettling.

She took a couple of steps forward and the bird didn't move. It had a dark body, mostly reddish-brown, with an amazing wingspan. The feathers were mostly black, with white tips at the wings. It looked sleek and dangerous, and Lila had seen those crystal blue eyes before.

"Oh, hey. I know you."

The raptor immediately took flight, but only long enough to cross the distance between them and flutter onto her shoulder. She—Lila was certain the bird was female—wasn't heavy at all, which was surprising; the thing was almost two feet tall, and the wingspan was amazing. *Guess it's true; birds are mostly feathers and air.*

Lila slowly turned and walked back to her nonbulance, like a girl in the 1950s trying to fix her posture by walking around with a book on her head. She tried not to think about the sharp, hooked beak that could have her ear off quicker than a straight razor. Or the talons that could slash through skin and muscle with next to no effort.

"Is there a plan besides 'make a distraction and then get the hell out of the way'?"

The bird screamed what Lila took to be "No."

"Right in my ear? That struck you as a good idea?"

She got another shriek for her pains.

Crashing through the huge windows of the Reflections Dance Academy was so easy she couldn't believe it. *TV told the truth for a change! Truly a wondrous day.*

She unbuckled her seat belt (thank you, George Cayley!) and hopped out of her nonbulance, fully prepared to—well, she didn't know what she was prepared to do, that depended on what was happening, and what was happening was that Garsea and Berne and Oz were whaling the fuck out of three men she'd never seen before. One of them was punching Berne and yelling about how his shirt was ruined, and Berne was acting like he couldn't even feel the hits, like he was being assaulted by a jar of marshmallow fluff. *Uptight* marshmallow fluff. Like he was waiting for the other guy to just knock it off already, so he could *really* go to work.

She heard gunfire and instinctively flinched, saw that Annette's guy had gotten one off but missed her, tried to step back to get a better shot (not a great close-up weapon…that's why God made knives), only to have the raptor swoop in and rake her talons across his face, blinding him in a slash and a flurry of feathers. Lila hadn't known men could shriek so high.

And then there were people everywhere, pouring in from where she'd driven through the front of the building like they'd been waiting for a signal—was she the signal?—and more coming from behind—the back entrance?—and she had no idea what to do because she could no longer see Oz, much less rescue him, and that was the *point*, that he was in trouble and needed her, except maybe he didn't, so this was now a piss-poor place to be and she had just decided to take cover in her nonbulance when a man in a turtleneck spotted her and just went crazy, spotted her and started toward her and screamed at her

"Who brought a fucking Stable into this?"

and then his gun was coming up but so was hers and she shot him and then she threw up.

Chapter 55

"Lila!" Oz stopped rearranging Mock's facial bone structure and ran to her. He didn't spare a glance at Turtleneck, who was on his back and clutching his chest and being the least aggravating he'd been all day. "What the hell are you doing here, *Jesus*, are you okay?"

She was leaning against her nonbulance, wiped her mouth, and took a couple of shaky steps forward. He caught her, steadied her, hugged her. She pulled back to look at him and he'd never seen a sweeter sight, not ever.

"I never shot anybody before. Just targets and pop cans and mailboxes I was mad at."

"You did it like a champ."

"Any other week," she said tearfully, "this would have seemed super weird."

"What are you doing here? For all you knew, you were driving right into danger!" He heard himself and rephrased. "You *did* drive right into danger."

She blinked, surprised by his tone. "Well, yeah. I mean, I assumed I was in danger. And acted accordingly."

"What?"

"Sure. That's my default. You haven't noticed this? House fires, gun-toting racists, shopping on Black Friday…always in danger means always prepared."

"How the hell did you even— Nadia."

"Yeah. After I shot Harry Harriss—"

"What?"

"—she called and I suggested she use my help."

(Nadia later relayed Lila's exact words with no small amount of glee: "Faulkner, let me help or I'll make a fucking nuisance of myself the likes of which you've never seen. Also I didn't send you all of the footage of Garsea's B&E. You missed the part with the sprinklers. If you want it, you know what you must do.")

"I fucking love you."

She sniffled into his shoulder. "You don't know me. But we can fix that. We just need to go on at least fifteen more not-dates. Sixteen, if you don't count *Meritage*. No," she said as he put a finger under her chin, tipped her head up so he could look into the lovely eyes she hid behind plain glass frames because she was weird and sneaky. "Don't you dare try to kiss me. I just threw up."

"Later," he promised.

"Agreed. Who are all these people?"

"Reinforcements."

"And who'd I shoot?"

"Someone who's fine with killing every Stable he sees."

"And who's *that*?"

"Judge Gomph." He understood her astonishment. The judge was in his early sixties, went about three hundred pounds, and was well over six feet tall. He was standing clear of the skirmishes, observing like a benevolent/merciless god (depending on whose side you were on), and it was impossible not to look at him, even in the midst of the mess.

Gomph had dark brown skin and small, bright brown eyes. His wide, kind face was creased with wrinkles; his hands were catcher's mitts. Nadia had once observed that he was so broad, he looked like someone had thrown a judge's robe over a mahogany table. Like most juvie judges, he was overworked, underpaid, adored cubs, and ate too much fast food. When Annette had stumbled onto the Sindicate, his first concern had been Caro and Dev's safety, then Annette's, and he'd backed everything she did—even the stuff he didn't find out about until later.

Judge Gomph was the reason Annette hadn't been arrested for

manslaughter, never mind tried. Even now, Oz wasn't sure how far his influence reached; he was simply grateful for it, given that he'd done some manslaughtering himself when he went to Annette's defense.

In the six months since the Sindicate was exposed, Gomph had repeatedly expedited paperwork and shielded IPA from Stable authorities as Annette, Nadia, and David tried to dig up any information on the SAS/Sindicate members who escaped detection, as they searched for other cubs to set free. *Protective* didn't begin to describe the judge. Neither did *imposing*, or *driven*, or *compassionate*, though they were a good start. Oz knew that when the judge found out about the SAS/Sindicate link, heads would roll, and not just metaphorical ones. And if Gulo or Mock sang a song that would expose more SAS members, Gomph's famous benevolence might even extend to them.

He wasn't sure what Gomph could do for a Stable who shot a Shifter

(two Shifters!)

and had more than a passing interest in finding out. He was torn between hugging Nadia for figuring out what had happened and bringing the cavalry, and throttling her until she squawked for endangering Lila.

"Judge Gomph?" Lila asked, still staring. He was lumbering toward the small group gathered around Turtleneck. "Is he a were-elephant? Are there were-elephants?"

"Yes. And yes. But it's rude to ask."

"Oh. Like asking someone how old they are?"

"Yeah. It's fine if the info is volunteered, but asking a Stable to their face is bad form. I'm telling you this because you're in our world now, there will be no escape, be resigned, and this is the stuff to figure out."

She pulled back and frowned. "Resigned, huh?"

"Yes."

She smiled. "Fair enough. But why is a judge here? Don't they usually put in an appearance months after the crime? Say, in a courtroom?"

"Other judges do that. You know the movie *Monsters, Inc.*?"

"Mike Wazowski!"

"Exactly. Remember Roz? Her cover was that she lived to bust balls over improperly filled out timecards, but she was really Agent #001, secretly foiling evil while making sure everyone's paperwork was filed. That's Judge Gomph."

He had a vague idea how Nadia and Gomph had known to show up and planned to get the details later. For now, he was too busy drinking in Lila, who had returned his hug while keeping her weapon close, and was always a bit dangerous, even when she was smuggling chili to cubs and polishing eyeballs.

There was an odd sucking noise behind them, which wiped the smile off Lila's face. She stepped out of his embrace

(*nuts*)

opened the back of her nonbulance, then came back lugging a large, blaze-orange duffel bag. "Help me with him, Oz. *Move*, gang."

"Why?" But he knelt as Lila examined the worthless shithead. Judging by her expression, she didn't think much of the whistling noise Turtleneck's chest insisted on making. Someone must have rolled him on his back, God knew why. *Let him bleed out.*

She unzipped the bag and Oz saw it had been divided into sections, with Velcro straps holding items in place as she spread the bag open. "Why do you have an EMT's kit? It's not an ambulance. You've made that super clear."

Around them, the fights had finished, though Gulo was still flailing. All at once, everyone quieted down, the way a lull sometimes falls over a party, so Annette's growled "Gulo, stay down. If you shift, *I* shift" was nice and loud. Oz almost hoped he would. He'd never seen a werebear and a werewolverine face off before.

Magnus squatted beside them. He was agreeably blood-spattered, having taken care of some of the reinforcements Team Turtleneck had been counting on. "C'n I help, lass?"

Lila had put on gloves, then grabbed a pair of utility shears and was cutting through Turtleneck's turtleneck. "Yeah. Call a real ambulance."

"Two minutes out," Gomph rumbled, standing over them.

Lila never glanced up, just slapped her hand over the wound. "Oz, glove up. Then check the left-hand pocket closest to you. That noise you heard? That's a sucking chest wound."

"Are you gonna try to stitch it closed?"

"No. See, what's happening is the bullet popped his lung, so air built up in his pleural cavity, that's what's making the sound. Berne, help me get him on his side." He did, while Gomph got the observers to take a few steps back. "No exit wound, okay. Roll him back, nice and easy…good. Okay, so we have to keep air from going in while letting extra air out. Oz, see the QuikClot in my bag? Red, white, and blue packet? Great, open it, and when I move my hand, you're gonna slap it directly over the wound. Ready? One…two…three."

Torn, Oz obeyed. He was pleased to help her, but unhappy about helping Turtleneck. Still, he wasn't going to argue. And while Gomph could pull strings for him, it wouldn't do to push it by ignoring Lila (as if that was possible) and letting the guy drown in his own blood.

"Good, now grab the tape. Berne, I'm gonna tape down the dressing, then tape all the way around his chest. He's sweaty and bloody, tape doesn't like sticking to either. So too much tape is almost enough. Okay, I want you to roll him on his side…now."

Lila finished just as more paramedics came through the door.

"They might as well have stayed home," Oz said, stepping back to give them room to work.

Lila stripped off her gloves while rattling off everything she did to the paramedics now examining Turtleneck. Then she turned to Oz. "Bite your tongue. That was the first time I did that in the field. Nobody was happier to see those guys than me. Y'know, since the patient is unconscious."

"Jeez, really? Your first chest suck?"

"Never call it that again," she said, trying not to laugh.

"You sure didn't show it. You'd make a great teacher."

"That's the secret," she replied, serious now. "You can't ever show you're scared. Even if you're positive you just peed a little."

"Well done, miss." Judge Gomph was looking Lila over. "Who are you, please?"

"Your honor, this is Lila Kai." From Annette, who rushed over to stick her nose in because she was Annette. "My mother's new neighbor, and our great friend and ally."

"*New* neighbor?"

"It's been a busy week, sir," Oz admitted.

"I look forward to hearing about it, Mr. Adway. And when you can, say hello to Mama Mac for me." To Lila: "Nice to meet you, Ms. Kai. I have several hundred questions."

"Hello," Lila said faintly, because everyone was intimidated when they met Gomph the first time. "On a scale of one to ten, with one being 'pshaw, no big deal' and ten being a stint in prison for attempted manslaughter, how much trouble am I in?"

"Three," Gomph replied, but going by the man's smile, Lila didn't have too much to worry about.

Chapter 56

"Oz, your poor hands!"

"You know they'll heal."

"Well, yeah," Lila replied, exasperated. "Most people do. That doesn't mean you have to suffer unnecessarily. Why should you have to heal *and* fight off an infection? Plus, Macropi will kill every one of us if she finds out you got hurt."

"She will," Annette agreed. "*My* hands are fine. If you were wondering."

It was hours later, and they were back in Lila's kitchen. Everyone had explained themselves to Gomph. Villains were hauled away shaking their fists (the ones who could, at least), which was as hilarious as it was stupid. Lila had told Oz and Garsea about Harry Harriss, who had disappeared. Since no one was in the least concerned, she figured that meant custody. Or the Shifter equivalent. Were there Shifter prisons? There had to be.

So many questions. The best part? I'll get the chance to ask every single one. The better part? They'll answer me!

"Garsea, your eyes were so red during the fight," Lila said. "Like two burning coals framed with L'Oréal mascara. Don't other Stables freak out when that happens?"

"I lie and say they're special contacts. Like mood rings for your eyeballs."

Lila snorted. She didn't even have to ask Annette if it worked. People were dumb. And speaking of dumb…

"Poor Harriss," she said as she ran cold water over Oz's bloody knuckles. "The elder, I mean."

"Is everything going to be awkward for him now?" Annette

asked. "Since the whole neighborhood knows what his son was up to?"

"Probably."

"Only if we make it awkward," Macropi said, coming in from the back yard. "Roy sends his profound apologies on behalf of his idiotically destructive son, Lila, and will be over in person to reassure you that Harry Harriss won't be bothering you any longer."

"He doesn't have to come over. Though, if he did, I would love it. Because I love it when people come over now."

Oz frowned while she blotted his knuckles dry with sterile gauze. "I can't tell if you were concussed when you crashed into the dance academy or if it's just your default sarcasm."

"Let's just say that while I don't actually love it when people come by, I hate it less. That's it. That's all the concession you're getting from me."

"And if you decide you still want to buy the Curs(ed) House," Macropi added, "I think you'll find Roy is willing to let it go for a song."

"Really? That's wonderful! Uh. Not that I care. I'm neutral. Whatever."

"Welcome to the neighborhood, you noble idiot." Garsea turned to Oz. "I know you gave Gomph a verbal report, but—"

"I know. Paperwork. We have so much of it. Still."

"By the ream. Though it's fairly straightforward. Ever since the Sindicate tried to kill us the first time—"

"That's an awesome and scary sentence, Garsea."

She smiled. "Who knew social work was so dangerous? Besides everyone in social work? But as I was saying, ever since, when we're in the middle of a case and needs must split up, Nadia and I check in. If a certain amount of time passes with no check-in, Nadia rings the rescue bell."

Rescue bell? Was that a literal bell? "Let me guess—the bad guys took your phones?"

"Yes. And the world's cleanest storage space had been tricked out to block Wi-Fi signals. So it wasn't half an hour before Nadia knew something had gone wrong. All we had to do was wait, knowing she was arranging a coup to stomp the coup."

"Where *is* that girl? I haven't seen her in too many weeks."

"She's coming over tomorrow, Mama. She knows you have to use up all the spring strawberries you got this morning. She's hoping for tarts."

"Good," Macropi replied, as she inspected the knuckles Lila hadn't bound yet. "Good Lord, boy, if it hurts that much when you're punching, you might consider stopping."

"There's no way you're lecturing me when Lila shot people. Ow!"

"I can do both." To Lila: "Annette tells me you're an EMT."

"Annette's wrong. I'm a paramedic. A bad one. Oz was walking around with bloody knuckles for how long before I noticed?"

"But it's...*not* an ambulance. The thing you drive."

"The thing that was hauled away, probably as Exhibit B in the court case that might never come up because you guys have centuries of practice staying off Stable law enforcement radar? Yeah. Which reminds me, can I borrow someone's car for the next month?" To Garsea: "That's right, it's not an ambulance. Why is that so hard to understand?"

"But you're a paramedic!" Mama exclaimed.

"Yeah, *now*. I got sick of people flagging me down and demanding I tend to their wounds and drive them to a hospital. So I got certified. There. Simple."

"Oh, no," Garsea replied. "Not at all."

Oz chuckled. "So instead of trading it in for *anything* else, you went out and trained as a paramedic." To Mama: "That's the level of stubborn we're dealing with. The Olympic standard of stubborn." He raised his hand to cut Annette off. "No one is saying you're not a talented amateur, Annette, but like I said—this is gold medal level stubborn."

"You can all stop talking about me like I'm not hearing every snarky word."

Lila finished with his other hand, and he flexed his fingers experimentally. "So you got EMT certified—sorry, paramedic—for spite."

She shrugged. "Yeah."

"Marry me."

"There's something wrong with you," she replied, but couldn't keep the smile off her face.

"Oh my God!"

Lila stared at the shed, which had been transformed. The kids had hauled out the old stuff, and swept and scrubbed everywhere, exposing the blonde wood that made up the walls and making the shed look bigger and brighter, even in the twilight gloom. They'd brought in old carpet remnants for the floor, and they'd found a rocking chair from somewhere for the corner (Lila suspected Macropi's place). There was a long shelf in the back under the sign (HOT CHOCOLATE HIDEOUT), which had been stacked with mugs, spoons, snacks, and napkins. The lawn lounge chairs had been folded flat and made into a bed with several inches of thick blankets, and the kids had stuffed a bucket with cut evergreen, making the shed smell like Christmas. There was a cordless space heater in the corner, putting the finishing touch on the cozy hideaway.

"She likes it!" Sally squealed.

"You did this?" she asked, stunned. "All this?"

"It was either that or homework," Devoss said.

"It was Caro's idea," Macropi added.

The teenager smiled, then looked down and shrugged. She scribbled and handed over a note. *Figured you should have a special place to make Flanders's cocoa. And yeah…it was either that or homework.*

"I love it," Lila said, and her voice didn't tremble at all. "I can't believe you did this instead of homework. Well, I can, but it's still a lot."

"Speaking of," Macropi said tartly, and began shooing the kids back to the house.

"But it's still the weekend!" Devoss cried as Macropi practically hauled him out by his ear. "And there's more to the story! Net and Oz and Lila got up to all kinds of cool crap today, and you *know* they've probably only told us half of it. Her nonbulance is gone, *disparou, andato!* Oz's hands are all taped up! Nadia left cryptic messages, and I'll just bet Gomph is involved, too!" Fainter and fainter. "Back me up, Caro. *'Stop screaming, Mama's making us leave so Lila and Oz can be alone.'* Oh. Gross. This isn't over!"

"Well." Oz coughed and pulled the shed door closed. "That was horribly indiscreet."

"And audacious."

"Right. Right!" He stood there, running his hands through his hair like he didn't know what to do with them. "Yes. I'd never—I mean, we didn't bring you down here to—there wasn't a sinister seductive plan being put in motion. That I knew of, anyway. The kids just happened to finish it today. It's part of the reason Caro and Mama went to town when Harriss tried to burn you out. They needed the finishing touches, and Target's great for that. Am I doing that thing where I talk too much? Also, if you hadn't shot him, I was going to use his rib cage for a xylophone, so it all worked oummmmmmm."

This because she'd had enough already and kissed him. He groaned and kissed her back and then she was groping behind her because she didn't want to break contact but she did want to get horizontal, and somehow they lowered themselves to the surprisingly comfortable blanket pile. Then she was grabbing at his belt buckle and he was tugging at her sweater and at first she hesitated, but his pants were around his ankles by now and if he didn't mind looking silly, she didn't, though she'd never thought of her scars as silly.

"Wait."

She made her hands go still.

"This morning the plan was to leave you be and wish you a long and happy life because we've caused you enough trouble—"

"Presumptuous."

"Yeah, that's what Annette said. But then you drove your non-bulance through a dance academy and shot an asshole and then saved that asshole."

"It *was* pretty heroic."

"But I want to know—well, everything." His hands were on her shoulders and he was almost vibrating with intensity. "I want to know everything about you, and I'll tell you whatever you want to know about me. But I also want to—to just put it out there: I want to be with you. I don't care in what capacity. I'll take you any way I can get you. Possibly forever."

"I don't know if I'm your *Rupa*. Or your *Kama*."

(The look of utter astonishment on his face was a thing of beauty.)

"Wh—how—I don't—how—Mama Mac?"

"Who else? You know how it is: you're hanging out on a stranger's porch mulling over the damage done to your home by the neighborhood racist and you decide to tell someone an origin fable while relentlessly matchmaking. Happens all the time."

"It's just a story."

"I know. And it can stay that way. Let's just see where this goes. Expecting each other to be their perfect physical and spiritual mate on such short acquaintance is ridiculous. Now take off your pants."

And then they were kissing again, and her hands went to his belt again, and the space heater might become superfluous because she was *very* warm, and how had she gone so long without realizing a man's scorching touch was nothing to fear?

"Oh please, please let me," he murmured into her neck, and then kissed her throat. "Please, I won't hurt you, I promise."

And that was just dumb because of *course* he wouldn't hurt her, not just because he was her Oz but because she'd put a bullet into his collarbone if he tried but if he didn't care about her scars then neither did she.

So she let him tug off her sweater and she got him out of his shoes, which TBH she should have started with instead of lunging for his belt like a sex-starved suburbanite—which she was—and then his pants, and relieved him of *his* shirt, and then he said something weird

"I'm getting rid of all my turtlenecks. I'm never wearing one again."

and then he pulled off her leggings and when she turned to toss their clothes toward a handy corner he laughed and laughed at her Harry Potter panties.

"*I solemnly swear that I am up to no good?*[13]"

"Shut up, you're the weirdo swearing off turtlenecks."

And then they were down to their underwear and scrambling beneath the icy covers because a space heater was all well and good but it was still early spring in Minnesota, and nearly dark, too.

They kissed and touched and stroked and nibbled and if someone had told her a month ago that she'd forever after think of sheds as erotic way stations, she'd have laughed 'til she choked.

After a lovely long time, they came to a mutual unspoken decision to back off a bit…well, no. She took a breath and said, "Let's back off a bit," and he groaned but complied.

"So fifteen and a half more dates," he said, and she giggled.

---

13. These exist! Amazon has *everything*.

"I could cut that down a bit. Make it an even dozen."

"Or three," he suggested hopefully. He had one arm around her and was tracing some of her scars with bandaged fingers. "There's another theory about *Kama-Rupa*, if you want to hear it."

"It can't be any weirder than all that's happened this week. That's not a challenge, by the way."

"Lone wolves need a mate and cubs, so they're drawn to another loner who needs to make their own family. And they're stronger together, so they make strong cubs."

"I don't want my own family. I don't like being around people. I don't even like kids that much. What?" she asked when he snorted.

"Mama Mac was right. You really don't want anyone finding out what a softy you can be."

"Mama Mac spends entirely too much time fretting about our love lives."

"But all kidding aside—"

"Oh, this should be interesting."

"—I'm so glad to be here with you."

"Me, too."

There was a long pause, which she broke. "Are you waiting for me to crack a joke? I won't. Not about this. I didn't think we could *have* this. I worried you might not want me once you saw my…" She wiggled her arms, and he snatched one back so he could go back to feathering kisses on the underside of her arm, just below the elbow. "Not that I thought you'd be shallow."

"Couldn't blame you if you did. The car. The suits."

"That doesn't mean you're shallow. You just like what you like. And if you can afford it, who cares? I just assumed you'd feel sorry for me and you'd break out the kid gloves and there'd be a lot of 'oh, the poor, poor Stable, best leave her alone, poor traumatized thing.'"

"Poor Stable?" he asked, astonished. "You?"

"I should have talked to you," she replied. "I'm sorry I assumed the worst."

"You've nothing to apologize for. My God, thanks to your choice in suburban neighborhoods, you could have been killed!"

"Multiple times," she added.

"Christ, don't remind me. You don't owe anyone an apology, and that includes the fucknut who tried to shoot you."

"Have you ever killed anyone?" She'd asked the question so abruptly, she was as surprised as Oz to hear it come out of her mouth. "I haven't, if you want full disclosure. Harriss and what's-his-face will live. But I was just wondering. You didn't seem put off by the violence. You didn't even look at the guy I shot. Those aren't criticisms," she added. "It was just…interesting. You've obviously been in fights. So that got me wondering if you'd killed someone."

"Not for months and months. You know that saying, 'it's like riding a bike'? It's not like riding a bike."

"You're gonna tell me all about it, right?"

"Yep. You're not worried about the gory details?"

"Nope. We'll save that for date two-and-a-half." To an outsider, Lila figured they sounded incredibly flip and far too casual about life-and-death matters. But it wasn't about being flip, it was about information overload. A lot had happened; they all needed to process. And she had questions. But now, just now, she needed a break from recent, potentially lethal events.

"Two-and-a-half? So it's official. The movie palace counts, and Meritage counts as half a date."

"Yep."

"Pretty arbitrary."

"Yep."

He turned and snuggled up behind her. "Tell me again about learning CPR and suturing and how to work a defibrillator for spite."

"A closed chest massage is surprisingly hard work. Tell me about werewolf birth control."

"Um. Okay."

"I've got the implant," she explained. "So I can't get pregnant, but it doesn't protect against STDs."

"Then I've got good news. Shifters can't catch Stable STDs and vice versa."

"That sounds made-up."

"What?" He propped himself up on an elbow as she rolled on her back to look up at him. "Why?"

"Because it's just the kind of thing a guy who hates condoms would say to get out of wearing a condom."

"It's true!" he protested. "Ask anybody. Well, maybe not anybody. Ask Annette or David. Keep Mama and Nadia out of it if at all possible."

"I'm choosing to believe you because you know I'm a trigger-happy firebug, so I don't think you'd risk lying about anything major."

"Anything *major*?"

"Well, obviously you'll still lie about dumb stuff like who used the last of the toilet paper or whose turn is it to go down on the other person."

"This is the sexiest conversation I've ever had about sex without actually having sex."

"That's because you're a lucky, lucky man."

"I know you're being sarcastic, but it's true."

And he dropped a kiss to her smiling lips.

Chapter 57

LILA KNOCKED ON THE FARMHOUSE DOOR, WHICH WAS YANKED open halfway through the second knock. "Hi!" she said. "Remember me?"

The farmer in whose field Sue and Sam Smalls crashed nodded and looked over Lila's shoulder, noting Berne, Garsea, and Oz. "The number one Realtor in Fargo. Did you get business cards? Have you come to show the field again?"

"No and yes. And I've come to confess."

"Yeah?"

"I'm not a real estate agent."

"No shit."

"You wound me, madam!" Lila shrugged. "Fine, you got me. I could be a Realtor, if I wasn't deathly allergic to closings and real estate licensing exams. Also, are you harboring a terribly injured man who bailed from the plane that crashed on your property and you're opening the door wider and you're beckoning us inside so the answer is yes. Excellent."

Wendy smiled, and it transformed her wary expression into something bright and welcoming. She was short and chubby, with long black hair pulled back in a braid, and small, wide-set hazel eyes. Her hands were beautiful, not at all the way Lila assumed a farmer's hands would look. Wendy had the delicate wrists and long, elegant fingers of a hand model. "Well, finally. Poor guy's been going stir-crazy all week. C'mon."

She led them past a sunny living room and up the stairs, walked to the end of the hallway, rapped softly on a closed door, then opened it. "Hey, Sam," she called softly. "Your friends are here."

Annette opened her mouth, then at a look from Oz, shrugged

and closed it. They filed into a small, nondescript bedroom that might as well have had "guest room" stenciled on the wallpaper: pale blue carpet, cream wallpaper, an end table with a lamp. One kitchen chair on the left side of the bed for a visitor. A lonely chair in a lonely room.

A painfully thin man with Sally's dark hair and eyes was tucked into the double bed. His skin was greenish-pale—too much time indoors—and he was wearing black wire rims with a cracked right lens. His left leg and right wrist were in casts, his face a rainbow (if rainbows were mostly yellow and green) of fading bruises. He smiled at Berne's pained gasp.

"There you are, Maggie. I've been waiting all week here."

"There was some confusion over whether or not you were dead, Sam." Berne crossed the room and shook the hand that wasn't in a cast. "My God, how are you?"

"You should see what's under the pajamas. I'm a walking rainbow."

"I'm so sorry about Sue."

"I know you are," he replied, clasping Berne's hand. "Thank you for coming for me. Introduce me to your friends." His tone was friendly, but as he looked at the others, he flared his nostrils, and his eyes narrowed when he zeroed in on Lila. "What's this?"

"Yeah, sorry. I don't have an 'other self.' There's just me." So it was rude to ask a Shifter what kind of werebeast they were, but a Shifter could smell out a Stable and comment? Bogus. *Eh, give the guy a break. Tough week.* "Your daughter's wonderful, by the way."

Sam smiled. "Takes after her mother, thank all the gods. How is she?"

"Stubborn. Strong-willed…"

"What'd I tell you?"

"…never believed you were dead…wouldn't give up your phone number until evil was mostly vanquished…" Which had been yesterday. Once Oz, Garsea, and Lila had sat down with Sally and explained that the men who hurt her parents had been caught, she turned over the last piece of info they needed to solve the puzzle.

Sam's smile faded. "I don't look forward to telling her about Sue."

"I never got a chance to tell her," Berne confessed. "By which I mean Oz told her when your plane went down that you were both dead, but I wasna able to update her after I identified Sue at the morgue. Oh, Christ, Dr. Gulo and the morgue—I have so many things to tell you—everything went to shite so quickly—"

"I know having to ID her was difficult. Thank you." Pause. "Dr. Gulo and the morgue?"

"What I'm sayin' is, your bairn knows her mother is dead, but she doesn't *know*, d'you understand?"

"Yes. Poor cub, she's got a tough road ahead. I know you—all of you—faced danger for me and mine. I'm more grateful than I can say." Then to Lila: "I'm sorry you got hauled into this, miss."

"I'm not sorry I got hauled into it."

"You're very kind, miss."

"Lila."

"Miss Lila."

"Ugh."

Garsea let out a small sound very like a snort, and Lila raised an eyebrow at her. Oz had crossed the room and was looking out the south-facing window. "Don't worry," Sam said. "Wendy made sure to put me in a room where, if I hobbled to the window, I wouldn't see my wife's tomb."

"You were right here the entire time," Berne marveled. "I should have checked the house. Stupid. Stupid."

"Give yourself a break, Maggie. No one could have predicted any of the last month's insanity. But you helped my daughter when she was at her most vulnerable. It's all I could have asked of you."

Berne shook his head. "Nae, Sam. Don't misunderstand, I'm liking that ye finally appreciate my stellar qualities—"

"Ha!"

"—but I didn't do much of anything. Oz and Annette deserve most of the credit. And Lila here did far more to keep Sally safe than I did."

"I gave her honey and pizza."

Sam chuckled. "Her favorites."

"So what happened?" Berne asked. "I heard Oz's theory. Now I'd like to hear the rest."

"Someone fucked with your plane, Maggie. And then they fucked with us. Sue put it together, but not fast enough to save herself. Can you believe how long those SAS pricks held a grudge?"

"Well, *now*," Berne admitted, and Sam laughed. It was weak and thready, but it was something. "Sally knows her mother was sick. But the wee lass didn't have any details, o'course. If you could… would you mind…?"

"Yes. Leukemia. Sue's white cells went into overdrive. We tried to keep it from Sally as long as we could, but Sue was already looking at hospice care options. The cancer… It was like a grass fire in a drought month." To Lila: "Our kind can fight off a lot of pathogens, but cancer isn't one of them. It kills us like it does anything else."

"I'm very sorry."

"Thank you, Lila. My wife knew she was destined to die in a hospital room with the smell of her own shit in her nose. She wanted to stick it out for Sally's sake, while at the same time she was torn about letting Sally watch her deteriorate. In a completely stupid and unexpected way, SAS gave her a third option and she didn't hesitate." Sam lapsed into silence and just lay there, struggling for the right words to describe the thing that tried to devour his wife and the people who tried to devour his daughter.

"She made you jump," Lila guessed. "It's why they only found one parachute. It's unbelievable to me that you survived. The fall should have killed you."

"It should have killed a Stable," he corrected gently. "Still, I'm not exactly unscathed, as you can see." This with a wry smile as he indicated the casts. "I gave Wendy and Kelly the fright of their lives, staggering up their driveway like I did. Tough work on a broken tibia, I can tell you."

"Kelly?"

"Wendy's wife. The gods smiled on me by making her a nurse. She's on-shift at the local hospital right now."

"So you found help, somehow talked them out of calling for an ambulance—"

"I bribed them. I agreed to buy their field. Wendy's been wanting to sell it for a decade."

"Okay, so Kelly the nurse filched supplies from the hospital to patch you up. And they helped you hide? You couldn't let anyone know you were alive until you knew who sabotaged Berne's plane," Lila said, thinking out loud. "You couldn't risk someone showing up here and finishing the job."

"And there was Kelly and Wendy to think of as well," Sam added.

Oz picked up the narrative. "You'd heard disquieting rumors to do with IPA—"

Sam nodded. "Yes, the trafficking thing. Sue thought there was more going on than anyone knew, but not exactly what."

"So you crashed, which confirmed your fears, found a den where you could lick your wounds, then called Sally—how?" Oz snapped his fingers. "Wendy brought you some burners."

"Yes. By the time I'd recovered my senses, I'd already lost a few days. I knew Maggie'd be coming to help Sally."

Oz cleared his throat. "Funny story, which is hilarious in retrospect. We thought Magnus—ha, ha!—might've been in on it."

"Hilarious, lad."

"Not without some justification," Garsea added. "The fire was started with avgas—"

"Fire?"

"We'll fill you in. We'll try to be linear and everything. So Magnus had access to avgas, and Sally told us you had specifically warned her to 'watch out for Maggie.'"

Sam frowned. "No, I told her to *keep* watch for him. It wasn't a warning."

"So it was more like 'don't worry, help is coming,'" Oz guessed.

"Yes."

This is why using small children to relay messages of dire import is a bad plan, Lila thought but didn't say.

"Well. Once I'd warned her, my nebulous plan was to lay low until I was strong enough to—" Sam cut himself off, shaking his head. "So much is still a fog. I was out of my head half the time. One night, Wendy caught me trying to leave to look for Sue in the field—"

"Good God," Garsea said in horrified sympathy.

"And that put me on my back for another couple of days. I never even heard you fly in."

"Take it easy. You've been through a shitshow."

"That's the official term," Oz added. "There's documentation and everything."

"Thank you, Lila. Oz. I'm sorry I didn't regain consciousness until you were long gone."

"You didn't miss much," Lila teased. "Just me being a terrible lookout. And Berne's amoebic dysentery."

"Ach, not *that* again…"

Sam laughed. "I figured you showed up to have a look for yourselves and scent the site. That was a stroke of luck for me. It confirmed my survival, put you back on your guard, and made you even more anxious to get to the bottom of things. And it sure livened up Wendy's afternoon."

"She suspected nothing!" Lila insisted.

Garsea snickered again, which Lila ignored because she was the bigger person sometimes.

"It was the lad's idea, Sam. I just flew them here."

"So your wife jammed you into a parachute and booted you out the door—"

"That's more or less an exact description of the sequence of events."

"—and then she just—" Lila cut herself off. She was trying, and failing, not to picture it. The chaos of the plane going down. Sam and Sue screaming horrible, loving things at each other. "I won't leave you!" and "Shut up and pull this cord after a ten-count!" and "Think of our daughter!" and "I am! Pull the cord!"

And then Sam would've been gone, shoved out the door to land who knew where, and in who knew what shape, and Sue would have ridden her old friend's plane all the way down to the mud.

That's why she wasn't in the cockpit and didn't have her seatbelt on. And why she didn't shift. Or even put her coat back on. She had no intention of living through the crash. Surviving it would have been Sue's worst-case scenario: critically injured and helpless, unable to help her husband or her daughter, and the leukemia doing its wretched, consuming work.

Awful as it was to contemplate, Lila felt like she understood, at least a little. *If I had to choose between a plane crash and dying for a month in a hospice… If it was a choice between throwing the bad guys off the scent while buying time for my daughter…well.*

It's not that it was a close contest. It wasn't a contest at all.

"We're here now," Oz said kindly.

"You are. Thank you." Then to Lila: "I'm in your debt for the rest of my life. If you ever need anything, call me first."

"Can't I just come see you? I feel like things get lost in translation when we rely on phones."

"Anytime. So what's next?"

"Sally's safe with my foster mother," Oz said. "She doesn't know we came for you. We weren't sure what shape you'd be in."

"Feels like I haven't seen her in years," Sam said, his voice suddenly rough as tears welled but didn't fall. "I've got so much to tell her."

"We've a lot t'tell you as well, Sam. The first of which is that the bastards who killed your wife are dead or wishing they were."

"Ah, that's the Maggie I was counting on." Sam let out a sigh and settled in. "Tell it all, my friend. And don't leave out the bloody parts. Wendy!"

Footsteps, and then she poked her head into the room. "Yeah, Sam?"

"We all know you've been eavesdropping in the hall."

"I didn't know," Lila confessed.

"Aw, c'mon, how could I not? I've put up with a hurt shapeshifter in my house for a week and all of a sudden a bunch of his shapeshifter friends show up? I'd have been crazy *not* to listen in."

"Agreed. Want to hear all the stuff that brought these guys to your farm before I go?"

"Kelly's gonna be mad if you're gone when she gets home," Wendy warned. "You were supposed to binge season ten of *Martha Bakes* tonight."

"Jesus wept. If these guys hadn't shown up, I'd still be leaving today. Somehow."

"That's the spirit, you old grump," Wendy said, and brought in more chairs.

Chapter 58

"Jesus." Lila sat up, brushing kernels off her belly and thighs. "Popcorn got everywhere."

"Don't care. Can't move."

They were in the movie palace, and Oz was sprawled, nude, on the blanket Lila had put down between the middle section and the nosebleed seats. Even though she was ridiculously sated, she couldn't look at him with anything but satisfaction. The long legs and big hands and feet had been accurate indicators of a big cock. One he knew how to use, which was just...delightful.

"I love your new math," he said dreamily, and she laughed.

Sam and Sally had been reunited a couple of days ago, the very definition of bittersweet: delighted to see her father, devastated to hear about her mother. They both needed to recover from their traumas, which wasn't the work of a day, or a year. They said their goodbyes and went home, and Macropi had made it clear that he and his daughter were welcome visitors to the big purple house.

With that last bit of business tied up, Lila decided that Oz spending nights on her couch counted as dates, and hanging out together counted as dates, and eating breakfast in her kitchen counted, and inadvertently meeting at the dance academy where she shot a man counted. And snuggle sessions in the Cocoa Cave.

"It wasn't new math. I just wanted to get laid," she teased.

"Happy to help. No. Delighted. Ecstatic. That's the one—ecstatic to help."

It didn't seem real, in all the best ways. Having wonderful sex—and how often is a first time wonderful? honestly?—in an empty movie palace was a fantasy, something you'd read about on an erotica website, nothing that could happen in real life.

But it had. Ohhhhh, boy, it had. She shivered, remembering Oz's mouth and fingers and cock, his tender, passionate skill, and her delighted response. She'd asked before. It had been on her mind, and she wouldn't pretend otherwise.

Sure, Lila. Are you worried I'll hurt you? Never in my life. But yeah, I've been with a Stable before. College and a couple of years ago. Have you been with a Shifter?

Not that she knew of. But then, how could she? She wouldn't have known what to look for.

You haven't, he decided. *A Shifter wouldn't have let you go.*

I can't tell if that's sweet or obnoxious.

It can be both.

"I have to talk," Oz said suddenly, "or I'll fall asleep and you'll hear me snore—"

"Again."

"—and it'll kill the romance. *God*, you're amazing. Everything you did and everything you let me do. Ummmm."

She saw his cock twitch and smirked. "Don't get ahead of yourself."

"This was perfect, and I've got no complaints about anything, not one single thing in my life, but is fucking in a movie palace going to be our default? I'm not complaining. Just trying to plan the rest of my life."

"Only until Macropi and the cubs move back." Repairmen had been busy at the purple house down the block; it looked like Macropi would have her home back in another few weeks.

"That's nuts. Nobody expects you to put them up until summer. You said it yourself the night of the fire—it was only for a couple of days. Forget it—I'm moving them into a rental. I'll pay in advance and present it as a fait accompli. Something nice, near all the stores Mama Mac likes."

"Presumptuous."

"If it's okay with you."

"No, that's what Macropi's gonna tell you. She'll probably whack you with something, too."

"Yeah." (The resignation in his tone was hilarious.)

"Get Devoss and Daniels on your side," she suggested.

He brightened. "That might work."

She made a mental note to bring a vacuum next time—how could one box of popcorn make such a mess?—then climbed on top of him.

"This is terrific," he said, his hands settling over her hips, "and I love your optimism, but I'm gonna need a few more minutes."

"You can have all the time you want. We both can."

"Corny."

"But truthful."

And she bent, and kissed him, and his arm came around her waist as he opened his mouth to her and she thought, *Who would have thought house fires would have brought me so much happiness?*

There was a lesson there.

Or maybe not.

"Okay, you're laughing while I'm kissing you. I won't lie. It's off-putting."

"Get used to it," she said, and then he laughed, too.

Author's Note

The Saint Paul restaurant Meritage is every bit as wonderful as Annette says. If anything, she downplays all the awesome. Though she was wrong to pooh-pooh the *salade Niçoise*.

Lila's booby traps were inspired by Andrew Vachss's *Flood*, the first in his incredible *noirey* (*noirish?*) series about New York vigilante Burke and his crew of disenfranchised badasses. If you haven't tried his work, do it. Now. The subject matter is bleak, but evil is always punished.

Teddy bear surgeons are a real thing! It's a legit job! Clearly every career decision I have made is wrong because somehow I am not a teddy bear surgeon.

My house burned to the foundation when I was eighteen. It sucked. Make sure you have lots and lots of insurance. Loads. So much that you find yourself saying, "I definitely have enough insurance." After you say that, go buy more insurance. Consider this your public service announcement of the day.

I made up the EZ-OUT collapsible ladder, but there are lots of fire escape ladders out there, they're not terribly expensive, and a kid can hook them onto a windowsill and get gone. Having one in each bedroom isn't the worst idea in the world.

Lila's Cocoa Hideout exists in real life! Visit mylifeonkayderosscreek.com/adirondack-style-hot-cocoa-bar.

Caro is entirely correct when she points out that the *Elfquest* series, by Richard and Wendy Pini, are "great #!#??# books."

Also, the grille of the 2020 BMW X1 Subcompact SUV looks like a pair of kidneys.

My indomitable and darling mother-in-law Elinor passed away last year. She's soundly missed, and it's strange to go on living in a world where she…isn't. All this to say that Lilydale, MN, does have an Eleanor Avenue, which I've changed to Elinor Avenue.

Don't miss book 1 in MaryJanice Davidson's
BeWere My Heart series

BEARS BEHAVING
BADLY

Available now from Sourcebooks Casablanca

Chapter 1

HE TELLS HER HE WANTS HER AND PROVES IT

his hands are everywhere his hands are magic they make the world fall away

and that is just what she craves and she is desperate to do her part she is wild to make the world disappear for him

and he is easing her onto her back and filling her up with all of him and all of her knows that is fine, just fine and the only thing she wants is for this to never stop

never stop

never

oh

oh my

oh

god

"Beautiful dreamer...wake unto meeeeeee... Starlight and dewdrops...are waiting for theeeeee!"

The world was falling away—no, was *wrenched* away. And by Stephen Foster, no less. "*Nnnnnfff?*"

"Sounds of the rude world...heard in the day...lulled by the moonlight...have all passed *awaaaaaaaay!*"

"Gah." She swiped, missed, found the thing, smacked it. Opened her eyes—and her fist—and the crushed components pattered to the carpet. *Oh, hell on toast.*

Annette Garsea, twenty-seven, single, IPA caseworker in need of a shower and a new alarm clock, sat up, pawed at her blankets, and finally freed her legs. She glared at the nightstand drawer, which stayed closed more often these days than her libido liked. Especially last night, when she had gotten home so tired she'd barely had time to undress before doing a belly flop onto her (unmade) bed and succumbing immediately. And even if she *had* made the time

(note: buy replacement batteries. lots.)

it wouldn't have made much difference. She and David had just missed each other...again. And even if she'd seen him, nothing would have happened. It wouldn't have changed anything, including the fact that her sex life was barren and mornings were...yuck. It was like thinking through honey for the first ten minutes. Which wouldn't be so bad if there was actual honey, but she hadn't had a chance to go grocery shopping this week. Eggs were good several days past their expiration date, right? Right.

He tells her he wants her and proves it...

From long practice, she pushed the fantasy away, stretched, yawned, padded though her messy den toward the bathroom. Showered, shampooed, watered down her conditioner again (at this point, it was water that vaguely smelled like conditioner), hopped out, toweled, ran a comb through her shaggy locks

(note: grocery shopping and conditioner and haircut)

and dressed. Black office-appropriate slacks she could stand, sit, and run in; ditto her shoes, which were plain black rubber-soled flats. Sports bra, dark-blue turtleneck. Dad's wristwatch. Or as her partner called it, "that quaint clock you strap to your body for some reason."

Breakfast. She loved their sun-filled kitchen, with bold, black appliances (easy cleanup) and lots of counter space (room to spread out the junk mail, tape, more mail, books, pens, junk mail), and the island, which was usually Pat's domain for his project *de la semaine*. She went straight to the fridge, took inventory of the pitiful contents, and grabbed staples. She sniffed at the eggs and, satisfied, cracked three, whisked them, added the last of the half-and-half, then swirled them into the softly bubbling butter.

"Oh, *Gawd*, I can't watch."

"So don't."

"And yet," Pat whispered, round-eyed, "I cannot look away. This is what people see just before they die."

"Stop it." Annette added chopped onions, ham, tomatoes, and sprinkled half a cup of cheese over the glorious mess. She let it cook for a minute, then grabbed a rubber spatula and ran it around the edge, lifting the bubbling, thickening omelet up here and there so the raw eggs could run beneath. A minute later she plopped the thing on a paper plate

(note: dishwasher soap)

and sat across from Pat, who took one look at Annette's repast

"Want some?"

and shuddered. "You've gotta know the answer is a vehement 'Oh dear God, not even on a bet.'"

"And yet." She took a bite, relishing the overcooked bottom and the undercooked top. "It's important to start the day off right."

"Self-induced salmonella is not starting the day off right. Are you okay?" Pat was 55 percent legs, 20 percent hair, and 25 percent heart, and had a horror of people discovering the latter. So before Pat could express concern—who'd know better than her lunatic roommate that Andrea's job was dangerous?—he had to insult her breakfast. "You got in late."

"One of my kids got pinched for shoplifting. I went out to make sure they had a decent bed for him."

"Let me guess."

"Don't guess. You know I can't talk about it."

"Dev Devoss."

"What did I just saaaaay?"

"You talk about that kid in your sleep. Seriously, you yell at him in your dreams." Pat drummed his fingers on the countertop, already involved in early-morning plotting. "I've gotta meet him."

"Never happen."

"And here I was the idiot hoping you were out on a date with Donald."

She almost dropped her fork. Pat had a tendency to read her mind, and she was in no mood to be teased for her recurring fantasy, which had now invaded her dreams. "David."

"I honestly don't care, Annette. Stop playing with your food before you eat it. That's literal *and* figurative, by the way."

"I'm not following."

"Call or text Derwood—"

"David."

"Still don't care. Call him or text him or homing pigeon him and then brutally and enthusiastically shag him silly."

Oh, sure. As if it were that simple. "And then?"

Her roommate looked taken aback. "How should I know? I'm all about the setup, not what comes after. Give him cab fare? Or a wedding ring? My point is—"

"I know what your point is." She brought the flat of her butter knife down on Pat's knuckle just as the duplicitous wretch was about to snitch some ham. "Nice mani, by the way."

"Thanks. Wouldn't kill you to sit still for one, either."

"Never. If I can't read during a procedure, I won't endure it."

"God help us if you ever need surgery, then." Pat inspected his nails, which were spade-shaped and the color of glossy pink pearls. "Got an interview."

"I figured. The suit and all."

Pat was wearing one of his brother's navy-blue pin-striped suits with a crisp white shirt and a pale-blue tie dotted with poppies that looked like blood clots. Though he wouldn't leave the house, Pat was a big believer in "dress for the job you want, not the job you have." Which led to some confusion the month he wanted to be a park ranger. ("I don't care if it's five below; this is what rangers wear!") And the following month, when he wanted to be a hippotherapist. ("If you're going to do physical therapy with horses, this is what it takes!")

"I'm letting you change the subject in your clumsy and obvious way because I've said my piece—"

"Oh *God*, if only that were true."

"—and because I want you to get what this means. No longer will I be the homeless parasite suckling at your 24-acre teat!" Pat declared.

"Okay, gross." Not to mention inaccurate. Pat insisted on paying $666.66 every other month, and he was far from homeless. "You know you don't have to get another job on my account."

"This isn't about you or your account. It's about me getting a job within these four walls before I go crazy within these four walls."

"Good for you," she said, snarfing the last of her runny omelet. "And stop with the matchmaking-roommate trope."

"I'm the original, dammit! Tropes come from me, not the other way around. Take. That. Back."

"Nuh-uh. And good luck on your interview. Knock 'em… uh…" *Argh*. Because once upon a time, she and Pat had knocked 'em dead. It was why he wore his straight blond hair shoulder-length, when his preference for years had been a buzz cut. "Knock 'em good luck."

"Gosh, it's such a treat to see your razor-like mind in action."

"You wait. 'Knock 'em good luck' will be in the national lexicon within the month," she said, and stifled an eggy, hammy burp.

About the Author

MaryJanice Davidson is the *New York Times* and *USA Today* bestselling author of several novels and is published across multiple genres, including the UNDEAD series and the Tropes Trilogy. Her books have been published in over a dozen languages and have been on bestseller lists all over the world. She has published books, novellas, articles, short stories, recipes, reviews, and rants, and writes a biweekly column for *USA Today*. A former model and medical test subject (two jobs that aren't as far apart as you'd think), she has been sentenced to live in Saint Paul, Minnesota, with her husband, children, and dogs. You can track her down (wait, that came out wrong...) at twitter.com/MaryJaniceD, facebook.com/maryjanicedavidson, instagram.com/maryjanicedavidson, and maryjanicedavidson.org.

BEARS BEHAVING BADLY

An extraordinary new series from bestselling author
MaryJanice Davidson featuring a foster care system
for orphaned shifter kids (and kits, and cubs)

Annette Garsea is the fiercest bear shifter the interspecies foster care system has ever seen. She fights hard for the safety and happiness of the at-risk shifter teens and babies in her charge—and you do not want to get on the wrong side of a mama werebear.

Handsome, growly bear shifter PI David Auberon has secretly been in love with Annette since forever but he's too shy to make a move. All he can do is offer her an unlimited supply of Skittles and hope she'll notice him. She's noticed the appealingly scruffy PI, all right, but the man's barely ever said more than five words to her... Until they encounter an unexpected threat from within and put everything aside to fight for their charges. Dodging unidentified enemies puts them in a tight spot. Very tight. Together. Tonight...

> **"Davidson is in peak form in this hilarious, sexy, and heartfelt paranormal romance."**
> —*Booklist* Starred Review

For more info about Sourcebooks visit:
sourcebooks.com

NIGHT OF THE BILLIONAIRE WOLF

USA Today bestselling author Terry Spear
brings you a shifter world like no other

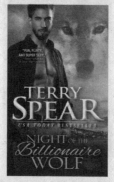

Lexi Summerfield built her business from the ground up. But with great wealth comes great responsibility, and some drawbacks she could never have anticipated. Lexi never knows who she can trust... And for good reason—the paparazzi are dogging her, and so is someone else with evil intent.

When Lexi meets bodyguard and gray wolf shifter Ryder Gallagher on the hiking trails, she breaks her own rules about getting involved. But secrets have a way of surfacing. And with the danger around Lexi escalating, Ryder will do whatever it takes to stay by her side...

"Fun, flirty, and super sexy."
—*Fresh Fiction* for *A Silver Wolf Christmas*

For more info about Sourcebooks's books and authors, visit:
sourcebooks.com